PRINCES OF LEGACY

ROYALS OF FORSYTH U

ANGEL LAWSON

SAMANTHA RUE

Copyright © 2024 by Angel Lawson Author, LLC and AngstyG, LLC

Lex cover photo credit: Michelle Lancaster, insta: @lanefotograf

All rights reserved.

No part of this book or cover may be reproduced in any form or by any electronic or mechanical means, including information storage and retrieval systems, without written permission from the author, except for the use of brief quotations in a book review.

❀ Created with Vellum

To the irredeemable bad boys.
Challenge Accepted.

FOREWORD

Queens!

We made it.

Apparently, like a pregnant Princess, we needed a bit more time to let this one gestate and get to full-term. We appreciate your patience and can't wait for you to read Princes of Legacy!

Like all Samgel books here's where we remind you that if you're new to this series, stumbled on it from a TikTok post or Facebook ad, you'll need to turn around and start at the beginning with Lords of Pain. Please read all the content warnings and make sure this is the path you want to go down.

As always, we ask family and friends to pretend this series doesn't exist. I mean, we love it. We're so proud of our little perverted chaos goblins, but face-to-face over family dinner can be a little awkward talking about the Throning or Cleansing, or the mechanics of a little brother-on-brother action. If you're one of Angel's daughter's friends, thank you, but just don't mention it at the tailgate. If you're Sam's hairdresser, keep reading!

Here's the short-list on what to expect inside Princes of Legacy:

- Breeding/Preg Kink
- Lactation Kink
- Medical Kink
- Edging/Withholding
- C*ck-Warming
- Group Play
- MMF (Look Closely at the Positioning of the Letters)
- Childbirth (and Complications)
- Blood Play
- Family Trauma
- Murder, Maiming, Torture
- Minor Minor Character Death
- Also, if you're sensitive to issues surrounding prior non-graphic childhood sexual abuse, drug addiction and use, degradation, public humiliation/exposure, physical abuse/punishment, and misogyny, you may want to bow out now. We're not pulling-punches!

If you want to dig deeper into the conversation of a like-minded community that digs breeding tropes, step-sibling romances, and revenge unaliving, join our Facebook group <u>Monarch's</u>, or our <u>discord</u>, where you can also find book-specific spoiler groups and chats.

Also, a reminder to check out our exclusive <u>Royals of Forsyth U</u> website for bonus content and links to our store, Royal Ink!

To Create is To Reign,
    Samgel

EX-KING: LIONEL LUCIA (SUPER DEAD)
CHILDREN: LAVINIA (DAUGHTER)
PLEDGES: CASH "MONEY" MALLIS (DEALER)

KING: SY PERILINI
(OUTGOING) DUKES:
NICK BRUIN, REMY MADDOX
QUEEN/DUCHESS: LAVINIA LUCIA
ARCHDUKE: CAT.
DKS MEMBERS: BALLSACK, KAZ
STAFF: MAMA B (MANAGER)
PAULY (MEDIC/TRAINER)
CUTSLUTS: LAURA, MAGGIE
FAMILY: TIMOTHY MADDOX (DAD),
SARAH (MOM), MANNY PERILINI (DAD),
DAVIS BRUIN (DAD)
LOCATIONS:
THE GYM (TRAINING/FIGHTS)
ROYAL INK (OLD ROYAL GAZETTE)

KING: TIMOTHY MADDOX
BARONESS: REGINA THORN (OUTGOING)
CHILDREN: REMY MADDOX (SON)
OLD BLOODLINE:
CLIVE KAYES (EX-KING, DEAD)
BENJAMIN KAYES (CLIVE'S SON)
WHITAKER KAYES (BENJI'S SON)
LOCATIONS: CRYPT
HOUSE OF NIGHT
MAUSOLEUM

KING: RUFUS ASHBY
PRINCES: PACE ASHBY,
LAGAN "LEX" ASHBY,
WICKER ASHBY/KAYES
PRINCESS: VERITY SINCLAIRE
STAFF: STELLA ST. JAMES (MISSING)
DANNER (SERVANT)
ADELINE (SPA OWNER)
FAMILY: EFFIE (BIRD)
MIRANDA & MICHAEL (DEAD)
PNZ MEMBERS: TOMMY WRIGHT,
RORY LIVINGSTON,
KRAMUS, DORY, LOEFFLER
LOCATIONS:
THE PURPLE PALACE
THE GENTLEMEN'S CHAMBER (STRIP CLUB)
THE GILDED ROSE

KING: KILLIAN PAYNE
LORDS: TRISTIAN MERCER,
DIMITRI RATHBONE
QUEEN/LADY: STORY AUSTIN
FAMILY: DANIEL PAYNE (DAD/FORMER KING/DEAD AF)
STAFF: AUGUSTINE ST. JAMES (MANAGER/STELLA'S SISTER)
MRS. CRANE (MADAM/BMF)
LOCATIONS: THE AVENUE (MAIN INNER CITY STRIP)

1

———

Verity

THE FIRST TIME I came into this room, it was with my heart in my throat and a pit of dread in my stomach.

Obviously, it's different now.

The glare of the bright overhead lamp, the sharp scent of disinfectant, the tray of shiny instruments, and the small sonogram machine rolled up next to the exam table. I used to find these things cold and sterile, full of only malicious potential. Now, it's a strange comfort to watch my Prince curl a familiar hand around the edge of the stool, rolling it closer to the exam table. The knowledge that the instruments are for his hands alone settles any unease. The smell of disinfectant is evidence of his diligence and meticulous care. The lamp is bright so he can see every part of me, always watching, analyzing. Even the snap of latex as he pulls on a glove is absent the nervousness I felt during my hospital stay—the nerves a result of all those strangers rallying to put their hands on me.

When Lex's fingers press into my abdomen, it elicits a different sort of shiver.

"Cold?" he asks in a smooth voice that I know all too well. His unbuttoned sleeves are rolled up to his elbows, revealing his strong, wiry forearms as he pushes each side of my belly. It's not the first time I'm struck by the fluid competence in his movements, nor the resonance of his quiet voice.

Outside of this room, we're the Prince and Princess—Lagan and Verity, expectant father and mother—but inside, he keeps the line drawn between doctor and patient.

Even now.

I shake my head.

He continues his exploration of my swollen stomach, tone clinically pensive. "Any pain in the pelvis?"

"No."

Another push, this time higher. "Belly?"

"No."

His fingertips drag against my skin as they skate toward each of my hips. "Lower back?"

"Lex..." I sigh, fighting the urge to squirm. "You know the answer to all of these."

"If you think I'm taking shortcuts with your recovery, then you got hit harder on the head than I realized." He stands over me, hands firm as he measures my belly, a lock of auburn hair falling by the side of his face. I reach up and push it back, revealing the scowl. "Any fluid discharge?"

"Just the ones that happen when you keep touching me like that," I complain, shifting uncomfortably.

Bed rest doesn't mean just *resting*. It includes all kinds of things I never realized I took for granted, like climbing the stairs of the palace. Lifting my books or gardening tools. Walking across the palace grounds. All of that's off-limits. My meals are brought to my room. Lex might allow me time in the garden, but only because the sunlight is good for me and the baby, and even that's supervised by Rory Livingston, a gun strapped to his side. The solarium is also off-limits until Lex confirms all of the bodies have been uncovered. But as much as those things suck, none are the biggest hardship that's befallen me for the past two weeks. That's been the other rule.

No sex.

The scowl shifts, his amber eyes growing heavy and knowing as he continues, examining my exposed body. "You're at twenty-two weeks. That's the halfway point. He should be about one pound. His senses are developing." His hands coast over the swell of my belly up to my breasts. Without missing a beat, he cups them in his large palms, a fat thumb rolling over each nipple. His tongue darts out, wetting his lips as they peak. "His eyelids are closed, so he can't see, but he can discern light from dark."

I swallow, throat clicking. "He's moving around a lot."

"A good sign," he says, lips curving into a slow grin. "He's strong. I know it."

The barely-hidden softness in his eyes is too much to bear, and I find myself reaching for that lock of hair again, rubbing it between my fingers.

It's stupid to miss someone I live with. Someone who's barely been nice to me until recently. Someone I can hardly get off my back now that he occasionally *is* nice to me.

But I do miss him.

He doesn't sleep in my bed anymore.

Neither does Pace—usually.

Lex's hands leave my body, and I feel the loss of them so acutely that I arch into the air. These exams are the only time I can get him to touch me until I'm cleared for physical activity, which depending on how paranoid he is, could be after the baby is here. Which means if I'm going to get some freaking relief, it may be now or never.

"Lex," I say, watching as he rolls the latex gloves off of his hands. "I do have one concern."

His forehead furrows and he turns back to the table. "What is it?"

"I've been experiencing this strange... ache." I touch my inner thigh, letting my knees unfold like a flower. "Right about here."

His gaze darts to my exposed center, jaw tensing with a tic. "An ache?"

Nodding, I plead, "Can you check to make sure nothing's wrong?"

He crosses the distance between us with a sure but unhurried stride, eyes never once leaving the apex of my thighs. Much like when he used to sleepwalk, it feels like I'm being stalked by a predatory animal, that spark of feral heat never far from the rippling surface of his control.

It's dangerous, tinged with the promise of violence.

I've never felt safer.

He comes to a rest at the end of the exam table. The light reflects off of his glasses, but I still feel the heat of his gaze on me as those muscles in his forearms flex, lifting blunt fingers to graze the sensitive inside of my knee.

"Show me." His voice is gruff in a way I'm not fully expecting. We've been doing these exams for two weeks—ever since I was released from the hospital—and he's always been infuriatingly impeccable. "Show me where it aches."

I don't have to look to know he's already hard. I see the strain in the hard set of his jaw, the ball of tension that only gets tighter when I reach down to brush against the hard bud of my clit. "It's right around here."

"Verity," he says, his tone full of warning. "This is risky..."

"I can get off with doctor supervision, can't I?" I take his hand off my thigh and move it between my legs. The instant his bare fingers meet the wet heat of me, a low, rough groan escapes his throat. "Or I can do it by myself. That, or we could always call one of your brothers in here and let them—"

He lurches downward, capturing my lips with his, cutting off the threat with his mouth. His palm cups my breast, while the fingers on his other hand make delicious circles over my clit. It's been *weeks* since I've felt anyone touch me like this. It won't take long.

"Fuck me," I whisper into his mouth. "Please?"

He jolts back, eyes flashing. "Absolutely fucking not."

Dr. Lex is holding on by a thread, and I reach for him again, this time grabbing the tie in the back of his hair and letting it fall.

Lagan.

This is what he keeps from me at night. It's the reason he gives me to Wicker or Pace in the hallway every evening before bed, leaving me with a slow, searing kiss before he goes to lock himself up tight in his room. Protecting me and our son from himself.

Lex growls, mouth dropping down to my nipple. The sensitivity is unreal, and fuck, even I'm turned on by how big they're getting. "Every night, I think about these," he mumbles mindlessly. "Wanting to bury my face in them—my cock. See my cum dripping down your pretty skin."

His words are so constricted with longing that it sends an explosion of heat to my belly. I think about it—Lex, at night, leaving me with one of those deep, tongue-fucking kisses, only to retreat to his room and bring himself off to the thought of it.

Jesus.

"Wick is going to lose his fucking mind with these." He grabs one in a big palm, pushing them together, and bows his head, again, breath hot on a peak. "So big and full, getting ready for the baby."

Whitaker Ashby has already lost his mind, but I'm not worried about him right now. I just want to feel— "Oh, god, do that again."

He obliges, swirling his tongue on my breast at the same time he flicks my clit. The sensation runs through me like a live wire. "Again," I cry, my orgasm close.

He suckles me, tongue lathing against my nipple, and I fall, the rush of release so good, so excruciatingly intense, that it almost hurts.

Releasing my breast, I continue to ride his fingers, only half-aware as he unzips his pants. His cock is thick—erect—a bead of cum seeping from the tip.

"You finished?" he asks, watching me writhe against his hand.

I nod, too spent to talk. He takes the fingers sticky with my release and grips his length, those muscles in his forearm shifting as he moves his fist up and down. Filled with endorphins, I look up at him as he brings himself to the edge, the muscles in his neck tensing with every stroke. I'm still not used to seeing him like this outside of those feral nights from before. This man isn't desperate. He's taken back control of his mind and body. He's clean. Healthy. The flush on his cheeks isn't new, but the sight of it is different. The smolder in his stare as he watches me. The way a wild lock of his hair billows in the breath being forced through his flared nostrils.

He looks like a column of flame, the edges of him licking out, gathering fuel. The sound he makes is deep enough to feel in my gut, the growl reverberating like a punch. He seizes, snapping forward to rest a hand on the table, right between my legs. The orgasm is swift, cum spilling from the tip of his cock in thick, ropey spurts that meet my flesh hot as fire.

I watch, hypnotized as he milks himself onto the slick crevice of my pussy, fist flexing with every squeeze. I can see the sense returning to his eyes, that line between patient and doctor, and the thing is, there's pain in it.

Hurt that he wants something he won't allow himself to have.

Reaching between my legs, I catch his release myself, guiding it to my hole.

He flinches. "Don't—"

But it's barely more than the tip of my finger pushing his seed inside. "That's what you want," I whisper. "Isn't it?"

It's hard for them, I think, to acknowledge the parts of themselves their father has built over his years of cruelty. Pace, and the way he seeks out isolation. Wicker, and the way he craves to binge on touch. And Lex...

Lex wants to *create*.

He never really got the chance, and now the thought of it alone is like a live wire to some primal, hindbrain instinct. And it's so powerful that he can't even trust himself to sleep beside me.

None of them can help it.

He watches me guide his seed inside with a slack jaw, his eyes tracking the movement as his own fingers join me, gathering up more of his release to feed carefully—reluctantly—into my hole.

"Verity," he says, voice thick and gruff as he cups a palm against my center as if he's holding it all in. "Do you ever think... after you have the baby..."

I wait for him to ask, the question lingering in his throat like a dangerous, secret thing.

But when he meets my gaze, I can see him pushing the words away, swallowing them up to hide them away. He pulls back. "Never mind," he says, shaking it off. "You just... *we* have to be careful."

Closing my legs, I shiver, the cold setting in. "I know," I reply, relieved he never actually asked.

The most important thing is the son growing inside of me. Delivering him into this world, healthy and happy.

I'm not sure how I'd answer the prospect of getting pregnant all over again.

"So, what's the verdict?" Pace asks, looking between us. He looks haggard and restless and messy, his dark hair unkempt and wild. His eyes look both glazed and too alert, and I wonder when he last got more than an hour of sleep. If it were anyone other than Lex's brother, I might assume he's been doing Scratch. But after Lex, no one in this palace would dare.

He just can't stop watching the monitors.

"Like you weren't watching," Lex says, ushering me into the sitting room and directing me to the chair. Used to be the examination room didn't have any cameras, much like the solarium. Pace has put a swift end to that.

"We were both watching," Wick says, flipping through one of the pregnancy magazines that randomly started appearing at the palace. "And that was a fantastic show, but it didn't quite confirm if the Princess is off bed rest yet, or if you two just wanted to bust a nut."

"Women don't have nuts," Pace says.

Wick shrugs, pausing on a page about breast pumps, "I said what I said."

"Lex," I say, also needing to know where we go from here. "Seriously. Is my bed rest over, or what?"

There's still a faint flush on his cheeks, the wrinkle in his brow a touch hunted. "As long as you're being truthful in your replies to my questions, I see no reason why you can't be released from bed rest—"

"Oh, thank god." I exhale. "I couldn't take another day in that well-appointed prison you call a bedroom."

Lex snaps, "Let me finish." He looks between me and his brothers. "You're released *with* conditions."

"Fuck it," Pace drops his head back, groaning, "what kind of conditions?"

Lex speaks directly to me. "Obviously, you'll still need to have a PNZ member with you at all times." I know they'd rather it be one of them protecting me, but with their focus on the dungeon right now, it's just not possible. "Keep heavy lifting under ten pounds. Maintain your diet and nutrition. Report any changes to me immediately—and I mean *anything*. Pains, aches, discharge, anything that seems like a red flag."

"Whatever you want," I promise, "I'll do it."

"Good girl." His approving stare is short-lived. "Also, no sex—"

"You've got to be fucking kidding me!" Wicker shouts. Unlike Pace, Wicker looks perfectly put together. Looking at him, one wouldn't even know that he spends most of his nights in bed beside me gritting his teeth. "You two just had sex. Like two minutes ago. She's still got her sex glow and you've got that dumb, post-coital look on your face."

Pace snorts. "So dumb."

Lex clears his throat. "As I was saying, no *vaginal* sex. Not yet. She needs a few more weeks of healing."

Wicker tosses the magazine aside and perches on the edge of the sofa, a relieved gleam in his blue eyes. "So licking the Princess' pussy is back on the table."

I look hopefully to Lex. "It is?"

Wicker answers thoughtlessly, "Of course, and obviously handjobs and blowjobs." This perks him right up, eyes darting to my chest and then back to Lex. "Where do we land on titty-fucking?"

Lex gives a clipped, long-suffering sigh. "Sure, Wick, *if* Verity feels up to it."

Wicker nods, rubbing his chin thoughtfully. "Cool, but what's the status on anal?" He doesn't even flinch when my throw pillow slams into his face.

"I am right here, you know!"

"You're always *right here*," he stresses, batting the pillow away. "It's driving me fucking insane!"

I wrestle down the instinct to feel stung. Wicker has been forbidden to touch me since I came back from the hospital. Since Lex can't sleep in my bed and Pace is too busy on guard duty to even *come* to bed, Wicker and I are alone all night, every night.

Not touching.

Not kissing.

Just sleeping.

I can see it wearing on him just as tangibly as the lack of sleep is wearing on Pace, both of my Princes turning brittle in the mornings.

Lex runs his hand over his face. "Listen, nothing enters the Princess' body for at least two more weeks." He glares at Pace, who has been quiet through Wicker's interrogation. "*Nothing.* That includes plugs, toys, *and* your cock."

Pace nods solemnly. "I heard you, brother."

"And you're okay with that?" Wicker's tone is shrill with disbelief.

I'm nearly as curious because I know he misses sleeping with his cock buried in me. If I'm being honest, I miss it too, and at this point, it might be the only way to even get him to sleep.

"What is wrong with the three of you today?" Lex bursts, brows snapping together in frustration. "We all agreed long ago that the most important thing is keeping the baby safe. We need to put our dicks—" he pointedly glares at me, "—and our *clits* aside, and do what's right for the pregnancy."

Feeling annoyingly cowed, Wicker and I both keep our mouths shut. But it's Pace who stands, walking over to press a kiss to my forehead. "I miss falling asleep inside of you." He smells like he's just taken a shower, clean and masculine, and when he grabs the hem of my shirt to push it up, revealing the swell of my belly, I'm not even surprised when he kneels to greet it. "I miss waking up and fucking you. I even miss doing it beside these two fucking headcases." He looks up to meet my gaze as he brushes his lips against the curve of my stomach. "But it's worth the sacrifice."

Behind him, Wicker scoffs, muttering under his breath, "Baby-whipped freaks."

"I miss it, too." I run my hand through his silky twists before cupping his chin. "But you're right."

"Well, Princess," he asks, looking up at me with his hands still cupping our baby, "what do you want to do with your new-found freedom?"

And there's really only one answer.

"I want to see him."

THE CORRIDOR DOWN to the dungeon seems darker than I remember. I clutch onto Wicker's sleeve as he leads the way, haltingly, as if he's reminding himself to go slow for my sake. A shiver wracks me as we meet the turn that leads to the cell I know all too well.

Instead, we turn left.

I can feel Lex's presence right behind me, the ghost of his touch lingering warm against my shoulder. I can't hear Pace, but I can sense him trailing us, his movements no more than a vague disturbance in the dusty air.

Wicker stops suddenly and I flinch to a halt, ears pricking at the sound of metal. A door swings open. The light beyond it is dim, but it may as well be the sun itself given the way my eyes burn to adjust.

"Careful," Lex says, his breath caressing my ear. "There's a step."

He holds my elbow as I find it, stepping carefully down into the room.

Behind us, Pace closes the door. "I don't like her down here," he says, not for the first time.

It is, however, the first time Lex turns to match Pace's grim tone. "Neither do I." His gaze meets mine, the line of his mouth so grave that it brings me up short. "You don't need to be here. You don't need to see what we've..."

But his words clip off, and a gnawing doubt grows in my belly at the look in his eyes. There's unease in the way he cuts his gaze. Perhaps shame.

"You've hurt him," I guess.

Lex meets my stare. "Yes."

"Badly?"

Pace raises his chin, a glint of defiance in his dark eyes. "Sometimes."

I look between them, deciding, "Good."

Lex parts his lips to argue, but Wicker steps between us, reaching for a switch. "Give it a fucking rest. This isn't some East End debutante we're dealing with here. She's West End. She can handle a little blood." There's a click, and then the room beyond a grimy glass window explodes with light. "Can't you, Red?"

My answer—*yes, of course*—gets stuck in the back of my throat at the sight before me. I breathe sharply and force myself not to look away, because Wicker is right. I can handle blood. I can stomach the sight of Ashby's mangled hand, two fingers missing. I can absolutely deal with the fact he's mostly naked, strapped to a metal table, torso slashed with whip marks.

This isn't the senseless violence of West End, I remind myself. It's not the Dukes having an ugly spar with another frat in the ring. It's not a bullet hole or a stab wound made for the purpose of *winning*.

This isn't victory.

It's justice.

The thought makes it easier to take the five steps to the window, peering through the dirty glass to get a better look at him. Rufus Ashby, no longer in his pristine white suit. The King of East End, completely absent of his poise and dignity. My father, little more than a sack of meat and bones.

I tilt my head, considering. "He looks…"

"Like a murderous piece of shit?" Pace asks.

"Well, yes but…" I try to find the words, assessing the changes as Lex watches me warily. Ashby's skin is pale—even worse than mine. And there are dark, sunken circles under his eyes. There's blood, certainly, and he looks smaller than I remember, but that's not quite the issue. I frown, finally putting my finger on it. "*Old*," I decide. "He looks old." His hair looks more gray than blonde in this light, as does the raggedy beard that's growing in.

"I'm not surprised." Pace's fingers flutter soothingly through my hair, the motion mindless, automatic. These last two weeks have built a few constants, one being Pace's distracted fixation with brushing his fingers through my hair. "Every day down here feels like an eternity. You know that, Rosi."

Swallowing, I ask the question there's no good answer to. "Will he… die?" A quick death wouldn't be just. To let him live, even less so.

"No," Lex answers instantly, snagging a clipboard from the hook beside the window. "His vitals have been steady, if not strong. None of his wounds are life-threatening. A couple signs of infection, but we're dealing with it." The tone is cold and curt. The contrast between Lex's clinical manner in my exam room versus Ashby's couldn't be more stark. "He won't die."

Darkly, Wicker adds, "Not yet."

"But he's in pain," I wonder, glancing at Pace beside me.

"Pain?" Pace's knuckle brushes the edge of my jaw, his lips curving into a slow, sinister smirk. "Fuckloads of pain."

Excellent. "I want to talk to him," I decide, moving toward the door.

To my surprise, it's Wicker who blocks the way, his blue eyes wide. "What? You can't go in there."

I bristle. "Why not?"

"Interrogation isn't all hack and slash," he insists. "It's easy to get in a man's skin, but getting into his mind? That takes time. Manipulation, incentive, reinforcement." Wicker's eyes dart down to my belly, a shadow crossing his features. "If you walk in there, you're going to give him something he wants. Something," he stresses, "he hasn't earned."

I straighten my spine, annoyed. "What about what I've earned? I've earned the right to ask my own questions! We put him in there together. We're supposed to be a team."

But Wicker just scoffs. "Why do you think I let you down here?" His hand flies out, punching a button on the wall. "Wake up, fuck-nuts. We've got your daughter down here."

Behind the glass, Ashby twitches, his eyelids fluttering open. The movement is small and contained when he twists his neck, his blood-shot eyes landing on the glass. "Verity?" he rasps, the hope clear in his voice. And then, quieter, "Michael?"

Wicker gives me a look that's so obnoxious he doesn't even have to say 'told you so'. "Tell us the combination to your upstairs safe, and maybe we'll let you see her."

Lex's gaze snaps to Wicker's, and then Pace's. There's an electric current of eagerness running between them. A bated breath. This is something they've been trying to get for a while, I realize.

But Ashby's face hardens at the request, and suddenly, he doesn't look like the frail old victim he'd seemed mere moments ago. He looks like the King again. The monster. "She's not worth it."

I spring forward, fist clenched as I speak into the microphone. "But our baby is, isn't he?"

Lex snags my hand, and when I turn to meet his gaze, I find a sharp, disapproving frown. "No," he mouths.

But when I look back at Wicker, his grin is chilling. "Yes," he mouths.

And that pretty much seals it. "Tell them the combination and I'll show you my stomach." I hold Wicker's gaze. It's probably not a good sign that he's so willing to use our son as a cheap interrogation ploy, but... "Tell them, and I'll show you your grandson."

It's barely the space between two breaths when Ashby lifts his neck, his red-rimmed eyes hard and wide. "Zero seven one," beside me, Pace scrambles to get down the numbers, "four two zero zero two." A ragged laugh rips from his throat. "You're all worthless if you couldn't figure that out. I'm even more disappointed in you than usual, Pace. If you were half the Prince you think you are, you'd know what this number means by now."

Pace looks both furious and lost as he glances at his brothers, only getting their confused shrugs in response.

But my eyes never once leave Ashby's gaunt face, a bitter taste lingering in the back of my throat. "It's my birthday."

That same ragged laugh tears through the speaker. "What, no celebration planned? It must be coming up soon. What is it, mid-June?"

Wicker's hand disappears from the button, an aggressive tilt to his mouth. "Do not *ever*," he grinds out, "tell him the date. Understand?"

I look at Pace, knowing the texture of the tally marks on his forearm well enough to give a slow, understanding nod. "Never."

He hasn't earned it.

And with that, Wicker wrenches open the heavy inner door.

The smell hits me before I even step over the threshold. It smells worse than death because it's actually life. Proof that his body still works. I push my palm over my nose, halfway to being sick as I follow Wicker through. Behind us, Lex mutters a curse, but they're different in here. No longer doting Princes. It's just like Wicker had said. A sensitive operation. Even the way they move is different, purposeful and precise, giving nothing away.

Pace sweeps in with such a lack of expression that it makes my breath quicken.

"Show me," Ashby demands, squirming in his restraints as he struggles to lever himself upright. "Show me my heir."

Exchanging a glance with Wicker, I reluctantly reach for the hem of my shirt, inching it over the swell of my belly.

Ashby's mouth forms a twisted grin. "He's still growing."

To say it's unpleasant is an understatement. I hate the way he looks at me, his cold eyes fixed on my belly with that repulsive smirk.

I hate the knowledge that I've been brought here to act as his *vessel*, just a cage for his next creation. I hate *him*.

So it's a triumph to see his face fall when I tug my shirt down, hiding our son away. "Where's Stella?" I ask.

Ashby scoffs. "She's clearly not here. If she were, she'd give you the proper attire for a Princess to wear in her second trimester." It's almost impressive how he can lay there bleeding, dirty, and bruised, entirely stripped of his dignity, and still manage to sound above it all. His lip curls in disdain as he stares me down. "You look like street trash."

The crack is unexpected, making me jolt in alarm. I'm not prepared for Ashby's strained, gnashed scream, nor the sight of blood bubbling up from the slash of the whip.

But it's satisfying, all the same.

"Manners, old man," Pace says, fist tight around the handle of the whip. "That's the mother of our child you're speaking to."

Behind me, Wicker slings an arm around my shoulder, deceptively casual as his other hand rests on my stomach. "Yeah, think about poor little CJ in there. We can't expose our son to that sort of filth."

I glance at him over my shoulder, brows knitted up in confusion. "CJ?"

Wicker grins. "Yes, little Clive Junior. It's tradition for a man to give his son the name of his patriarch. You know how much East End loves their traditions."

Lex's lips twitch, which is my first clue that he's not serious.

Ashby doesn't know that, though. His face transforms into ugly, sharp edges. "Under no circumstances," he grinds out, "are you to name my heir after a fucking Baron King."

"He's not your heir," I snap, "and we'll name him what we like. Maybe Clive." Eyes narrowing, I add, "Or maybe Davis. After Davis Bruin, you know? That's the closest thing to a patriarch I've ever had."

I'm expecting all three of my Princes to pull a face, but to my surprise, none of them do.

"Clive Davis has a ring to it," Wicker says, caressing my belly. "What do you think, Red? Should we hyphenate? Kayes-Sinclaire?"

Ashby roars, "Enough!" His restraints are pulled taut, the tendon in his neck bulging. "That's *my* blood. My heir!" He collapses back, exhausted. "I know you think you're in control, but I'm not alone. Danner—"

"Is locked upstairs," Wicker says cooly.

"Thaddius—"

"Is dead."

He shakes his head. "I don't believe it. He escaped."

"He did," Wick agrees, "but the network of PNZ alumni stretches far and wide. You saw to that. We contracted one to handle Thaddius." He tilts his head. "Would you like to see pictures?"

I've known for a long while now that Rufus Ashby is crazy, but I'm somehow still stunned at the depth of his obsession. Is this East End's true creation? I look at my Princes and wonder how long this obligation—this fanatical drive to breed—has been beaten into them. Is it just the Royalty, or is it the whole frat?

And why?

But these aren't the questions I need the answer to yet. I only need the answer to one. "Tell me where Stella is." Before he can argue, I offer, "Tell me, and I'll let you touch him." I rest my hand atop Wicker's, watching as Ashby's eyes grow impossibly more crazed. "I'll let you feel him kick."

"If these are the questions you're asking," he says, voice rough as gravel, "then I'm not worried. Obviously, none of you are prepared to lead a kingdom." He looks away, that same haughty demeanor taking over. "I'll get my heir, one way or another."

2

Verity

EVEN HOURS LATER, the memory of our father's gaze on my body makes my stomach churn. Worse than that were his words, because in a way, he's right. We're not prepared to lead his kingdom. The frat thinks Ashby is away on business until further notice. The only people privy to the knowledge he's currently sitting in his own dungeon are limited to rival royalty—the Dukes, the Baron King, and the Lords.

And, of course, my mother.

I'm rummaging through my bathroom drawer, looking for a tube of lipstick, when I hear a knock on the outer door. "Come in," I call, not hiding my frustration. "Where the hell did you go?"

I grab a handful of cosmetics and dump them on the counter.

"Should you be doing that?"

"Don't worry," I glance up at Ballsack's reflection in the mirror. "All of this is under ten pounds."

It's hard not to let my gaze linger on him. I've known Ballsack since he first pledged, just a scrawny little freshman with a spark of that wild, West End youth in his eyes. He's bigger now, having trained with the Dukes. More muscular and solid, maybe even bordering on imposing if one didn't know him. The soft cut of his jaw has given way to sharper angles and careless stubble. Every time he goes back to West End, he seems to return with another tattoo.

And he's quieter.

"I hear you've been cleared for tonight," he says, eyeing the pile of makeup. He'd always been one of the more easygoing recruits, just happy to have found a group that accepted him—a family. Losing Laura was hard enough. But Stella too? It's enough to break a lesser man. Eugene isn't weak, but he *is* angry, and that energy runs just beneath the surface. I'm scared. Not of him, but for him.

Desperate men and all that.

"Yes," I grunt. "Which is why I'm looking for my dusty rose lipstick."

I spin, turning to cross the bathroom back into the bedroom. I grab my school bag off of the desk chair and continue my search. Didn't I wear that shade for Sy's and Lex's graduation?

Ballsack follows, hands stuffed into his pockets, eyeing me warily. "Exactly why is this important?"

"Because I haven't seen anyone in weeks," I explain, harried. "Not only do I look like I shoved a beach ball into the front of my dress, but the lack of activity and sunlight has made my skin look like a vampire sucks me dry every night." I unzip a compartment and pull out whatever my fingers touch. Pens, pencils, art markers, erasers. "Dammit!"

He grabs my shoulders with firm, tattooed hands. "Verity, calm down. No one has any expectations of you. They're just excited you're coming home, even if it's only for dinner."

I look at his face, seeing the sincerity, and force myself to take a deep breath, exhaling slowly.

"Mama has been sending me over food every week, but it's not the same as actually being at Family Dinner." I return to my rummaging, unzipping another pocket. "Nothing is the same."

He doesn't respond, leaving us both in a stretch of quiet. That's the whole fucking problem; the quiet.

"I hate it," I confess, tossing out a pack of ginger gum. "I hate how quiet it is without her here. Everything feels *wrong*. There's no way I should be able to walk from the bathroom to the bedroom without her in the background going off about some random thing, like..." I huff. "I don't know, one second she's talking about this cute Matryoshka doll she had as a kid, and the next thing you know, she's explaining how 'decimation' was a punishment for mutiny in ancient Roman legions, and the path from A to B shouldn't even make sense, but—"

"Because one soldier out of every ten would be randomly killed," Ballsack says, eyes solemn and sad. "It's one of the games she used to play as a kid, but she didn't have toy soldiers. All she had was—"

"The Matryoshka doll."

Ballsy gives a heavy nod.

I'd become used to the incessant, non-stop chatter. The way she flitted around, expertly assisting me as my handmaiden. She had an instinct. A way of knowing *what* I needed exactly *when* I needed it, but it was more than that. She knew what they expected of me.

"Being Princess—living here, having this life..." I look around the room, remembering that not too long ago, it was a more literal prison than not. "It was unbearable. And she made it better. Easier. She took care of me after the ceremonies when I was bleeding or covered in gross frat boy fluids. She held my hand when I took the pregnancy test, checking the results when I was too scared to look for myself. She brought me tea and crackers when I suffered through morning sickness. And she was there when I was in danger and scared, trying to protect me." I swallow, meeting Eugene's pained eyes. "I took her for granted, I realize that now. She was the thing—the friend—I didn't realize I would miss until she was gone, and it sucks, Ballsy. It sucks so fucking bad."

After a long beat, he says, "I know."

I walk over to the bed and sit on the edge. "I saw Ashby today," I say, picking at a fingernail. "The guys finally took me down there. I got to ask him about Stella."

There's a beat of silence, and then Ballsack's hopeful, "And?"

It's agony to meet his gaze, giving a small shake of my head. "He wouldn't give an answer."

Ballsack's face falls. "Apparently, her sister has been talking to some cop."

My head snaps up in shock. "Auggy went to the cops?" I try to reconcile the former escort, now Hideaway manager, talking to the authorities. Royals are notorious for handling issues internally, and South Siders especially.

"No," he shakes his head, "she's *fucking* a cop, which is weird too, but she's South Side so who the fuck knows what they're thinking. Probably some customer or someone dirty, taking a cut." He shrugs. "Anyway, she filed a missing person report."

I blink. "Wow."

Shrugging, he says, "I already told your Princes. You know, in case they come around asking questions."

"Good idea."

My eyes land on the bedside table. There's a stack of pregnancy books on top, the spines cracked and worn. A pair of Lex's reading glasses are sitting on top. Leaning over, I pull open the drawer, pushing aside a bottle of lube and a cluster of hair ties. The rose gold tube catches my eye and I grab it.

"Ah ha!"

The thin ghost of a smile touches his lips. "You think she put it there?" he asks.

"Not a fucking chance. This is what happens when I'm left to my own devices. The lipstick gets mixed in with the lube."

He grimaces. "More information than I need, Princess."

With the lipstick in hand, I rise and cross the room. "We'll find her," I say, knowing this down to my marrow. There's no other option.

Ballsack doesn't seem as confident, collapsing into the wingback chair by the window. "We haven't found Laura. Or the Livingston girl. Or—"

"We'll find all of them," I amend. "And when we have her back, everything will be better. You'll see." But as I'm putting on the lipstick, I catch his reflection in the mirror, the way he drags a heavy hand down his face.

"Verity," he begins, looking impossibly more exhausted. "Can I... tell you something? Something I haven't told anyone." The words are imbued with a graveness that makes me turn to him, but it's the sorrow in his eyes that makes me hold my silence. "Stella... there are things we don't know about her."

I frown. "What do you mean?"

He sighs, reaching up to rub his neck. "She was secretive. Not... outwardly. She was good at hiding it. But I could tell. Sometimes she'd hide her phone, or I'd walk into her room and she'd get this look on her face. Pale, and kind of like I'd caught her doing something."

Mind whirring, I perch on the edge of the bed. "I don't understand."

"I don't think it was anything bad," he rushes to add. "She'd never betray you. Or me. Or the Dukes, or... honestly, even the Princes." A small, sad smile tugs at the corner of his mouth. "She has a really pure heart. You've seen that, right?"

My chest clenches. "I have."

"But there was something in her life she didn't want us to know," he goes on. "I never pushed. I mean... fuck, there's plenty of things about my life in West End I kept from her." He meets my gaze head-on, even though the curve of his brow is reluctant. "But a couple nights before she went missing..."

My heart jackhammers in my chest, sensing there's a clue. "What?"

His shoulders sink. "You were locked in the dungeon, and she was a mess, Ver. She was trying to get a message to..." Suddenly, Ballsack glances up into the corner of the room, looking away just as quickly. *The Monarchs,* I realize. "Well, she wanted to organize some kind of rescue mission. We both did. But we also knew it was futile," he insists, seeing the fear in my expression, "and that it'd only make things worse for you.”

“I made that decision to go in there.”

“I know, and it’s not my job to interfere with Royal business. Sy would agree. What happens between a Royal female and their men is between them, but when she came to my room that night, I figured she wanted to talk about that: getting you out.”

Confused, I wonder, “But she didn’t?”

He shakes his head. “She was really quiet. *Weirdly* quiet. And serious. The kind of serious that can make a guy nervous, you know?” He links and unlinks his fingers, drawing my gaze to the motion. The word ‘WEST’ is tattooed across the knuckles of one hand. It’s his newest ink. “She said we couldn’t see each other anymore. That things were getting too complicated—East, West, South, North. She said...” His words bite off and he looks up, shrugging. “Well, it doesn’t matter. She dumped me.”

“Oh, Ballsy...” I’m not sure how to respond to that. To any of it. “Did she say why?”

He leans back in the chair, shrugging. “No. I guess she just wasn’t into me enough to risk upsetting the Lords. I mean, I was willing to make it work. Lavinia and her Dukes did. You and the Princes are.”

Reluctantly, I muse, “It’s not exactly the same. Lavinia was being sold around the different territories. Nick saved her from that. And me... well, nothing about my situation is normal. I had no idea I was Ashby’s daughter when I agreed to the Masquerade. But Stella was just a sweet South Side girl sent to keep an eye on me.” I give him a sympathetic glance. “Kind of like you.”

He groans. “I already feel like a pussy for getting kicked to the curb, Ver, thanks for making it worse by implying I’m sweet.” He balls his fist. “I’m officially DKS now, you know. I’ve had blood on my hands.”

“That’s not what I meant and you know it.” The last thing I meant to do was hurt his pride even further. For one thing, bruised egos make men in this town react badly.

He shakes his head. “Look, I wanted you to know—just so you don’t think I’m hiding anything from you. But otherwise, I’d rather not have the world know I got dumped, because it doesn't actually matter." Lifting his chin, his words are quiet but hair-raising. "I'm going to find out what happened to her and who's responsible, and then I'm going to make them regret it."

I see it then, maybe for the first time.

The DKS.

My blood runs cold at the casual malignance in his gray eyes, and it doesn't matter that I know him in my heart as the sweet, scrawny West End pledge who first stumbled into the gym. Right now, I believe he's capable of the threat.

Slowly, I nod. "Good."

THE MOMENT WE WALK IN, the gym falls into a sudden, uncomfortable hush. I've seen a lot of Family Dinners over the years, so naturally, I figured that first night with Lavinia Lucia as Duchess was as weird and tense as one could possibly get.

Boy, was I wrong.

At the head of the table where Sy Perilini—the King of the Dukes —is sitting, Remy is bent over, pointing to something on a sheet of paper. Beside him, Nick Bruin is in an intense staredown with another DKS, their elbows both planted on the table as they engage in an arm wrestling match.

All of them pause at the sound of the doors slamming behind us, every gaze in the gym lurching to us.

Beside me, Pace is as stiff as a board. "No one said the whole frat would be here," he says through clenched teeth. "That wasn't the agreement."

"It's *family* dinner," I point out, squeezing his hand. "Of course they're here."

But Pace just scowls, a baffled crease appearing between his eyebrows. "DKS isn't family."

I frown, glancing at his stony expression. For my Princes, family doesn't mean DNA. It means secrets, isolation, and suspicion. It's a club so exclusive that it only includes the three of *them*. The Princes have never seen their PNZ brothers as anything other than mildly inconvenient subordinates. Struggling to find the words, I explain, "Family means something different in West End. The Dukes have always been close with the frat. They work together, live together, and fight together. They'd die for each other."

He makes a low, derisive sound. "That's stupid. How can you trust forty men and their fuck-toys?"

My eyes narrow at his description of the cutsluts. "Because they're good fighters and loyal friends, and they respect the King they've chosen. Even the girls." But truthfully, I'm just as tense. It's not so much about the Dukes, but more about the way everyone's gaze dips down to my pregnant belly. Some of the cutsluts visibly recoil at the sight, turning away. A pregnancy for a cutslut isn't the honor it is for one of the girls in my court. It would be devastating. Even Remy and Nick stare at me for longer than is entirely polite. However, "I'm safe here," I tell him, turning to peer up into his dark, suspicious eyes. "You said you'd try."

"What does it look like I'm doing?" he snaps. The sharpness of his tone makes me flinch, which is the only thing that finally draws his attention to me. "Fuck." He turns to me instantly, cupping my cheek in his hand, and pitches his voice to a silky hush. "Don't look at me like that, Rosi. Not here. Not in front of them."

Frowning, I search his eyes. "Look at you like what?"

"Like I scare you." His thumb caresses the corner of my frown, and when he bends down to brush his lips against mine, it's easy to wind my arms around his neck, melting into the kiss. Initially, Lex was supposed to be my escort, and while it would have been good to have his calmer energy at my side, I told him it had to be Pace.

He needs to see this more than anyone.

"You're not scary, you're just protective. It's sweet," I decide, but then amend, "annoying, but sweet."

He smirks into the kiss, shifting the package tucked under his arm. "Well, kick me in the balls or something, because if anyone here tries to protect you from me, I'm going to start stabbing Dukes again."

I swat his bicep, ordering, "No stabbing this time! Remy's still pissed about the scar."

Shrugging, he wraps an arm around my shoulder, facing the room with a bracing inhale. "No promises."

As if we weren't off to a bad enough start, the moment we approach the table, Nick saunters up to fix Pace with a scowl. "Pretty sure the rules were to leave your heat at home." He glances pointedly at the gun peeking from Pace's waistband.

Pace drags me closer, eyes narrowing. "I'm escorting my Princess and unborn child into a rival territory." He gives Nick a challenging look. "Don't pretend you'd come unarmed if it were your pregnant Duchess standing in this gym."

Nick's face does something complicated, his eyes shifting to his brother. "Probably not," he concedes.

Eagerly, I ask, "Is she here? Lavinia?"

Remy jerks his head toward the back. "In the kitchen with your mom."

But as soon as I take a step in that direction, Pace takes one, too. And when the Dukes see Pace following me to their Duchess, Nick and Remy jolt forward to do the same.

"Oh, for Pete's sake," I groan, turning to my Prince. "It's just the girls and my mom. Sit down and have a beer, okay?"

Pace's eyes harden. "There's no fucking way I'm—"

"I'll take Ballsack with me," I insist, but before my eyes can find him, the door to the back opens, Lavinia stepping out.

She spots me instantly, handing a tray of food off to Kaz, one of the established DKS members. "There you are," she says. "We were starting to think you wouldn't make it. Your mom's become a real basket case."

"Sorry." I give a rueful smile, resting a hand on my stomach. "As soon as we hit the Avenue, my bladder decided I needed a rest stop. This one," I jab a thumb at Pace, "had to do a security sweep that took forever. Reminder to self: don't ever pee in South Side."

Just then, the woman in question struts through the door, her face lighting up when she sees me. "There's my Ver Bear," she squeals, sweeping me up into a bracelet-jangling hug. She smells like home, cinnamon and jasmine, and I pull in the scent greedily. Briefly, I wonder if my son will ever press his nose to my shoulder and be reminded of comforting, soft things. "Let's get a good look at you." Mama steps back, touching my stomach. "How's he doing?"

"I just had a full checkup," I assure, grinning. "Lex says he's doing great."

The corners of her eyes tighten, Mama's mutter dripping with disdain. "Lex says, huh."

Sharply, I clear my throat, turning to Pace. "I doubt the two of you have been formally introduced. Mama, this is Pace, my Prince." I nod between them. "Pace, this is Mama."

My mother has never liked the thought of me with another boy, and while some part of that must have been her intention to groom me for Duchess, I now know a bigger part was due to her own experiences as a young woman in Forsyth.

"So you're Pace Ashby." She stares him down like he's the scum beneath her shoe. "Your bird's got a filthy mouth."

Pace's jaw tightens. "Filthier since you had her." I jab an elbow into his side, giving him a pointed look, and watch as he visibly struggles to swallow down his instinct to lash out. With a crinkle, he extends the gift he's kept tucked close, as if it's some shameful, embarrassing thing. "We... appreciate you looking over her." To his credit, he almost says this with a straight face.

Mama B takes the gift with a dubious scowl, immediately tearing the wrapping paper away. Once revealed, she cradles the sparkly bottle of rum in her hands, lips pursed into a pensive moue. "Looks expensive."

"Disgustingly," Pace confirms, glancing around the room. "It was distilled in the nineteen hundreds. The glass is inlaid with topaz, and there are only twenty confirmed bottles in existence. It's one of the most sought-after, collectible rums in the world."

She sneers down at the label. "It's *his*, isn't it?"

A shrug. "Yours now."

Mama hums and I all but die when she just grabs the polished wooden cork and *pulls*.

"Mama!" I hiss, but thankfully, it doesn't just pop open.

She strains with the effort of trying though, animosity burning in her glare.

And then Pace, as if he's on some weird, dutiful Prince autopilot, reaches for the bottle and effortlessly yanks the stopper free for her. Snatching it back, Mama holds his stare as she tips it up, taking a long, aggressive swig.

I shake my head in disbelief. "That's a five-figure bottle of rum! You can't just—"

But Pace doesn't miss a beat when she hands it back to him, smoothly taking a pull from the mouth of the bottle.

Almost in unison, they pull a face.

"Always knew this'd taste like ass," he mutters, handing it back.

Mama replaces the stopper. "We don't coddle our liquor around here," she says, handing it to the first passing DKS member she sees.

Kaz's eyes twinkle in delight. "Fuck yeah, booze!" Pace's incensed stare follows as Kaz takes it to the table like a bear parading its kill.

"Well, come on," Mama says, ignoring Pace as she bodily ushers me into a seat. "The girls and I made lasagna tonight. Remington's trying to learn to cook. I'm not sure my kitchen will ever recover." She catches my excited glance at the buffet table. "I'll bring you a plate."

"*I'll* bring you a plate," Pace interjects ridiculously. What are they going to do, poison me? But then he starts for the buffet and I have to snatch his arm.

"Not yet."

He looks around, realizing no one has a plate, and gives me an uncomfortable look. "We're not going to have to say grace or something, are we?"

"The King and his Queen serve themselves first," Mama says, eyeing him like an alien.

Everyone waits patiently as Sy and Lavinia approach the buffet, filling their plates. I catch the glance she casts toward Remy, whose attention is fixed on a sketchbook, and I don't miss the soft grin on her face when she piles up with extra garlic bread. *Smart.* There's no way there'll be any left by the time he surfaces.

After that, I'm expecting the frantic energy of the ensuing free-for-all, but Pace isn't. He goes tense, strung tight as the DKS and cutsluts clamor for the buffet, their voices rising to a deafening pitch.

I place my hand over his, noticing it inching toward the gun. "How about I fix the plates?"

Pace slides me an insulted look. "I spent eighteen months in the Forsyth Pen, Rosi. I'm not scared of hungry frat boys." And with that, he sweeps into the buffet line.

Dinner itself is a strangely lonely affair. Mama talks my ear off for a bit regarding her summer project of clearing out the old garage—although it sounds more like DKS' summer project with all the suckers she's talked into doing the actual labor. But other than that, no one talks to me or Pace. At the head of the table, the Dukes cast us the spare, discomfited glance, but none of them pull me into conversation.

I know it's not about me.

It's about the Prince at my side.

I remember the first time I saw Pace eat a meal at the palace. The dining room there is so formal and cold, but seeing him huddled possessively over his plate had set some part of me at ease, and reminded me of home.

He doesn't look at home here, though. "Stop," he mutters, fork scraping across his plate.

"Stop what?"

"Stop looking at me like you're waiting for me to lose it." Despite this, he eventually whispers, "They seriously just go up and talk to him while he's eating? Whenever they want?"

I laugh, watching Sy's long-suffering expression as a boisterous sophomore stands beside him, gesturing wildly. "Yeah, pretty much."

Pace nearly seems offended on Sy's behalf. "He's the King."

"He was their friend before he was their King," I explain. What I don't tell him is that it doesn't make sense to me for *any* King to spurn his people. Even back when Saul was at the head of this table, he often came to dinner and openly invited any DKS to approach him, regardless of the fact he was an arrogant pig.

Maybe it's just what life with Ashby does to a person. I've only been in the palace for five months, but I feel the way his imposed coldness sticks to my bones like a disease. I watch Pace shrink away from the warmth of my home—my people, my *family*—and it doesn't just make me sad.

It scares the crap out of me.

The thought of raising our son in all that stiff coldness is galling.

It becomes a mission then, the thought of making the palace into a home blooming outward in my mind just as delicate and thorny as the roses in its garden. Maybe it's impossible. Perhaps all the grand rooms and dark nooks of the palace are too obstinate and haunted to shed any warmth into.

But now that its halls are free of Rufus Ashby, I resolve to try.

As soon as Pace disappears through the door, Lavinia asks, "You've heard about Auggy's G-man?"

I nibble on a wafer, my chair turned to give me a view of the training area. "Ballsy told me she filed a missing persons."

Lavinia sits beside me, but directly on the table, her boots resting on Mama's abandoned chair. "It's weird," she sighs. Across the room, three different sets of recruits are sparring, the sound of fists on various padded surfaces ringing through the room. "Remy's got a lot of family on the force, but this guy's a fed. It's annoyingly hard to get any intel."

Nervously, I point out, "Now would be a really inconvenient time for someone like that to come poking around the palace."

"Tell me about it," she groans. "But Remy's got his cousin sniffing around, and I don't think Auggy would bring someone into the fold if she thought he'd cause trouble for the Lords. You know how it is in Forsyth. People can't stay out of the Royal fray for long."

I don't blame Augustine for using any avenue available to her. For all the Lords' talk of keeping what's theirs, they haven't found anything about Stella. I can't deny that I'm beginning to lose faith in the whole thing. It's almost like no kingdom wants to take responsibility for her. She was born South Side, but she worked East End and spent plenty of time in West End.

As I'm pondering the unfairness of it all, Pace returns from the bathroom, his dark eyes glued to me as he crosses through the training area.

Offering him a little wave, I don't get up, allowing him to have a little space. To my surprise, he stops at one of the smaller square sparring mats, watching Dillon and Grant circle one another while Pauly coaches them on technique.

Lav follows my gaze. "He seems to be relaxing a little finally. Can you imagine the Dukes escorting me to a Princes' ball or something? They wouldn't make it ten minutes before starting a brawl."

"Oh, that happens anyway," I shake my head, thinking of Wicker destroying the gender reveal cake. But I do consider the idea. "Remy could probably handle it. His father would've raised him to attend nicer affairs."

"True. He's more comfortable than you'd expect at the country club." Her gaze shifts to where all three Dukes are sitting in the next row, hunched over a cleared table and discussing logistics for the fight on Friday. "He certainly looks delicious in a suit."

Remy's got that long, lean body that looks amazing in almost anything he wears.

"Family Dinner is definitely different from dinners at the palace, which are as stuffy and oppressive as you can imagine, but..." I tilt my head, inspecting my Prince. "The guys spent years in boarding school, and then Pace did that stint in prison. I don't think this is as unfamiliar as he wants to act like it is."

With his arms crossed over his chest, Pace studies the training session with shrewd, curious eyes. He's probably surprised to learn the Dukes aren't fueled merely on adrenaline during a match, but actually take the time to work on their skills. Dillon and Grant are both excellent fighters, and I'm assuming if they're training with

Pauly tonight, they must be in matchups at tomorrow's Fury. Pauly has them run through different sets of drills; punching, blocking, and defense.

"You're leaving your left side open," Pauly tells Grant. The junior pulls his elbows down in response. "And you," he calls out to Dillion, "you're wasting opportunity! His weakness is your gain!"

Grant clearly doesn't like being called weak and reacts with a sudden flurry of motion. Dillon pulls his fists up, protecting his face, dodging and weaving so that Grant can't get in a hit, but the junior manages to force his opponent up against the edge of the mat before he takes a hard swing.

Dillon ducks at the last minute, the swing flying into the empty space over his head. Grant, caught up in the momentum, propels forward—right toward Pace. The Prince's hand flies up, catching the punch mid-swing.

"Oh, shit," I jump up, or try to. Lumber is more like the word.

"Fuck." Her eyes dart to her Dukes, but they didn't notice. I start around the table, watching the dark smirk lift the corners of Pace's mouth. He thrusts Grant back into the ring, and Lav's hand reaches out. "Wait."

"What do you mean, wait?" I hiss. "Pace is the type to bring a knife to a fistfight, remember?"

"Just..." her fingers wrap around my wrist, "just give it a minute."

A minute is all Pace needs to filet Grant, but Pauly gives an impressed grin. "Nice reflexes. You train?"

"I play hockey," Pace replies gruffly, eyes narrowed at Grant. The frat boy shakes his fist and wiggles his fingers, glaring daggers.

"That's right, that's right." Pauly nods, sizing Pace up. "You're the one who stuck Maddox during the Fury."

Pace shrugs, raising his chin. "Yeah, so?"

Pauly has always been a no-nonsense sort of guy, so he meets Pace's challenging stare with one of his own. "So with reflexes like that, you don't need to mess with blades." The older man chews on his bottom lip, then jerks his chin. "Get over here. I'll show you."

My heart thunders as Pace remains frozen. This could go badly.

Pauly is a good guy, a solid trainer and medic, but Pace isn't one of his DKS.

To my surprise, Pace takes the step onto the mat.

"Holy crap," I mutter, twisting my way out of Lav's grip. I don't plan on interrupting but I do move closer. Just in case. "This is going to be a mess."

Lav follows, her voice low. "I don't think so. Pauly has a disarming way about him."

"Tell me," Pauly says, waving both Grant and Dillon off the mat as we get close enough to hear. "Why'd you pull the knife on Maddox during the Fury?"

"Because," Pace's smirk is jagged and mean, "he was being an obnoxious prick."

The trainer snorts. "Is that what you're telling yourself?"

Pace's eyes narrow. "What the fuck does that mean?"

"You're fast," Pauly says casually. "Obviously your reflexes are good, and everyone knows a hockey player can give and take a punch—"

"Get to the point, old man."

He fixes the Prince with a look. "You're used to wearing all those pads. How much weight does that add? Ten? Fifteen pounds?"

"Fifteen to twenty-five," Pace admits smugly.

"Damn," Pauly whistles, "it's like you're used to fighting underwater, which out on the ice, makes sense. It gives you balance, but in here?" He spreads his arms across the blue mat. "I bet everything feels slightly off. You get sloppy. Desperate."

Pace's jaw hardens. "I'm not sloppy."

The trainer shifts, his body moving into a fighter's stance. "Then prove it."

The gym has grown quieter, and as I glance around, I realize DKS —and the Dukes—are watching. Waiting to see what Pace will do. There are a lot of expressions in the ranks. Some look amused. Curious. Hostile. The last thing we need is some impromptu Fury breaking out.

So when Pace reaches for his waistband, smoothly drawing his gun, my stomach jumps into my throat. But he just releases the clip, jerking his chin. "Hey, Ballsack."

Ballsack is uncharacteristically alone, sitting on the steps leading up to the catwalk. But his gaze rises at the sound of his name, and he doesn't hesitate to rise to his feet, crossing the distance to take Pace's gun.

Pace meets my eyes, faltering. "Will you—"

"Don't worry," Ballsack says. "I'll watch her."

An odd feeling washes over me as Ballsy slides up on the table next to me and Lavinia, my Prince assuming a fighting stance. He looks up at Pauly and says, "Okay, old man, show me what you've got."

Uneasily, Pace says, "We should get going."

"Just a few minutes, okay?" I drag him up the metal staircase, pretending I don't feel his hand on my hip steadying me.

"Should you be climbing these?" he asks. And then, when the railing jiggles, "Should *anyone* be climbing these?"

"I'm not lifting anything," I reply, reaching for the knob of the door the stairs have led us to. "And Lex said some sun is good for me."

That's exactly what we find when we step out onto the roof of the gym. The sun is a harsh glare in the western sky, slowly dipping into the horizon. I take Pace's hand and lead him over to a bench that faces the sunset. I sense him scanning the area for any potential threat, but there's nothing up here except the other warehouse roofs that make up West End. The clock tower rises in the distance, the hands announcing the time as 8:17. On the other side of the roof, the raised boxes filled with dark, leafy green plants shoot upward.

"The Dukes growing weed up here?" Pace asks, nodding over at the plants. "Oh wait, those leaves don't look right."

"That was my vegetable garden, although Mama's taken over while I've been gone." I sit and pat the bench. We put the bench up here a few years back. It's comfortable, with a back to lean into and a soft cushion on the seat. He takes another sweeping glance around the rooftops before he's satisfied, and sits next to me, pulling me into his side. He smells warm and musky—a little like sweat from training in the ring. After being holed up in the palace for weeks, my senses are on overload. "That tomato sauce from the lasagna? That was from last summer's crop. These will come in over the next few weeks and we'll start canning." I look over at the beds, remembering the summer we built it. "Well, I guess she'll do the canning alone this year."

He lifts my hand and spreads my fingers apart, threading his with mine. "So you've always had a green thumb. Guess it's in the Sinclaire genes."

"I guess." I look over the rooftop. "It was just nice to get some fresh air every once in a while, get away from the sweat and testosterone downstairs." His thumb rubs soothingly over the side of my palm. "I didn't really make the comparison but, yeah, I guess maybe it's in my genes." Lifting our hands, I place them on my belly. "It's weird what we inherit from our parents without even knowing."

His dark eyes follow our hands, tightening at the corners. "Yeah, I wouldn't know much about that."

"We'll get Ashby to talk." I press my fingertips under his chin and lift his gaze to mine. "We're going to find out the truth about Odette and your real father. I promise."

The sun sinks another notch and the sky turns from blue to pink. Pace's large hand palms and rubs my swollen belly, and he muses, "Whatever we get out of him, it's going to have to be soon. You heard Perilini."

Sy had come over after Pace and Pauly finished sparring and told him that the Princes had been summoned to a meeting with the Kings the next morning.

"When you came back to East End and we made that call, the Kings were willing to give us time to sort this out, but the clock is ticking." He cuts his eyes toward the tower. "They're going to want this settled, quick and clean." The dip in his voice makes it apparent that such a thing isn't possible.

"We need more time," I argue. "This isn't a regular mark down in the dungeon. Ashby's a master."

Sighing, he swings his gaze to mine. "This isn't something you need to worry about. Your job is to stay healthy and prepare for our son." His hand moves up, cresting boldly over my breast, and he drops his forehead to mine. "Fuck, Rosi, I want to be inside you more than I want to breathe."

They've all been hesitant to touch me since I got hospitalized—scared. The attack in the garden, the fact they almost lost me and the baby, turned them into these new, reluctant men. I sense their hunger—their need to be with me—but it's been set aside to give us time to heal.

It's *killing* me.

"I miss you, too." I brush my lips across his. "Waking up without you inside of me... I don't like it."

It's hard to explain how what had once been an intrusion became so achingly familiar. I think it's probably a lot like carrying this baby. I can't imagine anything else. It's not *just* the sex. It's that, for a brief moment, when things had begun feeling more settled between us, their touch became soothing instead of bruising.

I want that, more than anything.

Pace dips forward to kiss me, parting my lips to thrust his tongue inside. The kiss is hot and slick at first, but then harder, a touch of desperation in the way his fingers run down my throat, grazing over my collarbone. My nipples tighten into painful peaks, and I arch my back to brush them against his chest. A groan of frustration builds in his throat, roughing his muttered words. "Fucking Lex and all his fucking cockblocking rules."

"Hey," I run my hand over the hard bulge in his pants, "we can do other things."

Pace's eyes dart over his shoulder to the door that leads back downstairs. "And risk those animals coming up here and catching me violating the girl they think of as a sister?" He shakes his head. "I don't think so."

"After Remy decided to shoot off fireworks during the Fourth of

July last summer and almost burned down the whole building, Mama put a strict no DKS on the roof rule," I suck on his bottom lip, getting his focus back on me. "Including Dukes. Although I'm pretty sure she really just wants some peace and quiet from the nonstop rowdiness in the gym."

That's the green light he's been waiting for, and his fingers move to the buttons making the V down the front of my dress, pushing them loose. My tits hang heavy between us and his eyes glaze. "You know, I've always been about the pussy," he tells me, shoving aside the cups of my bra to fondle me with a surprisingly gentle touch, "but one day, when the baby is here, and you're full up with milk, I'm going to fuck these sweet tits. Cover you with my cum." He licks his lips, then bends, taking one peak into his mouth.

"Oh, god..." Stars blind my vision. Holding Pace's head against my chest, I moan, the sensation spreading.

He pauses, looking up, "Am I hurting you?"

"No." I breathe, "they're so sensitive. I'm going to come from this if you don't stop."

"You for real?" A dark flicker crosses his eyes, and he plucks the right side between two fingers. "Just from me sucking them?"

"Mmhmm." I bite down on my bottom lip and dig my nails into his shoulders. "Or that. Anything. It's insane."

There's a dark, frantic energy in his eyes that sends a shiver down my spine. "Then let's get you off."

Dropping his head, he latches on to one side, sucking and licking the nipple. On the other, his hand cups the tight swell, toying with the peak. My hips rock up, the orgasm building despite the lack of stimulation between my legs. It's a heady drunkenness, the rush cresting over me in an unrelenting wave. It's like nothing I've ever felt before, both extreme and muted. Sharp, yet dull. Bright, yet dimming.

It's too fast, like a memory of an orgasm instead of the real thing.

But it's still enough to send tremors through my body.

"Jesus *fuck,* you weren't lying," he growls, placing his hand over mine on his erection. He sounds dazed, even though his eyes are too alert, scanning the rooftops before ducking to suck a kiss into my neck. "I want to get my cum into you so bad, Rosi. You can take it, can't you? In your pretty mouth?"

Still catching my breath, I'm stunned by how much the thought captures me. "Yeah, just—"

Instantly, he's popping his fly and pulling himself from his pants, his long, dexterous fingers wrapped around his shaft. He strokes himself as he watches me, licking out to wet his lips. "You don't have to take it all," he says.

But I will.

I always do.

It's never about the journey for Pace. He jerks himself off like it's just an inconvenient prelude to the real thing, and when he jolts to his feet, I know he's close.

I grab his hips, faced head-on with the sight of his obscenely hard cock. "Look at me," he rumbles, tipping my head back. His hand is warm and gentle on the base of my skull, and I give a long, slow blink at the corrosive heat in his eyes. This is what Pace likes. Something soft and sweet. The innocent sweep of my tongue against the head of his cock, inviting him inside. The way I open for his cock—not wide, not narrow, but just enough.

Just for him.

I hold his stare as his cock gives a strong, aggressive throb between my lips. But it's not that first salty taste of him that makes me shudder. It's the way his face collapses in awed rapture. The curl of his forefinger beneath my chin, so gentle. The way he doesn't break my gaze, so fixated on the sight of his cock spurting onto my tongue that he doesn't even think to scan the rooftop for threats.

I swallow every drop.

3

L^{ex}

I'VE NEVER BEEN to the old Forsyth courthouse without Father until now.

The first time he brought me here, I was seven. One of Daniel Payne's South Side soldiers had brazenly assassinated one of the Counts in a drive-by shooting. It'd been a huge scandal at the time—not just because of the audacity of the Lords to attack a rival so boldly, but because it exposed the Kings' lack of control over their ranks.

But they were younger back then, new to their kingships, exuding the brash confidence of the newly empowered. They were men. *Kings.* And I wanted nothing more than to bask in their superiority. I observed Father engage with these men on equal footing as they deliberated over consequences for LDZ, but I couldn't help but fixate on the Baron King, his unsettling mask sending shivers down my spine.

It wasn't just the gleam of the twisted horns, the sunken cheeks, or lack of mouth. It was the efficacy of the illusion. With the black suit and gloved hands—even the neck hidden beneath dark fabric—no part of him was visible. The mask was all he was. The devil made flesh.

Even as a child, I couldn't shake the feeling of dread, wondering about the enigma concealed behind the facade. I knew he was affiliated with the dead, the person Father called when something messy happened in times of that youth-fueled chaos.

In my imagination, the Baron King transcended the others, almost supernatural in nature. One of Death's emissaries, haunting the nocturnal streets of Forsyth, seeking souls to add to his crypt.

Just like my parents.

Now, stepping into the stuffy, ornate room of the courthouse as a man in my own right, I catch sight of him, the Baron King, sitting at the head of the table. His features are still hidden behind that golden mask and black suit, but this evening, I'm distinctly lacking that old sense of awe. There's nothing supernatural about him. He's no longer a man shrouded in mystery. He's undoubtedly human. Flesh and bone. Not just a King, but a father.

Remy's father.

And a killer of fathers.

I can only speculate about Wick's inner turmoil. He sure as hell gives nothing away as he strides in behind me with an air of nonchalance. He leisurely unfastens his blazer and settles into the chair beside me at the elongated table. Among the three of us, he's the most skilled at navigating interactions with nobility. Pace, on the other hand, visibly tenses, his discomfort palpable, especially after having to relinquish his weapons before entering the room.

"I hate this place," he announced when we arrived. "Nothing good ever comes out of a courtroom."

"I'm not sure why we have to justify what happens in *our* territory, anyway." Wick scowled as he handed off his pistol to one of the lesser-known BRN members manning the breezeway. I don't know him, but the long, gnarled scar slashed across his throat was as conspicuous as the metal in his face, piercings scattered like violent speckles across his features. I certainly didn't miss the nod he sent to Pace when Wicker groused, "It's not like we're digging around the Barons' crypt."

"We knew they'd want an update." I'd kept my voice low while trying to reassure my brothers. "This isn't some low-level PNZ we've got holed up in the dungeon, or even a fucker like Oakfield everyone's happy to see taken care of. We've got a King down there in the midst of a mutiny, and that makes other Kings nervous."

Especially Kings of the old generation.

They're disappearing like smoke.

All of that logic holds up until we find ourselves face to face with the reigning Kings: Killian Payne, Simon Perilini, and Timothy Maddox, hidden beneath his mask. I strive to summon the same confidence that propelled me to the head of my class in Forsyth, the assurance that secured my place in the medical school of my choice. The steady heartbeat, the unwavering self-assurance, the deep-seated belief that I have every right to be in this room.

After a nod from the Baron King, Killian clears his throat. "Word's gotten out that Rufus hasn't been seen for seventeen days." Normally, Payne makes it clear that he has little to few fucks to give about the larger matters in Forsyth, preferring to focus on his own territory. But I see the frustration in his eyes as he continues. "According to people in the community, he missed the annual report at Forsyth Mutual Bank, skipped a poker game at the Gentlemen's Chamber, and failed to attend the symphony's Summer Solstice event—of which he's one of the acting chairs."

"He sent me to the Solstice event," Wick says with a wave of his hand. "The guest cellist from Milan was dreadful. He could barely manage the bow work." He sniffs with displeasure, looking the very picture of snobby ease. "As was the strawberry shortcake. It was like eating sandpaper."

"One of these is explainable," the Baron King's flat voice carries down the table. "Three is a problem, especially with something like the annual report. Rufus hasn't missed one in twenty-two years.

Trudie Stein has been asking enough questions that my associates are asking *me* questions." He pauses before adding with heavy disdain, "This mutiny is sloppy work, boys."

"Apologies, *Your Grace*," Wicker's sarcasm is as thick as the bald hatred in his glare. "We've been focusing on issues inside our house, like trying to force a psychopath into accounting for the five bodies he buried in the solarium. Or," he glares at Killian, "telling us anything he knows about the current missing women in Forsyth."

"As well as attending to our Princess and child," I add. "Who, by the way, are both healthy and improving every day. Thanks for asking."

Not missing the barb, Killian levels me with a scowl. "We're well aware of the shit East End's been through this past month, but ruling as a Royal means more than focusing on your own house. As much as I couldn't personally care less, being the leader of a territory in Forsyth is about balance and presentation. It's about assuring the members of your community—*in and out* of your house—that things are running smoothly. People need a sense of safety, dependability, and reliance. Rufus, for all he might be a piece of shit, was a consistent presence that made not only East End feel secure, but the whole fucking city."

My nostrils flare with a restrained sigh because Payne isn't wrong. Father is the devil PNZ knows. His absence is making people jumpy and suspicious. Clearly, we've been too absorbed in our own family dynamics. "We're prepared to spread the word immediately that Father, along with his personal valet, is on an extended business trip." When no one argues, I continue, "What started off as a week-long excursion to Asia turned into a much longer affair."

"What kind of business?" Killian asks.

"His kind," Pace responds. "After the assault on the palace and the attack on the Princess and our unborn child, we've been forced to elevate the security of East End. He's found that the best in the business are not located in the US, but overseas."

"Security is your specialty." Sy eyes Pace. "So why didn't you go with him?"

"With Verity on bed rest?" he snorts. "Like hell."

"I don't see the connection." Sy leans back, his massive arms crossing over his chest. "It's not like you protected her before."

"This shit again?!" Pace's hands slam down on the table and he bolts to his feet, the chair kicking out behind him. "Our commitment to the Princess is unwavering, and I'm sick and tired of West End acting like we're holding her against her will. She chose to honor the contract."

I reach for the back of his shirt, trying to get him under control.

"You say that," Sy says, shrugging, "but she never got hurt in West End."

Pace's eyes flare hot. "Because I never took my eyes off of her when she crossed into your crusty, rundown territory."

Sy's face hardens. "Are you implying you've got West End wired, Ashby?"

"If our woman and child are there, then you can bet your ass I've got it under surveillance."

This time, when I yank at his shirt, he relents, dropping back down into his seat with a huff.

Pace has spent the last two weeks researching exactly what he says Father is doing on his trip—just from inside the palace. The security surrounding the property is now military grade. Upgraded cameras cover every inch of the exterior. There are no weak links. No blind spots. No places for Father to bury bodies unnoticed. Pace has all of our devices synched, so honed in on the Princess that we can pinpoint her exact location at any time. And that's just in East End. I'm not even sure what all he's doing outside our territory, but I'll put nothing past him. Not when it comes to protecting Verity or our baby.

"Do you hear this?" Sy says, looking between Killian and Maddox. "No one is going to believe that these three idiots can handle East End without Daddy's involvement."

Wicker scoffs. "You just want Verity to come back to West End."

"Maybe we do," Sy growls. "You're not fit for protecting her, let alone her baby."

My jaw clenches. "I think you mean *our* baby. And we can protect both of them just fine."

"Then maybe someone," Killian grinds out, "can finally fucking tell me why a South Sider disappeared in your territory."

"Stella St. James disappeared in North Side," Wicker corrects.

Killian gives a malicious smile. "How convenient."

"Not especially," Pace replies. "Ballsack and I have been going over footage for the last three fucking weeks. What has South Side been doing? Involving the feds?"

Killian balks at the accusation, straightening in his seat. "We had nothing to do with bringing that agent here. Augustine acted as—"

"As one of your senior staff members," Wicker offers, picking a piece of lint from his knee. "This mutiny is going to get a lot harder with them sniffing around, so kudos for that."

Killian looks close to murderous, his eyes bugging out. "While we're on the subject of staff members acting suspiciously, maybe you'd ought to look at your own."

Pace snorts. "What's that supposed to mean?"

"It means there's a common denominator in at least two disappearances, and the Lords are done beating around its bush."

Sy's the one to stiffen though, leveling a slow, threatening stare at his fellow King. "Don't you even fucking say what I think you're saying."

Killian raises his chin and says it anyway. "Two of the missing girls were involved with Eugene Warren." He nods at Pace. "The same man you let in your palace with this pregnant Princess you're so intent on protecting."

"You motherfucker," Sy growls. "Ballsack had nothing—"

"Enough!" The Baron King's voice commands the room, sharp and strong from behind his golden mask. His hands, hidden by black gloves, ball into fists. "We are not," he seethes, "here to discuss the missing girls or your petty squabbles over the Princess. Verity Sinclaire is a problem of your Father's making that's trickled downstream. Staff members, arranged heirs, breeding with women who bear questionable allegiances..." His eyes burn with anger through the mask. "All of it is irrelevant to today's meeting."

We quiet, everyone sinking back in their chairs.

Brusquely, he continues, "The majority of Forsyth doesn't give a damn if Rufus is alive, dead, or holed up in an opium house in the South China Sea." He jabs the tip of his forefinger into the table, the movement swift and powerful. "When we talked on the phone fifteen days ago, I signed on for a mutiny in East End, not an indefinite interrogation of its King. People are talking, and to restore balance, you'll need to give proof of life or crown someone else. Either way," he grits out, glancing at Killian and Sy next, "I'm not going to Royally father all of you into honoring your kingships. Grow up and lead your goddamn kingdoms!"

I think of Father, bloody and scarred down in the basement, and wince. It's not going to be that easy.

I take a deep breath. "How long do we have to give proof of life?"

The Baron King's incensed eyes snap to mine. "One week."

"And if we don't cooperate?" I ask.

"Then someone in your house will choose for you," Killian says, rising from his chair. "PNZ is watching. If you don't rise to the occasion, then one of them will."

"You can photoshop him into a picture, right?" Wicker asks, slamming the door. He's twisted around, looking at Pace in the backseat. "Like some fucked up image of Father surrounded by underaged Thai girls?"

"I *can*," Pace says, inspecting his gun before tucking it behind his back, "but we can do better than that."

"Better how?" Wick's forehead creases, and then he cackles. "Oh, Thai *boys*. Yes, that *is* so much better."

The problem isn't proof of life to the Kings, who wouldn't blink at an image of Father's gaunt face and oozing wounds. It's the rest of Forsyth we have to convince. We need something to buy us time.

"Well, whatever we're going to do, we better figure it out fast," Wick says, slumping against the car window as we approach the palace grounds. The new sensor that Pace installed in the gate to trigger as we turn into the drive isn't the only upgrade. Two armed guards nod as we pass—both alumni. Wick and Rory vetted each and every current and former PNZ for security positions. Anyone with lingering loyalties to Father didn't make the cut.

"They're on a rotating schedule," Pace says, nodding as we pass. "Two hours at the gate, two hours patrolling the perimeter, and then two hours watching the cameras."

I park the car in the turnaround in front of the house, sighing. "I know this is the least of our problems, but clearly the Lords think Ballsack had something to do with Stella." Cutting the engine, I turn to look at my brothers. "That's something we should probably keep to ourselves for now."

Pace blinks. "Why?"

"Verity," I answer, glancing at Wick. "She's... protective of him."

Wicker gives me a long look. "You sound like a jealous boyfriend." And then, pulling a face, "Gross."

Tightening my fist around the steering wheel, I insist, "I'm not jealous. I just don't think it'd do her any good to add another do-gooder campaign to her list of projects. She's already helping to volunteer for the search parties and the social media blitzes. Plus..." I don't really want to say the next words, but as I look out the windshield at the palace grounds, I can't help but wonder. "Maybe they have a point."

Pace's response is swift and annoyed. "Fuck that."

"He's West End," I point out. "We don't know what kind of shit he's mixed up in. And you heard him on the monitor yesterday. Stella dumped him right before she disappeared. That's suspicious as fuck and you know it."

But when I meet his gaze, it's the strangest thing. Pace, the most ridiculously paranoid and suspicious person I know, doesn't look the least bit swayed. "I don't care where he's from," he says. "I know when a man is desperate to find something. That street rat has been at my side for weeks, pushing me to look harder, and he's not even fucking remotely ready to give up."

Before I can argue, Wicker cuts in, "Fuck it—whatever. We'll keep it to ourselves. Lex is probably right, anyway. She doesn't need another friend to worry about, does she?"

This seems to convince Pace more than anything, but even when we walk into the house, he's still giving me that look of his, like I'm disappointing him.

"What?" I snap when he grabs my arm, stalling me. I'm not about to apologize for seeing things from all angles. If anyone can appreciate that, it should be him.

But instead of pressing me about it, he eyes Wicker, who's disappearing down the hall. Pace raises his eyebrows. "You need to talk to him."

I follow his gaze, deflating. "Why me?" I ask, watching my brother duck into the kitchen.

"Because I've already told him what I think about him going in there every day. It's a stupid risk that he shouldn't be taking." Pace rolls his eyes. "He didn't care about my opinion. Maybe he'll listen to you."

"Fine. I'll talk to him." I tuck a loose strand of hair behind my ear, wondering how it is that, even with Father out of the equation, my days are still chock full of bullshit like Royal meetings and brotherly mind un-fucking. "You'll check on her?"

"Yeah," he says, already pointed in that direction. "I'm going to see if she and Effie want to get some air."

"Nothing strenuous," I remind him. Parting, Pace climbs the stairs and I go look for my other brother in the kitchen. I find him standing at the center island, pulling items out of the refrigerator and setting them on the counter. There's bread, fruit, and a piece of salmon from last night's dinner.

Leaning against the counter, I start, "Wick—"

"Hand me one of those cookies, will you?" He points to the glass-covered dessert stand. "He likes chocolate chip."

"Wick," I try to measure my words carefully, "we talked about this. Danner can't be trusted. He's loyal to Father."

Deciding what to do with Danner has been the one thing we've struggled to agree on since Father was locked away in the dungeon. Danner isn't just Father's closest confidant. He and his family have worked for PNZ since its inception. The original King hired his father as a valet and his mother as a cook for the palace, and when he came of age, Danner stepped in. There are few secrets he doesn't know, which is the only reason Pace and I have kept him locked in his room instead of making other, more permanent, decisions.

If any part of this mutiny involves breaking the cog that turns East End's worst institutions, then Danner is a part of that. There's no getting around it.

Wick on the other hand…

He raises a slow glare in my direction. "Maybe he's loyal to Father, but don't forget, he's also the one who actually took care of us."

"It was his job, Wick," I remind him as he slathers butter on the bread.

"His *job* was to feed us and make sure we had clean clothes and practice uniforms." His jaw tightens. "Danner took care of us by bringing us the salves and ointments to heal the cuts on your back after father whipped you within an inch of your life. He visited Pace every week he was in prison and kept his commissary account in the black. If there's a man in this house who's earned the right to be called 'Father', it's not the one down in the dungeon."

I rub my temples, a headache setting in. "Look, I won't deny Danner cared for us, but—"

"Danner," he cuts me off, "is the one who took me to get tested for STDs after events like Mayfield." He swallows thickly. "I understand your concern. I hear it, but I can't turn my back on him. He was a pawn to Father's whim as much as we were."

That's when I decide this is the worst discussion of the day, by far. Wicker, with his set mouth and tired eyes as I try to convince him to abandon feelings for the only man who ever gave a shit about him? It makes my chest hurt as badly as my head.

But he's not the only one struggling.

This past month has been the hardest of our lives, and that's saying a lot. Standing up to Father, taking him to the dungeon, putting Verity and the baby before anything else in our lives... It's unfamiliar. *Uncomfortable.* And Danner has always been the constant.

"People need a sense of safety, dependability, and reliance..."

Killian's words come back to me, and that's what this is. Danner is to us what Father is to East End. Not *good*, just familiar.

But the main thing I can't tell Wicker right now is that Danner didn't do all of those things because he cared for us. He was taking care of us because we were assets of the crown. Father needed us under control, but healthy. He needed us to be fit in order to give him an heir.

"I don't think this," I wave my hand around the food he's arranging on the tray, "is about Danner at all."

"Here we go," he mutters. "Enlighten me. What do you think this is about?"

"I think you're avoiding any and everything to do with the fact you're the biological father to Verity's baby."

He snorts, not even looking me in the eye. "Is that supposed to be a shocking announcement? Because it's not. I've made it explicitly clear that I never wanted to be a father. I don't want the obligations, the responsibility, or the dirty fucking diapers. Not to mention the crying. Have you ever heard a baby cry?"

"Have you?" I counter.

He blinks. "I mean, on TV. At restaurants. Once, on a plane to that tournament in Alberta," he shoots me a glare, "for six fucking hours."

"What about Verity?"

"What about her?" He slices strawberries into a small bowl.

"You've been avoiding her, too."

His jaw drops. "*I've* been avoiding her? I sleep beside her every fucking night! And where the hell are you and Pace? Too obsessed with keeping her safe to bother realizing she's in that big, stupid bed waiting for you."

"You know what I mean," I say, avoiding the accusation. "You don't come to the exams, you weren't even remotely interested in her last sonogram, and whenever you aren't in bed with her, you hardly touch her."

"Hey," he points the sharp tip of the knife at me, "that's on you. You're the one who created a buffer around her bigger than the palace's security fence. I've just been following orders."

"For sex, Wick, not for all of the other things she needs right now. Like support, help, conversation, the decisions she's about to face as the baby gets closer."

His lip curls disdainfully. "Oh, like picking out baby furniture? Or maybe selecting a nice wallpaper for the nursery—something that'll cover the blood stains still on the wall." He rolls his eyes. "Because no thanks. She can call one of the girls in the Court to come do that."

"You haven't even been around when we read up on the baby's progress and how her body is changing." I grab a strawberry. "Dude, you haven't even asked what piece of fruit the fetus is now."

He drops the knife with a clatter and flattens his palms on the butcher block. "Tell me, Doc. I'm dying to know. Mango? Coconut? Pineapple?"

"Eggplant," I smirk.

His lips press together. I can't tell if he's pissed or just trying really hard not to laugh. "That's a vegetable."

"Technically, it's a fruit," I tell him. "It has seeds and comes from a flowering plant, which makes it a—"

"Great." He lifts the tray, everything arranged nicely. In contrast, Father is lucky to get a bowl of soggy oatmeal once a day—just enough to keep him alive. "I'm all caught up."

My face falls at the utter determination in his eyes. "Well, if you insist on going in there, then I'm coming with you. Maybe we can find out something useful for once. He needs to understand that keeping him alive and safe comes with conditions."

"Fine," Wick says, eyes narrowing at me as he lifts the tray, "but don't be a dick about it."

~

I DON'T REMEMBER a time when Danner didn't always look pale and wrinkled, like he may be a step from death's door. He's always looked old, and it's no different now when I unlock and open the door from the outside with the key. He's sitting in the recliner near the window that overlooks the back of the estate. A copy of the monthly Financial Times sits on a table next to his chair, along with a cup of tea.

"Afternoon, boys," he says, mid-rise.

"Don't get up," Wicker says, striding into the room. He sets the tray on the small kitchen table that's been pushed against the wall, and starts unloading the plates. "I know you like salmon, so I had the cook save you a piece from last night's dinner."

"Thank you, Whitaker." His cloudy blue eyes glance over to where I'm standing in the corner, arms crossed over my chest, watching. "I didn't expect you to come see me, Lex." He chuckles. "Chaperoning your brother?"

"Just came in to see how you're doing," I say, deciding to play the game. Being rude to Danner will get me nowhere. "How are you feeling?"

"Fine, overall." He stretches out his right leg. "Muscles a little tight, and my digestion likes to act up before bed."

It's no secret Danner is lactose intolerant. "Any problems with your sciatica?"

He smiles. "Turns out not having to carry things up and down a staircase all day saves the back."

"Father shouldn't have had you doing those things," Wick says, dropping into a wingback chair. "You're not a pack mule."

"Keeps me spry." I notice that his hand shakes when he lifts his teacup. "I assume Pace is well."

"He's fine."

"And your Princess? She should be about twenty-one, twenty—"

"Twenty-two weeks," Wicker finishes. I shoot him a glare, but he continues, "Fetus is about the size of an eggpl—"

"The Princess' condition is none of your concern, Danner," I snap, cutting Wicker off. *Jesus Christ.* How can he be so diligent about

Father's interrogation, but Danner apparently gets all the information?

Rookie moves.

Danner meets my gaze. "You're right, of course. I've lost the privilege of taking care of her and you." He looks between us, a sad smile on his lips. "I know you don't want to hear it, but I've hoped that finally having an heir would soothe your Father's temperament. He tried desperately for years to have another child, but every attempt was futile. As you know, there's so little about a King's world that's beyond his control. But the creation of life? That's in the hands of a higher power. Verity and you boys were his last chance. Everything he did was out of desperation."

"Don't." My voice is hard. "His actions are *not* defensible."

"Of course not," he says quickly. "I'm just providing some perspective on the actions of a man as complex as your father."

"Was it desperation that led to him burying those bodies down in the solarium?" Rage surges through me, something I used to have under control, but has risen closer to the surface with every trip down to the dungeon. "Was it desperation that had him whore Wicker out? Or lock Pace up for almost two years? What about my beatings? Did he do that out of desperation, too?"

To my disgust, Danner nods. "All of it, Lagan. Every step. Every move. These were all the actions of a terribly desperate man."

Anger is one match strike away from a lit fuse. I try to cloak it with a cool facade, with the demeanor of a physician—steady like a surgeon—but at times like this, it's impossible to hold back. "So that's why there's five dead bodies buried in the solarium? Because Father was desperate?" I scoff. "Bullshit. He's nothing but a monster."

He frowns at the language, but I notice he doesn't even make an attempt to argue. "Have you made progress on identifying the bones?"

I weigh how much I want to tell him versus how much he can tell me. "Not as much as I'd like," I admit. "Whoever placed them there did it with some care, which makes it easier. But excavating the bodies, tagging and sorting, is a big task, and we currently have bigger Kings to fry."

I do know that they're all female. And young—approximately eighteen to twenty-four. There are no obvious signs of trauma or violence. No bullet holes or broken bones. No cracked skulls. The bones themselves are old, having been in the ground for several years, and there's no indication they belong to the current missing girls. I'm aware of all of this, but I don't reveal it.

"I'm sure you'll figure it out," Danner says. "You're a smart boy."

Impatiently, I reply, "I think you can help me figure it out a lot faster. Who do the bones belong to?"

"Your science hasn't told you?" There's a trace of mocking in his tone that makes me want to glance at Wicker, as if to say, *see?* It's a brief glimpse of the truth—the man Danner actually is. "I thought your father gave you access to the Forsyth DNA profiles. Surely, the answers to your questions are there."

"Danner," Wick interjects, his voice calmer than my own. "It may improve your position if you cooperate."

The old man takes another long sip of tea, his throat shifting as he swallows. "Ask. I'll answer if possible."

I take my shot. "Why were they left here, in the solarium, and not disposed of by the Barons?" That's the part that really gets me. It's not that Father's responsible for the deaths. My brothers and I were molded to be his weapons. We know firsthand just how casually he decides to end a life.

But he hid it from the Royalty, which was built to handle such things neatly and quietly and without complications. There are precious few reasons he'd circumvent those sorts of established procedures, and none of them are good.

"Even the Baron King and his shadows have their... moral limits." Danner's eyes are steady. "Innocent girls seem to be one of them."

"Innocents?" Wicker asks, leaning forward.

"As innocent as one can be," Danner clarifies, "after going through the throning ceremony and taking the role of Princess."

"So it's true," I say. "They're princesses." The age of the victims and location of the bones had made me suspect as much, but it's nice to have confirmation—something to help me narrow down the search.

"Each and every one." He glances at his wrinkled, age-spotted hands. "Failed, of course. Of no use to East End."

Wick and I share a look before he stands, moving closer to Danner. "Nothing you're saying makes sense. Why would Father kill a failed Princess? Don't they just get sent away?"

"Usually," Danner says, but then there's a stretch of silence that bothers me. It's like he's choosing his words a little too carefully. Tactically. "But there for... a time, there were some princesses he chose to offer a chance at... redemption."

Wicker recoils. "Tell me this isn't going where I think it's going."

"All princesses are chosen as vessels for a reason," Danner explains, looking at me now. "Strong genes. Excellent behavior. Icons of purity and motherhood."

"It'd be such a waste, wouldn't it?" My grin is brittle, carved from the hot, wild thing that's always throbbing in my chest when I look at Verity. "Letting those fertile *vessels* just waltz out of East End, unused?"

Danner gives me a serious nod. "Indeed."

"So he'd rape them."

His mouth forms a disapproving frown. "Every Princess gives her consent to—"

"Her Princes." Wicker bites out.

Danner's eyes soften. "The covenants are very clear about our King's place as head of this household."

Uninterested in hearing more of the Royal spin, I ask, "So, he dumps his seed into East End's finest disgraced princesses, hoping to get his precious fucking heir out of one of them, and then what? Why kill them? What happened?"

"The day after Michael died, I found Master Ashby in the water." Danner's eyes seem far away, lost in a memory. "It was winter. Cold and gray. Made my bones hurt something awful. I saw him out there, just standing in it, chest-deep. Not moving. I thought at first he was trying to end it. I panicked," a shaky, wrinkled finger rises, pointing out the window, "waded out there myself, splashing around like a fool. And you know what I saw when I grabbed him?" He looks between me and Wick. "Nothing. He never cried for Michael, you know. There wasn't anything there to give. He just became... empty. A shell of a person." A slow, wistful smile touches his lips. "Until the night he brought Whitaker home."

My fists clench. "Oh, bullshit."

"It's true," Danner stresses. "Suddenly, he had a purpose. Not an heir—not really—but enough to make him want one again." He reaches out to grab Wicker's hand, the move making my chest burn with hot fury. "My boy, you were a miracle."

It's manipulation, pure and simple, and I worry that Wick's too blinded by affection for the old man to see it.

But suddenly, he tugs his hand away from Danner's grasp, face twisted in disgust. "I wasn't a miracle. I was stolen. I was cut away from my real family. I was a fucking *pet*."

"You were a boy without a father," Danner replies. "He was a father without a boy. In another life, maybe that would have been enough." A shadow fills his expression. "But it wasn't. Instead of filling Michael's place, you reminded him of what he could have had: a blood heir."

Frustrated, I snap. "You didn't answer the question, Danner."

"Oh, but I did." Danner takes a slow, shaky sip of his tea, "You just didn't listen to the answer."

I give Wicker a tired look. *Great*. Cryptic horseshit. This isn't any better than interrogating Father. At least when we do that, there's a sense of satisfaction at the whip slicing into his flesh. "Who were the princesses?" I ask instead. "I'm going to find out eventually. Might as well save East End the lab fees."

"Oh, I couldn't remember their names if I tried," he says, waving this off. "It was so long ago now—so many girls in and out of this palace. They're all 'Princess' to me."

"Here's a name you'll remember." I watch him closely. "Odette Delisle."

There it is.

A twitch of his eyebrow.

"Doesn't ring a bell, I'm afraid."

Deciding I've had enough of this game, I jerk my chin at my brother. "Let's go."

Wick doesn't argue, and although he still says a quiet goodnight to Danner, I sense a change in him as we exit the room. At the back staircase, I ask, "Are you okay?"

"Peachy," he says, climbing the steps with those long legs. "Finding out Father was inspired to kidnap, rape, and murder failed princesses because you're not good enough is an excellent way to end the day." We get to the landing of our wing and he turns to me, bitterness in his eyes. "Maybe I'll go fuck out my shame with my own Princess, who's undoubtedly curled up in that massive bed right now, sneaking the candy she has hidden in the weapons chamber." He cuts me a look. "Oh wait, that's not allowed either because even though we're not in the dungeon, we're all fucking trapped."

Melodramatic much?

"You see, this is exactly why we didn't want you going in there. Danner can't be trusted. He's a liar and a manipulator, just like Father. That story about finding him in the water? It's bullshit, Wick." I don't know the truth, but I'm not letting that old man mindfuck my brother any worse than he already is. "He found an opportunity to get you off-balance, and it worked. Father *is* a raping, murderous monster, and Danner is programmed to make excuses for what he does."

Wick stops in front of our shared bedroom. "What about you? Did that throw you off-balance?"

"Enough that I'm going to ask Pace to lock me in tonight." I've been better lately, but the long days, sober life, and lack of sex has me on edge. Adding in a dose of white hot rage from the news Danner just told me is enough to spill out in my sleep. "Go to her." I grimace. "And be nice. Don't take all this shit out on her."

"Fine." He heads toward her room, then tosses back, "But I'm getting a handjob at the very minimum."

An hour later, I'm exhausted. I strip down and turn on the shower, spinning the knob to make it as hot as possible. The room fills with steam, and I think about the bones. I don't doubt that Danner's telling the truth about them belonging to failed princesses. Father would believe he had the right to them until they were no longer of value, and in his twisted mind, that may have been after he'd tried to create with them. With the way the females are valued in East End—Forsyth as a whole—no one would have questioned where they went after being disgraced.

Stepping into the shower, I ease into the scalding water. I set my back to the spray, palms flat on the wall, and let the burn wash over me.

I've been too busy—too distracted by Father being down in the dungeon, taking care of Verity, and handling the needs of East End— to really focus on identifying the bones. Danner's mocking may have been a diversion, but he's right. The proof *will* be in the science. However, if I'm lucky, digging through the files for a match may not be necessary.

Shutting off the water, I dry off and change into a pair of sweats before sliding on my glasses. I open my kit, grab what I need, and take it into Pace's room. He sits behind his monitors, each one focused on a different part of the palace, interior and exterior.

Standing over him, my gaze goes directly to the screen in the center—it's the largest—the one covering the Princess' room. She and Wick are in bed, asleep, the image of them captured in infrared. He's got her pulled close, because despite whatever tensions run between them, Wick is an aggressive cuddler. His face is buried in her neck, his arm wrapped tight around her body, although I notice that even in sleep, he avoids touching her stomach.

Fuck, I miss being there beside them.

The feel of the three of us all in the bed at once, surrounding her, and keeping her safe—we didn't get many of those nights before everything went to hell in a handbasket, but it was enough to make me crave more. Unfortunately, right now, I don't trust myself. Not until Father's been handled.

"Hey," I say, dragging my eyes away from the screen, "look at me."

Pace turns, frowning as I unwrap the sealed package I brought in with me. "What the hell is that for?"

"I need a sample."

He eyes me suspiciously. "Don't you have one in the system?"

"Yeah, but ask me if I trust that system. At least when it comes to those bodies down there." He stares at the swab, jaw clamped shut. "Open up, brother. This is one mystery we can solve."

Pace relents, opening his mouth, and I take a sample from the inside of his cheek. Once I'm finished, I secure the swab in the tube and place it back in my kit. "I'll run it against the DNA profiles in the morning."

"So you believe Danner," he says, turning back to the monitors.

"Do I believe he was using failed princesses in an attempt to create an heir? Absolutely." Arching an eyebrow, I add, "But do I believe it was some redemption story they all agreed to? Not a chance. I'd bet anything he had them locked downstairs."

"Yeah, me too." He glances over his shoulder at me. "Thanks for asking about her."

"It was a long shot." I rub beneath my glasses, eyes stinging and gritty. Everything about me feels tired and edgy, like I'm about to burst out of my skin. "You going to be up tonight?"

"Yeah, I've got an idea for this proof of life thing." He glances over at me. "Why? You need a chaperone?"

"More like a warden. Hey," I ask, nodding to the center screen, "does she really sneak candy when I'm not looking?"

Without the slightest hesitation, he says, "Yes."

I groan. "Seriously? That's not on her meal plan."

"Dude, it's been a stressful few weeks—for all of us. Don't even think about taking those from her." Behind Pace's head, there's movement on the screen in Verity's room. There's no volume, but the camera catches her rolling around, pushing Wicker onto his back.

"What's she doing?" I ask, moving closer to sit on the arm of the couch. Wick's eyes flutter open as she slings her leg over his body.

"Looks like Rosi's horny," Pace says, leaning back in his chair with a smirk.

"They can't fuck," I point out. "Her body isn't ready."

Physically, maybe not, but from what we're watching, hormonally is a different story. Wick's eyes are glued to the woman straddling him. He's frozen, watching as she strips off her gown, revealing her full tits and swollen belly.

"Chill, her panties are still on." Pace shifts in his seat, adjusting himself. "Trust him."

Wick snaps out of his stupor and surges up, pushing her hair off her face. He leans into her, kissing her long and slow. Verity takes his hands and places them over her tits.

"Fuck *me*. They're so fucking hot together, aren't they?" Pace exhales. "Her nipples are insanely sensitive. I made her come yesterday just by sucking on them."

"It's hormones," I reply, even though I'm barely paying attention to the way my mouth forms the words. "Estrogen, primarily."

Wick pulls the band out of her hair, letting the red waves fall down her back. Her hips rock greedily. I knew she was horny, her body flush with hormones, but watching her glide her body over Wicker's reinforces the concept. It reinforces why I can't be alone with her, because my brother, despite his hypersexuality and impulsivity, knows how to control himself. But this hot, wild thing clamoring around inside my chest? It's primal, beyond sense or logic or concepts like love.

And it'd tear her apart just to find a place to plant its seed.

4

erity

Nights in the palace have grown painfully quiet.

It's not the same kind of quiet it used to be, with the guys sneaking around, trying to keep things from their father. There was fear in that quiet. Pain. Secrets.

But this silence is unique and fragile, as if the smallest breath could shatter it.

I wish something would.

I'm not sure when the prospect of sleeping in a quiet bed began disturbing me. Maybe it was all those lonely nights in the hospital, so scared for the delicate life growing inside of me, but ever since I came back to the palace, it feels like something's missing, and I've been unable to shake this strange *hunger*. Not for sex, although with the way my hormones have been raging, it certainly wouldn't hurt.

The hunger is for the way it used to be—even briefly. The sensation of the four of us packed in tight, wrapped around one another, had been an aching comfort. It's taken me a long time to put my finger on it, but I think it must remind me of home. The warmth of bodies, the press of shameless limbs, and heady breaths. West End has an undeniably physical nature. I never really considered it before I was thrust into East End, with its cold dinners and stiff, formal rituals.

Then there's the baby, his size making it harder and harder to find a comfortable position. And if I do settle down, he'll press on my bladder, giving me the urge to pee every forty-five minutes. My sleep is always restless now, as if my limbs are seeking the closest warm body and only finding *his*.

Not that Wicker isn't a fantastic cuddler.

I can't tell what rouses me tonight, but I know that when I surface from the foggy veil of sleep, it's the breadth of him against my back. Wicker always smells clean, but there's an edge of something spicy buried beneath it, sharp as a razor. I don't even need to open my eyes to know it's him.

Also, his erection is drilling into the small of my back and turns into a small, mindless, rut.

It's not the first time. Usually, I just jostle him with a jerk of my body, and he grumbles something soft and frustrated into my neck before aggressively flopping to the other side of the bed.

Tonight, that hunger throbs between my legs.

It's the first time I've felt a warm, sticky wetness accompanying the pressure.

"Wick?" I whisper, arching my back into the sleepy curve of his body. "Wicker, you awake?"

All I get in response is his gritty chuff, his arm tightening around my middle. Against my backside, his cock gives a strong twitch, the wetness surging. I groan at the realization of what's happened, pressing back into his lazy, mindless thrust. He's the most difficult to be around these days. Mostly, he's absent, always busy down in the dungeon or sweeping the palace grounds. Aside from our quiet, fragile bedtime, he hardly spends any time with me at all.

And the hunger *burns*.

I wonder, as I roll toward him and straddle his hips, if this is how Lex feels when he's sleeping. Does the need for touch burn like an inferno through his veins? Does he look down at me like I'm watching Wicker, hoping to see a gaze staring back? Does it twist painfully in his gut when I don't?

But then Wicker's blue eyes suddenly blink to life, his cock hard against my center as I rock into him. "Red?" he rasps, pushing his hair from his eyes. "Can we fuck yet?"

"No," I say, pulling off my nightgown. Everything feels unbearably slow and far too heavy. It hurts to hold myself up, the gravity dragging me down into the expanse of his warm chest. Even the blink of his eyes as they settle on my exposed breasts seems to take a century.

"Oh," he breathes, fingers grazing my bare sides. "Brutal, Red. Can't fuck you yet. Lex said."

Holding his gaze, I feel ripe and too warm, rocking down against the bulge in his boxer briefs. "This'll do."

He hisses at the motion, grinding his head back into the pillow. Strong hands grasp my hips, fingertips bruising as he drags me up the length of his cock. "Jizzed in my shorts already. *Jesus.* Fucking junior high shit. That's how desperate I've become."

"You complaining?"

The air between us is full of hot exhalations, and suddenly he's rearing up, licking a hot path from my collarbone to my nipple. My belly protrudes between us, but he manages to avoid it carefully, like it isn't even there. "Would you care?"

Freezing, I thread my fingers through his hair, pulling until his dazed blue eyes lock with mine. "I'll always care, Wick."

He stares at me like that for a long moment, his left palm cupping the weight of my breast.

And then he falls back.

"Come on, then," he rumbles, guiding my hips into a slow, aching rhythm. "Ride me."

It's never difficult with him, as if our bodies have known what they wanted long before our brains ever caught up. It's like being possessed, my hips working of their own accord in long, rolling writhes. I can see his building pleasure in the slack part of his mouth. The way the tendons in his neck strain when he rocks up into me. The pinch of his eyes as he watches the sway of my breasts, so quiet.

"No one touches me like you do, you know," he murmurs, skating his fingertips up to my nipple. "You gonna come like this?"

God, he has no idea.

One brush of his fingertip over my nipple has me trembling, but it's the hardness against my center that drives my movements, the fabric between us damp with arousal. Mine? His? Ours?

Wicker already came in his sleep, but he's still hard.

Still throbbing.

Somehow, I'm not expecting it when he surges up to kiss me, a hand tangled in my hair. It's sloppier than I'm used to from him, all serrated teeth and clipped grunts, and when I palm his chest, it's rock solid. Tense. Strung so tight I can practically feel him vibrating with restraint.

"You won't hurt me," I promise, willing him to let go, "if that's what you're thinking about."

His mouth curves deliciously against mine. "Nah, I'm just thinking about how much I want to fuck your tits, Red." He punctuates this with a gentle pinch to my nipple, rolling the peak between forefinger and thumb, and I whimper.

Honest to god *whimper*.

"Fuck, you're so hot when you're like this," he says, panting. He never stops spurring me on, the hand on my hip moving to the small of my back, forceful as it yanks me into him. "Never had as many wet dreams as I've had after meeting you."

It's his dirty mouth that tips me over the edge, along with my wet panties and his touch. The combination is too much, and the orgasm trips through me, like releasing a series of locks. I feel it all over—from my nipples, down my spine, to the throbbing heat in my clit. Wicker grunts, stilling my body with his big hands. He pumps furiously, back arching as he comes a second time, then falls flat on the pillow.

"That shouldn't have been as hot as it was," he admits, throwing an arm over his forehead as his chest rises and falls. His eyes cut to the top right corner of the room. "Hope the boys enjoyed it."

I laugh, endorphins rushing through my body. "A dry hump? Not quite the X-rated material they're used to."

"Rosi, you're not watching the right porn." Gently, he rolls me off his body, onto my back, bending my knees. His nose wrinkles at the front of his shorts before he discards them. When he climbs out of bed to walk to the bathroom, I can't help but watch the way he moves, naked and shameless, the muscles in his ass shifting like art.

For a while, the faucet runs, and then he returns with a wet cloth. "It's warm," he tells me, easing off my soiled panties. It's not even awkward when he wipes away the sticky mess. "Don't do that with Pace. We'll be cleaning up spunk for a week."

Cleaned up and back in my gown, I settle back on my side, pulling one of the extra blankets to my chest. Wick gets back in and quickly clears the distance, dragging us together.

I feel his hand rest on my thigh.

"You never touch my belly," I say, feeling his heartbeat against my back. "Does it bother you?"

Softly, he confesses, "Not in the way you're thinking." His eyelids are heavy, gaze wandering aimlessly around the room. "I wish it were Lex's."

He's right. That's not what I'm thinking. "Why?"

"Because he's ready for this and I'm not." I expect him to move but he doesn't. If anything, he draws me closer. "Lex grew up ten years ago—probably right after the first beating. He still remembers what it was like to have parents. A family. He's talked about it before, how it was a feeling he had. This security that was there one day and gone the next. I don't even have that."

I rest my hand on his, linking our fingers. "Just because you didn't have something doesn't mean you never can."

His chest twitches with a snort. "I'm not a creator, Red. That's not what I was made for."

I think about this for a long moment, watching his chest expand and contract. "Creation and death are two sides of the same coin."

The words from my attacker that night in the garden still haunt me. They're Ashby's words, too. "You're the coin, Wicker. You're more than one thing."

His fingertip taps mine in a mindless rhythm. "That's the problem, Red. I don't know what I am anymore. So what the fuck am I supposed to tell this kid? Is he an Ashby? Is he a Kayes? Is he a Sinclaire?" He exhales, the line of his brow more troubled than I like. "Some day he's going to wonder where he belongs."

"He belongs with us," I say, matter-of-factly. "Kayes, Ashby... those are definitions made by other men who never knew you. We're building our own family. Our own legacy. One where this child will have three fathers, and he'll know each and every one."

I know what I'm saying sounds like a fantasy, out of reach, but in my heart, I believe it. I believe Wicker can be a good father. He just needs to believe it himself.

"I think..." he starts, then stops. To my surprise, he looks at it—my belly—and slowly lifts a hand, resting his palm right there in the middle. Something complicated passes over his features. It's not quite a frown, and even less of a grimace, but it still makes my heart sink.

He looks so *lost*.

Pulling back, he clears his throat. "I think I just need a little time to adjust to it all." And then a rough, "Sorry I can't be as into it as them."

I'm the one who frowns then, using my own palm to chase the fading heat of his on my belly. "You don't need to be sorry, Wick."

The sad fact is that Wicker has been forced to be with many women, but this is the first time it's created something. And though I mean the words, it still sits heavily in my chest, because the two of us have this in common. For a while there, this baby had been a wound for me, too. Painful, festering. The product of abuse. Evidence of hurt.

I can't heal Wicker. Neither can his brothers or our son.

But maybe I can give him a place to start.

∽

"THAT ONE, TOO," I say, pointing to the large portrait on the landing of the stairs.

Lex purses his lips, head tilting as he inspects it. "Why that one?"

"He's creepy," is my answer.

The man in the painting is middle-aged and stick-thin. His eyes are hollow and he's holding a rose like it's a weapon. I don't even know who he is. Maybe he's an Ashby. Maybe we're related. Maybe this is some distant granduncle or something.

I shudder. "Put it with the cherubs."

Shrugging, Pace drags the ladder over and climbs the four rungs to reach it, smoothly unmounting it from the wall. Something inside of my chest unwinds when he stacks it with the others, face down.

"What's next?" Wicker asks, only half paying attention. He's leaning against the wall in an annoyingly artful curve, a half-full beer bottle dangling from his hand. "Wanna take down the drapes? Pull up the carpet?"

Actually, I kind of do.

I've been taking them all throughout the second floor, removing the portraits I hate. Sometimes Pace or Wicker will chime in with their own opinion—they really don't like still lifes—and they'd go into the pile. But mostly, I'm just trying to erase it of *him*. Unfortunately, de-Rufus'ing the palace is probably an exercise in futility.

We'd have to burn it down.

"The drapes," I agree, smirking at Pace, who grabs two fistfuls of the heavy brocade covering the window and gives it a powerful yank.

Suddenly, the landing is bathed in colorful light.

It really is a beautiful palace, the window bearing a geometric stained glass design. Burning it down would be effective, but a real shame.

We'll just have to make it our own.

Hands on my hips, I nod decisively. "Let's go to the next wing."

It's not the best way to spend a summer's day, but also not the worst. I stand by as Pace, Lex, and a couple of PNZ members labor through it, removing paintings and ornate tables, crude figurines, and creepy busts. Somewhere in the middle of this, guys begin losing their shirts, tucking them into their waistbands. A fine sheen of sweat covers Lex's brow as he and Rory push an old armoire to the end of the hall. I watch him specifically—Lex—and the way his muscles shift and ripple as he pushes. It doesn't even matter that he pulled off his shirt to reveal a white tank top.

He's magnificent.

I'm used to seeing him do such precise, delicate things that it's almost easy to miss the pure, masculine power of his body.

There is *rippling*.

"You've got a little something..." Pace says, thumbing at the corner of my mouth. "Oh, that's just drool."

I try to snap out of the lust-fog, sending him a tepid glare. "Shouldn't you be destroying more drapes?" He groans when I point out the tall, gargantuan window in the library, its windows covered with heavy velvet.

"You're just trying to make it hotter in here so we'll sweat more," he grumbles, stalking over to the window in question.

Well, it doesn't hurt.

Wicker, however, does almost nothing. "Does this," he asks, pointing to his cheek, "look like a face for manual labor?"

I roll my eyes. "You've lived under Ashby's elaborate roof your whole life. Now he's out of the equation, this place belongs to us. Don't you want to make it yours?"

Plainly, he says, "It *is* mine. I don't need to gut it to feel better."

"Really?" I step up to him, arms crossed. "So that painting in the foyer—you know, the one with the Prince standing over the dead Baron—you don't feel any desire to burn it?"

His lip twitches. "Father didn't kill my father." Brow knitting up, he backtracks, "*Ashby* didn't kill my father. You know what I mean. I think that painting is hilarious, though. It's perfectly *him*. More about the illusion of victory than anything real." Tipping the bottle to his mouth, he takes a long swig of the beer. "I know you're new here and all, but I came to terms with my world a long time ago, Red."

"Oh?" I arch an eyebrow. "So you haven't even considered taking it down and pissing on it?"

He pauses, the bottle poised against his lips, and then hums thoughtfully. "Hm."

I jerk my chin at the staircase, holding back a laugh. "Go on."

But the moment he pushes off the door he's been leaning against, I stop him. "Wait. What's in here?"

Wicker turns, making a face. "That room? That's—"

"The nursery." Pace approaches, dragging the slain drapes behind him. "It's been closed off ever since the vandalization incident."

Lex returns, mopping his brow with his discarded shirt. "According to Father's calendar, we're supposed to be cleaning it out right about now, calling the decorator, anointing it with oil."

I check his expression for seriousness. Honestly, I can't tell. "Is that last one true?"

"No." His lips twitch. "I mean, I don't think so."

Turning to the door, my stomach flutters as I reach for the knob, swinging it open.

The smell alone makes me stumble back, Pace's strong hands catching me. "Oh my god," I choke, pushing my wrist beneath my nose. "What *is* that?"

"That," Wicker says, smirking, "is the smell of rancid pig's blood."

"They never cleaned up the blood?!" I gawk into the room, but it's not what I'm expecting. There's not any blood visible. It looks clean enough, if overly bare. There's an old, ornate crib against one wall with no mattress or bedding. Against the other wall are a long antique cabinet and a rocking chair. There's an empty iron clothing rack on the other side, and the walls are a dull, faded orange and lilac color.

But then I realize the orange is just the blood stains.

"It got into the base and floorboards," Lex comments, ducking his head inside with a grimace. "We're going to have to strip it down to the studs."

"Like hell we are," I squawk. "My baby is *not* sleeping in here. The grossness of rancid floorboard blood aside, it's like a mile from my bedroom. How am I supposed to hear him crying?" Turning, I notice the tense, grim looks on their faces. "What?"

Lex pushes a lock of hair behind his ear. "Well…. usually, a Princess' handmaiden would sleep next door." He jerks his chin to the room. "That door beside the crib connects the rooms."

A lump grows in my throat as I inspect the room, imagining Stella waking in the middle of the night to pad her way in here, reaching down into the crib, and shushing our son with her soft, lilting voice. It's difficult to shove it back down. "Well, I don't have a handmaiden anymore," I reply, clearing the ache from my throat. "And even if I did, I'm not letting some other woman mother my baby. That's absurd."

Lex nods like he agrees with me, but, "It's just… there aren't any free rooms in our wing."

"Is anyone else going to say it?" Pace looks between the three of us, raising an eyebrow. "We don't need to live in this house of nightmares."

I shuffle my feet, frowning. "Where else would we go?" I see the way they look at one another, my emphasis on *we* not having gone unheard.

"Our trust funds are still locked," Lex says, sighing. He braces his hands against each side of the door jamb, his biceps flexing with the motion. "I have years of med school and residency ahead of me. It'll be a long time before I can pull enough income to support us all."

Wicker takes another pull from the bottle, snorting. "Fuck, I've barely chosen a major."

"We don't need a whole palace." Pace crosses his arms, looking pretty serious about it.

But I eye Lex and Wicker, and know they're wondering the same thing. Who would take the palace, if not us? Would Danner stay here? The next set of Princes, totally unchecked? A place like this needs staff, upkeep, and money, but most important of all is the *idea* of it. The Purple Palace is an institution just as much as a home— exactly like West End's clock tower. There's power in living here and the minute we walk away, there's a power vacuum that someone will fill.

Lex snorts, tossing his brother a skeptical look. "So you're ready to give up the military-grade surveillance of our massive estate? Because the baby is going to be here in three months."

Pace reaches up to rub his neck, forehead knitted into a pensive frown. "Okay, maybe you have a point."

Wicker mutters a curse, drawing our attention to him. "Fuck it. He can have my room." At the ensuing, stunned silence, Wicker just shrugs. "Pace needs his room for the equipment, and Lex needs his for the lock. But let's be real, I almost never use mine. It's mostly just there to hold all my clothes." He freezes, eyes widening. "Wait. Is there any chance we can expand her closet?"

Lex rubs his chin, amber eyes lost in thought. "You know, if we knock out a doorway beside the bathroom, we can connect her room to Wick's, easy peasy."

That lump returns to my throat again when I face Wicker. "You're sure you're okay with that?"

He glances around, looking panicked. "I'm serious about the closet situation. Do you have any idea how many clothes I have?" He rolls his eyes, though. "But yeah, if it'll get me out of having to pull up these floorboards, consider the room all his. No skin off my back."

I grin at him, hoping he can see the softness in it. "Thank you."

It was barely fifteen hours ago that we were in that big, half-empty bed, somber and quiet as Wicker visibly struggled to reconcile the concept of fatherhood.

With a lazy salute, he saunters away, loudly stressing, "Closet space first, Red."

A SHIVER RUNS through me as I peer into the darkened room on the other side of the glass. The open wounds he had when I came down a few days ago have started to scab over, red and raw and angry. According to Pace, my Princes have altered their approach, shifting more toward sensory deprivation than physical torture.

"If this makes you uncomfortable," Lex says, ever observant, "we can do it another time."

"It's not the situation," I say, rubbing my arms to quell the goose-bumps. "My body can't regulate the temperature these days. One minute I'm hot. The next I'm freezing."

"Here," Pace says, shrugging off his hoodie. It's marked with 'FU Hockey' over the heart, the number three stitched on the sleeve. The shirt he's wearing underneath is sleeveless, revealing the lean, hard muscle in his inked arms. He drapes the sweatshirt over my shoulders. "This'll piss him off, anyway. Just another reminder of who you belong to."

His scent lingers, and that does more to bolster my courage than anything else. "Thank you."

"Bulky, too." A hand comes down on my shoulder and spins me around. Wicker stands before me, catching the ends of the zipper between his long fingers. He drags it slowly up, covering my belly and stopping just below my breasts. "Father loathes a tease—especially when it's hiding his heir." His eyes linger a beat longer than necessary on my cleavage, and he licks his bottom lip. "You ready?"

I nod. Asking Ashby about the women in the garden is easy. Until now, they've been faceless, nameless victims, left to rot into compost. I want to know who they are as much as anyone else, but I have a bigger question for the fallen King, one I've been too angry and frankly too fragile to ask until now: who the hell did he send after me that night?

"Let's do this," I tell him, ignoring the concerned gaze of my other two Princes.

After an arm wrestling match, three rounds of rock, paper, scissors, and then some unspoken game involving punches that I couldn't quite follow, I made the ultimate decision about who I wanted to go with me into the torture chamber with Ashby. There are two primary reasons I chose Wicker. One is because he's the baby's biological father, a Kayes, and that alone is enough to spark Ashby's innate jealousy. And two, Wicker is the least protective of the baby. I need someone with me who understands the mind games Ashby is playing, and Wicker is fluent in pretentious bullshit.

"Be careful," Lex says, taking one last chance to frame my belly with both hands. "He'll manipulate you any way he can to get information about him."

"I can handle myself." I'm not afraid of him. I'm afraid of the anger that surges every time I think about the risk he put me and his unborn grandson in just to prove some deranged and delusional point. That he, over my Princes, should raise my child. This man truly knows no bounds.

Wick opens the door at the same time Pace flips on the overhead lights. The chamber is flooded with the glare of fluorescents, and a small cry of surprise echoes off the stone walls. I walk in first, Wicker right behind me, closing the door with the latch snapping into place. Instantly, I'm reminded of my own time down here. The cold, damp chill. The musty scent is now co-mingled with the coppery residue of blood.

"Verity," Ashby says, eyes squinting. "You came to see me."

"Weird." I sniff the air.

"What's that, Princess?" Wicker asks, pulling over a chair for me to sit across from the blinking, bound man.

I ease down, resting my hand on my stomach. Wicker moves to lean his back against the door, his eyebrow raised in exaggerated interest. "You'd think the way Rufus goes on about bloodlines and legacies, that Royal blood would smell different." I sniff again. "But it's exactly the same as everyone else's."

"Ah, I see you came ready to play," Ashby says, his eyes acclimating. He frowns as I come into view, taking in my body head to toe. Other than the hoodie, I'm in a comfortable pair of stretchy leggings. Commoner clothes. "I guess that's why you're dressed like a West End hooligan. Prepared for a fight?"

"I'm not here to fight with you. I'm here for answers."

He raises his chin, just as haughty as ever. "You know my parameters. Update me on my grandson, and I'll see what I can do."

"Wrong," I reply. "You're the one tied up, emaciated, and reeking of piss. You're definitely the one running out of time. Give me what I want, and I'll consider providing you with an update."

His eyes shift from me to Wick.

"Am I really running out of time, Whitaker, or are you? There are procedures in place. I'm sure you've been called in by the Kings by now, ordered to give proof of life."

Wick picks at the ever-present scabs on his knuckles. "The other Kings are well aware of your current status. They aren't too bothered, really. They have questions of their own, particularly the Baron King, who made it quite clear he's alarmed about the dead bodies in your solarium—bodies he wasn't tasked with removing. And as for Perilini and Payne... well. They'd be almost as happy as us to see you rot down here for eternity. The new generation of Royals aren't very impressed with you."

If it bothers him to hear this, he does a good job of hiding it, sniffing dismissively. "And what about those outside of leadership? People are talking, aren't they? By this point, I'm missed, and not just by the society types. Have your PNZ brothers started whispering about your slapdash coup? I can think of a few boys who'd be more than interested in a mutiny. Thomas has had sour grapes since I named the three of you my Princes."

Wicker, god love him, in all his arrogant beauty, lazily pushes off the door and walks over to me. He strokes my hair, brushing it off my neck, then plants a slow kiss on the skin beneath my ear. It's inappropriate as fuck, but chills run across my skin, and I'm glad my nipples are covered by Pace's thick hoodie.

"That's your problem, you know that? Always underestimating us. Thinking we're too common, or inbred, or subservient to make it on our own." Wick straightens. "Proof of life is in process and will be delivered to the Kings as directed. The residents of East End and Forsyth are content with the fact you're on an extended business trip. No one will blink when you're not seen for another month, and by then, we'll have you replaced entirely. Now that we're clear on that," Wick nods down at me, "why don't you ask your question, Red."

Ashby sighs heavily, as though we're wasting his time, but finally shuts up long enough for me to ask, "Who did you hire to attack me?"

"That's your big question?" He scoffs. "A common thug."

"Yeah," I say, leaning back, letting my stomach protrude. "I don't think so. There was something about his voice. His choice of words. He sounded quite educated."

"Impressive," he replies, "although I can see why to someone raised with non-Royals it would be distinct."

Wicker tenses next to me, and I know if I don't want this to end in a pummeling I need to get him to talk. "So? Who was it? It couldn't have been anyone who liked you very much. I'm willing to bet you had a different agreement from what went down."

For all my Princes and I are expendable to him, there's one thing I can trust for certain:

Rufus Ashby would never want this baby to die.

His lips are cracked and peeling, split in the center, drawing my grimace as he speaks. "The man I hired wasn't just a test for the boys, but for the other houses as well. I found a weak link in one of Forsyth's strongest foundations." His cracked lips form a thin line. "But you're right. I'm displeased that he took it so far. You and the child were never to be harmed, and if I weren't locked down here, I'd have already dealt with the matter swiftly and decisively." He lifts his chin at my stomach. "Now. Tit for tat, Verity."

I glance at Wicker, and he gives me a curt nod.

Straightening in the chair, I pull at the zipper, revealing the entirety of my stomach. Ashby grins, a strange, feral expression transforming his face. "Such a strange thought, isn't it? To know there's life growing just beneath all that skin and muscle? So much potential..."

I give Wicker an uncertain look, but he just gives a minute shake of his head. So, I ignore the comment. "So I was right. He is Royal," I say, trying not to squirm under his gaze. "What's his name?"

Ashby's eyes narrow. "I'll need to know how much weight you've gained, the fetal heart rate, and I want to know if he's active. The fall you took..." A coldness seeps into the hard angles of his face. "That wasn't supposed to happen. He wasn't supposed to get hurt."

Lex prepared me for comments like these. "He'll try to make himself out to be a victim," he said. "He'll try to act like you're on the same side."

It's what makes it easy for me to school my face and square my shoulders. "You'll tell me the attacker's name if I give you this information?"

"Yes," Ashby says, eyeing me greedily. "I promise."

"As of this morning, I've gained fifteen-point-two pounds." Ashby's expression brightens with every word, like a thirsty man being given water. "And the baby's heart rate is 136 beats per minute..." I glance at Wicker, whose jaw is tight, his eyes watching his Father carefully. "And yes, the baby is active. Mostly at night—"

"That's enough," Wick says. "Give us the name."

Our Father grins. "That heartbeat is strong. Virile. Just like an Ashby."

"Spit it out," Wicker barks.

"And, fifteen pounds..." Ashby repeats, his eyes calculating. "You're thin, however, which would put you somewhere between twenty-two and twenty-four weeks?" I know the math he's doing isn't about the baby. It's about the passage of time, how long he's been down here.

Wicker's large frame steps between us, his broad shoulders and wide back dominating the space. His fist balls and he swings, cracking his father in the face. "Stop fucking around and talk!"

Head turned, Ashby spits, a gob of blood splattering on the floor. Red-tinged drool oozes down his chin. "Violence has never suited you, Whitaker."

"Yeah, well, neither does patience," Wicker responds. "Your daughter asked you a question."

"Fine. You want a name?" Ashby looks up at me, craning his neck, and there's a spark in his eyes that I haven't seen since the day my Princes tossed him in here. "William," he snarls. "His name is William."

WICKER RUSHES me from the room, and Pace shuts off the lights, sending our father back into pitch-black darkness.

"What the fuck?" Lex seethes once we enter the observation room. "William? As in one of the Barons?"

Pace doesn't look convinced. "He knows the Kings have blessed the mutiny. He could be trying to sow discord between us. You know how Father—"

"No." Wicker wears a path from one side of the room to the other, flexing his fists in tight, tense bursts. "He's doing it again."

Shivering, I hug my middle. "Who? Ashby?"

His blue eyes blaze into mine. "Maddox. That motherfucker!" With a crash, he sends everything on the low table to the floor. Pliers, the whip, a large knife. I skitter back, stunned. "First my grandfather, then my dad, and now my son. He won't stop until he's exterminated my whole fucking bloodline!"

It's rare for Wicker to lose his cool. The only times I've truly seen it are during the gender reveal, and when he stopped his father from whipping me in the study. Even then, there'd been a sense of detachment, a lost boy trapped in a man's anger. But standing here now, his face red and his forearms strained, it's not just anger rolling off of him in waves.

I swallow, resting a shaking hand on my stomach.

It's the first time he's ever called the baby his son.

"This," he spits, thrusting a finger at my stomach, "is a declaration of war."

"Calm down," Lex says, pinching the bridge of his nose. "We don't know enough, Wick. Father said this was about testing weak links. Maybe he wanted to see if the Barons are as loyal as everyone thinks. *If* he's even telling the truth," everyone in the room knows that Ashby could be lying, "that means whichever William this is, he could be undermining Maddox as well. We need evidence. We need *facts*."

"Fuck, fuck, fuck. This is a fucking disaster." Pace stops muttering and looks up, resting his hands on his hips. "Obviously we have to kill him."

"Which one?" Lex asks.

Wicker is quick to offer a solution. "All fucking three of them, and their King, too."

I can feel the energy of the room ramping up, teetering on the edge of spiraling out of control.

And then a knock sounds on the door behind me.

Three raps. Then two.

Pace looks at me, jerking his head to the door, and I emit a relieved sigh when I swing it open, revealing a jittery Ballsack. "Oh, thank God." Then I see his face, the dark set of concern marring his features. My heart skips a beat, dread building in my stomach. "What's wrong?"

"We have a problem." His gaze goes from mine to the men behind me. "There's an FBI agent waiting for you at the front gate."

5

P^{ace}

IT'S loud with the sounds of summer when we walk down the drive toward the gate. The sun is low, the sky a blaze of oranges, and the cicadas are screaming—along with the crickets and the frogs. The palace grounds have a certain scent in the summertime, wet and ripe. It's the roses and wisteria, but also the musty scent of the moat and the surrounding trees.

It's such a fucking ridiculous place.

I stand by the fact that we don't need a goddamn castle to raise a kid in. Some people in South Side and West End probably raise their kids in shoeboxes, and they do fine. Hell, Verity herself was raised in a shack behind that ratty gym. It's stupid for four people and a baby to live in a place like this. It's too big to ever be a home. Too many nooks and crannies. Too many linear feet for an intruder to gain access to.

That said, as we approach the large wrought iron gate, I can't deny that the palace has its benefits. The man waiting there has a large ledger tucked beneath one arm. The other lifts a cigarette to his lips, and the pull he takes is hard and aggressive, like he's trying to get as much nicotine as he can out of the single draw before he tosses it to the ground, stamping it out.

"Ashby," he greets us, voice like gravel despite the fact he's fairly young. Maybe in his early thirties. "Ashby, and Ashby. Shouldn't there be one more of you?"

"No," I say, the three of us reaching the gate.

He's dressed in a dark suit. Behind him, a nondescript sedan is idling, no one in the passenger seat.

So he's working this alone, then.

"Agent Knight," he says, smoothly pulling the bottom of his blazer aside to flash the badge. Beside it is a gun in a holster. "Mind if I come in and talk for a minute?"

"You're fucking right, we mind." My words to the agent are firm and without politeness.

Lex inhales deeply. "You'll have to excuse my brother. He's not a fan of your profession."

"Who is?" Agent Knight covers his badge once again. "I'm here about—"

Wicker clucks his tongue. "What are we, idiots? We know why you're here."

Stella. Although, it could be other things. Like the man we've got locked down in the dungeon. Or Danner, who hasn't been seen in weeks. Or Chuck.

Shit. We've been busy.

"If you want through these gates," I tell him, "get a warrant."

"East End never changes, does it?" He scans each of us, eyes lingering on Wicker's head. "Even after all these years, it still smells like hair gel and bullshit."

"If you want to smell our hair gel," I say, slowly, so there's no confusion, "get a warrant."

A small grin curves the corners of the agent's lips, as if he's amused, but there's an air about him, like he thinks he's better—

smarter—than us. Ballsack's intel says he was sent in from the State office or has connections in Forsyth. He's staying down on the Avenue in that shitty flop hotel, but spends most of his time over at the Hideaway fucking the Madam.

"People who don't cooperate tend to have something to hide." He looks around the grounds, clocking the various security cameras and sensors I have in place. "What are you hiding behind these ridiculous gates and all the security?"

"It's mostly brocade drapes and cherub paintings." Wick draws his attention off me. "But what about you, Agent Knight? Got any secrets? Because the way we heard it, you're only here for the South Side trim. Are the feds paying for pussy now, too?"

"Whitaker, right?" Knight asks, opening the ledger. His eyes scan it quickly. "Everyone I've spoken to so far has described you like a poodle, which confused me at first, but now I get it." His lips curl. "Well-groomed, yippy little barks, and largely ineffectual."

"Emphasis on largely." My brother grabs his crotch. "And you've been talking about me? I'm flattered."

Knight ignores him and turns to me. "You're Pace."

I lift my chin. "And you're wasting our nice evening."

"Doesn't have to be a waste." He flips a piece of paper over in his ledger, giving me an intentional view of what's underneath. My court documents. "Just got out of an eighteen-month stint in the Forsyth Penitentiary for wire fraud, right?"

This guy.

"Agent," Lex steps between us, aware I'm about to pop off, "we know our rights. You're not getting past the gates without a warrant. Go downtown, talk to the judge, and get one signed. Then we'll happily let you in."

There's a reason Lex is the smartest. He operates on facts and not emotion like me and Wick. There's not a judge in the whole damn town that'll issue a warrant on Ashby's Palace. Each and every one is a frequent flier down at the Chamber. Father's got more dirt on these men than our gardener's boots.

Agent Knight shrugs. "I'm just trying to find the girl; Stella St.

James." He digs through the folder and pulls out a sheet of paper. It's one of the flyers Rory's been passing around. "It's my understanding you've been looking for her, too."

"Sure, Stella's a sweet girl," Lex says, "and yeah, we've put in the effort to find her. Trust me when I say that no one in East End wants to fuck with a South Side asset. But she didn't go missing in the palace." He nods outside the gate. "She went missing out there."

"True," Knight says, his gaze ticking back over to me, "but she worked here, and this house isn't the only place you've got cameras, is it? I hear there's footage of the day Stella went missing."

I stare blankly. "And?"

He stares boldly back. "And it seems like it'd be in both of our interests for you to share that so I can have it officially examined."

"Sure," I say, with a small shrug, "when you get a warrant."

Wick barely conceals a snort.

"Let me get this straight," Knight says, his tone shifting from friendly good cop to something darker. "Six women have gone missing in Forsyth and instead of feeling concerned about that, you're impeding the investigation."

Straightening my spine, I crowd up on him. "You don't get to show up at our house and accuse us of not doing enough to find Stella. These women have been going missing for months, and we're the only ones doing anything about it. Those flyers have been posted for weeks and not one single law enforcement agency has shown up until now. And instead of organizing a search party, you're in our faces doing fuck-all. Why is that?" Blood thrums in my ears. "You're not here because you give a shit about the missing girls. You're here to rack up credit from a whore you've gotten too invested in."

Knight's olive complexion turns a deep shade of red. He snaps the ledger shut. "Fuck you."

"Get a warrant for that, too," I mutter, done with this bullshit. I turn and walk back toward the palace, my brothers following close behind.

"Christ," I hear Knight say down by the gate, "you Royals are real pains in my ass, you know that?"

He has no idea how much of a pain we really can be if we have the time to put our minds to it. But we've got much bigger and more pressing things to deal with, like finding a man named William.

~

"THIS IS IT?" Verity asks, looking out the window. "I thought this place was abandoned."

Father's club is in a nondescript brick building. No windows, no neon signs. "It's not a trashy strip club out on the highway for truck drivers and pathetic men from the suburbs to haunt," I tell her. "It's an exclusive club for the powerful, wealthy, and connected in Forsyth."

Dubiously, she guesses, "People who happen to enjoy doing business while women dance and serve them mostly naked."

"Well," I grin, "obviously."

It's my idea to bring Verity with me to deliver the proof of life to the Baron King. Wicker obviously couldn't come without triggering WW3 and Lex wanted to stay back and make sure Father didn't have any life-threatening injuries. But now that I see her sitting next to me in a pale green, summery dress that has flowy little sleeves and a sexy tie nestled under her breasts, I'm not sure I want to take her into this den of sin.

"Stop looking at me like that," she says.

I look at her *exactly* like that. "Like what?"

"Like I'm a fragile flower who can't handle a strip club." She smooths her skirt out over her knees, but her belly is so big now that the hem keeps riding up, revealing the creamy skin of her thighs. "I started hanging out with the cutsluts when I was in elementary school. There's little I haven't seen or heard." She gives me a pointed look. "And it's not like you guys handled me with kid gloves for the first half of our relationship."

My lips tip up. "You're kind of a badass, aren't you?"

She opens the door. "You just figured that out?"

Leaning over the center console, I grab her arm and pull her back into the car. The kiss is hard and forceful, opening her mouth with a tug on her lower lip. She tastes so fucking good. There's this thumping in my heart, a beat different than I've ever felt before. Not for my brothers. Not for anyone.

She's appropriately breathless when I pull back, holding her face in my hands. "Look at me, Rosi." When her dazed eyes blink open, they're sparkling with the reflection of the dash lights, hypnotizing me. "I need you to follow my lead," I whisper. For a moment, my whole world feels contained to the sheen of her lips when her tongue sweeps out to wet them. "We can't let emotion lead with the Baron King. Where he is, the shadows aren't far behind."

She gives a slow nod. "I understand. But you, too, right?" At my raised brow, she points out, "You're the one who was talking about killing them all."

"Rosi, if you know anything about me, it's that I have the patience of a saint. Sure, I'm decisive. When I make a decision that's that. Like how I knew the first time I saw your picture that you belonged to me." I push a soft tendril of hair behind her ear. "We're here to give him proof of life. And then, to get the Williams."

When we enter the bar moments later, natural light and sounds vanish, consumed by the dark moodiness of the club. Despite Father's lack of presence, the place is packed, a testament to a well-run business. In the back of the room, I see a group huddled around a gaming table. That's where I find the Baron King, gold mask firmly in place, tucked in the back corner, holding cards. I recognize the others as Mayor Kenneth Strong, Louis Mercer, and Judge Marjorie Klein. Lex wasn't kidding when he said that Father has dirt on every judge— even the women.

There's a fifth person at the table, a young woman with dark eyes and blood-red lips. She's perched on Maddox's lap, head resting on his shoulder.

The Baroness.

I nod at Monroe, the barkeep, as we pass, going straight to the darkened booth in the back. Father's table. It's empty unless he's here —or well, unless *we're* here. It's a place to do business off the books, much like the Barons' Crypt or the Lords' Hideaway. It's the equivalent of making a deal on a napkin. Maybe it won't hold up in a court of law, but it sure as hell will out on the streets.

I help Verity ease around the curve of the booth, the pink light overhead giving her skin a warm glow. Before we even take our seats, a server approaches, likely noting the importance of the table. Her dress is beyond skimpy, the top a tight corset to show off her tits and the skirt flaring out in a ruffle. Unsurprisingly, Father has a thing for a sexy bar wench.

"Pace Ashby." Her eyes are steely as she juts out her hip, a tray tucked beneath her arm. "It's been a while."

"Autumn." I throw my arm over Verity's shoulders and glance down at her belly. "I'm sure you heard we've been a little busy over at the palace."

"I heard. Congratulations." She makes no attempt to hide the bitterness in her tone. "Although that's not the only gossip going around."

"Yeah?" I jerk my chin. "What else have you heard?"

Autumn *is* bitter, but she's East End, through and through. She'd never deny a Prince what he seeks. Eyes rolling, her shoulders sink. "The King hasn't been in for weeks. No poker. No meetings." She taps her fingers against the silver tray. "He hasn't even been by to see his favorite girls."

Verity looks up at me, mouth gaping. "Rufus hooks up with these women?"

I stroke her cheek, thinking it's kind of sweet how innocent she can be sometimes. "If that's what you want to call it."

"His personal little harem," Autumn says, but also pulls a face. "Not me. I don't meet his standards."

"Failed Princess," I not-so-quietly whisper in Verity's ear. Reaching over to stroke the swell of her belly, I tell Autumn, "No worries, the King will be back soon."

"Great." She looks anything but thrilled.

"In the meantime, grab me a beer? Rosi will have something non-alcoholic. Something... *sweet*."

Autumn's mouth forms a tight purse. "Of course."

"And send a round of whatever they're drinking to the front table. Judge Klein is looking a little thirsty." Even though Her Honor is more focused on the dancers on the stage than the card game. I lean back, placing my hand on Verity's thigh under the table, and notice her green eyes following Autumn's backside as she walks off. "You know her?" I wonder.

But Verity shakes her head. "No. I mean, I saw her around when she was Princess, at the Furies and stuff. It's just..." She trails off, looking away. "Never mind. It's nothing."

I tilt her chin to face me. "It's something. Tell me."

She turns, glancing over at Autumn by the bar where she's placing our order with Monroe. "Back then, I didn't know what she'd been through. The throning and all of that." She frowns. "Were you there when it happened?"

"Nah," I assure. "I was a little busy serving my sentence in the Pen last year."

Her frown deepens. "But Wick and Lex were."

"I assume so." I watch as Autumn takes the first tray of drinks across the room and delivers them to the poker table. Maddox picks up his glass of top shelf and glances over at us. Message delivered. "You know she didn't mean anything to them."

Groaning, she insists, "It's not that I'm jealous. I just..." She truly seems like she's at a loss for words, finally settling on, "I just know she went through all of that, and now she's here. She went from the top of the Royal game to... this. It's just really sad, isn't it? How this machine can just chew you up and spit you out?"

Probably like me when I see people I was in prison with, like seeing DK the other day on my way into the courtroom. It's like meeting a fellow combat soldier. Names, territory lines, kingdoms, loyalties... for a second, it's like they don't even matter. There's a connection you can't dismiss.

"If it makes you feel any better, I heard she wasn't dethroned. And hey, at least she's not buried in the solarium."

Verity cuts me an unamused glance. "Neither of those things makes any of this better, Pace."

I shrug. "Fair."

Autumn returns to the table with my bottle of beer and a red, fizzy-looking drink for Verity. "Shirley Temple," Autumn says, placing it in front of her. "I delivered your other drinks."

"Perfect." I reach into my pocket and pull out a roll of cash, grabbing the money for the drinks and adding a fat tip on top.

Autumn notices, eyes widening for a long, awkward pause. Ultimately, she stammers out a quiet, "Wow. Thanks."

I squeeze Verity's leg under the table. "Thank her."

Their eyes meet, and sure enough, I see a flicker of understanding pass between them.

"May she reign," Autumn says, and it doesn't even sound sarcastic.

Jesus, sometimes it's absurdly obvious that we're not just Royals, but royally fucked.

After Autumn saunters off, Verity takes a sip of her drink, sucking in a cough. "Jesus, that's sweet."

All I want to do is lick that cherry syrup off her lips, but then a shadow hovers over the table.

"Regina," a quiet rumble sounds from behind the mask, "be a good girl and wait for me by the bar."

She keeps her eyes cast down, hands folded in front of her. "Yes, Daddy."

Maddox watches her walk away, his dark eyes chilling from behind the mask. "It'll be a shame to see her go at the end of the summer. I'd only just gotten her trained up right. That's the bitter pill of Kinghood. You get them just long enough to make them sufferable, and then they're on to greener pastures." He sighs, as if to say 'what can you do?'

Verity's wide eyes say enough about what she thinks about those two.

There's something that's always bugged me, and the chance to ask the question is the only thing distracting me from the fact the man in front of me might be responsible for Verity's stint in the hospital.

"What's with the Barons' whole daddy roleplay thing, anyway?" I ask, sipping from my glass. "What, you sucked so bad at the real thing, you have to make up a fantasy about kids who actually love you?"

It's the first time any of us have touched on the 'mutually assured destruction' that was given to us the day we made our deal with the Kings.

The Baron King—Maddox—adjusts the golden cufflink on his jet-black suit, appearing unbothered that I know his identity. "The last place a father in Forsyth would look for love is from his own children. No one knows that better than the two of you," he says, greeting Verity with a nod while lowering himself in the seat normally occupied by my father.

My smile drips with disdain. "Just seems a bit creepy and incestuous, is all. You should consider your public image."

Maddox doesn't even blink. "You've fucked the boy you call your brother." He tilts his head toward Verity. "She's fucked the boys her father adopted, and all of you are fucking your sister." A tsk. "Glass palaces, Pace."

I'm not sure what he sees in my expression, but internally, I'm wondering how the everloving fuck this piece of shit knows anything about what me and Wick have done behind closed doors.

Whatever he sees, it brings a low, ominous chuckle from behind his mask. "Oh, I've been keeping tabs on the Kayes heir for a while now. In truth, I'm surprised he's not here. It seems like an opportunity he'd be eager to pursue—looking me in the eye."

Verity squeezes my hand, and I realize I'm vibrating with anger. "He's a little busy handling that Forsyth fatherhood thing."

"Pity," Maddox says, the word glaringly insincere. "I assume that if you're interrupting my game, you have something for me?"

It's difficult to look him in the eye with the storm cloud hanging over me. It's entirely possible this man is responsible for almost killing my Princess and our child. And the thought of him watching

Wicker? It makes me want to fly over this table and stab him in the fucking eye. But I meant what I said to Verity before.

So I slide over a tablet and a thin manila folder. "I think you'll find this satisfactory. Tomorrow's Royal Gazette, online and in print." He opens the tablet to a color image of Rufus Ashby standing in front of a shiny modern skyscraper in Indonesia—Jakarta, specifically. "This should satisfy anyone questioning Father's whereabouts. As you can read, he's busy checking out operations for a new cybersecurity firm that only began launching operations on Saturday."

The 'shopping job was easy enough. It took a little more effort to make a believable paper trail, but it should hold up to scrutiny.

It's impossible to tell what Maddox is thinking behind the mask as he reads the article. "You have flight records? Credit card statements? Banking logs?"

I give him a long, derisive look. "Don't insult me."

Humming, he scans the papers in the file folder. "A video would have been better," he laments, but despite the daggers I'm staring, he shuts the folder. "However, I agree that this should keep Trudie Stein from calling my office every fifteen minutes, and allow me and the other Kings a shred of plausible deniability if the truth comes out." He hands me back the tablet, but keeps the folder for himself. "And how is your dear father? Are you going to need our services soon? The crypt always welcomes fallen crowns."

One day, hopefully yours.

"Not yet," I say, feeling the slight uptick in my pulse. "We've been encouraging him to share some of his darker secrets with us."

Maddox folds his fingers against the tabletop. "More women buried in the backyard?"

"Actually, no," Verity grits out. "Something *current.*"

There's a tense beat, and then Maddox's clipped sigh. "Why do I get the impression you have something else to annoy me with?"

Keeping my temper in check, I inhale deeply. "We've known for some time that the attack on our Princess came at my father's command. It was a test for me and my brothers—to be sure that we're fit for parenting an heir." I twist my neck, stretching my muscles. "The actions of a crazed, desperate man."

"Seems like it." He nudges his drink aside, still untouched. His mask doesn't even have an opening for his mouth.

"But whoever he hired, they went off script, and we've had some trouble figuring out who he contracted." I don't even blink in fear of missing a tell. I scrutinize him for anything. A blink. A twitch. A fucking exhale. And I find *nothing*. The pointed horns of his golden mask gleam in the ambient light, but whatever's beneath it is hidden. Leaning back, I continue, "Luckily, after some persuasion by my brother, Verity was able to get a name."

A sigh. "And that name is?"

Verity's the one to pitch forward, hurling the name like an accusation. "*William.*"

Slowly, Maddox unlaces his fingers, back straightening. "Impossible."

To drive home just how possible I believe this is, I take the knife from the sheath strapped to my belt and stab it right into the middle of the manila folder—a bare inch from his hand.

The resounding *clunk* draws a flinching sea of stares.

I tighten my grip on the hilt. "I'm going to need a little more convincing."

I'm clocked into my periphery on a good day, but right now, it might as well be a laser focus. It's how I catch the movement in the shadows near the back, without even having to break Maddox's eerie stare. There's another to our left, and while I don't see the shadow shifting behind me, I can sense it, like a prickle on the back of my neck.

Beside me, Verity's throat clicks with a swallow.

But Maddox just raises a hand, gesturing casually with two fingers. "I don't know anything about a contract," he says, the figures in the dark corners bleeding away, "and I never gave such an order. My Barons are as faithful to me as the shadows."

Verity audibly gnashes her teeth. "For someone keeping tabs on the *Kayes heir*, it certainly seems like you have a motive."

"I don't keep tabs on Whitaker because I'm threatened by him," he replies, glaring at her from beneath his mask. When his gaze shifts to me, it's thin and flinty. "Your father is lying."

"*One* of you is lying," I correct, falling back to leave the knife buried between us. "And since he's the only one whose balls I've had hooked up to a car battery this week, you'll understand if his words hold a little more weight."

Maddox's voice twists into a mocking tone. "Well, you'll excuse me if I don't have a car battery handy."

I grin. "I do."

"Who's going to kill Rufus?" he asks, catching me off guard. "Someone needs to take the crown and it's clearly going to be one of you. After you're finished getting your pounds of flesh, who's going to be holding that knife?"

Shrugging, I reply, "You'll know when we need you to know."

"Well, that's unfortunate," he sighs. "If I were speaking to a King right now, there'd be a mutual understanding."

Verity snorts. "And what kind of understanding is that?"

But instead of answering her, he stares at me. "Do you know why my house sigil is a pentagram, Pace? There are plenty of rumors. Some say we worship the devil with blood magic, but that's ridiculous, and everyone at this table knows it." He tips his head down, eyes intense. "Do you know the true reason?"

"Can't say I care."

"Of course, you care." There's a grin in his voice. "It's your brother's birthright. Maybe even your son's."

Verity goes rigid at my side. "Why the pentagram?"

When he reaches out to clutch the hilt of the knife, yanking it free from the table, I jolt in front of Verity.

But he just rucks up his sleeve, slashing a shallow cut into his flesh.

I snap, "What the fuck are you—"

"Five points," Maddox says, dragging his fingertip through the pooling blood. He then presses it to the table, drawing a crude star with the blood. "One for each Royal house. North, south, east, west, and nowhere." The blood smears against the wood as he drags it down, completing the star. "I realize this must be difficult for you to comprehend, considering who raised you, but there's a reason the Barons don't claim territory. It's the same reason I'm wearing a mask right now. It's why Clive Kayes wore one of his own." Locking onto my glare, he draws a slow, bloody circle around the star. "Unlike the rest of you, we're servants of Forsyth—of life and *death*. Not ourselves."

"That's horseshit," I argue, sneering at the display. "Every Royal house serves itself."

"Then let me speak this language you know so well. My son—my *real* son—sees this girl," he nods toward where Verity is peeking over my shoulder, "as a sister. Harming her and her baby would be unforgivable in his eyes. That trumps your flimsy motive."

The puff of laughter that tumbles from her lips is dry and harsh. "You've done enough unforgivable things to him. I don't think it'd make much of a difference."

Maddox slams the knife back into the table—this time, in the middle of the pentagram. "If Rufus is telling the truth, this goes deeper," he says, grabbing his drink. I watch, frustrated as he tips it over his bloody wrist, the expensive alcohol washing the blood away.

Verity wonders, "What do you mean?"

But he's already standing, fixing the black cuff of his shirt. "I'll call the Williams to the crypt tomorrow and see if there's any legitimacy to Rufus' claims."

I give him an incredulous look. "And we're supposed to take your word for it?"

"A Baron always honors a promise made in blood." Maddox gestures at the drawing on the table, and then at Verity. "Ask your fists and their fury. She'll tell you what this means."

When he stalks toward the door, half of the patrons around the room—at the bar, by the stage, even some in the middle of playing a game—stand and begin exiting with him. These, I know, are his shadows.

In the midst of the display, I give a stunned, gawking Verity an unimpressed glance, reaching to tug the knife from the table.

"Fucking drama king."

6

―――――

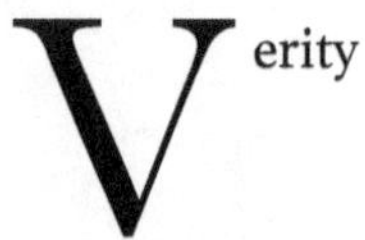 erity

For the rest of that week, we almost get into a routine.

Mornings in the dungeon, afternoons in the garden, evenings spent pouring over design plans for the new nursery, and nights spent with Wicker wrapped around me like a vine.

Of course, the peace couldn't last.

"It should be me," comes a voice from beside the bed. "You know I'm right."

I'm beginning to get used to Wicker popping out of walls, but I still toss him an exasperated look when he appears from behind the panel. "I don't want another argument," I say. Things are still fragile since last night, when I made a proposition that neither Pace nor Lex took very well. Wicker hadn't seemed to care at the time. "And should you really be using that right now?" I glance at the door, pitching my voice to a whisper. "With *people* in the house?"

The whirr of the drill whines down the hall, followed by the sound of plaster hitting the floor. It's been like this all day. *All day.* Starting at 7 AM.

"Seemed easier than going through that obstacle course out there. You're the one who wanted a new nursery." He notices the suitcase on the bed. "They aren't going to see anything."

The baby will be here in less than three months. And since Lex seems to think we're already cutting it close if we want the nursery to be done first, we've had to accelerate the timeline on my nursery plans. Early mornings, late nights. All of this despite the man we're currently holding prisoner down in the basement.

"I still think this is a bad idea," I sigh, rubbing my temples.

"Going to West End?" he asks, sliding a look toward the half-full suitcase. "Probably."

I shake my head, throwing another pair of socks into the bag. "You know what I mean."

"The construction is proof of life." Wicker shrugs, completely uncaring about the team of contractors hammering two floors above our torture victim. "Father would never let the baby come without tearing up the palace to make it perfect. The less of a fuss we make, the more suspicious it'll seem."

I know he has a point.

It's just that I'm tired.

Once Wicker offered up his room, the three of them got busy, digging through Rufus' files for his contacts. All of us then spent the following week meeting with an architect, contractors, and designers. There's a benefit to being Royal, especially with access to a King's fortune.

Money doesn't buy quiet, though. Or sleep. It doesn't soften the loud footsteps going up and down the hall, or the incessant radio chatter the workers turn on the minute they arrive, or this knot of nervousness in my stomach that they're going to find out what we're hiding below.

The construction chaos isn't just in our wing, either. They rolled out paper covering the floor from the kitchen entrance up the back-stairs and hung thick sheets of plastic in a futile attempt to keep the dust out of our living quarters. Pace pretty much wrapped his office in plastic wrap.

So when I realized the date—that it's time for my month in West End—I won't deny seizing it with a complicated gusto. I fold another shirt. "I have to get out of here, Wick."

A loud crash echoes down the hall, and he grimaces. "Convenient that Dr. Lex decided he should be the one to go with you, while we get to stay here and 'hold down the fort.'" He uses air quotes on that last part before flopping onto the bed. He picks up the small purple massage ball that helps with the cramps I've been having in my arches and tosses it in the air. "Take me with you instead, Red. I'll feed you burritos. I even promise not to complain about sleeping on what I assume is a dirty mattress from some warehouse alley."

"Thinly veiled insults about my family will get you nowhere." I stifle a yawn. "But nice try. Lex has already worked out the deal with Sy to run the annual blood drive at the gym, so there's another reason for him to go with me." I shoot him a look. "Unless you want to join in the organization of dozens of volunteers, setting up the bus, and everything else?"

He considers it, or pretends to, and then decides, "Better me than Lex."

I frown, walking to the dresser to get my toiletry bag. "You're worried about him?"

"Sending my brother into enemy territory completely unprotected?" The look he gives me is mocking, all wide eyes and guileless expression. "What's to worry about?"

It's all I can do not to groan. "The Dukes aren't anything like the three of you seem to think. Maybe if you'd stop treating them like the enemy, you'd see that." I give a pair of leggings an aggressive shake. "And then maybe we could actually work together to find Stella, Laura, and Rory's sister."

Before he can refute this, there's a distant slam.

"Son of a—" The sound of plastic ripping and cursing precedes Pace ripping through the barrier between the hall and my bedroom door. He finally makes it through with a scowl on his face and Effie's cage in his hands.

"*Decay,*" she chirps an exuberant greeting, "*beautiful decay.*"

"What?" I ask, laughing. "That's new."

"It's that goddamn radio." He carries the cage over to the window. "They listen to it all the time. She's fucking obsessed with that one DJ."

"Oh, that Royal Noir show? Yeah, I like him."

"Well, I can't take it anymore." He strokes Effie's beak and faces us. "It's so fucking noisy this week, I can't get her to settle down. She already curses too much, the last thing I need is for her to become fluent in a second language."

Artis, the foreman, is Czech.

Pace finally sees the suitcase. I know he does because he suddenly freezes.

"Maybe Lex and I can take her with us," I offer, ignoring the storm brewing in his eyes. "I know Mama will be happy to see her again."

Wick glances between us, a smirk flirting at the corner of his mouth.

He's enjoying this way too much. "Yeah, bro, let her take your most precious possession with her into a rival territory."

"You're really going through with this." Pace's words fall like a boulder, dull and flat and twice as heavy.

I wince at the coming headache. "We talked about this. The Princes have a contract with the—"

"They'd honor your decision," he snaps. "You know they would. If you tell them you want to stay in the palace, they'd tear up the contract."

Gently, I remind him, "I made a contract with the Dukes, too."

Pace scoffs. "That's not why you're going."

"You're right," I say, throwing my hands up. "I'm going because I'm tired. And because I miss being somewhere I don't have to constantly worry about our torture victim being found."

Finally, Wicker cuts in, eyes rolling as he tosses the massage ball in the air. "Give her a break, Pace. This shit is obviously stressing her out. That's not good for the baby, right? Let the Dicks worry about protecting her for a while. They're gutter rats, but they're well-armed gutter rats."

I send him a glare. *Not helpful!*

The look he gives me in return? Butter couldn't melt.

"You just want her to leave so you can avoid acknowledging the baby for the next few weeks," Pace snaps back.

His expression hardening, Wicker replies, "I want her to leave so we can handle our shit without worrying about her." He pushes up, propped on his elbows as he levels me with a stare. "Look, no offense, but this baby thing is putting a real damper on our extracurricular activities."

"None taken." I think. *At first.* When it begins flaring in my chest, I blurt, "I've been really on board with the torture stuff, thank you very much."

He snorts, giving the massage ball a squeeze. "Chill, Red. No one here doubts your commitment to Sparkle Motion. But let's stop bull-shitting ourselves. Our focus has been divided."

"And now it won't be?" Pace runs his hand through his hair, frustration evident in his tone. "What about Lex? What if he's sleeping and we're not there to pull him off you?"

I feel my face soften at the knowledge I hold, deep down. "Lex would never let himself hurt me, and everyone in this room knows it —even if he doesn't."

"And what about William?" Pace's eyes blaze with fury. "What about the fact someone's snatching Royal assets, and the last one to be taken was driving your car?"

There's nothing being said that wasn't gone over last night. "I'm safe in West End," I insist, for the millionth time. I'm expecting the same old rebuttal—blah blah, gutter rats—but I'm not anticipating the way he springs forward, words slicing through the air like a knife.

"When are you going to get it?!" he roars, uncaring that Wicker has jumped from the bed, grabbing him by the arm.

"Hey, chill," Wicker tells him, but Pace jerks away from him.

"You're not safe anywhere!" he snaps. "And if that hasn't sunk in yet, then the last place I want you and our kid is somewhere I can't protect you. Someone has to think of *him*."

"I am thinking of him!" But before I can make him even angrier by mentioning that this baby has family in West End too—family he's entitled to, and family that will protect him—I see the icy shutters falling over Pace's eyes.

"No, you aren't," he says, the coldness in his voice cutting. "Just like you weren't the night you ran out of here, right into William's stupid fucking trap."

For a moment, it feels like all the air has been punched out of my lungs. "That's not fair," I say, struggling to inhale. But when I glance at Wicker, his blue eyes dart away from me, the cut of his jaw suddenly tense.

Clearly, he agrees.

Pace allows his brother's silence to speak for itself. "What's not fair is that every time you make some rash, half-cocked decision to step foot into danger, you're taking us with you. Not just our baby. Not even just my brothers. The Dukes, too. Your mother. Lavinia." A new arrogance curls his mouth into a snarl. "Stella."

The name lands exactly as he means it to, painful and jarring, snatching my breath away. It twists inside my chest, this knot of agony and shock, and I'm taken by the thought that Pace would have hurt me less if he'd punched me.

"How dare you." My vision blurs, tears filling the edges, but I can see Wicker stepping between us, a hand fisted into his brother's shirt.

"That's enough," he hisses. "You're not putting that shit on her!"

Pace doesn't break my stare. Not until the first tear makes a track down my cheek. "I didn't mean—" The words bite off, and then he clenches his teeth. "Whatever. Doesn't matter what I think, right?" His chest jumps with a clipped, humorless laugh. "This is the deal we made that day in the solarium. You get to do anything you want, and we get to deal with the consequences." He makes a snide, mocking bow. "May she reign."

"Fuck you," I spit, but Pace is already retreating from the room, his footfalls nearly as loud as the hammering down the hall.

Wicker sucks in a long, fortifying breath before turning to me. "He didn't mean it like that."

But he did.

It lingers, this ghastly, unspeakable thought that Stella was taken because of me. Pace didn't put it there. It's been haunting the corners of my mind since I watched her on Pace's monitor, driving into North Side and never returning.

Turning back to my suitcase, I zip up the sides, more determined than ever to get some space. This isn't a place of creation. It's a fucking palace of destruction and it'll destroy anyone and anything inside its walls.

"IT'S PRETTY NICE HERE, don't you think?" I pat my face dry and analyze my skin in the bathroom mirror. Ugh. Everyone talks about the pregnancy glow, but no one talks about the persistent acne. "I'll even pretend I didn't see you hiding guns all over a few hours ago." I squeeze a glob of toothpaste out on the brush and shove it in my mouth.

My fight with Pace still burns angrily in my chest, but I'm resolved to ignore it, letting the familiarity of West End and Royal Ink's loft apartment soothe the wound. Crossing into the territory earlier that afternoon had meant Nick and Remy patting down Lex for weapons and finding too many. They were unhappy about it, but I convinced them to let him keep most of them.

Maybe Pace hurt me, but he did it with the truth.

Nowhere is safe for me.

Which means nowhere is safe for *us*.

After a long moment, Lex's flat voice rings out from the bedroom. "There's only one room."

Sighing, I spit into the sink, staring into my own reflection. "I know."

There's a long pause, and then, "The couch will be fine."

"Lex," I start, the words garbled around the toothbrush, "this is stupid; just sleep in the bed with me."

It's been a month since the attack, and even by Lex's own metric, I'm cleared for just about anything. But he treats me like spun glass.

Or rather, he treats *the baby* like spun glass.

Lex strolls into the bathroom, shirtless and in a pair of pajama bottoms that hang low on his hips. His chest is covered in a scattering of light auburn hair, with a darker thatch that runs below his belly. He's wearing his glasses, peering down at the back of a pill bottle. "I think you should add one of these to your daily supplements."

Distracted by his—Jesus, *everything*—toothpaste slides down the back of my throat, and I gag.

"Ver!" He drops the bottle on the counter and rushes over, one hand on my back, the other on my stomach.

"I'm fi—acgh-ne." I gag again and then spit out the toothpaste in the sink.

Lex turns on the water and I bend, scooping water into my mouth with my hands. Coughing a few more times, I finally get it together. When I look up again, my face is red, and the concern he'd shown before has darkened into something sharp and complicated.

"What?" I ask, wiping my mouth on the handcloth. "I'm fine."

In the mirror, his eyes dart down. "What are you wearing?"

Following his gaze, I pull at the big T-shirt I found in the back of the closet. "Oh, this?" It's faded and worn, an oversized, black Forsyth Fury shirt with a growling bear on the front. "It's super soft and big enough to cover our little head of lettuce here," I say, referencing this week's produce-to-baby scale.

I search his eyes as he spins me around, putting my back in the reflection of the mirror. Expressionlessly, he points to something there. "It has Perilini's name on it."

I crane my neck and see the peeling letters. "So?"

"So..." He meets my gaze, brows crouched dangerously low. "I know we have this little truce, and you think it's fun that we're all playing nice, but you don't belong to them, Verity. And when a woman wears a man's shirt, *with* his name on it, there's an implication."

"Oh, for the love of—" I just can't help it.

I laugh.

That dark eyebrow-crouching grows more severe with each snorted chuckle. "This isn't a joke. Who you belong to in this town means something." It isn't until I see the tendon straining angrily in his neck that I swallow down my amusement.

I lift my shirt, revealing the ever-growing swell of my belly. "I think this is a bigger implication of who I belong to. One I can't take off." His gaze roams the taut, pale skin of my stomach, and his jaw tenses. There's this spark of fire in his eyes that grabs me like a fishhook, right between my thighs.

Goodness gracious.

Jealousy looks good on Lex Ashby. "It's not the same and you know it."

"It's comfortable," I say, tossing the towel on the counter and walking past him into the bedroom. "And that's my biggest priority right now."

One of the cruxes of being in West End is that I know, somehow, Pace has his eyes on me. The feeling used to be a phantom thing, a suspicion I figured I was conditioned to after months in the palace. Now, I know better.

There's a camera on me right this instant.

I know it like I know Lex is about to stalk out of that bathroom, fists clenched.

A moment later, he does. "Take it off."

"No." I turn, walking out into the living room, aware of him following me. There are a lot of big windows in here. Pace would have had trouble getting tech into the loft, but somewhere else?

I pull my hair up, putting my back to the window.

"Verity." Lex's voice comes low and full of warning, and when I glance up, a dark smirk freezes on my lips. He's by the kitchen now, idly inspecting a series of frames on the wall. "You shouldn't provoke him. He's having a hard enough time already."

"A hard time doing what?" I ask, remembering the searing bitterness in Pace's eyes when he bowed to me. *May she reign.* "Letting me make my own decisions? Trying not to own me? Not lashing out when he doesn't get his way?"

Lex slides his gaze to mine. "Not coming in here and taking you back to his cell." The word he uses is like a bucket of cold water, and he notices. "It's the only way he knows to keep the things he cares about safe. He can't help it, but he's trying."

Shaking my head, I let my hair drop, covering the name on the back of my shirt. "He doesn't see reason."

Lex fingers the corner of a frame, his amber eyes scanning the text of the old newspaper article inside of it. "The two of you have that in common."

I look toward the bedroom, and for a moment, I wish it was Wicker here with me. He'd touch me, even though it'd be hungry and full of frustration. He'd be curling around me in bed right about now, half-asleep, yanking me aggressively into the breadth of his chest.

I'm not sure I can sleep alone anymore.

"Can you take those down?" I plead, watching Lex inspect all the articles about the Forsyth Carver. Rubbing some warmth into my arms, I explain. "They freak me out."

Lex raises an eyebrow, tipping his head toward my chest. "Can you take that off?"

"Come to bed," I challenge, fidgeting coyly with the hem, "and you can take it off me yourself."

The shutters slam over his eyes, and with a tightly contained inhale, he begins taking the frames off the wall. "I have to sleep out here," he says, gesturing to the couch. "You have to tie me up."

It takes me far too long to realize the rope slung over the arm of the sofa has an actual purpose. I blink at it, jaw going slack. "Oh my god, you can't be serious."

He stacks the frame neatly on the counter. "That was the condition of me coming."

"Lex, this is ridiculous."

"Look," he suddenly snaps, rubbing at the bridge of his nose, "it's been a long day in another territory. I'm in a strange place without my brothers. I've seen three other addicts from group. And *my Princess* is wearing another King's clothes." When he turns to me, there's a flash of something dark and barely contained in his eyes. "I don't know what I'll do."

I approach him carefully, slowly, like a cornered animal, and when I reach up to cup his cheek in my hand, I don't miss the slight twitch of his body—the incremental flinch. "You're really worried."

His eyes fall closed. "I don't want to hurt you," he whispers, voice ragged. "Either of you."

It's why, with a lump in my throat, I follow his instructions, eyeing the long, lean cut of his body as he stretches out over the length of the couch. His feet hang off one end while his head rests on a silk throw pillow.

He raises his wrists, expression inscrutable. "Thread it through that pipe."

I do as he orders, the rope rough against my palms as I wind it around the large pipe. It's sturdy in that old way—maybe cast iron—and has been painted a glossy, if scuffed, white.

Then I tie his wrists.

"Tighter," he commands, giving the rope a gentle tug. Obeying, I cinch it hard, wincing at the loss of circulation he's about to experience. It's only as I'm standing back, drinking in the absurdity of the visual, that he makes a soft, frustrated sound. "Shit. Forgot about my glasses."

Sighing, I reach down, gingerly plucking them from his nose. Folding them up, I place the glasses on the leather ottoman, and then reach for the blanket on the back of the couch, covering him.

He stares up at me, giving a slow, heavy blink, like he's surprised I'd do something so odd as to take care of him.

It's the reason I lean down, brushing a kiss to his mouth.

At first, the only movement I feel is the way his arms flex against the binds. The quick sharpness of his inhale. The way his body tenses when I sling a leg over his hip, straddling him.

And then I feel his tongue sweep out against mine.

The kiss is hot and slick, but also infuriatingly measured. I can feel him growing hard beneath me, and when I rock down into it, a gritty sound erupts from his throat.

"Don't," he rumbles, jerking his head to the side. There's a spot of color on his cheeks, mouth pressed into a tight line. "You'll make it worse."

"I could make it better."

He frowns and I give up, my stomach sinking as I rise, my own cheeks feeling ablaze with embarrassment. I'm not sure why, but some part of me had been certain that having Lex here, away from the cameras and security and medical equipment—out of the cell— would make things different.

But that's the problem.

The pitch of my voice is soft, curious. "Is this all I am to you?" I wonder, cradling the swell of my belly. The question isn't made bitterly. I never know where I stand with these men. "Am I just a... responsibility?"

His jaw hardens when he glances at me. "Trust me, Princess. Things would be a lot easier for both of us if you were."

I turn the lights off when I leave, my heart in my throat, and crawl into bed alone. Ashby's damage runs deep. He broke his sons in ways they'll never comprehend. Not just with whips and punishments, but the places inside.

Places I'm not sure I'll ever be able to reach.

I always have the worst dreams when I'm in West End.

It shouldn't be the case. This is still home for me, the place where I feel safest. But something has twisted that sense of comfort into a nervous unease. I know these streets. I know the buildings. I know the shape of the clock tower on the horizon. I know the way the cracked asphalt looks in the summer, waves of heat rolling off it. I know the people, the sky, the scent.

But West End doesn't know *me*.

Not anymore.

It's why I wake with a start, a vague notion of worry gripping my lungs like a fist. I don't remember the nightmare, only that I felt incomprehensibly alone, adrift in a vast, empty sea, whose waves I can still hear breaking through the fog of sleep.

It takes me a moment to realize I'm not hearing the breaking of waves.

It's breathing—low and ragged, animalistic.

The dark shape looming in the doorway is familiar, as is the little tinge of terror creeping into the edges of my awareness.

Oddly, there's also a sense of relief.

"Lex," I whisper, turning toward him. It doesn't even occur to me to wonder how he escaped the binds. His hair is loose, a slash of orange streetlight from the window cleaving him across the chest. I meant what I said to Wicker and Pace earlier in the day. Lex would never hurt me, and that's something I trust all the way down to my gut, even though it twists in anxiety.

So when that first footfall sounds, his heavy eyes and rippling muscles coming toward me, I don't fight.

He wouldn't like that.

It shouldn't surprise me that the first thing he reaches for, clawing with a violence that unnerves me, is the shirt. He plants a knee on the bed and grabs the hem in his big palms, curling them into fists.

The fabric rips like paper.

I gasp, slamming my hands over his fists, but by the time I realize he's ripped it clear up to the neck, splaying the two sides of the fabric apart, he's already wedging himself between my thighs. The dark glaze of his eyes is entirely without reason or thought, a man driven only by instinct. His fists dig into the mattress on either side of my shoulders, the fabric of my shirt still clutched within them. I feel like a specimen who's been peeled open for empty eyes, unable to move under the pressure of his grasp.

"Lex," I try, straining against the binds of the shirt. "Lex, wait."

He forces my thighs apart with his own before mindlessly pushing his hardness into the apex of my hips. When I shove at his chest, trying to make room between us for my belly, I'm greeted by his snarl, teeth bared, body slamming into me once again.

I respond with a firm, "Lagan!"

He freezes.

Lex's eyes are dazed, eyelids heavy with sleep as he stares down at me. A lock of his auburn hair is caught on his lip, billowing out with every puff of breath, and he shudders when I reach up to free it. Dragging my fingertips down a heaving chest, I tuck my hand into his waistband, only needing to think for a second before easing them down his hips.

"It's okay," I assure him, knowing what he wants—what he needs. Lex would never allow himself to take it, because I might be more than a responsibility to him, but whatever *that* is, it's not nearly as important. "You can have it."

When I push at my panties, working them down a leg, they're already soaked.

"Here," I whisper, grasping his hot, rigid length in my hand. It's easy to guide him, to rub the swollen head of him against all my slickness and want, to strain up to taste the tense line of his mouth as he takes the cue, punching his way inside.

The cry he makes is soft, rough, and desperate.

So is mine.

After weeks of emptiness, the fullness burns, my muscles tightening against the intrusion. I dig my fingernails into his hips, stilling him with an urgent, "Lagan, stop." And just like I always knew he would, he obeys—even though the low, animalistic whine in his throat reveals his strain.

I adjust to him slowly, reacquainting myself with his cock, the thickening and stretch. He's propped above me, and one squirm of my neck puts his bicep right into my line of sight, the muscles rippling with restraint. Biting down on my lip, I rock up, taking every inch of him with a groan.

"God, yes," I gasp, finally working my arms from the shirt. I use the new freedom to frame his face, looking into his glazed eyes. "Go slow, Lagan. Fuck me slow."

His body jolts, forehead knitting up into a scowl as he drags his cock back, drilling forward once again. I can't even think of a word for how good it feels to have him inside of me again. It's liquid warmth, a fullness so big that it could choke me, and I rock back into it greedily, winding my legs around his strong hips.

"That's it," I say, watching the way his face collapses in ecstasy. "This is what you want, isn't it? You want to fill me up, give me your seed…" It feels illicit, me being the one to whisper these dark, dirty things against the warm curve of his cheek. He turns his head on his next thrust, his lips dragging clumsily across mine, and I give him what he wants, licking at the seam of his mouth.

It parts for me instantly.

The kiss can hardly be called a kiss. With every rock into me, his back bowing with tightly contained shoves of his hips, a growl builds in his chest. I can hear it knocking around in there, can taste the shape of it on his tongue, can smell the scent of it in his sweat. He's a bow strung tight, his body vibrating with power, and yet…

He fucks me so gently, spearing his cock in and out, but never slamming down on me.

The tears that spring to my eyes are ridiculous, pointless things, but I'm powerless to stop them. "I knew you wouldn't hurt me," I tell him, knitting my fingers into his silky-soft hair. "Because I'm yours, aren't I?" I gaze up into his dead eyes, and the longer he's silent, fucking into me like a mindless thing, a worry niggles at my chest.

Maybe I'm wrong.

Maybe I'm just using him.

Maybe I'm the one being driven by something primal and impulsive, the knot in my belly tightening with each thrust of his cock, clit throbbing for the friction of him against me.

And then a ragged, slurred sound emerges from his throat.

"Mine."

I gasp, pulling him closer. "Show me," I beg, fisting a hand into his hair. I make sure his eyes are locked on mine when I command, "Come for me, Lagan." Quieter, like a dirty secret, I plead, "Put your baby in me."

His mouth slackens the moment he hears the words, body crashing into mine with a hard, forceful punch. The sudden rush of slick heat pulsing inside sends me over the edge, and I come with him, neither of us blinking as we come together.

As we meet.

As we *create*.

It's almost agony to feel his cock slip free, but he soothes it by collapsing on his side next to me, curling protectively around the swell of my stomach. The breadth of his hand cradles the bump, and in the next moment, his eyelids are falling closed, a satisfied sigh fluttering a lock of his hair.

As I fall back asleep, satiated and full, I realize that nothing—not a stockpile of weapons, high-tech security, or even the damage these men can do with their hands—feels as safe as I do at this moment.

Tight in Lagan's arms.

THE CUTSLUTS ARE afraid of Lex.

It's not an abject fear. They don't whisper about him or scurry off when he's near. They just... avoid him. In a primal way. These are women who have been around fighters and criminals, men who'd sooner slam a woman up against a wall than actually speak to her. But Lex isn't like that. He's tall and sometimes physically imposing, but he doesn't harness it the way DKS does. It's not his use of physicality that unnerves them.

It's the lack of it.

"We're expecting about two hundred people to come through today, so we'll need to keep the lines moving." Lex stands in front of the group of volunteers, looking neither in his element nor out of it. We've been here a week, and it's like the Lex I've grown used to doesn't even exist. This Lex is mechanical and concise, eerie in his stillness. *Robotic.* It's as if he's taken all human emotion out of the equation. "If you have any questions, refer to the pamphlet Forsyth General provided to you. If you see me about to stick a needle into someone, don't bother me. If you see me drawing blood, don't bother me. If you see me having just drawn blood, don't bother me." His amber eyes pass over the crowd. "Don't bother me."

Greta shivers when his gaze passes over her.

"Not exactly inspiring the community spirit," I mutter to Maggie, who shakes her head.

"I'm definitely not bothering him."

Stretching my shirt over my belly, I follow Lavinia over to the table near the front doors of the gym. On a fight night, this is where Fury business takes place, but today, we'll be checking in donors.

"That shirt is fucking adorable on you," Lavinia says.

"It's like three sizes too small." I tug at the hem of the T-shirt Remy designed for the inter-frat blood drive, trying to keep it from riding up, but it's useless. The bear on the front is comically distorted, its little crown laboring under the swell of a boob. "I look like one of those badly inflated balloons."

"They're ready."

I look up and see Lex standing over the table, amber eyes fixed on the clipboard in his hand. His hair is pulled up in a neat twist, and unlike everyone else, he's dressed impeccably in dark, fitted slacks and a crisp white button-down. He's been on his guard ever since we stepped foot over the boundary line, but even worse since our first night here, when he had that sleepwalking episode.

I hold up a shirt, pouting. "Please?"

He glances up, catching sight of the snarling bear. "No."

"It's festive," I argue. "It'll put people at ease to see you dressed a little more... er, casually."

He must sign something, the flourish of the pen tightly contained. "Why would I want to put people at ease?" he wonders, flipping another page on the clipboard. "Tension will make the veins pop."

I give Lavinia an exasperated look. "Dr. Nightingale over here."

Lex pointedly ignores the jab. "I hate to admit it, but the gym really is a great place for this." He'd been concerned, of course, when I'd suggested it. Usually, these things take place over at the hospital, but after the tweaker high on Scratch ruined the party last Christmas, he was open to a new location, one that could be well-guarded. "As long as there are no surprises."

The gym allows for the various stations required for an event like this. There are curtained-off areas along the back wall with cots and a hospital worker taking the actual blood. Over near the kitchen is the recovery area where Mama commands an army of cutsluts as they organize juice and cookies. Sy and Kaz work the gate, checking for weapons, while Lex oversees the medical logistics, counting donation kits and supplies, and making sure all the blood gets to the refrigerated truck that goes back to the blood bank tomorrow.

Across the room, Rory and Maggie man a table together stacked with flyers I had Pace make with photos and details of each of the missing girls. No one is supposed to leave the gym without a stack to pass out or hang on light posts or shop windows when they leave.

"Mama loves to host a community event," I assure him.

"Everyone will behave," Lavinia promises, "I've made sure of it."

But when I lean down to grab the bag we packed this morning, he snaps forward, saying, "Hey, wait." Lex walks around the table and grabs the bag himself, resting his other hand on my belly. "Don't overexert yourself, okay? No heavy lifting. No standing around for more than a few minutes at a time. Got it?"

I'm so happy to see this brief flash of *my* Lex that I don't even roll my eyes. "I've got it," I assure, grinning.

Reaching into the bag, he pulls out a bottle of water. "Stay hydrated."

"She's in good hands, Doc," Lav says, obviously taking pity on me. "I'll keep an eye on her."

He frowns, not convinced, but when his finger nudges my chin, forcing my gaze to his, I get stunned stupid at the flash of warmth. "One last thing," he says, placing his hands on my shoulders and spinning me around. He reaches for a roll of tape on the table and Lavinia's eyebrows lift in question. I shrug, also confused, until I hear the sound of tape ripping off the roll, and feel him lay the long strip across my shoulder blades. The firm press of a pen follows as he writes on the tape.

"There," he says smugly, dipping down to brush his lips against my cheek. "My woman. My baby. My name."

I swallow in understanding. He'd just marked me for everyone to see.

"And for what it's worth, you make that hideous shirt look gorgeous."

The low, silky whisper immediately brings a flush to my face. "You're obligated to say that as one of the fathers of my baby," I say, aware of Lavinia watching us.

He shrugs and replies, "Doesn't mean I'm wrong," before sauntering off.

Lavinia and I are both quiet as we watch his retreat. Halfway across the gym, one of the nurses approaches and they both head toward the blood drawing area. Once he's gone, Lavinia turns to me, a wide grin on her face. "Girl, holy shit."

"What?"

"That." She points at him, and then back at me. "You two."

"What about it?" I unscrew the cap of the water bottle.

"He's been a machine since he got here, but one second with you and he turns into a fucking teddy bear?" She laughs, head shaking. "He adores you. And the baby. It's so cute, I could literally barf."

"He's a Prince," I remind her, feeling my cheeks heat. "He's programmed for fatherhood."

"Maybe, but that look? All the sweet things?" She blinks. "He loves you."

I can't explain my reaction, which lands somewhere between annoyance and panic. "Stop. We're barely into the acceptance phase of this thing. We're fulfilling roles. Creating legacies." I say these words, these Ashby-isms, but they sit wrong in my chest. The Princes love one another—that bond is undeniable. And I know they care for the baby. At least Lex and Pace do. And things have changed between us, but I can't imagine these men being capable of loving me. That's not what a Royal relationship is about. Not in East End. "They're not Dukes," I tell her, "raised on passion and emotion. Their life has been hard." She snorts, raising her eyebrow in disbelief. "Not like that.

They're rich, obviously. Spoiled, in their own way. But having Rufus as a father wasn't a picnic. The kind of things he inflicted on them..." I swallow hard. "He left marks they'll carry for the rest of their lives. The good thing is that they're determined not to let that happen to their son, which is the most I could hope for."

Lavinia knows what it was like to grow up with an abusive father —a King—and I see it reflected back in her cool, gray eyes. "I hear what you're saying, but you can't see what I see." She nods toward the front door where Sy pats down a donor. In a freaky moment of synchronicity, as if he actually senses her attention, he glances our way, giving her a wink. "That look Sy just gave me? That's the way your doctor daddy looks at you."

The looks I catch Lex giving me are analytical. Controlled. Occasionally, down in the exam room, when it's just the two us under the bright glare of the light, my legs up in the stirrups... heated. But the other expressions I see more than anything else are a mixture of fear and worry. Protective.

The morning after the incident on our first night here, he woke up, bolted out of bed, and spent an hour checking me over for bruises and internal injuries. I got to watch, groggy and heart-heavy as he hurled curses at himself, checking the baby's heartbeat obsessively, not missing how he tossed Sy's shredded shirt in the garbage without another look. Even now, a week later, I still sometimes catch him looking at me with that angry, agonized divot between his eyebrows.

Now, he makes me lock my door at night.

"Why does it bother you?" she asks, catching something far too telling in my expression. "Wouldn't you rather have... er, *created*... out of love rather than some Royal strategy bullshit?"

But we didn't. Even if Lavinia is right, and I doubt that much, this baby wasn't created in a moment of love or even longing.

Maybe it wasn't even created out of Royal obligation.

"Where do you want these?" Remy appears in front of the table with an armload of cardboard boxes. Another person comes up behind him, the stack of boxes too high to see their face, but I can recognize Wicker's muscular arms anywhere.

"Oh, the rest of the T-shirts!" Lavinia jumps up, completely unaware of the turmoil she's created inside my mind, and shows the boys where to unload the boxes. "Back here."

I stand and move to help Wicker but he clucks, "Don't even think of it, Red." He cranes his neck around the edge of the box. "I already got a lecture."

"Join the club," I sigh, trying not to see the flash of blue in his eyes and think of *that* night. The Royal Cleansing. "I was just going to tell you that you can put them on the table. We'll sort them by size."

But he just drops the box like a sack of bricks, dusting off his hands. "Fuck it. Someone will take it."

I can't help but snort when he slumps against a nearby donation bed, palms propped out casually, legs crossed at the ankle. He looks like a model posing, and terrifyingly, I don't even think it's intentional. "Why did you even come if you weren't going to help?"

Reaching up, he rubs the back of his neck. Much like Lex, he's foregone the unspoken mandate of conformity, wearing nice pants and a dark button-down. To anyone here, he probably looks downright formal, but I see the details. The top two buttons of his shirt are undone, giving me a peek of the white tee underneath, and it's untucked, the fabric a little rumpled. I get a bit caught up on the wave of his hair, the way it falls over one eye. Practically messy, for him.

If Wicker is good for anything, it's driving me to distraction. "Do you need something?"

"I uh..." He hedges for a moment, but ultimately says, "Never mind."

I narrow my eyes, glancing around to make sure no one can overhear. "If this is your weird way of asking me for a blowjob or something, the answer is no." I swallow. "Not here."

A low, velvety chuckle falls from his lips. "Chill, Princess. I know you miss waking up to the feel of my cock drilling into you, but I'm not here for that." His gaze dips to my chest. "Well, I wasn't. What do you mean 'not here'?"

"Spit it out."

"Alright." He glances over at the kitchen. "You think your mother's got any of that banana pudding in there?"

"Good grief." I sigh. "I should have known."

He gives me that wide-eyed, innocent look he thinks he's good at. "What?"

"*That's* why you volunteered to come today. For my mother's pudding." Truth be told, I woke up this morning and found myself a little excited for his arrival. Lex hasn't been chilly—not necessarily—but I understand what Lavinia was saying before about him being a machine. He goes through the motions, but I've missed that spark of heat in his eyes. The way he touched me our first night here, desperate and determined.

Deadpan, he replies, "No, I totally came for community solidarity."

Honestly, I thought it was for the possible blowjob. "I don't know what she's got in there, Wick, but you can go ask."

He grimaces, stuffing his fists into his pockets. "Yeah, um, I thought maybe you could do that for me."

"I'm a little busy doing the actual community solidarity thing." I open up one of the boxes on the floor and pull out a stack of the white shirts every donor receives, setting it on the table. "What's the big deal? The worst thing she can say is no." He shifts on his heels. "What?"

"Look, your mom is fucking scary. She's got this vibe like..."

I cross my arms over my chest. "Like what?"

He gives the door to the kitchen another fleeting look. "Like she wants to claw my eyes out and de-ball me. Kinda like you for the first three months you lived at the palace."

"You're not wrong," I admit, a shadow cast over my thoughts. "You *are* the man who took my virginity. Brutally, I may add."

Wicker does this thing where his expression sort of just... *snaps* into blankness. There's a quick blink, and then his spine straightens. It's like he's getting ready for an attack, shoulders squaring, features hardening. "It's not like I wanted—"

I hold up a hand, struggling to tamp down this new, yet so

familiar burn in the back of my throat. "There's no time for this right now, but if you get through the day without starting any kind of trouble, I'll ask her about it."

I'd blame Lavinia for putting the question in my head, but it wouldn't be fair. Maybe it's always been there, this gut-deep sense of dread that Wicker and I have created something out of hatred and hurt. That I'm going to look into our son's eyes one day and see something horrible and tainted reflected back at me.

"Turn her around. I should have never fucked this bitch face-to-face."

"Yeah?" He grins, yanking me out of the memory of the cleansing. It's the only reason I recoil when he reaches out, fingering a lock of my hair. "Is that BJ still on the table?"

I ignore the flash of surprise in his eyes at my flinch. "Don't push it."

"I haven't," he says, brow knitting up in confusion. "In fact, I've been really fucking good about not pushing it, so what's your problem?"

"Nothing. I just—" I push a fist into my lower back, stretching an aching kink at the base of my spine. "I'm just tired. Forget it."

Although he gives me a long look, he seems happy to let it go and walk away. I return to my task, needing something to busy myself with.

"Now that one," Lav says, tossing a shirt in the medium pile, "the way he looks at you?"

"What about it?"

"I've seen that before too." She turns to watch Wicker approach Lex in the middle of the room. "He's not ready yet, but when he finally is..."

She trails off, but honestly, I'm dying to know. "What? What happens?"

"It's going to feel like falling off a cliff."

7

———————

L^{ex}

By the time we get back to West End's tetanus factory masquerading as living quarters, my neck is fucking killing me. Nine hours of staring down at veins isn't the most ergonomic way to spend my day. Frustratingly, there's also a nagging presence in the back of my brain reminding me of the Scratch dealer we passed on the way here, and the more the day drags on, the less I'm inclined to ignore the tickle in the back of my throat.

When I shove the key into the loft's door, prying it open with a bump from my shoulder, my body feels heavy, like weights have been tied to my limbs.

Still, I help Verity inside first, hefting my bag with one arm as the other presses a hand to the small of her back. Over time, she's gotten more inclined to accepting these small, proprietary gestures, which is good, seeing as how it's getting more and more difficult to be around her without touching some part of her.

Usually her belly.

The loft has a strange smell. Old, like dust. There's also an edge to it, metal and the tang of salt. Rust and paper. We've been here a week and no one is more surprised than me to find I miss home. Part of that is the professionally contained bedroom I can lock myself into, not to mention the impeccable medical facility built into the palace, but maybe what people say about the Princes is right. Perhaps we really are spoiled.

I miss *my* silk pillows.

As I'm dumping my bag and emptying my pockets, I watch her carefully. She goes to the fridge, swinging the door open to stare at the contents for a long moment. Verity does this new thing where she'll pick at her lips when a craving hits her. She does it now, bottom lip pinched gently between forefinger and thumb as she gazes at the selection. I've had it stocked with vegetables, fruits, and easy proteins since our second day here.

Her chest swells and shrinks with a long sigh.

She opens the freezer.

My mouth twitches as I watch her work through the mental steps of what it is she wants. Her hair is pulled up into a messy bun, the back of her neck flushed. She's been hot all day. She's not hungry. We ate at the gym just two hours ago, with seventeen DKS members, twelve cutsluts, her mother, and Remington Maddox.

I kick off my shoes. "Ice cream."

Without even meeting my gaze, her eyes pop wide, a delicate, longing 'ooh' floating off her lips. "Mint chocolate chip," she moans. And then, with a pout, she lets the freezer door swing shut.

No, I don't stock the freezer with ice cream.

"There's yogurt," I offer.

She cuts me a horrified look. "It's not the same."

"I'll get some tomorrow," I promise, unbuttoning my shirt.

She shrugs like she doesn't care, watching as I collapse on the couch. A jaw-cracking yawn takes me, and I know there are things I need to do—brush my teeth, check the baby's heartbeat, get her a pint of mint chocolate chip—but I can't bring myself to do anything other than reach for my hair tie, letting my hair loose as my eyes flutter closed.

I hear more than see her shuffling around the room, the sounds growing closer.

The instant the weight of her presses into the couch against my hip, I reach for her, splaying my hand across her stomach. I don't feel him moving. He must be resting. Maybe he had a long day, too.

"Can I ask you something?" The sound of her voice, small and confusingly fragile, is the only thing that could make my eyes flutter open. Her tired eyes stare back, fingers fidgeting with the hairband around her wrist. It's only now that I realize she's taken her hair down too, the red locks cascading over her shoulders.

My thumb sweeps soothingly against her belly. "Of course."

She glances down, catching the motion of my hand, and stills it by placing her own hand on top. "Remember back when you were... making deposits?"

Something in me stirs at the quick flick of her eyes to mine. The timidness. The blush rising to her cheeks.

God, I want to feel her beneath me.

Haltingly, I answer, "Yeah."

"Why did you..." A crevice appears between her eyebrows as she works through the stilted nature of her words. "Why did you always make me look at you?"

I blink, fighting the urge to pull my hand away. Instead, I squirm, clearing my throat. "I don't know."

She finally meets my gaze, leveling me with an unimpressed stare. "Yes, you do."

With a resigned sigh, I think back to those long weeks. Most of the time, filling those syringes meant sitting in a dark room, desperate to get it over with—to *come*—out of nothing but obligation and a fear of failure. There was no passion in it, only desperation and persistence. I'd think of her, of course. Sometimes, I'd have Pace pull me up a clip of her and Wicker. More often than not, I'd put myself in his place, imagining I was the one emptying my balls into her with the same untethered grunts.

But mostly, it was just a battle with my body, fighting to stay hard.

"Because if my seed took hold," I begin, struggling to put something so absurd into words, "I wanted to know it was done with... *more* of me than just a lousy nut into a specimen cup."

Okay, it definitely sounds stupider when I say it aloud.

Looking up, I catch her watching me back, her head cocked curiously. "Why?"

Unsettled by the confusion in her eyes, I look away, my gaze falling on the coffee table. It's a chaotic mess consisting of my laptop, the heart monitor, nursery invoices, the framed articles I'd taken off the wall for her, and a stack of old newspapers that I found in the closet. Fittingly, these things have become a sort of clock for me. Rotations of my day. Mornings with the heart monitor strapped to Verity's belly. Afternoons spent pouring over spreadsheets and lab results. Evenings coordinating with the contractors over the phone. Nights—long nights that seem like they'll never end—spent flipping idly through all these clippings of Forsyth's history. This building has all kinds of tattered shreds of it lying around.

It's why I relent, turning my hand to lace our fingers together. "Because I'm not like Wicker or Pace. My blood isn't Royal, or warm, or full of potential, and I—" I look down, fixated by the sight of our entwined hands, resting against our son. "I didn't want to create a life out of emptiness. A life like mine."

Her face goes slack, lips parting. "What?"

"It was dumb. Superstitious, I guess." It's never easy being faced with things I can't quantify, and I frown as I consider her belly—the life stirring inside of it. "But what is a soul? Does it even exist? Is it just a pretty name we give to the concept of sentience, or is it something that transcends science? And if it is, are we imbued with one at birth, or is a soul something we build ourselves? Can we inherit a soul? And if we can, does that mean we can also inherit the absence of one?" Exhausted, I rub my eyes, confessing, "I don't know. I just *don't fucking know*. But with my history, if there was a chance of that moment, the spark of creation, having any impact on genetic nature, then I wanted to at least—"

A loud, wracking sob shatters my meandering train of thought. I lay there, stunned, as Verity rips her hand from mine, covering her crying face. There couldn't be a more concise validation of those fears than this. I feel it in the pit of my chest, this dull, painful throb that I'd put her through it. It's why I'd been so happy to find out our son was made from Wicker.

Wicker, whose biggest problem is that he has *too much* soul.

But really, who'd want to look into these dead, empty eyes while creating life? It's harder than I thought it'd be to say, "I'm sorry I made you look."

Her hands fly away from her face, revealing red, tear-stained cheeks. "No," she cries, the agonized twist of her expression tugging at something painful. "Looking at you was the best part of the whole thing, Lex. I'm... I'm so glad you made me look." She sucks in a sharp, shuddering breath, her green eyes brimming. "But Wicker didn't."

For a moment, all I can parse are those words.

"... the best part of the whole thing."

And then I push up, sweeping the hair from her wet cheek. "Hey, what are you talking about?"

She grimaces, but I don't let her twist away, thumbing a tear from her cheek. "I found out I was pregnant after the cleansing," she explains. In my periphery, I see her hands tangling the hem of her shirt up into fists, wringing them. "What if that's how we made him, Lex? What if it was *worse* than empty? You were all so mean and hateful, and you... you didn't want to create with me. You hated me. You wanted to *hurt* me." She untangles a fist only to push it against her diaphragm. "That hurt is still *in here* somewhere." With wide, shining eyes, she presses a ragged whisper into the space between us. "What if it's *him*, Lex? What if we bring this child into the world and I can never look into his eyes and see anything but pain?"

Her words sink into me like a knife, the thought so gutting that it's a physical impulse to recoil from it.

Instead, I pull her close, gathering her shuddering body up to mine. "Fuck, Verity..." She smells sweet and ripe, her hair like silk against my cheek. I want to fucking *hit* something. "You know how hard I've worked to analyze this pregnancy." Every last deposit. Every ovulation. Every menstruation. Temperatures. Hormones. "You trust that, don't you?"

Her breath hitches with another cry. "Yes."

Nodding, I command, "Then I need you to trust this. Look at me." Pulling away only enough to frame her face in my hands, I hold her watery stare, willing her to hear me. "That's just not possible, Ver. Our son was conceived before the cleansing."

She makes a quiet, miserable sound. "You can't know that."

"I thought you trusted me." But really, why would she?

She pulls in a sniffle, searching my eyes. "How can you even be sure?"

"I pinned it down before…" I reach into my pocket, pulling out my phone. I began tracking her cycle that first night I put a deposit in her, and I bring up that calendar. It's packed with tags and times and details she's probably not even aware of herself. With only the slightest hesitation—it might put her off to realize how closely I've been tracking her—aware that it may seem obsessive, psychotic even, I turn the phone to show her. "It had to have happened the last week of January. See? That was almost two weeks before the cleansing. You wouldn't have even been ovulating that day, Verity."

She drags a wrist beneath her nose as she inspects the data, brow furrowing. "And you… you're sure? You're *positive*?"

I do her one better than that. "I'd swear it on Wicker's life." I tuck a lock of hair behind her ear, trying to catch her gaze again. "And hey, you and Wick had some good sex in there, didn't you?"

She does this little half-laugh, half-grimace that makes her nose wrinkle cutely. "I think so," she croaks. She's still inspecting the calendar though, her forefinger landing on January 27th. "That night… Wicker and I went to that dumb party." It's tagged in yellow; a Wicker deposit. She glances up at me, a glow of hope in her green eyes. "We had sex in the pool downstairs. It was… it was the first time he looked at me while we were…"

I catch on, whisking a teardrop from her jaw. "I bet that's the one that did it."

"Yeah?" She looks so hopeful, that I can't bring myself to tell her we can never actually know.

But I believe it. "Yeah," I agree, gathering her close again.

She comes with me when I pull her down, tucking her head beneath my chin, and I let her keep the phone, her fingers slowly browsing all the daily details and timelines. For a little while, it's perfect. The warmth of her against me, pressed between my side and the back of the couch. The weight of her thigh, slung over my leg. The press of her stomach—our son—resting against my hip. The rhythm of her breaths tickling against my collarbone.

By the time I speak, the phone has gone black, her breaths evening out, and I know she's close to falling asleep. I should rouse her, tell her to lock herself inside her room, protect herself from me.

But selfishly, I don't.

"I'm sorry we did that to you." The whisper is little more than a breath, but I know she hears it. I don't say that Father engineered the circumstances, or that I was too high on Scratch to stop myself, or that I was just protecting my brother from someone I thought would hurt him.

It doesn't change anything.

I stare out the large windows facing the east and imagine Pace sees us right now, watching as I stroke my fingers through her hair, trying to soothe a hurt we both imparted. My last thought before slipping under a weightless doze is that I hope he'll call to wake me up.

It's NOT a phone call that jolts me into a panicked awareness, though.

It's the sound of sirens.

Once I realize this, I exhale, wrapping my arms around a still sleeping Verity. West End, I've found, is always a little more chaotic at night, and distant sirens are just a part of its atmosphere. It's one of the things that fascinates me about Perilini's territory, the way West Enders let the city be part of their lives. It's not done that way in East End. We have the Purple Palace, which is set back from the city. We've never heard traffic from our bedrooms, even when we were living in the Golden Row. But out here, the sights and sounds of western streets are married to the buildings they border. It's loud and jarring, the sirens swelling, but I find myself growing used to it.

What I'm *not* used to hearing is the sudden series of slams against the loft's door.

It jolts Verity awake, but it practically propels me off the couch, my hand ducking under the couch for a gun.

"Go to your room," I order, racking the slide. "Lock the door. Don't come out until—"

"Verity?" Another loud bang against the door precedes Remington Maddox's panicked voice. "It's us, open up!"

The look I give her says in no uncertain terms that this doesn't change the spirit of my command, and with a shocked scowl, she obeys, scurrying into the bedroom.

Laying abandoned on the couch, my phone begins ringing.

Pace's ringtone.

Turning to the door, I lift a finger that I know Pace will see. "Maddox?" I call. "What do you want?" I just saw Remy a couple of hours ago, leading some of the frat members to the refrigerated truck behind the gym with the coolers holding the blood bags. He seemed a lot more calm than he sounds now.

"Open the fucking door!" he screams.

Screams.

It goes against every instinct in my body, but with another glance toward the window, I clench my teeth and unlatch the lock.

The second I crack the door, all of them slam through, pouring in like an avalanche. Maddox is first, then Perilini, Ballsack, and one of the DKS members I've begun recognizing as a soldier, Kaz.

They're carrying a bloody Nick Bruin with them.

"Lock it!" Sy barks, but no one waits for me. Kaz slams it shut behind them, popping the latch.

I watch, frozen, as Sy dumps Nick on the floor because he's fucking *choking* him. "What the hell are you—"

But no.

Sy isn't choking him.

He's applying pressure to a wound.

The same wound that's saturated Nick's shirt, down to the waist, with dark, sticky blood.

My phone goes off on the couch again, and I rake my fingers through my hair. "Shit."

"Nicky, stay with us," Sy's snapping down at him, but Nick's eyes are unfocused and cloudy, his face pale.

Remy looks like he just ran a marathon, soaked in sweat and blood. He's staring down at his shaking, blood-covered palms, panting out some wild-eyed nonsense. "Crimson and black," he gasps. "Ruby and onyx. The river didn't lead to the sea."

A stone-faced Ballsack leans close to translate this gibberish. "Oakfield's brother caused a ruckus during a drop. Nick took a piece of shrapnel, I think."

I survey the scene with growing disbelief, wondering if those sirens I heard were meant for them. "And you brought him here?" I ask, anger swelling my chest. "With my pregnant Princess in the next goddamn room? What if he comes looking for you?!"

Kaz begins, "We've got some guys outside—"

But Sy cuts in, his voice sharp and tearing, "My fucking brother's dying here, so could you please *shut the fuck up* about your pregnant Princess?! This is our property, and we need a place to hide out until—"

"Oh my god." Whipping around, I realize—unhappily—that Verity's come out of her room. Her green eyes are locked on a motionless Nick, her face almost as pale as his. "Oh my god, is he..."

It's a testament to Nick's condition that Ballsack checks, squatting to put an ear to Nick's mouth, before answering. "He's still breathing. We can't take him to the hospital, because—"

"Because it'd out you idiots as the gun runners involved in a local shootout," I say, ignoring the phone still going off on the couch. "Jesus Christ..."

"Pauly and Vinny are on the way," Remy says, nodding. "She'll make him better. She always makes him better."

The look I give him isn't subtle. This isn't some slice he's taken during Friday Night Fury. He doesn't need a cutwoman or a gym medic. He needs a whole goddamn surgical team.

There's a sharp intake of air, and then Verity zips toward me, dragging me toward the kitchen. "Save him," she hisses.

I gawk at her. "With what?!"

Her gaze keeps darting behind us to where Nick is lying. "You keep people alive; that's what you do. Pace said—"

The phone's still ringing.

"He's a King's brother," I hiss back. "For fuck's sake, he's a *Bruin*. If I try and fail..." Shaking my head, I can perfectly imagine the consequences waiting for me. It'd be the same if it were one of my brothers. "It'll start a war. West End will never forgive me."

Her face falls when she reaches out, touching my chest. "Earlier, you said... you said you were sorry for what you did to me." Green eyes blaze into mine. "You're sorry because you're not empty, Lex. You have a soul. And... and one day, I'll be able to forgive you for what happened that night, because deep down, I don't really believe it was you." Her face hardens as she strains closer. "But if you let Nick die on that floor without even trying, then I'll be the one who'll never forgive it. And then maybe you'll prove yourself right because no one with a soul could do that."

I search her face, and though I'm not proud of it, I wonder if she'd get that same anguished, desperate fire in her eyes for us. *For me.* "They're family for you," I realize.

Without hesitation, she answers, "Yes."

Looking over my shoulder, I see Perilini giving his brother's cheek a firm slap.

Nick's unresponsive.

Muttering a curse, I start moving a stack of pregnancy and nutrition books from the dining table, snagging my glasses from the counter. "Get him on the table," I call out, snapping my fingers. "You," I say to Kaz. "Make a call to the frat's best fighters and shore up security downstairs." As they're lifting Nick, Sy's hand still tight against his jugular, I begin scrubbing my hands in the kitchen sink. "Ballsy, go in the bathroom, get all the towels and alcohol you can find. Ver."

"I'm here," she says, voice crisp and urgent.

I point to the couch. "Answer that phone. Put it on speaker."

She scurries to grab the phone, and as soon as she does, Pace's winded voice rings out. "I'm walking out the door now."

I scrub harder. "Then go back inside. I'm going to need my red bag." Glancing at Nick's lifeless body, now splayed over the kitchen table, I add, "The blue one, too."

"Blue, yeah," Remy rushes out, stroking Nick's forehead. "Hear that? We're gonna make you blue again, Nicky."

I give Ballsy a nervous look, but he just shakes his head, mouth set into a grim line. There's blood every-fucking-where, so when Verity holds the phone closer, I tell Pace, "And bring the ambulatory pump. He's going to need a shit-ton of blood. Maddox! Are you with us?"

When I glance back, rinsing my hands under the hot spray, Remy's snapping upright, fists flexing. "I'm here. What can I do?"

"Remember where we took all those blood bags?" I ask, pleased to see his quick nod. "Find Nick's, Sy's, their parents', and whatever else is labeled 'type-O'."

Remy's shooting out of the kitchen before I can even think to tell him he'll need to break into it.

He'll find out eventually.

When I get to the table, Sy spears me with a glare. "So help me god, if you tell me to do something that isn't sitting here with my brother, I'll knock your pretty fucking teeth into this table."

"I need to see the wound," I explain, reaching for the hand he has over Nick's neck. A shirt, I realize, and Sy's own, going by the fact his chest is bare.

But when I touch it, Sy growls.

Like a fucking *bear* and everything.

The ridiculousness of it hits me, and I snap, "Has your Duchess ever re-attached a limb before? Because I have." When he finally looks at me, I see the fear in his eyes. It's an all-encompassing panic, and I'm bombarded by these flashes of memory.

Wicker standing over me after a rough whipping.

Pace standing over Wicker after that fight on the ice.

Wicker and I sitting outside the door to the dungeon for days, waiting for Father to release Pace.

"I'm not letting anyone lose a brother," I promise, easing his hand away from the compress. "Let me try."

Sy looks like he wants to let it go, but it takes a long moment for his hand to obey him.

When he does, the blood gushes out.

Immediately, I replace the shirt with a clean towel, applying pressure. "Pace? You still there?" Verity's across from me, the phone still in her hand. Her face is drawn and slack, even though she couldn't have gotten more than a brief glance at the wound.

"In the med room," Pace says.

I inspect Nick's motionless face. "Get the black box, too."

There's a long pause, and then Pace's muttered, "Fuck."

"What's in the black box?" Verity asks, eyes wide and glistening.

I spare Sy a quick glance, knowing better than to bother lying. "Resuscitation equipment."

Just in case.

THERE WAS a time when I wanted to be a surgeon so I could heal people.

It's been a long time since I've felt it, though.

The dream became a job, and then the job became an ambition, and then the ambition became a duty. Over the last few years, I've cut into way more people who deserved it than didn't, and at some point, I stopped paying much mind to my knowledge being more of a weapon than a gift.

But right now, hunched over a lifeless Bruin, I begin feeling the strangest of things.

Like I really want to save him.

Not because Verity or West End wouldn't forgive me if I didn't. Truthfully, not even really because I'm convinced Nick Bruin's life is precious or whatever nonsense. There's no real incentive. No contract. No money. No Father on the other side of the door demanding it.

I want to save his life because I want to prove I can.

For a good ten minutes, I can do nothing but apply pressure to the wound, monitor his vitals, and make an order of operations, which Verity scribbles down for me on an old scrap of dusty newspaper.

"Vitals and transfusion first," I say, giving the wound another quick look. It's a clear slice in the carotid artery. Either the universe is on our side, or Nick's worse off than I thought, because the bleeding has slowed to a sluggish trickle. "I'll suture after he's more stable."

Luckily, the first knock on the door is Pace. He strolls in with a scowl, dark eyes going to Nick's bloody body first, eventually landing on Verity, who hasn't stopped pacing.

As soon as their eyes meet, she does.

"Just a head's up," Pace says, dumping the red and blue bags at my feet, "these streets are fucking crawling with five-oh."

Rory Livingston trails in behind him, setting the black box down at the end of the table. "Also, the ten flashy fighters you've got posted out front are going to start drawing heat real soon."

"Hold this," I tell Sy, eager to get to my supplies. Once his hand replaces mine, putting pressure on the towel, I get to work unloading equipment, asking, "Doesn't Maddox have connections on the force? Can't he put in a call?"

Sy hasn't paced once, choosing instead to stand back and stare at his brother, fists flexing rhythmically. It's a bit surprising how still and quiet he's been since I took the reins, almost like he's giving me room to do my best.

It very slightly feels like a threat.

"If you think the heat out there is bad, then the Forsyth PD is basically a tire fire," he explains, eyes never leaving Nick's slack face.

"That goddamn Fed has his dick buried in every hole of the department."

"That's why you couldn't take him to the hospital." Verity's question emerges in a small, shocked whisper, and when I glance at her, she's gone ashen.

As he applies pressure, Sy's thumb slowly strokes Nick's bloody jaw. "We can handle local heat, but federal intervention will mean the end to every Royal house." He finally glances up, catching everyone's stare. "It'd mean the end of Forsyth."

I try to catch Pace's gaze, but he's locked on Verity, and it's like a storm cloud is floating over his head, eyes dark and shadowed. Not exactly the reunion I wanted for them. I'd planned to stay here with her for a month and then take her home, put her and Pace to bed, and let things work themselves out.

Now, her owlish eyes are suddenly brimming with tears, locking with Pace's over the distance. "You were right," she gasps, clutching her chest. "This is all my fault. He's going to die because Stella went missing, and she went missing because someone wanted to take *me*."

With every word, her voice rises, hysteria bleeding into the edges, and it's a good thing Pace springs into action because I'm too tangled in the ambulatory pump to calm her down.

"Rosi, stop," he rushes out, gathering her up into a forceful embrace. Her shoulders hitch with a sob, and I'm reminded of the two of us doing much the same thing mere hours ago, right on the couch.

Her hormones must be going into overdrive this week.

Pace murmurs gentle words into her temple. "We don't know why she went missing. I'm the one who was wrong, okay? I was trying to scare you because I didn't want you to leave. This isn't on you, and neither is Stella. Understand?" I don't miss that he reaches down, splaying a wide palm over the swell of her belly.

Despite the situation currently happening on the kitchen table, some part of me unwinds in relief. He's been insufferable all week, but my brother has always been too stubborn to apologize.

I plug the pump into the nearest socket, calling, "Pace." And ignoring the fact Perilini is right beside me as I say this, I look my brother in the eye and command, "Take her to bed. The stress isn't good for either of them. Give her what she needs."

Pace pulls her closer, his hand wrapping around the base of her neck. "You're sure?" At my nod, he exhales, a slight shudder moving through him. "I've got her."

It bothers me less than it should as he leads her into the bedroom, closing and locking the door behind him. I'll never really understand it—the way having him inside of her evens her out, makes her soft and pliant and calm—but it's something they both need.

Plus, it'll distract her, which is good.

If I'm going to save Nick Bruin, I'll need complete focus.

"Remember when you came for me and Remy that night? In the water?" She's sitting in a chair on the opposite side of the table. It's been dragged all the way up to the edge, but Lavinia Lucia's cheek is pressed to the table, her mouth up against Nick's ear. Her eyes are bloodshot and puffy, tears still occasionally tracking down her temple. She's tangled their fingers together, their joined hands resting on his tattooed stomach. Every few seconds, she'll tense with a sob that she refuses to let free. "He knew you'd find us, Nick. That you'd never let us fly away. I need you to come back to us now. Follow my voice, okay?"

Sy's begun pacing finally. He walks back and forth in front of the large windows, eyes scanning the rooftops above and streets below. "Is he still breathing?"

He also keeps asking these annoying questions. "Yes," I sigh, squinting as I place the next suture. The skin of his neck is all torn to fuck, but thankfully, the artery itself is a rather clean laceration. At the head of the table, the ambulatory pump is feeding the seventh unit of blood into Nick's veins.

Remy is sitting cross-legged in the middle of the floor, his head in his hands.

At least he's quiet.

I work like this for a long while, the Duchess' soft, lilting voice a background mantra to the hum of the pump and the beep of the blood pressure monitor. Ballsy dug out some rusty old hood lamp from a storage closet downstairs and it pains me to think of how much more sterile this all could be.

As I tie off another suture—almost done with the hard part—I glance up at the monitor to see how his pulse is doing.

Nick Bruin's blue eyes are staring back at me.

I freeze for only a split second, holding his blank stare, and then get back to work. "You took a gnarly piece of shrapnel during the shootout," I explain, keeping my voice low and matter-of-fact. "Right now, I'm suturing the hole in your carotid artery. I need you to be very still. Don't speak."

It's only then that the others realize I'm not just talking for the sake of it.

A lot of things happen at once. The Duchess jolts from her chair, the legs screeching against the floor. Sy sprints towards us. Remy bolts to his feet.

"Nick?" Lavinia cries, squeezing his hand.

Sy looks like he both wants to vomit and punch something, and it's very hard to tell which is the greater impulse. "He's awake? You're doing that while he's conscious?!"

"Please," I grit out, feeling sweat spring to my forehead, "calm down. This is precision work I'm doing."

"Oh, god." Lavinia lifts their joined hands to her lips, brushing a kiss to his inked knuckles. "Does it hurt? Are you *hurting him*?"

I'm saving him, I want to snap back.

I don't.

Nick's eyes cut to mine, and I don't even need words to understand the command in them. They're saying, "Yes, this hurts like a motherfucker." And they're also saying, "Keep going."

Bruin's lost a lot of blood. It took every unit from his family—can't say he and Sy's father don't share blood now—plus a few other donations. That much blood loss can cause all manner of brain damage. So, I begin asking him questions. "Today's date is July ninth. Blink once for yes, twice for no."

He blinks once.

"You used to work for Rufus Ashby."

Two blinks.

"You worked for Daniel Payne."

One blink.

The Duchess takes the next one, leaning over him with an agonized expression. "My father's dog, the night you broke in..." She swallows. "His name is Angus."

Two blinks.

She exhales, relieved.

But I keep pressing. "The mayor of Forsyth is Kenneth Strong. Thumb up or down." Slowly, Bruin lifts the hand Lavinia isn't clutching like a lifeline, twitching his thumb up. I glance at it before asking, "You suck at finding cover from active gunfire."

Nick raises a finger, but it's not his thumb.

My lips twitch at being flipped off. Seems like he's fine, so I tell him what I'm doing, ignoring the anguished chuckles of his family. "I'm tying off the last suture now, then I'll close up your neck. I know a surgeon in Northridge with decent facilities. I'll call him in the morning and see if he can take you for a few days—"

"Like fuck you will," Remy says. He never washed the blood off of himself, and right now, he's caked in it, elbow to fingertips, all down the front of his shirt. "Nicky stays in West End. With us. With DKS." He waits until I look up, catching his gaze, to add, "With you."

I pause, glancing at Bruin. He looks sluggish, but that spark of life in his eyes hasn't dimmed. Still, I wonder, "Why?" I'm looking into this guy's neck. One wrong move and I could end it all. Why trust me with the life of a legacy like Bruin?

Remy gives me this look, like it's the most obvious thing in the world, and then points to the counter, where all my supplies are littering the surface. "Because you got the blue bag."

I follow his gaze, confused and yet... strangely not. The blue bag has stuff like the heart monitor, O2 meter, and diagnostics. These supplies aren't just for keeping someone breathing *for now*. These are the kinds of things I wouldn't bother bringing down into the dungeon.

"Because you saved him," the Duchess concludes, drawing my gaze to hers.

Sy nods toward the bedroom, adding, "Because she's our family, and you're her family." He dips his chin in a grim nod. "Family is the only thing we trust."

Dragging in a deep breath, I reach for another suture kit and a bundle of gauze. "Yeah," I mutter, getting ready to finish this up. If there's anything I can understand about the Dukes, it's that. "Yeah, okay."

Dawn bleeds over West End like a slowly leaking puncture, the sky flowing from black to orange. Outside, there's a sour moisture in the air, smog mingling with summer, and the streets are quickening with buses on their early morning routes. I dodge one as I cross the street toward the corner store, stepping inside with an exhale. The air conditioning is on full blast, even at half past six, and I'm already feeling the sticky sweat clinging to my neck evaporate as I wrench open the back freezer.

It isn't until I reach the counter, sliding the carton of mint chocolate chip ice cream toward the cashier, that I realize I've forgotten my wallet.

"No worries," the haggard man behind the register says. He gestures out the window. "Word on the streets this morning is that the visiting Prince is to be treated like Royalty today." He slides the pint of ice cream back, eyeing the smear of blood over my white tee. "To the victor, my friend."

So it's with an odd sense of confusion that I wander back onto the streets of West End, pointing myself toward the old newspaper building. I haven't slept in twenty-four hours, but it's more than the exhaustion wearing me down.

When I return to Royal Ink, Ballsack, Remy, and Pace are waiting just outside the door, sharing a thick blunt. "I found him," Pace says, only hesitating briefly before offering me the blunt. "Oakfield's hiding out in a building that borders South Side."

I take the blunt dazedly, giving the glowing cherry a long look before attempting a drag. It feels like fire going down, burning my lungs. I'm not sure I like it.

"You're going now?" I ask.

"We were waiting for you," Pace explains, tipping his head toward the door. "She's supposed to be sleeping, but..."

"You didn't want to leave her alone," I say, understanding. She wouldn't be alone. Sy, Lavinia, and Rory are probably all up there with her. But none of them are her Princes. I adjust the paper bag, already soggy from condensation, and pass the blunt to Maddox. "Call me if you need backup."

Pace nods, and then they're off, the three of them disappearing into the alley—a Duke with a grudge the size of a skyscraper, a soldier with nothing to lose, and one of the most skilled torturers Forsyth has ever seen.

Brice Oakfield is in for a world of pain.

When I reach the loft, I pause in the entry, gaping at the sight before me. "You shouldn't have moved him!" I snipe, but all I get in response is Lavinia Lucia's annoyed grunt as she squirms closer to Nick.

Nick, who they've moved to the couch.

The couch, which apparently fucking pulls out into a sleeper?

Why didn't anyone tell *me* that?

Annoyed but diligent, I check the IV and monitors, making sure they haven't jostled something important in the move from the table to the couch. Sy and Lavinia bracket his sleeping body, all of them half-naked and way too comfortable considering that their Duke isn't out of the woods yet.

I really wish they'd let me hand him over to the surgeon in Northridge.

Thankfully, everything looks in place, so I leave them be, shoving the ice cream into the freezer. I didn't just buy the ice cream because I promised it for Verity. I bought it because I was buying time. The events of the last twenty-four hours have proven more than ever that life is short, and we can't fuck around hoping for another opportunity.

Grabbing the stack of papers off the coffee table, I carry them into the bedroom and find Verity, propped up against the pillows, a book tenting the curve of her stomach.

"Hey, you're back," she says, setting the book aside. "Pace told me to wait here."

"I saw him out front. Ice cream's in the freezer," I say by way of greeting. "Want some?"

Her nose wrinkles. "As much as I want to say yes, I think it'll give me heartburn all day if I eat it now." She watches me kick off my shoes and yank the bottom of my shirt free. "You sleeping in here?"

"Not sure I have much choice," I unbutton and shrug it off, leaving on the white tank underneath, "there's a pack of Dukes sleeping in my bed."

"A sleuth."

"Huh?" I unfasten my pants and let them drop to the floor. Yeah, I'm stalling.

"A group of bears is called a sleuth," she says, eyes dragging away from my legs to the stack of papers I left on the dresser. "What's all that?"

My eyes linger on it, tightening. "That's something I want to talk to you about."

It'd been startling to see them when I first arrived at the apartment. Someone—the Duchess, I think—had started a collection of the articles, tacking them to the wall. Morbid curiosity with serial killers is nothing new, and the Royal Gazette's documentation of the Forsyth Carver was thorough. It just feels different when it's your history, your story, pinned to the wall as a novelty.

In East End, we don't put our pasts on display. Those records are sealed, only to be brought out by Father as a reminder of our inferiority, validation for his need to assert control over us. Our blood—our genetics—are inferior, none more so than mine, and he seemed to think that he could punish them into submission.

The time we've spent alone here in West End has brought us closer, and it's time Verity knew the truth about her Prince.

I grab the top paper, which bears a big, bold headline announcing, *"Forsyth Carver Slays Wife, Himself, Child Found Among The Bodies."* I hand it to her, watching her forehead furrow in distaste, and comb my hair back from my face.

"I was two," I begin. "All I remember are the blood, flashing lights, and a faint memory of a police badge, but—I can't be sure that isn't false. What feels the most real is something that's more of a... a sensation," I place my hand over my chest, "like being ripped away. Like a tether being cut."

"You?" she says, recognition falling into place. She sits up, face going slack in shock. *"You're* the baby they're talking about here? The Carver's child?"

I nod and pull out a separate file. I'd found it in Father's belongings after we locked him in the dungeon. It's worn and stuffed with official-looking papers from the police, federal agents, and psychologists. There's a profile inside, listing the characteristics of a psychopath, along with notes in a familiar script. Lists from Father's ledgers. Dates. Timelines. Rufus had been tracking him for years. Watching him hunt the co-eds of Forsyth, not only out of interest, but because he knew exactly who he was all along.

Reluctantly, I explain, "My biological father was a Prince. No one noteworthy—a faint line that gave him enough credibility to earn the position. Father—Rufus—as much as he goes on about bloodline, that's never his real priority when choosing the Princes. In his mind, the Ashby legacy is the only one of importance." I feel the oddest combination of disgust and intrigue as I hold the pieces of a puzzle —*my puzzle*—stuffed inside this folder. "Father must have seen something unique in him. That's his gift, you know. The ability to see a flaw and cultivate it. Nurture it. The value of Wicker's legacy. Pace's paranoia and fear of rejection. My detachment and precision—which we know are inherited." I shake my head. "It was no accident that Ashby was there to adopt me days after my parents' deaths. He'd been waiting for the opportunity to create his own family, one misfit at a time, and when the Carver committed murder-suicide, it gave him the opportunity."

"You're not a misfit," she says, dipping her head to hold my eyes. "And you're not detached." She reaches for the file, slowly tugging it from my hand. "You're the glue that holds you and your brothers together."

"That's debatable, Princess." I laugh darkly. "What I do in the dungeon, what I did to you... those things were as instinctive to me as blinking."

Her eyes flare angrily. "Those things have been trained into you by a madman." She pulls me to her, moving us both to the center of the bed, until we're lying, facing one another, nothing between us but her round belly. "You're a good man, Lex, despite the blood that runs through your veins."

My eyes flutter at the feel of her fingertips against my face. "You don't know that."

When I blink them open, she's watching me unflinchingly. "I do, because the blood that runs through my veins belongs to that madman. If you're lost, then so am I." She touches my lips. "So are Wicker and Pace. And this baby? He's ruined before he takes his first breath." She stares at my mouth, eyes shining. "You're the one who told me he was created from something good—even if it was just a glimmer of connection between me and Wick. I believe that, Lex. I have to." She lifts my hand and flattens it over her stomach. "There are times when I'm not sure how you all feel about me—whether or not you still hate me for upending your lives—but there's no doubt in my mind that you love this baby, and I have to believe that he feels it."

I reach for her—not the baby, but Verity—twisting her around to cradle her back against my chest. "I don't hate you, Verity. Not even fucking close," I whisper in her ear, but I can't articulate what I *do* feel. I'm exhausted but raw with the uncertainty of our lives caught in eternal bedlam. Violence and death. Creation and hurt. It claws at my chest like a wild animal threatening to get loose.

"What does that mean?" she asks, fingers stroking the fine hair on my knuckles.

"It means I'll always protect you and our child. I'll take care of your family, East and West." I swallow the emotions close to the surface. "Just promise me that you'll always be here. That you won't get taken away, severed, like a…"

She twitches. "Like a tether?"

"Yes." The word emerges in a gust of breath, a sudden urge to be connected to her consuming me in a maelstrom of need. I run my hand down her hip to the hem of the loose dress and push it up, finding cotton panties underneath. "Let me inside, Verity," I tell her, reaching into the flap of my shorts. My cock is hard, pulsing, the tip slick. Desperate, I shove her panties aside and nudge against her pussy, almost slipping inside. "You're wet," I tell her, knowing it's too much to be just from her own desire. "He was in you?"

"Before he left," she says, arching back into me with a hitched breath. "He filled me up, told me to wait for you."

With an exhale, I sink in, engulfed like a warm hug, understanding that my brother knew what I needed before I did. That I was too tired to fight anymore. To fight her. To lash out with the darkness I feel inside.

After the blood, stress, and fear, I needed *this*.

A tether.

Rising up, I fuck into her, plunging in as deep as I can go—as deep as she'll take me. Her fingers curl into the sheets, her breath coming in hot, rapid bursts. I drop my hand between her legs and find the spot I know will set her loose, rolling my fingers across the volatile nerves.

"Right there," she cries, face burying into the pillow as I fuck her slow, drawing this out as long as I can make it last. "Don't stop, Lagan. Don't stop."

"Never," I tell her, realizing that I mean it. I am *never* letting this woman go.

8

icker

THE BOW FEELS good in my grip as I run through the chords of the song. It's been weeks since I've played. Typically, my performances are scheduled, pretentious events set up by Father—usually, a precursor to nights I'd rather forget. If not that, they're somber hours down by Michael's grave. Rarely do I play for myself, and even this isn't exactly for fun.

Indulgent, but not fun.

I glide through the string work of *Kashmir*, a pace so furious that my forehead beads with sweat. I've adapted it for a cello-only piece, and judging by the expression on my father's face across the room, he isn't impressed.

Good.

I finish with a dramatic flourish, using the bow and my fingers to extinguish the resonance. The small stone room almost vibrates from the silence that follows.

Setting my cello on the stand, I rise, walking over to the worktable against the back wall. I don't reach for one of the dozens of sharp objects. Instead, I pour myself a glass from the expensive bottle I took from Father's collection and then pick up the bowl and spoon.

Carrying both back over to my chair, I muse, "It's weird. I never thought sixty-year-old Scotch would pair so well with banana pudding."

Father stares at me from behind the bars of his cell. He looks smaller every time I come down here, the weight slipping off him with each passing day. Despite the indignity of it all, he never loses the smug mask of pompousness. He's perched on the edge of his cot, posture perfectly straight, the scrubs Lex gave him to wear hanging from his frame.

Finally, he asks, "Are you enjoying yourself?"

I scoop a glob of the pale yellow pudding onto my spoon, making sure to get some of the cookie, and shrug. "This isn't my first choice, but if I have to sit down here and babysit you, I may as well add a little pleasure to my pain." I swallow the spoonful of dessert and groan. "*Fuck me*, those West End women know how to cook."

I'll admit that when Pace rushed over there to assist Lex in some 237 crisis, I wasn't happy about it. The higher level PNZs can run things upstairs, overseeing the final stages of construction and keeping security tight, but only *we* can deal with Father and Danner.

So I figured if the cats are away, the mice will play, and here I am playing classic rock on my cello, drinking Father's Scotch, and enjoying this banana pudding that Verity's mother must lace with Scratch.

"I'm aware of what you're doing, you know."

"What's that, old man?" I dip my pinky into the whipped cream and lick it off.

"You think you can annoy me to death." His voice is dull, bored. "Good effort, but we both know it'll take more than Led Zeppelin and stealing my Scotch to do that."

"True," I admit. Picking up the glass of cut crystal, one Father bought in Austria, I eye the brown liquid inside. "But Lex told me you can't lose any more blood right now, so it's the best I've got." I sniff the liquor, inhaling the rich scent just like he taught me, and take a measured sip.

"So why were you the one who got left home alone to, as you put it, babysit me?" His lip curls. "Where are your brothers and your sister? Doing something important? Something that requires Lex's intellect? Pace's knack for analytical persistence? My daughter's pedigree?"

Truth be told, I *am* a little irritated I got left here alone in the quiet of this haunted mansion. There's a reason I keep busy— running, playing hockey, lacrosse, creeping through the secret passageways. I'm always moving. Talking. Fucking. Whatever it takes.

The quiet—the stillness—allows the demons too close to the surface.

But I had a much better reason to come down here. I want answers of my own. Ones that don't involve my brothers or Verity.

"Maybe they thought that with my impulsivity, I'd end this once and for all. Put us all out of our misery at keeping an abusive asshole around. But," I drain the glass, savoring the last drop, "since we're here and alone, why don't you answer some of my questions?"

He doesn't even blink. "Which are?"

Before I answer, I shrug off my jacket and walk to the corner where Pace's camera records our every move and every word. I lift the jacket over the lens, covering the device. It's motion-sensored and should stop the recording. This moment is between me and Rufus. No one else.

I face him, arms crossed over my chest, and ask a question I've never had the guts to before. "Why did you do it?"

"*It?*" His lips pull back, teeth bared. "You'll need to be more clear, Whitaker, if you want me to answer."

I swallow, hating the words that he wants me to say, but I know how to play this game. *Tit for tat.*

"Why did you sell me at Mayfield?"

His eyes light up at the question, at the perverse pleasure of making me ask. "Oh, but how could I not? You were an exquisite child. Porcelain skin, sharp cheekbones, and those thick, pouty lips. Such a body…" His gaze takes me in, head to foot. "Some children are created beautiful and then transition through a gangly period before settling into mediocrity. Not you. Your beauty was obvious from the start. Transcendent. A *diamond*." Bile rises to the back of my throat as he speaks, and I will it back, allowing him to ramble. "That special moment when carbon creates the strongest of gems. Beautiful to look at. To touch. Unique. Everyone wants one to hang on their arm or adorn their body with. And because of all that, your value only appreciated over time."

His explanation resonates; I feel the truth in every word, but something is missing. It has to be. "You're telling me this isn't because of who my father was? The fact I'm the only living Baron legacy? That you weren't afraid that one day I'd have too much power, so you decided to reduce me into another one of your cheap commodities?"

"I won't pretend it didn't give me some satisfaction. The heir to Forsyth's shadows, so exposed and *handled*?" A ragged, malicious laugh rips from his throat. "If only your grandfather could have seen how you bloomed under the warmth of their attention, all your petals spreading for them *like a rose*. I liked to imagine Clive rolling over in his grave, again and again." He raises a slender, elegant hand to make a rolling gesture.

I gnash my teeth. "I wasn't blooming, you arrogant fuck. I was enduring."

"And this was all the power that befits you," he continues, eyes sparking. "The greedy Forsyth society, the *non*-royal, could barely keep their hands off you. Having grown up inside the walls of my palace, having attended the best boarding schools, having been a leader in PNZ…" He tsks, arching an eyebrow. "I don't think you can appreciate the appeal that the aristocracy has to the common people in this city. They'll do anything for an association—a piece of Royalty —and Mayfield provides that."

"You didn't sell me off for tea and biscuits," I snap. "You sold me off, as a child, to women and men for their pleasure."

"And you were always very good at giving them what they wanted." He cocks his head, scrutinizing me. "Which makes me think you're protesting a bit too much, aren't you?"

The nausea transforms into rage and I slam into the cell, grabbing onto the bars. "As if I had a choice! Any infraction, any complaint or defiance, was met with punishments doled out to Lex and Pace!" A rumble of anger rises in my chest. "Don't delude yourself into believing I was your willing victim—that *any* of us wanted to do what you asked. All we ever wanted was to protect each other."

He rears forward, delight sharpening his features. "And that is why you're weak, Whitaker. Self-preservation should always be the highest quality for a Royal, but despite being a spoiled brat, you've always put your brothers before yourself." His eyes narrow to small slits. "It's why the Baron King handed you over when he ascended to the dark throne. He sensed it. It's why I hoped either of your brothers would be the one to plant his seed in my daughter." He rises from the cot and stalks toward me, caught up in his ranting. "You fought the creation process every step of the way. You don't understand the value of what it means to bring an heir into this world—what it means to East End. It's why locking me in this cage is foolish, and the beginning of the end for my kingdom." Venom spills with every word. "You're an abomination to my kingdom. A bastard. An unwanted orphan created from mixed blood and deception. You don't have what it takes to be a leader, much less a father. You were made to *serve*. As a whore. As a brute. As a tool. Nothing else."

There is nothing my father loves more than a monologue, but I've always known his hubris would be his downfall. Even locked in a cage, emaciated and withering away, he still thinks his words carry weight.

He's right.

His words do carry weight.

But I'm not as weak as he thinks.

I thrust my arm into the cell and grab him by the shirt, yanking him into the bars. He slams into them, eyes widening when he sees the switchblade I've pulled from my pocket. I push the lever, the dramatic click revealing the sharp-tipped knife.

"Whitaker," he warns, no doubt seeing death flash before his eyes. "What would Lex say?"

"He'd understand," I snarl.

"So, it's going to be you, is it?" Father chuckles, the sound almost chilling. "Because whoever kills me takes the crown, you know. Do you really think PNZ would follow *you*—a mutt?" Humming, he locks onto my stare, musing, "How long would it be before they figure out who you really are? They'd never suffer a Baron legacy in this palace. Mutinies are all in good fun when you're on that side of the cage. How will you fare in here with your brothers, I wonder? Your Princess?" He grins. "Your son?"

Yanking up the top of his scrubs, I reveal the hard plane of his chest and press the tip of the switchblade to it. "The only reason I never wanted to be a father is that I didn't want to be anything like you," I say, the first drops of blood spilling from the cut I carve into his flesh. "But that's because you know nothing about being one. And I may not have what it takes, but between the three of us, we'll do a hell of a lot better than you."

He takes it with gnashed teeth, his blazing stare as unrelenting as my own. "You're astonishingly like your own father," he snarls, pain in his eyes as I bring the blade down. "He was also a Royal failure who hated his child."

I dig the blade in a little deeper near the center. "I guess my fathers have that in common."

A small, agonized sound rumbles in his chest, but he clamps down on it. "You don't know anything about your real father, Whitaker. Oh, everyone likes to talk about your grandfather, the mysterious Clive Kayes. But haven't you noticed no one ever has a word to speak about his son, young Benji?" His eyes spark and wince. "I'll let you in on a secret, little Prince. This flaw that flows through your veins wasn't given to you by your father at all." He leans closer, as if inviting the blade to sink deeper, and speaks the words with a low, malicious sneer. "It's the whore he created you with."

I pause, the tip of the knife finishing the final line.

It's hard to stab someone in the chest. People don't tell you that.

The sternum is tough and takes a lot of focused pressure to get through. It's not something a man like me does on a whim. It requires patience and choice. The gut is always the better option, quick and devastating and so damn messy.

Right now, I'm thinking that I have the time to spare.

It's difficult to shove him back into the cell. "You're going to die in this palace," I promise, casually wiping the blade of my knife. The last glimpse I catch of him, Rufus Ashby is hissing in pain and anger, the stubs of his bloody, missing fingers prodding the pentagram on his chest.

WHEN I WAS YOUNGER, I used to imagine having the palace all to myself. I'd ride Pace's skateboard down the grand banister, use the second floor corridor as my own bowling alley, and invite every hot girl or boy I knew over for rowdy, erotic parties.

The reality is disappointing.

After the contractors all leave, everything is unbearably, eerily still. It settles into the pit of my gut like an ominous thing. There's a monster below me and a wild card above me. I can while away all the hours I want torturing Father or visiting Danner, but every move I make feels wrong, like I should be doing something else. Something important. Something... *useful*.

Gross.

Nearly three weeks pass in this vacant, restless limbo. There are no meetings to attend, no dates to escort, no lacrosse or hockey practices. There's just me in the solarium, my fingers pressed to the strings of my cello as I search for a sound that'll quiet the shout trapped in my chest. Every night I go out there, settle the instrument between my legs, and play.

I play so hard that my fingertips scream.

The days are endless, but these nights—trapping myself inside that glass casket—are without measure or purpose. The only obligation I have is watching Pace's bird while he's out, so I take her down there with me, watching as she makes all these furious, clumsy attempts at flight. Over and over, she bats her wings, struggling to reach the highest branch of the camellia tree, but never quite making it.

You and me both, pretty bird.

I keep a beer at my side, the bottle sweating as the notes bounce off the glass, but never even touch it as I search for that *thing*. That important thing. That *useful* thing.

Goddamn it.

I ignore it for as long as I can, this pressing need to *do*. It's a sickness, festering away inside of me like an infection. I know Father was the one to put it there, but it doesn't make it go away. It hovers just behind me, always lurking.

I'm almost grateful when Pace barges into the kitchen one night, telling me, "Dude, look at the news." Instead of waiting, he turns his phone to me, showing me the screen.

The headline of the article declares, "Missing niece of Forsyth University's Dean Hexley found alive."

I snatch the phone, reading on.

"Arianette Hexley. She was one of the six missing girls," Pace says, an energized glint in his eyes. "They found her up at the river—said she was missing for three weeks. I mean, she's unaffiliated with any of the frats, but—"

"The dean's niece," I agree, glancing up. "She's prominent."

"It could be that she was just off on a bender somewhere or just a runaway or something."

"I'd run away if Hexley was my uncle." That guy is an ass-kissing douche.

"Right?" Pace is already shoving his phone in his pocket, backing out of the room. "I told Ballsy that I'd see what I could find out, if there are any details the press is holding back."

"Good idea, the more prominent, the more eyes, and the last thing we need is another surprise visit from the FBI."

"That's the fucking truth." His eyebrow lifts. "Are you good here?"

Here?

Alone?

"Of course I'm good," I roll my eyes. Everyone here has a role, mine is watching over two old men making sure they don't die before we have the chance to kill them.

I'M MORE excited than I expected when the day finally comes to drive through the streets of East End, headed west. The air is sticky and humid when I arrive at the boundary line, baffled at the sight that greets me in the distance.

Three Dukes, seven of their DKS soldiers, and—I get out, whipping off my sunglasses to make sure I'm seeing this right—all three of Perilini and Bruin's parents.

And they're *shaking Lex's hand.*

As I goggle at this, Verity crosses the parking lot, sauntering towards me with a grin. "Hi," she says, which would be well and fine, except then she launches herself at me. A slender arm captures my neck, her pale cheeks already pinkening by the time she springs up on her tiptoes to assault me with a kiss.

Grunting, I catch her hips, surging into the warmth of her lips and tongue like a starving man. Maybe *this* was that thing I've been scratching so desperately to find because suddenly, I'm spinning her, pushing her up against the driver's side door, and taking my time memorizing the feel of her body, the new curves and swells, against mine.

When she dips back, her eyes widen, a smile blooming as she glances between us. "Wow, he's doing somersaults in there. I think we woke him up." She laughs, the sound airy and musical, and for a long moment, all I can do is follow her gaze to the roundness of her belly, stunned in more ways than one.

The last time I saw her, she was hard as stone, barely willing to offer me a graze of her fingertips. I'd be lying if I said it didn't bristle, that day in the DKS gym when she flinched away from my touch. It left me expecting more of the same distance. Her belly is so much bigger now, this gigantic, inescapable obstacle between our bodies.

Whoa.

That's, like, profound or something.

And now she's lifting a Tupperware container, eyes glinting in satisfaction. "I brought a souvenir."

I blink at it before snatching it out of her hands. "Your mom made me banana pudding?" Surprising, considering Mama B has had nothing but spite for me since the first day I met her.

It's probably poisoned.

Eh.

I'd still eat it.

But Verity just snorts, shoving my shoulder. "This might come as a surprise to you, but I can actually follow a recipe myself."

I jolt back. "*You* made it? For me?" Alarms sound in my head, my hackles immediately rising as I back away, giving her a suspicious once over. *Too nice*, my brain screams. *Look out*. "Do you want something?" I skeptically wonder. "Did something happen with Lex?"

A little bit of that breathless joy in her expression falls. "Of course not. I just..." Biting her lip, she looks away, her gaze fixed on a piece of broken glass on the asphalt. "I guess I missed you. A little."

My eyebrows hike up. "You missed *me*?"

A small, put-upon groan expands her throat. "Oh my god, never mind."

But before she can flee, I trap her against the car, not even trying to tamp down my smirk. "What did you miss?"

She pulls a face, but I don't miss the way her eyes glaze over when I bend down, dragging my lips against the warm curve of her cheek. Swallowing, she fists a hand in my shirt. "Your insufferable ability to turn the smallest gesture into emotional blackmail?"

Humming, I argue, "Although I'm good at that, I don't think that's it." I nose in below her ear, sucking a gentle bruise into the skin there. I barely realize I'm feeling her up until I register the heavy weight of her breast against my hand.

Her tits have gotten bigger, too.

Fuck me.

She shivers so hard that it vibrates against me. "Definitely your mouth."

Before I can cajole her into elaborating—a list of bullet points would suffice—the sound of Lex's footsteps breaks my concentration.

"You're not fucking her against the car," he mutters. And he's a real jerk about it too, sounding all long-suffering like he hasn't had almost a month alone with these blushing cheeks and full tits. "Her family is still watching."

Sighing, I extricate myself painfully. It doesn't escape my notice that he's said nothing about *not* fucking her. Just not against the car. So instead of humping her like a dog, I play the part of the perfect fucking gentleman, wrenching the door open for her, helping her inside.

"What was all that about?" I ask Lex, nudging my chin in the Dukes' direction.

Lex follows my gaze, shrugging. "I saved Nick Bruin's life."

"Oh." My nose wrinkles as I shut the door behind Verity, desperately trying to ignore the sight of her thighs pressing together. "Why?"

Lex gives me a look. "Can't have you being the prettiest man in Forsyth, can I?"

I balk, jaw dropped in outrage. "Dead or alive, in no universe is he prettier than me."

Lex doesn't argue—really, how could he?—but he does grab my arm, fixing me with a seriousness I'm not expecting. "Hey. You good?" We've kept in constant contact, of course. Daily video calls with Pace. Nightly check-ins about Father. Morning meetings about construction and the frat.

One thing rings true. "It's been a long month," I answer, feeling confusingly frayed about it all. Having too much time on my hands, I've now learned, is not all it's cracked up to be.

Lex shakes his head. "You aren't lying."

I clap his shoulder, voice thick with sarcasm. "Glad to be coming home?"

"Weirdly?" He reaches up to scratch his freshly shaved chin. "I think I am."

Well, that's not the answer I was expecting. "How is she?"

The question comes on the crest of a wave of doubt. This new thing where she hugs me and brings me treats is only slightly less weird than that flash of warm excitement I saw in her eyes as she did it.

Since when is Red excited to see *me*?

Lex rolls his eyes. "Yes, she can have sex again, Wick."

"That's not what I—" But I clamp down on the protest, unable to really express this unease curling through my belly.

Whatever Lex sees in my expression, it makes his soften. "I think it did her good, seeing them for a while." Reaching up, he rubs his eyes. "She's still sleeping like shit."

Scrutinizing him, I decide to keep the news of the envelope in my pocket to myself. For now. "Who isn't?"

Getting into the car, I think to myself that it just fucking figures.

I've spent all month doggedly ignoring the pressing, desperate need to do something.

In the end, it found me.

THE MESSAGE CAME by courier yesterday, a black envelope with two names written across the front in gold ink.

Whitaker Kayes Ashby & Verity Sinclaire

Inside, in the same pretentious script, is an address written on a thick black card. On the back, a brass skeleton key is attached, with a delicate number engraved into the metal.

237.

"A mausoleum number in the cemetery?" she asks, shifting her scrutiny to the key. "Seems a little macabre."

Verity sits in the passenger seat and studies the thick black card as if there's another, hidden message that she can't see. She's wearing a cream-colored, summery dress that criss-crosses over her chest, making her tits look like two overripe melons. There's a tantalizing little tie above her hip. One little yank and the whole thing would fall off.

"Seems on brand to me." I roll my eyes and adjust the semi I've been sporting since she threw herself at me in that parking lot. Sometimes, it barely even matters that I haven't had a good, hard fuck in months. Other times, like right now, it barrels into me like a goddamn tornado, sweat springing up on my forehead.

It gets worse when she's near, smelling so damn good, her body all round and inviting. Any other time, I would have taken her right there in the car, on the way home. It should say something really fucking significant that I didn't, waiting until she and Lex settled in before dragging her away with the promise of an evening frolic into Baron territory.

I can't spend another night alone in that fucking solarium.

Annoyed, I grumble, "God, I hate the Barons' insufferable flair for the dramatic."

I feel her gaze on me and when I look over, sure enough, Verity's staring at me with her jaw dropped.

"What?" I ask, shifting into a lower gear as we approach the wrought iron gates of the cemetery.

"*They* have an insufferable flair for the dramatic?" she asks. It's followed by a snort in the backseat, and I shoot Ballsack a hard glare in the rearview mirror. He shrugs, and I don't have time to stop the car and beat the smug look off his face before Verity adds, "I'd tell you to look in the mirror but you'd get so hung up on your reflection that whatever is waiting on us would be long gone."

I don't bother responding, mostly because there's no room for error. The cemetery is neutral territory, unclaimed by any of the five Forsyth frats while also being maintained by the Barons. But being the rightful Baron heir with his Princess in the vehicle, I can't be sure this isn't a well-designed trap.

Ballsack seems to have the same concern. "I'd feel a lot better if your brothers were here," he says, not for the first time.

"I can handle this," I say, gritting my teeth. There's no safer feeling than having Lex and Pace at my six, but this is one of those things.

I have to do it myself.

Not even thinking to question this, Verity says, "We need to get out of the North Side and over into BRN," and points to a sloping hill where the Baron's sprawling plot overlooks the entire cemetery. It reminds me of Effie perched on the top of Pace's bookshelves, acting as a sentinel overlooking the room. "I think 237 should be up there."

But I don't need a number to find our destination. A massive black mausoleum sits at the peak, towering over the headstones. Even from a distance, the pentagram etched into the marble is visible in the rising moonlight, and the name KAYES set in gold underneath.

The King of the Barons is leading me home.

Verity, growing quiet next to me, seems to understand this as well. I steer the car down the narrow gravel road, stopping just beneath the mausoleum.

"Jesus, that's creepy," Ballsack says, looking up at the onyx building. It has a peaked roof and thick columns framing a door made of intricately welded iron. Four thick marble steps lead to the entry. "This is where he sent you?"

I cut the engine, allowing the silence to engulf us just as thickly as the impending darkness. Truthfully, I don't remember anything about being a Kayes. It's just a name I had and molted away like dead skin. How can someone feel a connection to a place they've never called home?

But as soon as I look at the mausoleum, that frenetic scream trapped inside my chest transforms into an inexplicable stillness. I've never worn the name. I've never mourned it. I've never breathed it, bled it, or claimed it.

But it's still *mine*.

Grabbing the key from Verity before stepping out of the car, I take a moment to absorb the spectacle of the cemetery. The serene rolling hills. The grass, bright green from the afternoon summer rains. I see the dotted rooftops of other mausoleums in the different territories, each aligned with an important bloodline in Forsyth. But none have the grandeur of the tomb that houses my grandfather, Clive Kayes. Even decades after his death, he still carries a presence in this town.

Unlike Verity and Ballsack, places of death aren't unusual to me. I wonder briefly if this familiarity is nature or nurture. I've spent countless hours playing the cello in front of Michael's headstone, surrounded by the scent of warm earth and quiet misery. But there's a thrum in my blood, an acknowledgment as I hold the heavy key in my hand, that this is where I belong. Of a life stolen from me by a deranged, vindictive man I now have trapped in a crypt of his own making.

Walking around the car, I open the passenger door and help Verity out. It's reckless to bring her along, even if the envelope was equally as addressed to her. When Lex and Pace find out...

Her green eyes lock on mine as she takes my hand, her palm soft and dry as a goddamn bone. "I can handle this," she says, parroting my words from before. Her legs are smooth, bearing a new warmth of color after her trip to West End. Pace says there's a garden on the rooftop of the gym. Exposed natural sunlight, not like the filtered canopy in the solarium. I like the idea of her up there, staring across Forsyth as she drinks in the light. She belongs there, not here, lost in all this death and darkness.

But as much as the Kayes name is mine, it also belongs to the life growing inside her. Perhaps more than anything, I need her to know —*to understand*—what the weight of the name means.

Ballsack gets out of the car and moves to the back, opening the trunk. He pulls out a black duffle bag of supplies I brought from the dungeon. None of us are exactly sure what Maddox called us here for, but I have a suspicion.

"You sure you want to do this?" I ask her. "Because I don't know what's waiting inside, but I'm pretty sure it's going to be unpleasant, and you just stopped puking every fifteen minutes."

"I haven't vomited in a month, thank you very much." Her eyes dart to the black building, lip disappearing between her teeth. "I'm not sure I have a choice. Both of our names were on that invitation."

She's right about that. When William came after Verity, he

slighted both of us. Her, personally. Me, because that child, like it or not, is mine.

"Eugene," I say, not forgetting the dig from earlier, "keep an eye out."

He rolls his eyes, leaning against the trunk. "Got it."

Taking the bag from him, my Princess and I climb the steps, approaching the dark, heavy door.

Slotting the key into the lock, I turn it.

It opens with a heavy creak, musty, cold air rushing out to greet us like a quiet exhale. It's dark inside the room, other than the faint light filtering in through a window made of stained glass. In Baron fashion, the window has been designed to project a pentagram along the back wall. Dust motes float within the ethereal rays, billowing toward the black of darkness when we disturb the air.

An altar sits underneath.

I hold my arm out, grazing Verity's belly. "Let me check it out."

I can't discount that this is a setup, a retribution for accusing one of the Barons of harming my child. Maybe Father was lying about hiring William. It wouldn't be his first misdirection, but it could possibly be his last.

Turning on my flashlight, I let my eyes acclimate, searching the dark corners for the King's Shadows.

But there's nothing except more dust and marble, this time with engraved brass plates marking the tombs of past Kayes. Long benches sit underneath, a place for visitors to mourn. A muffled sound draws my attention back to the center of the space, where a large, black tomb sits above ground. On top is a bundle.

No. A *body*.

Bound with rope, a black hood covers the head of our victim.

"What is that?" Verity asks, her footsteps following closely behind. Of course, she didn't wait. Approaching the body, I scowl at the display and yank off the hood.

"Well, look at this, Princess," I say, staring down into fearful, pleading, beady eyes. "Seems the Baron King left you a birthday gift. A bit late."

"What kind?" she asks, her voice lilted, coy.

"A William." I grab his neck and lift him into the light, ignoring the grunt he makes. "Look familiar?"

Her green eyes squint through the darkness. "I'm not sure," she says, studying his body. She approaches, moving close, but I thrust out a hand before she can get within distance. Frowning, she commands, "Talk. Say something."

He's not gagged, which is a real shame considering the first words spilling through his gnashed teeth are, "*Fuck*. You."

My punch snaps his head back, slamming it into the marble tomb. My knuckles ache, but it's worth it to see the first drop of blood slide over his lip. "You're talking to my Princess. Show some respect."

Verity's hand rests on my shoulder, and she says, "Repeat after me: two sides of the same coin."

He hisses when I jostle him with a violent shake. "Two sides of the same coin." His lip curves, eyes sharp as a dagger when he adds, "Do you believe in fate, Sinclaire?"

Recognition flickers in Verity's green eyes, but it's quickly replaced with fear. "It's him." She steps back, hands protective over her stomach. It's not the knowledge that this is the William who hurt the Princess and my baby that triggers my rage. It's seeing that fear, the insecurity, in Verity's eyes.

Verity Sinclaire isn't a coward. She's tough. A fighter. West End, through and through. She's taken every single thing we've thrown at her for months without a flinch. But whatever this piece of shit did to her that night was enough to make her afraid.

And that makes me very, *very* upset.

The anger that runs through me is toxic, a poison that fuels every cell in my body, but it's the stillness that drives me. I turn away from the traitor and reach into the bag on the floor, taking out a narrow black box. That's the real difference between East and West. A Duke would be pummeling this guy's face into ground Baron right now.

A Prince takes his time.

"We know my father hired you to scare my Princess, and trust me, he's paying for that betrayal. But I need some answers, Willie." I set the box on the tomb and open the lid. Inside is a set of knives, each with a different blade. The handles are made of jade, a deep green that reminds me of the Princess' eyes. One has a fine, scalpel-like point. The other is jagged like broken teeth. Another with a hook on the end. The box came from Father's office, from the same cabinet where he stored his whips. He always did appreciate things like these. Ceremonial tokens.

It seemed appropriate to bring them tonight.

"I need to know why a Baron, a man known for his loyalty to his King and to his house, would step across territory lines and harm not just another house's woman, but a pregnant Princess." I pick up the blade with the hook and touch the tip with my finger. A bead of blood comes to the surface. "Why would you do this, when the consequence of being discovered is certain death?"

William sneers up at me. "I don't fear death."

"No," I agree, licking the blood off my finger, "you respect it. Or so they say."

"You don't respect death," Verity says, pushing past me. "You crave it. I remember every word you said to me that night. How you'd like to split me open, pop my stomach like a balloon, and let my insides spill out."

He laughs, and it's interesting. I've threatened a lot of marks down in Father's dungeon, but none of them have laughed at the prospect. "I remember you running scared, *begging* me not to hurt you or your child." His eyes go dreamy, like he's lost in the memory. "You were perfect."

I lash out, the blade slicing down his cheek. At first, there's nothing but the flap of flesh, but then the blood sluices down his cheek. "I don't believe you were acting for your King. Any Royal knows better than to risk starting a war between the houses." I watch him, disgusted at this part of my heritage—my grandfather's legacy. "You just wanted to kill something important for the thrill, didn't you?" When he doesn't answer, I press on him, catching the hook on the edge of his mouth, giving the slightest tug.

He inhales, erratic and fearful—*pained*. Good. Tenderly, he speaks, "That *thing* growing inside of her is an abomination. Unlike you," he snarls, "I love my King. He earned his reign through the trial of death. You think loyalty means blindly following orders?" A ragged, sinister laugh spills from his bloody lips. "Real loyalty means protecting your King, even when it angers him. That abomination inside of her is a threat to his reign. It should be flushed out like the parasite it is and left bleeding on the—*agh!*"

His agonized shriek emerges in perfect accordance with the depth of my blade, sinking into his side like butter. "If that whole stunt was an act of loyalty, then wow," I say, voice flat, "you really suck at killing."

He gasps as I twist the knife. "It wasn't time! It wouldn't have been an earned death! I needed her to fight back so I could show him." I can see in his eyes when he understands that's what he is to me. An earned death. "I needed to prove I could be his kin."

There are two types of acceptance when a man is looking down the barrel of his death. The type that clams up, ready to go down carrying his secrets. Then there's the other kind, the type that wants to get it all off his chest. Willie is a talker. All he needs is a nudge.

"Then why not go after me?" I spread my arms at the black tomb. "I'm the real blood kin."

"You're more Ashby than Kayes. Everyone knows it." He shudders, blood burbling from his mouth, but when he meets my gaze, there's the oddest thread of grief in it. "Don't you see? The Baron King is lost. His son abandoned his legacy to become a leader in a rival house. His wife is locked away. The men he came to power with—the old Kings —they're dying or wounded. There's no place for him here anymore. He won't accept it, but my King needs a death to keep his throne." William's eyes turn hard, flicking toward Verity. "An *earned* death."

I drop the blade and both hands snatch out to circle around his throat. His skin is slippery with blood, but I clench tight. "You're about to see how a death is earned." He gasps, his air cutting off, eyes bulging, lips turning blue. So close. So fucking close.

A small, cool hand wraps around my blood-soaked wrist. "Wick."

Glancing over, she gives me a stern look. She wants to know more.

Fuck. With another squeeze, I release him, watching him gasp for air. Verity wastes no time. "Did you hurt anyone else? Have you been kidnapping and hurting other girls in Forsyth?"

Struggling to breathe, he shakes his head. "No one—" He swallows and I know it's as much blood as air. "No one else matters enough to bother." He makes eye contact with Verity and I pick up the blade with a serrated edge, deciding that I'm going to cut his eyes out next. "Until Ashby approached me, I only had fantasies. He gave me the opportunity I'd been looking for."

I twirl the jade handle in my hand, warming the stone with my fingers, and walk around the tomb. "Your King left you here for us. You would call it an opportunity. I call it a gift." I purse my lips. "Maybe even a peace offering. But, unlike you, I won't be squandering it." The rage simmering under my skin bubbles to the surface. I stop at the head of the tomb, and grab William from behind. "This is for hurting my Princess." He grunts, but the following cry is lost when I slash the jagged blade from one side to the other. Blood sprays, but the action feels better than any fucking release in my life. "This is for my son, the *true* Baron heir." I plunge the blade straight into his heart. I yank it out and immediately thrust the blade in and out of his lifeless body. "For violating the sanctity of my home and for being a fucking betrayer of yours."

Something inside unleashes. Something feral and pure. This rage that I have for everything that's been building up. Father. Mayfield. The obligation of being a Prince. Verity. The baby. *My baby*. Everything that is out of my control is channeled into every sharp tooth in that blade, jagged and raw, tearing into flesh. My hands are slick, coated in blood, and my shirt drenched. Never again will this man be a risk to my family.

"Wick!" Verity's voice is distant, somewhere past the hum of violence. I raise the blade over my head. "*Whitaker!*"

I snap my head in her direction.

Splatters of blood are sprayed across her face and body. My eyes go instantly to her belly, assessing, making sure.

"He's dead," she says, taking a tentative step toward me. "He can't hurt us anymore."

My breath comes out in ragged bursts. "Are you..." I point to her stomach with the blood-stained blade and then realize what I'm doing, dropping it to the ground. The metal and jade clatter against the marble floor. "Is it—" I swallow, tasting blood. "Is it okay?"

"He's fine," she promises, taking another step to me. "Want to see?"

I eye her belly, round with life. I've avoided it. Ignored it. Thrown countless tantrums about how that 'thing' has ruined my life. But just now, I killed for it. *Him.*

For us.

She takes my hand, the one I'd just used to brutally slaughter a man, and presses it, bloody and bruised, against the hard surface. The tiniest movement flutters underneath, and I exhale.

Creation.

Her eyes are wide, watchful. "What about you? You okay?"

A trail of blood drips down her neck, traveling between her breasts. Swiping my thumb over the blood, I smear it across the expanse of her chest. Her nipples tighten and peak in response. I tug at the neck of her dress, revealing the swell of her full breast. For the first time I see them for what they are—proof her body is preparing itself for my son.

"I want you," I tell her, realizing the truth of it as I say the words. "I want to taste you. Fuck you. Feel your body wrapped around mine."

I don't wait for a response, taking what I need by grabbing the back of her neck and pulling her mouth to mine. Fingers digging into her hip, I kiss her hard, desperate, the urge to consume her overwhelming. Verity reacts by sinking into me, her hips rocking forward. My cock thickens, perverse, and aroused in this death chamber. Maybe I truly am a Kayes, getting off on the brutality of death. But in this instant, it's not death I want, I crave warmth. Life.

"Wicker," she pushes up on her toes, licking a hot path under my chin, "please."

Dragging her away from the tomb, I push to the altar, and with one hard yank on the tie at her side, the dress falls, revealing her body to me. She's round everywhere. Her tits. Her hips. Her belly. I touch them all, my blood-stained hands marking every inch of her body. Her panties are thin and soft, but I push my fingers into the warm, drenched heat. "Jesus, Red," I groan, not knowing what made her so wet, the fact we've been apart for so long, or the bloody scene in the middle of the room. "Death gets you off, eh?"

She tugs at my shirt, pulling at the placket of buttons. Her mouth presses hot kisses against my chest. All I want is to be inside of her, so I lift her up, setting her on the edge of the altar, and spread those legs wide. The moonlight shines through the stained glass, casting her hair in a fiery halo. I barely get my cock out of my pants without coming. There's no preamble, no fucking foreplay. I ease between her thighs, press my cock against her entrance, and punch inside, burying myself in the heat of my woman.

"God, Wick. *Deeper*."

I don't feel like a God. I feel like a man—skin and bones, flesh and blood, capable of defending what belongs to me. I take Verity, take what's *mine*, slamming my hips into her ruthlessly, getting harder with her every breathless cry. She holds onto me, clenching with every thrust.

When I come, burying myself inside of her with a pained grunt, it feels just like death should be. Earned. Warm. Final. But Verity and I aren't death. We're something much more complicated and difficult to earn.

She and I are creators.

I touch the roundness of her belly, the reality of it banging around my ribcage like some wild, unfettered thing.

This is my son.

I brush my lips against hers.

This is my Princess.

I gasp for air, tasting the tang of blood and the edge of old, rusty death.

This is my legacy.

9

erity

MY FIRST NIGHT back in East End, I fall asleep so quickly that it's hours before I realize Wicker and I aren't alone in the enormous Princess bed. A part of me was afraid to even expect Pace and Lex. Before I left, neither of them would sleep in here, both practicing their own forms of obsessive vigilance.

But that was before Pace took me to bed in the Royal Ink loft, sliding so carefully inside of me that he never moved an inch once he was seated. On the other side of the door, Lex was saving Nick Bruin's life, but for Pace and I, the world was whittled down to the curl of his body against mine as I finally fell asleep.

It was also before Lagan emerged from slumber, rough and desperate. Possessive. But not cruel. Not like Lex was so afraid he'd be. To Lex, I'm a duty, but Lagan sees me as his woman. I think both of us understand this now.

So I'm more surprised than I should be to hear their quiet, gravelly voices through the fog of sleep.

"Wicker," Lex whispers. "Shut up."

Since Wicker is wound around me like a vine, his voice is louder, my ear pressed to his sternum. "I didn't say anything." He sounds confused.

"I can hear you thinking." Lex sighs. "It's like nails on a chalkboard."

Against my other side, Pace mutters, "Seriously. You'd think someone who just got spectacularly laid would *go to sleep*."

"Don't blame me," Wicker hisses. "Lex is the one who instituted the 'only one fuck per day' rule, and both of you got some long before I did. Fair's fair."

My lips twitch, but I don't give away that I'm slowly rousing.

"We have to go easy on her cervix." Lex's voice is imbued with a familiar exasperation. Truthfully, this whole 'one fuck per day' rule is news to me. Maybe that was part of the discussion they had when Wicker and I returned from the cemetery, bloody and lust-drunk. Lex had dragged his brothers off for what I expected to be a dressing down for the two of us going off territory without backup other than Ballsy.

There's a flutter against my stomach and then the warmth of rough fingertips. "I was just wondering..." Wicker's voice is stilted, hushed. "Do you think he'll look like me?"

Lex answers this a little too quickly. "Statistically, without knowing her exact genotypes, there's a seventy-five percent chance he'll be blonde."

Wicker's touch on my belly lingers. "No shit?"

There's a slight jostle behind me, and then Pace's voice. "Green eyes, you think?"

Lex hums. "Eye color is more complex than a simple Mendelian trait, but for the sake of simplification, yes. Green eyes are inherently dominant over blue."

"Fitting," Pace says, snorting, and then I'm shaken as Wicker lobs a punch over my shoulder to his brother's forehead.

"*Don't,*" Wicker hisses, "wake her up. She went through a lot today."

"The Princess goes through a lot *every day,*" Lex replies quietly, "but what's different is you asking about genetics and hereditary traits. Since when do you care about all that stuff?"

There's a long beat where I'm sure he's not going to answer, but then he does. "What happened in the mausoleum. It was… intense."

"Torture and murder usually are," comes Pace's deep voice. "Even when we pretend like they're not."

They fall quiet, the admission a weight too heavy to consider, but I think I know what Wicker is trying to say. He had an awakening in that cemetery. A rebirth, maybe. It's like, for the first time, he stopped running. From everything: his past, his bloodline, his child. Instead, he faced his truth head-on. I felt it when he asked about him, checking to make sure we were both okay. When he didn't panic, but remained strong. For *us.*

There's never been a doubt about Wicker's loyalty to his brothers. They're his life. But I wasn't sure if he'd ever be able to carve out space for me and this baby—at least, not without resentment. But since that moment in the mausoleum when his blue eyes met mine, wide and full of steel, it's been different. It's the same look I see in Lex's eyes when he examines me, or in Pace's when he holds me close.

It means this baby and I are his.

Still, when we left that cemetery, he was raw, and I suspect he's not ready to articulate this, not even to Lex and Pace.

"He's going to look *tired,*" I gripe, abandoning the ruse. When I open my eyes, I'm greeted with the bluish glow of a large tablet, which has been propped on the bedside table. It's shifting automatically through security streams of the palace. I drag my eyes away and look at Pace. "No. Not in bed."

His eyes shutter. "Then I'll leave."

"No, you won't." I grab his wrist. He could easily get out of my hold, but he doesn't. "You told me once that this ridiculous, ornate Princess bed was made for one thing: creation." I run my hand over my belly. "I'm creating right now, growing your child, and I need your attention and focus here," I tilt my head toward the screen, "not there."

"The house is secure," Lex tells him, "with both your security measures and guys from the frat pulling shifts."

This doesn't seem to make Pace feel much better. "There's always *him*."

A stretch of silence engulfs us before Wicker casually offers. "We should kill him."

"Not yet," Lex says.

"Why? Father's useless to us," Pace grumbles. "He hasn't given us any usable intel in weeks, and he's clammed up even more since Wick used him for carving practice." The glare Pace sends his brother is some strange mix of annoyance and pride, which explains almost anything anyone needs to know about the Ashby brothers.

"It's also starting to smell down there," Wick adds, unhelpfully. He's got me pulled up against his side, his hand flat against my hip, not quite touching the baby, but not-*not* touching the baby either. I consider it progress. "I'm with Pace, let's end this."

"It's not that easy and you know it." Lex shifts to recline against the headboard, raking his hair from his face. "There are rules and procedures. If we just kill him, there will be outright pandemonium. A sub-mutiny."

"Why would they care?" I ask, although I'm in agreement about the mutiny. There are some guys, particularly Tommy, who won't be onboard.

"Just because we know Rufus is a princess-murdering, sex-trafficking, egomaniacal psycho doesn't mean the rest of PNZ or East End sees him the same way." Lex reaches over to the nightstand, plucking a book from the tall stack that's collected there. The cover is dark purple, with a gold emblem on the front. "Maddox was right. Rufus kept East End running smoothly. He managed a balance between the territories that provided comfort. When the rest of the frat finds out that we've had him locked up in the dungeon all this time, they're going to have questions, and I don't know how many we want to answer." He passes the book to Wicker, who purses his lips at the cover, emblazoned with the words 'PNZ Pledge Book'. "If we're going to dethrone Rufus, we need the backing of every single member of PNZ."

"We have most of them," Wick says, not bothering to open the pages. "Rory obviously. Giles and Turner will sway the other guys from the hockey team. Maybe Mitchell. But yeah, there are a few that are a problem."

The guys share a look—a look obviously regarding me.

"What?" I press, eyes narrowed.

At first, no one speaks, but then Pace releases a hard sigh. "They don't like you, Rosi."

"Me? What did I do?"

Wick snorts. "Well, let's see. You hit Heather with a frying pan. Got all the girls in your court to dump their boyfriends..."

"She was flirting with you, knowing you belonged to me. And those guys! Every last one of them came on my face!" I refute. "They gave me dead, black roses! I'm the victim here."

There's a sudden frisson of discomfort, so thick that it's almost visible as it ripples through us, at the mention of my Royal Cleansing.

Lex doesn't meet my eye as he takes the pledge book back from Wicker, clearing his throat. "Tensions were high, and conventional wisdom is that a Princess should be compliant and cooperative." He raises an eyebrow. "You were anything but."

"As far as they see it," Pace adds, "you were an outsider—a West Ender, for god's sake—who took the Princess spot away from one of their girls. And because of Father's manipulations, we took their spots away from rightful legacies."

Rolling my eyes, I read the clues. "So what you're saying is that in order to get PNZ on board with killing Rufus, I need to win them over." I think of Tommy standing over me, cock in hand, a mean snarl on his lips as his seed spilled on me. I don't want to win him over, but I do want Rufus' reign to end. I remember the bodies down in the solarium—what they endured. What they sacrificed. Far worse than I had. "Fine. I'll do it."

"Do what?" Pace asks.

Wicker frowns. "How?"

I nestle back into the blankets, already feeling pretty good about my idea. "By embracing my reign as Princess and heir, and instituting a new East End tradition."

Pace's mouth slants unhappily. "A new tradition? What would that be?"

"The thing that brings any well-organized frat together." I grin. "Family Dinner."

All three of them groan in such perfect unison that it's all I can do not to laugh. Wicker bursts, "Red, come on."

"We don't do that kumbaya shit here," Pace argues. "Forty snobby pricks trying to make small talk over a casserole every week? It'll be torture."

Lex mutters, "I've seen some torture that would be preferable." Pausing, he adds, "I've *done* some torture that would be preferable."

"It'll be perfect." I aim my glare at Lex. "And since you won't let me *do anything*, it'll give me a project to keep me busy. I'm not spending the next month in East End twiddling my thumbs."

"It's not like we have much choice," he says, which sounds enough like an approval for me. "We'll get started on it tomorrow. Right now, the Princess and baby need some sleep."

Pace glances back at the tablet, and Wick says quietly, "She's right, bro. Give it a rest. Father and Danner are locked up, and the William is no longer a threat."

"There's always another William," Pace mutters, lifting a hand to rub his eyes. "And dozens of shadows. They're like cockroaches. You can't be sure."

"Oh, I'm sure. That creep was trying to impress his King, and given what we know, it didn't work." Wick's hand is heavy on my hip. Stabilizing. "But I have a feeling the Baron King is about to clean house. What about you, Red?"

I lean into him, breathing in the scent of his aftershave. "Definitely. Will wasn't entirely wrong when he said his King was lost. If he's going to find a place in the new Forsyth order, he's going to have to make some changes, too." Or maybe William just meant Timothy Maddox himself is lost. I don't know. It sounded sad more than anything else. I look up at Pace, who still seems unsure. "We're all here, sleeping on top of a bed loaded with weapons, attached to a panic room. Stay in bed." I meet Pace's gaze, an ache stirring deep inside. "Stay with us."

It's an invitation, and I like the way his hands feel on me as he rolls me back to Wicker, his fingers plucking my panties aside. Lex, on the other side of Wick, opens his mouth to admonish—to lay down rules—but I shake my head. "It's past midnight," I point out. "It's a new day."

Pace is too worried, too focused on the outside of this house. I need him here—with us. Lex must understand because he simply nods and lies back on the pillow he shares with his brother.

"Look at me," Wick says quietly. "I want to see your face when he fills you up."

I meet his eyes at the moment Pace enters me, swift and deep, stretching me with a gasp.

"Night, Rosi," Pace whispers, his mouth brushing the shell of my ear as I drift off surrounded by my men.

It ends up not being a dinner. These are Princes, after all.

We settle on a luncheon, but I reject the cook's suggestion of tea and sandwiches, because men are men, regardless of what territory they reside in. They're hungry. They want to be fed something hearty and filling. And more than that, they want to be *served*.

Unlike my mother's family dinners at the gym, there are no ancient folding tables and hard metal chairs. Lex took me to the storage closet off of the ballroom the next morning, which I found to be filled with everything we needed: large round tables, gold-plated chairs with soft cushions, and stacks of white linens.

"You can't seem like you're changing it too much," Lex said, pointing out the crates of plates and glasses. "The key here is making them feel comfortable—familiar—while showing them what you can offer."

So when Saturday afternoon arrives, I survey the room. It's the same room the masquerade was held in, with its high ceilings and chandeliers. Only now, I've had some of the guys open the heavy brocade curtains, filling the room with summery light. Sunshine catches on the crystals overhead, making everything sparkle and shine.

Ever since we locked our father in the dungeon, it's like the palace is waking up, spreading its arms, and indulging in a long, invigorating stretch. No longer are the corners dark and dusty from disuse. I can't enter a room in this place without angrily chasing away the shadows, unable to shake the feeling the mortar and stone have been prisoners to him, too.

I want to erase every mark Rufus Ashby has made on this place.

But Lex is right.

I can't do it all at once.

"You're really taking this seriously," Pace says, sliding up behind me. His long arms engulf me, tugging me into his broad chest, and I don't need to glance up to know he's following my gaze to the display of tables that we've been arranging since yesterday. He groans. "Are those golden name cards? Christ, you really are an Ashby."

I swat the hand that comes to rest on my belly. "Fuck off."

"Ah," he says, bending to press a kiss beneath my ear. "There's the Sinclaire."

Shivering, I try not to get distracted. "Are they here?"

He hums, the exhale tickling at my hair. "Most of them. They're waiting outside to be frisked."

"Oh." I frown, straining my neck to catch his gaze. That's when I realize Effie is perched on his shoulder, her dark eyes frantically taking in the room. Pace has been taking her places with him more and more. Reaching up, I give her feathers a gentle stroke. "Do you think frisking our guests might start this whole thing off on the wrong foot?"

His dark eyes hold mine. "I think if we're doing this whole ridiculous thing to earn their trust, then they can fucking well put in the effort to earn ours."

I grimace. "Maybe you have a point."

A shrug. "I usually do."

"*Gentle*," Effie coos. And then, a harsh, "*Fucking bird.*"

Glancing at her, Pace tisks. "No. Effie's going to be a pretty bird today. We're having company. Best behavior, okay?"

I watch as she looks at him, almost like she's trying to decide if he's serious. "*Pretty bird?*"

He nods. "Yes."

"*Pretty fucking bird.*"

Pace sighs in frustration, but I can only give a delighted laugh. "It feels good to have her here," I say, beaming when Pace nudges her onto my shoulder instead.

"Then you look after her," he offers. "Maybe you can stop her from cussing people out."

Feeling bolstered by the weight of her on my shoulder, I take a steeling breath, nodding. "Start sending them in."

I've tried not to think a lot about my time as Rufus Ashby's pet Princess, but through the balls, parties, and meetings, I've come to learn a thing or two about what it means to lead East End.

It's about faking it.

"Thanks for coming, Matt!" I tell a stone-faced Matt Kramus as he enters the ballroom. When that gets no reaction, I greet the guy who filters in behind him. "I love that shirt." Nothing, not even a twitch. To the next guy, Loefller, I offer, "Great work with the midge team this summer!" and he just gives me a sour look.

By the middle of the line, I'm feeling more than a little discouraged.

"You're not him."

I glance over, realizing Wicker has sidled up to me. He looks impeccable in a way that always stuns me. There's not one hair out of place. His navy shirt, the top two buttons undone, has the sleeves rolled up, but even that sense of effortlessness feels carefully considered.

He gives Effie's head a soft pat, keeping his voice low. "As someone who's done my fair share of schmoozing, let me give you a tip, Red. The secret isn't getting all of them to like you. That'd take years."

I huff, crossing my arms. "Well, we don't have years, so what do you suggest?"

He catches my gaze, smirking. "Getting the guy at the top to like you."

"I already did that," I mutter, eyes rolling. "Three times." One of them is lingering in the corner by the balcony doors, his amber eyes tracking every frat boy who waltzes in. Across the distance, he catches my gaze, trapping me beneath his too-intense stare.

"We might be at the top *royally*." Beside me, Wicker glances toward the back of the line, jerking his chin at someone. "But when it comes to the frat, he's the one with sway."

I follow his gaze to Tommy, just as he approaches us, giving me the stink eye. "Princess," he all but sneers.

With Wicker at my side and Lex watching from across the room, I don't even question the instinct to sneer back. "Asshole."

She'd been so good the whole line, but now Effie latches right onto the word. "*Asshole*," she snaps at Tommy.

Tommy scoffs, strutting into the ballroom without another glance back at us.

"Nice work," Wicker says, hands folded primly behind his back. "A true diplomatic touch."

I give Effie a stroke of solidarity. "That guy's a fucking dildo."

Effie squawks. "*Fucking asshole*," and I wince. Pace is going to kill me.

"Tonight," Wicker says, snagging a single-stemmed white rose from a passing tray, "he's your opponent." Wicker tucks the rose behind my ear, grinning. "To the victor, Red."

～

God, I hate this guy.

Hate him.

From the second I sit down at his table, just me and him, he does nothing but glare at me. No barbed words. No insults. Just *glares*. All around us, the rest of the frat seems chilly but at least happy enough to indulge the pretense. I've already been to four tables and it was *fine*. Loeffler was stiff, but still greeted me. Baxter stumbled around a flaccid attempt at conversation about the nursery construction. Decker even shook my hand.

Not Tommy.

He sits in front of me with his arms crossed over his chest, looking like a sulking schoolboy. It's a shame Pace took Effie back when the food was being served. She'd tell this prick what's what.

He hasn't even touched his food.

I get a good three minutes into this glaring contest before I break. "*What* is your problem?!"

His lips pull back into a menacing grin. "The email said I had to be here. It didn't say I had to make conversation."

I look over my shoulder, making sure none of my Princes are around before I hiss, "Why are you such a jerk?"

"Why are you such a bitch?" he snaps back.

"Maybe because my back hurts." I lean against the back of the chair, trying to stretch out my spine. I've been on my feet all day trying to pull this whole thing off. "Or it could be that you've been nothing but an asshole to me since I stepped foot in East End! What's your excuse?"

"Don't pull the pregnancy card on me, Sinclaire." His eyes shift wistfully from his empty glass to the bar across the room. "You really want to know?"

"Enlighten me."

"You assaulted my girlfriend with a frying pan."

I roll my eyes. "She tried to fuck my Prince."

He looks distinctly unimpressed. "Everyone on the Court tries to fuck the Prince. It's tradition. You'd know that if you belonged here." The last part is laced with venom. Good. It's time to hash this out.

"Well, where I come from, if a girl tries to fuck your man, you kick her ass."

"Of course they do." He snorts. "Barbarians."

"Oh, I forgot," I glare at him, "real class means strapping girls down and coming on their faces, right?"

"See, this is the problem." He straightens up, resting his elbows on the table. "Heather, and all the other girls you took the title from, never would have been in the situation for a Royal Cleansing because they would have given anything to become Princess. And if they required punishment, they would have taken it with humility and grace. Everything with you is so goddamn dramatic. It's all one fight after the other, and now you've got the Ashby brothers so cuntstunned they can't fucking see straight." The muscle in the back of his jaw tics. "If you don't want to uphold the duties of Princess, the good and the bad, then maybe you should go back to your shitty West End gutter."

That little speech does nothing to adjust my attitude toward him. In fact, I'm one step from going full Whitaker Ashby Gender Reveal tantrum on him, but instead of throwing cake, I quietly explain, "I'm not going back to West End. I'm the Princess and I'm carrying the heir to this kingdom, which means there's no going back. Not for me, and not for you. So here's what's going to happen." I take a deep breath and hope that Lex isn't monitoring my blood pressure right now. "You've got ten seconds to look me in the eye and tell me what your goddamn problem is so we can fix this."

He glares at me.

"Ten," I start. "Nine. Eight..."

Finally, he snaps, "You're the reason she left me."

"Heather?" I ask, dumbfounded. "You're really broken up about being dumped by the same girl who was trying to fuck Wicker a few months ago?"

"She's on the Court," he grinds out. "It's trad—"

"Tradition, yeah yeah." I sigh, rubbing my forehead. "Look, I'm sorry Heather broke up with you." From the aggressively skeptical scowl, it's obvious he's not buying my apology. I insist, "I actually am. Believe me when I say there are no two people better suited for each other."

"She blocked my texts," he confesses, looking away. "And when I went by the house, she had one of the other girls tell me she wasn't there, but her car was out front."

I stare at him for a moment. "Have you tried anything else?"

"I've sent her flowers," he growls, the vein in his temple popping. "Dozens upon fucking dozens of flowers. I bought her one of those diamond-studded coffee mugs that are impossible to find, a necklace that's worth more than my car, and her favorite designer shoe in every color and sheen."

"And nothing?"

"Not anything!" He throws his hands in the air. "No 'thank you'. No 'I missed you'. *Nothing.*"

I blink. "Tommy... that's fucking amazing!"

"Amazing?" His eyes bug out. "I just saw her flirting with some fucking LDZ at the sorority mixer last weekend! She's moving on. Or worse—*rebounding*. How is that amazing?"

It's all I can do not to laugh. "It means she doesn't want to be bought off."

His expression scrunches in confusion. "She's East End. They *all* want to be bought off."

God, he's so dumb. Are all men this dumb? I speak slowly. "Heather may like shiny things—you're right, most of us do—but when you fuck up by coming on some other girl's face with glee, it may require a little bit more. Especially when she wants you to prove you actually care about her."

"What are you talking about?"

Leaning forward, I fix him with a firm look. "I'm going to do you a favor here, Tommy, and help you get Heather back." I inhale sharply. "And in return, we're burying this feud."

His mouth turns down into a small pout. "You don't know anything about her."

"I know she's a woman. More importantly, I know she's a Forsyth woman." His eyebrow lifts. "You have to speak the language of Forsyth."

"What does that mean?"

"It means you find that LDZ who was flirting with her," I say simply, "and you beat him to a pulp."

He scoffs. "That's something a DKS would do."

"Exactly." I grin, explaining, "The Dukes may be a little rough around the edges and have no use for crystal stemware or caviar, but they understand fighting for what's important. Is she?" I wonder. "Is she important to you?"

He answers aggressively. "Yes."

Nodding, I continue, "Then trust me. Heather's waiting to find out if she's worth fighting for." I look around the room, at the guys hesitantly milling around the room, unsure of their future. "And for what it's worth, they're waiting to find out if you think PNZ is worth fighting for, too."

He glances around, finding Pace scowling at him from across the room. "They're mutts," he mumbles. "They shouldn't have even been eligible to become Princes."

"Well, they did," I argue, trying not to snap. "And whether you want to believe it or not, no one in this room has earned the position more."

Arms crossed, he sinks further in his chair. "I would have been a better Prince."

It's impossible to look at this imposing, ornery, *moping* figure before me and see anything more than an angry little boy. In fact, the more I look around me, I see it in most of them. Matt Kramus looks harried and uncomfortable, tugging at his collar. Loeffler hasn't even glanced up from his phone since he sat down. I even see it in my own men, Wicker fidgeting with a fork so hard that he accidentally flings it into his champagne flute, the glass shattering.

Without missing a beat, he covers the mess with his napkin.

All this time, I've struggled between the dueling instincts to wear my role of Princess like a Duchess or an Ashby, but the truth has been staring me in the face the whole time.

These men don't need a King.

They don't need a Princess.

They need a mother.

"Theodore Loeffler!" I bark, watching the man in question flinch with his whole body. When his gaze jolts to mine, I command, "Put that phone away or I'm going to take it."

His jaw drops. "But—!"

"*Now*." I channel my own mother, the look I give him brooking no argument. And then I turn to the man beside him. "Matt, please go help Rory with the plates."

He gapes at me. "Why?"

"Because you're bored and I asked nicely." I lift my chin. "But mostly *because I said so*."

There's a long moment where he looks around, assessing the others, and I get this notion that we're on the edge of a knife. *Are we obeying her?* his expression asks.

Ultimately, he huffs, "Fine," and the tension falls out of me like a sack of bricks. For the first time this afternoon, I turn to the man in front of me and don't feel intimidated one bit. "Tommy, eat your lunch."

He pulls a face. "I don't like chicken."

"Then why didn't you get the salmon?" When all he does is shrug, I roll my eyes, reaching out to slide his plate to my place setting. "I'll take this. Go get another plate."

Still, he argues, "I'm not hungry."

This man's sulking could put Whitaker Ashby to shame.

"Two bites. That's all I'm asking." I say, the threat clear in my voice. "If you still don't like it, then fine."

To my amazement, he heeds it, even if it's done with a sharp, annoyed groan. The next time I look over at his plate, the salmon *and* chicken, are clean.

All bark, no bite.

Who knew?

Things go a lot smoother after that. I go around the room, digging my fist into the aching small of my back as I make sure everyone's getting enough to eat. It's so much easier than trying to be King Ashby or Lavinia Lucia, imagining what my mother would say to Baxter, who's got a hacking cough.

Stopping at his table, I don't bother asking as I put the back of my hand to his forehead, cringing. "You're burning up, Dory! Why aren't you at home, resting up?"

His bleary eyes blink up at me, a frown etched in his brow. "The invitation said it was mandatory." The words are said in a ragged voice, and the more I look at him, the more I see how frayed he is, nose glowing red.

"Come on," I sigh, motioning at Lex. "Let's put some meds into you and get you home."

His mouth goes slack. "Really?" When all I do is shoo him from his seat, he slumps away with a hoarse, "Thanks, Princess."

It'd be a lie to say they warm up to me. Wicker was right about that much; it'd take years to get into each guy's good graces. But he was wrong about Tommy being the only way. Maybe I don't need to be *liked*.

Maybe I just need to be respected.

As I'm in the powder room scrubbing Baxter's germs from my hands, rolling this concept around in my head, I'm startled by the sudden pounding of feet passing through the hallway to the foyer.

When I duck my head out, almost getting pelted by the blur of Rory whizzing by, I see Pace and Ballsack rushing out the front door. "What's going on?" I ask, barely catching Rory before he's followed them out.

"That FBI agent is at the gate," he says, face pale, winded. "And he's got half of the fucking police force with him."

My stomach sinks, a million thoughts rushing through my mind. *We should have killed Ashby*, comes a little voice that sounds a lot like Wicker. If they search the palace, we're all screwed.

Stomach churning, I follow Rory outside, realizing that most of the frat—my Princes included—are already at the gate, arguing with Agent Knight.

"—no jurisdiction here," Pace is fuming, Lex looking annoyed beside him.

"Oh, we just heard there was a party going on," the agent says, glancing at my approach. He's smacking on a piece of gum, carelessly tossing his jacket over the hood of the cruiser parked up against the gate. "Don't worry, though. We brought a present and everything—something you've been wanting for a long time." He lifts his clipboard, offering Pace a chilly grin. "A warrant."

I can practically feel the blood draining from my face, and when I reach out, tangling a searching hand in Pace's shirt, I can sense the tension vibrating off him in waves.

But he's perfectly calm as he reaches through the bars to take the paper, his dark eyes glancing over the words. "Not for the palace," he says.

Lex exhales, leaning over to give the warrant a closer look. "Wait. This is for..."

"Eugene Warren," the agent calls out, gaze seeking behind us. "You're wanted for questioning in the disappearances of Stella St. James and Laura Walker. You're going to come with us."

"This is bullshit," Lex starts, "you've got nothing on him."

"Unfortunately, I do," Knight hisses, getting into Lex's face. He's tall, similar in height to Lex, and when they're next to each other like this, it's clear that the agent's broad shoulders and rigid frame are ripped with muscle. "And while I've been working this case, I've been learning a lot about this little town and its history of violence. I've been reading about a very similar murder spree that happened two decades ago. Ever hear of that?" He asks, then answers himself quickly. "A serial killer dubbed the 'Forsyth Carver'. A man who slaughtered girls in much the same way. Seems a little coincidental."

The muscle in Lex's jaw tightens as he bites out. "The Carver is dead."

Knight nods. "Maybe we have a copycat. Someone who has something to prove? Or maybe someone with the same genetic makeup is back at it again."

"If you're implying something, spit it out, Knight."

"Just spitballing. Stranger things have happened." The agent glances over his shoulder and commands, "Let's do this, boys!"

In unison, officers begin exiting their cruisers, swinging the doors open and standing. *Just* standing. But the threat of force is unmistakable, and when Pace glances over his shoulder, I follow his gaze, finding Ballsack at the back of the parting crowd. He looks hunted and angry, two fists jamming into his pockets as he stalks toward the gate.

"He hasn't done anything," I argue, swinging my glare at the agent. "And he doesn't know anything either."

Knight shrugs, looking far too pleased as Pace slams his hand down on the button to open the gate. "Then he has nothing to worry about."

"It's fine, Verity," Ballsack says, lifting his chin. "Maybe it'll even help."

The stone in my gut says otherwise, and Pace must feel the same way, because he grabs his arm and commands, "Say nothing. Not one fucking word. You have your rights."

"Let's go, Warren," Knight says, and two of the cops approach him, grabbing him roughly by the collar and bicep. "Can't wait to hear how you explain this away."

"Pace is right," Lex calls out, expression grim at the way Eugene is being handled. "Keep your mouth shut and your fists clean. We'll call Perilini."

He's shoved in the back of a patrol car, and they're gone as fast as they arrived, dust blowing up as their tires race off the bridge. Lex is already on the phone, storming back to the palace, but Pace reels me to him, his hand resting on top of my belly. "He's smart," Pace says. "He won't say anything stupid."

I turn into him, face pressed against his strong chest, and can't help but worry. Eugene has been by my side ever since my first week in East End. He's seen the good, the bad, and the ugliest of it all, and just like Stella, he's never once wavered. These are people who have helped me claim my own power.

So why am I so powerless to help them?

10

P ace

"THIS IS BULLSHIT," I say, checking my phone again. "He should be back by now." Verity promised she'd text me the moment Ballsack was released from the station, but it's been thirty-two hours. How long are they planning on keeping him?

In the driver's seat, Wicker downshifts, turning onto an old, overgrown road. "He's probably sleeping off the interrogation in West End or something."

"The Dukes would have told her," I point out. Wick's caught only a brief glimpse of what Verity's life is like in West End, but I spent the last month going back and forth, running supplies to Lex as he nursed Nick Bruin back to something resembling health. I've seen the way the Dukes are with her. A little too close, in my opinion, brotherly or not. But they wouldn't leave Verity hanging.

I suppose that's the difference between my brother and me.

I observe.

Wicker *does*.

Case in point...

I peer through the break in the trees, unable to miss the looming structure. "Huh."

"What?" Wicker asks, opening the glove compartment and stashing his gun inside. I know he has the blade from Father's office in his boot. He seems partial to it lately.

Shrugging, I swipe the gun before he can close the compartment, sliding it into my waistband. "I'd heard the Baron King did Royal business out of an old church, but I always thought it was an urban legend or something."

Wicker scoffs, tossing me a look. "There's no such thing as an urban legend in Forsyth. Every ridiculous rumor you hear is not only true, but the reality is probably even more absurd." He stares out at the stone chapel, craning his neck to look up at the steeple, the cross missing at the top. "And that's a lot more than just a church. It's the House of Night. It's probably the oldest building in Forsyth."

It'd be a lie to say it doesn't worry me a little, seeing this new flash of energy in his eyes whenever anything Baron-esque comes up. The way he's looking at this building, with all its vines and stones, has an unnerving hunger to it. If I thought it'd make a lick of difference, I'd drag him back, but the hard truth is that there's nowhere better to drag him to. Are the tattered remains of Wicker's Baron legacy any better or worse than the ones waiting for us in East End?

"Well, we either need to take care of our business or get the fuck out of here," I say, "before someone notices two relatively under-armed Princes are lurking outside the King's office at night."

Coming into BRN territory wasn't on my bingo card for the day, but Wicker casually announced his need to run an "errand" after dinner. It was obvious to everyone but him that he wasn't going alone, so a coin flip later, here we are. "I still don't get why you couldn't have this delivered by courier the way he had it sent to you." Wick and I stand at the edge of the stone pathway that leads to the front door. "There's no reason to do this face to face."

"This was the return address on the envelope," he tells me, as if that was some kind of invitation. "You're welcome to wait out here."

I point between him and the church. "You think I'm letting you go into the Baron King's creepy, decrepit forest armpit without backup?" I'm still pissed that he and Verity went to the mausoleum alone. The whole thing could've been a colossal disaster. I know Wicker thinks I'm too paranoid, but there's a reason for it. It's a bit of a stretch to say he's lived a charmed life, but there are few situations Whitaker Ashby doesn't think he can't charm himself out of unscathed.

When he glances at me though, he stalls, releasing a measured breath. "Look, I can't explain it, but this is just something I need to do. It's like..." He makes a frustrated gesture. "It's like closure or something."

"Closure," I repeat, brow arching. "Okay, so you're *not* planning on claiming your right to Clive Kayes' throne, leaving the rest of us to rot away in East End."

Wicker's forehead scrunches. "And give up my cars?" He laughs when I reach out, slamming my fist into his shoulder. Still, I see the flash of disappointment in his eyes. "Jesus, do you really think I'm that fickle?"

"You?" I ask, deadpan. "Fickle?"

He rolls his eyes. "I know you were committed to this whole fatherhood and mutiny thing on day one, but the road is a little more winding for the rest of us. This," he nods at the chapel, "is a pit stop."

Thinking that I can probably understand that, I take a deep breath, nodding. "Then let's get this over with."

As Wicker lifts his fist to rap on the door, he mutters, "God, you're such a jealous freak." And before I can argue, the door is swinging open, revealing—

I draw in a sharp breath, reaching for my gun, but it's only a short thing.

The guy in the doorway looks just like a William. Slick hair. Unsettling eyes. Black suit, completely murdered-out. Tattoos just below the collar of his black shirt, which is straining at the biceps, even though he's fairly lean. He's a bit baby-faced in a way that might be disarming if his stare wasn't made of razor blades.

But he's not any of the Williams I know.

Wicker snorts. "Looks like the King appointed a new Baron already. William, is it?"

The guy looks from me to Wicker, a twitch of disdain on his lips. "No." He doesn't elaborate.

My brother shoots me a look. "See? As if I could ever survive being that terse."

I start, "We're here—"

"To see the King," the guy says. There's something about his voice that niggles in the back of my mind, but I can't quite place my own familiarity with it. He turns, walking off and leaving me and Wick in the doorway. Once he's halfway down the entry, he turns and fixes us with a blank stare. "Well?" he asks. He may be terse, but that one word speaks volumes, infused with some pretty thick implications as to our intelligence.

My bones are instantly met with a chill, and the weight of the gun on my hip feels strange as I step into what used to be the narthex of the chapel. We'd certainly never invite another Royal into the palace armed.

But I'm not handing it over if no one makes me.

Small alcoves set with votive candles flank each side of the small entry, and straight ahead, through a carved, arched double doorway, is the chapel itself. Pews sit in solitary, vacant rows, all facing the altar at the front. Before I can get a better look, the Baron turns down a hall and leads us to a smaller version of the arched doors.

The room is long, with high ceilings and more arches, but this time on the windows. Stained glass obscures the view to the outside. The purpose of the room itself seems to be a library of some kind, and that's what stands out to me most.

The room is practically stuffed to the gills.

Thick, old-looking books fill the shelves that line the walls, and binders and boxes cover every other available surface. Where everything in East End seems coated in a gossamer sheen, this appears to carry a layer of history. But there's an obvious system to the chaos, each stack and row aligned with some system of intent. For a blink, I wonder if this is a *Maddox* thing. A speck of mania, the kind that's evident with his son. I look to Wicker to see if he's thinking the same but his gaze is across the room, focused on the far wall.

Maddox stands in front of it, his fingers laced behind his back, seemingly unaware that we've entered the room.

The wall in front of him is much like the meticulous collection filling the room. A finely organized web of maps and photographs, mugshots and lists, scribbled notes, and official-looking government paperwork.

I only manage to zero in on one name—Arianette—before the Baron announces us. "He's here, Father."

"So soon?" The King unwinds his fists to reach for a heavy rope. Immediately, a curtain falls over the wall. He's dressed more casually than I've ever seen him, his signature black suit jacket draped across a chair in the corner. His sleeves have been rolled up, revealing muscular forearms and an expensive watch, which sits right below a faded tattoo of a pentagram. My Father always wielded his power through intimidation and instruments. But the Baron King looks strong, like he could dole out the abuse himself.

When he turns, I see Wicker's hands curl into tight fists in my periphery. "Take it off."

The King's head tilts. It's impossible to read his expression under the mask he's wearing, the two horns gleaming. "I conduct my business in this place as the Baron King, not myself."

"We already know your identity," I tonelessly remind him, keeping an eye on the Baron. "There's no reason for pretense."

"Very well." The King answers by reaching up, plucking at some buckle beneath the cowl, and lifting the mask from his head. Maybe because I've glimpsed them through the mask this whole time, the green eyes are the first thing I notice. They're not a pale green like Verity's, but deep emerald. His dark hair has gone gray at the temples, and there's a bit of attitude in his features, sharpened and aloof, just like all the other Kings I know.

"I was wondering how long it'd take you," he says, hanging the mask on a hook attached to the shelf. "From what I understand, you and the Princess received and were satisfied with your gift."

"We did. I wanted to *thank you* in person," Wicker's hand dips into his pocket and he pulls out the key, "and return this."

"Ah." Maddox turns to the Baron. "Hunter, you may leave us. Prince Ashby and I have some further business to attend to in private."

"Pace is staying," Wicker quickly adds.

"Suit yourself." Maddox shrugs, waiting until the Baron—Hunter —has exited the room to nod at Wicker. "That key belongs to you and your biological family. Why are you bringing it back to me?"

"I got what I needed." Jaw tight, Wicker sets the iron key on the long table in the middle of the room. "And besides slitting your traitor's throat, it was the realization that I know who my family is, and they're not rotting bones encased in marble. Now that I've finally looked the man who killed my first family in the eye, I think we can consider our business done."

Maddox's mouth ticks up. "Is that what you think I've done?"

"You killed my father." Wicker lifts his chin, doing just as he'd wanted. Looking Maddox—not the King, not the mask, but the *man* —in the eye. "You killed *my father's* father."

Blandly, I muse, "Probably killed more."

Maddox's gaze shifts to me, that same malicious grin ticking upward. "Probably. But then, so have you. Rufus is dead, or presumably will be soon. One of you will take the position of King. Patricide under the weight of a crown." His eyebrow lifts. "That would make us contemporaries."

"I've seen what the Kings do," Wicker says, disdain thick in his voice. "Squabbling over petty negotiations, dividing territory lines, keeping brothers and pledges in line. But most of all, you're all in the flesh trade; whores, fights, trafficking, breeding." Every muscle in Wick's well-honed body tenses. "I'm not interested."

For so long, Wick buried the trauma he experienced from Mayfield, but I think the prospect of having his own child has brought it bubbling to the surface. I get it. Seeing Father on the other side of the dungeon bars, my truth hit me like the coiled tip of his whip.

I'll never be caged again. Not by him. Not by anyone.

"I can't say I blame you," Maddox says surprisingly. "It's lonely at the top. Isolated. As much as I'm loath to admit it, Payne and Perilini may have the right idea. They're not doing this alone. They've surrounded themselves with their family." He chuckles darkly. "Perilini even has *my* family. The irony is that what they've created is what I tried to do in my own house. With the Williams, and before that, with my wife, Amber, and our son."

Wicker and Verity told us what the Baron had said moments before he died on top of the marble casket. How the King was lost without his son and wife, and that William's attempted assassination was to give his King a death—*a purpose*. Is that what we're looking at here? A man with no purpose?

My gaze flicks over to the curtain and the board he covered when we walked in. I'm not sure what that was all about, but it doesn't seem without intent. If the kingdoms are a chess game, then Maddox has memorized the board we only just realized existed.

"The Baron confessed he was working outside your direction," Wicker says in that artificial way of his, like Maddox should be grateful he's not being blamed.

And he fucking well should be.

Maddox exhales, looking away. "Will's loyalty was misguided. He'd developed a fanaticism that went against the order of my rule. He'd felt I'd grown soft by not acting after the announcement of a potential future Kayes. He worried about an uprising, or worse, a claim by you. But if I've learned anything from my son, it's that the new generation's loyalties lie not with blood, but with emotion." I can't tell if he's impressed by this or not. Maybe just resigned. "In any case, while you were getting your vengeance, I was getting something of my own."

"A new baby Baron?" I ask, scoffing. "Doesn't seem like much of an upgrade."

Maddox braces his hands on the table, shadows blotting his eyes. "Hunter? Oh, I choose my darklings meticulously, and this one will have a very specific role to serve." Before I can question that, he goes on, "I was referring to intelligence, however. The way young Whitaker here left that body." He feigns a shiver—of delight, of disgust. Hard to tell. "We dragged him out in sacks. That's how I knew."

Wicker stiffens. "Knew what?"

"The baby your Princess is carrying." Maddox grins, and for a moment, it's hard to believe he's anyone's father. There's no warmth in the steel. No paternal comfort in the aging lines of his face. "It's yours."

My heart ticks up, and I don't even think before snapping out, "He's *ours*."

Maddox raises a flattened hand, tipping it back and forth. "Emotionally, I'm sure. But genetically, biologically, he is a Kayes. Relax," he continues, eyes darkening. "If I had an interest in murdering infants, you'd never have known one another."

Wicker grinds out, "You don't have any proof," and Maddox scoffs.

"I don't need a DNA test to know that. To kill someone with your bare hands so violently, so *artfully*..." The energy of the room crackles with tension. "That's an act of love. A *father's* love. I'd know it anywhere." Maddox tips closer, his low voice full of power. "It's almost exactly what Benji Kayes looked like when I got through with him."

I catch Wicker just before he lunges. "You backstabbing piece of shit!" he snarls.

Maddox steps back, as if the line connecting them has snapped. "And this is exactly what you can expect from Forsyth when you've finally taken Rufus' crown. To the victor go the spoils? That's a fantasy," he sneers, meeting my gaze next. "You'll be the monsters now, Ashby. No one will care about why it happened. They won't assume it was deserved. Are you ready?" He looks between me and my brother. "Are you ready to be the ones in the mask? Because separating those parts of yourself is what it'll take. Not fancy luncheons and desperate appeals to your frat."

"If you're trying to scare us into giving up," I growl, allowing Wicker to shake me off, "then you're going to be disappointed."

"I want you to succeed!" I'm not expecting the sharp boom of Maddox's yell, nor am I prepared for the slam of his fist on the table. "You—all four of you—are children of Royalty. You're different facets in the legacy of Forsyth. Stop putting on a play and start leading your fucking kingdom!"

If I didn't know better, I'd think this asshole was trying to give us advice. Wicker must feel it too because he suddenly asks, "What is this?"

"What is what?" Maddox asks.

He throws his arms out. "This! All this sentimental talk. The gift. The key. The reminders of my bloodline. The fact you let me and my brother walk in here, fully armed, and without any notice."

Maddox makes a sharp, annoyed sound, reaching up to rub the bridge of his nose. "Is it a bad thing that I trust you not to murder me in cold blood on hallowed ground?"

Wick ignores this, his Adam's apple bobbing before he says, "I'm going to ask you something, and I want the truth." He doesn't give the King a chance to respond. "Are you my real father? Is that what this is about?"

I reel back, not expecting that. I know the branches of family trees in Forsyth criss-cross through the generations; Verity is proof of that. But I didn't see this coming. My heart lunges in my chest, suddenly terrified of an answer I didn't anticipate needing to know.

Maddox deflates. "No. Your real father is dead." His response is without hesitation, thank fuck. Wicker exhales, but I'm not sure it's out of relief, because it's obvious he's touched on something when Maddox continues, "But we are bound, Whitaker, through both blood and deceit."

"What the fuck does that mean?" I ask because I'm not sure Wicker can.

Maddox pauses in a way that makes me nervous. It isn't until I see a crack in the facade that I realize how cool he's always played it. Right now, he looks like he's searching—desperately. "Did Rufus really never tell you about your father?"

Wicker takes a sharp breath. "You know our father buries secrets the way pirates bury gold."

"He always was good at that." Maddox seems to think about it for a long moment, nodding at two chairs in a seating area near the stone fireplace. Then he grabs a bottle of Scotch off of the shelf under an ornate stained glass window in the crucifix design and carries over two crystal glasses, setting them on a wooden table. He fills them, liberally, and takes the seat across from ours. Wicker lifts his and sniffs, and before I can slap it out of his hand, takes a long swallow.

Even Maddox looks disappointed in the lack of self-preservation on display, meeting my gaze before taking a long drink—proof that the Scotch is untainted. Having no time for formality, I throw mine back all at once, trying to figure out what we're doing here. It feels like I've been watching these two dance around this moment since the first time we met the Baron King at a tribunal.

Maddox must feel the gravity of it too, because he begins, "I suppose I should have expected this moment ever since I put you into Rufus' arms, almost twenty-two years ago. This is something you'll come to learn about Forsyth. We always answer for our sins, one way or another."

If there's one thing that being Rufus Ashby's sons has taught us it's that when a King speaks, we should listen patiently. These bastards love to hear themselves talk.

Glancing into his glass, he goes on, "I'm not sure how your own initiation as Princes feels, but taking the journey down the wicked path changes you. It's not rare for a Baron or Baroness—or even a King—to fall victim to the doctrine of death. You no doubt saw a bit of this in Will before taking his life."

Wicker is eerily still and I don't like it. It's almost as if being in this place is gripping some deep-down, familiar part of him. "He was a fucking wack job."

The corners of Maddox's eyes tighten. "Your father, Benji," he says, the words emerging slowly, thoughtfully. "It consumed him. Corrupted him."

I snort. "Convenient."

"You think I killed him for ambition," Maddox tells me, shrugging. "Everyone does—it's a tidy little story. One people respect. But actually, Benji was my second cousin, once removed. Oh, yes," he says, seeing Wicker's reaction. "Our families were close. We grew up together. Prep school, summer camps, shared holidays in Europe, and eventually Forsyth U. We served as Barons together, but although Benji was the heir, I couldn't have possibly cared less. I was majoring in business and didn't want to be tied to the parameters of royalty anyway. In fact," he adds, gesturing with this glass, "I graduated, guided our Baroness off the wicked path, and had a son with her. I built a family. An *empire*. And all of that without ever needing *this*." He lifts a hand, showing us the golden gleam of the pentagram on his middle finger.

"But Benji..." Maddox's eyes darken. "He didn't just want to be a King, you see. He wasn't satisfied with worshiping death. He wanted to *become* death. His choices weren't without risk. His actions..." His sharp jaw tightens. "They weren't made from ritual, they were blasphemous. *Selfish* and inhumane. It would have been fine if he'd kept it to his followers, but when I found out Benji's true mission..." The tension in his neck snaps when he cracks it, electricity squirming over his skin, as if he's shaking off the memory. "Well, he had to be stopped."

My knee starts bouncing. "What mission?" I ask.

But Maddox pauses, pouring out another glass of Scotch. "I want you to know I gave Clive, your grandfather, an honorable death."

Steadily, Wicker replies, "There's no such thing."

Maddox gives him a significant look. "You know that's not true."

"So what, you shot him in the head?" I wager, already losing patience. "Made it quick? Who cares?"

But he shakes his head. "I gave him a much higher honor than that. The honor of claiming the sin." His green eyes shift to Wick. "By hiding that his own son was the one to put the blade into his neck."

Wicker blinks, brow furling. "You mean... my father killed Clive?"

"Surely," Maddox drawls, "a mutiny against one's father can't surprise you, of all people."

"You expect us to believe you murdered Wick's father because he killed your King?" I bring my hands together in a slow, mocking clap. "A true hero of the ages."

Maddox releases a chuckle that bleeds with malice. "Oh, that's not why I killed him." The laugh clips off, his face hardening. "I killed Benji because he corrupted my wife. He chained her to the wicked path, found the flaw in her mind, and twisted it until it devoured everything I loved about her."

Wicker's mouth parts on a rebuke, but before he can, Maddox leans back in his chair, holding up a finger.

"They wanted me to kill you." The words are chilling, aimed at Wicker. "Saul Cartwright, Lionel Lucia, and Daniel Payne; the new Kings. They were willing to back my taking the throne, but with one point of advice. They all told me to get rid of you."

Wicker's teeth click shut. "So you gave me to *him*," he growls.

Maddox sips far too casually at his drink. "He was the only one who disagreed with them. Rufus had just lost his son. For however little you might think of him—and however well-earned that opinion may be—he wouldn't entertain the thought of killing a *creation*." He dips his chin. "I knew he'd keep you and raise you as his own."

I jolt up from my chair, the anger writhing like a snake in my chest finally striking. "You were wrong," I snap, unable to hear any more of this bullshit. "He did kill him. Night after night. *Used* him. He put Wicker on a fucking platter for Forsyth to consume, and you sit here on the land you stole from his family, pretending you did him a favor? And for what? Because some goth fuckboy stole your *girl*?" Disgusted, I shake my head. "You're worse than a monster. You're *weak*."

Maddox holds my stare, seeming unfazed by my outburst. "You're right, Pace." Setting down his glass, he rises to meet me head-on. "A stronger King would have ended it then. But I was blood-sick and drained, already facing what I'd have to do to my wife by locking her away. But then..." He cocks his head, as if he's searching within himself now. "Even that's not completely honest. The truth that took me so long to face, Whitaker, is that I could have killed you. If you were nothing more than Benji's heir, I would have thrown you into the river and let death make its claim." Worse than the words is the way he says them, so indifferent to the possibility of infanticide. "The only thing that saved you was the love I had for Remy. In the end, I couldn't do it." His eyes fix like lasers on Wicker, and in them, I see something aged and weary. Something horrifically *sad*. "I just couldn't bear the thought of killing my wife's creation."

For a brief moment, the earth might as well stop spinning. I'm suspended in the gravity of what Maddox is saying, and for some reason, all I can hear is Lex's voice whispering inside my mind.

Green eyes are inherently dominant over blue...

The Maddoxs' green eyes.

Wicker's blue eyes.

"Kayes or not," the King confirms, turning away, "you're still my son's little brother."

11

P^{ace}

It's raining when I drive us out of there.

The dark path from the House of Night to North Side might as well be a mud pit by the time we reach the highway. I mutter curses as I struggle through the downpour, lightning cracking in the distance, but it all feels distant and dull.

Beside me, Wicker is a mess.

He doesn't say as much, but he doesn't need to. He still has that discomfiting stillness about him, and he doesn't speak. Not one fucking word. Not even to argue about me driving his precious car.

The fist constricting around my lungs doesn't let up until we reach East End, with its sparkling lights and well-kept roads. It might be the first time I've ever thought of it as home, deep down inside. A magnet drawing me back to the chimney stacks in the distance.

When we arrive, I cut the engine, the sound of rain pelting the roof of the car a stark contrast to the silence within.

In my periphery, I see Wicker's lips part with a halted breath. And then, "I *flirted* with him." When I glance over, his expression is twisted into a disbelieving grimace. "I hit on my *brother*?"

I wait until he meets my gaze to lift an eyebrow.

He blinks. "Yeah, okay, that actually tracks."

I don't bother rushing inside, letting the rain soak me as Wicker whizzes past, his jacket tugged up over his head. I already know what's waiting. He'd texted them before we left the chapel, something short and lacking the weight it deserved, I'm sure.

By the time I reach my room on the second floor, they're already assembled there around the monitors, Lex and Verity, and a restless Wicker.

"Wait." Rosi's green eyes are wide as they track Wicker's pacing form. "Just... wait."

"Are you sure?" Lex asks, forehead creased with skepticism. I get it. It's mind-blowing.

"You're welcome to do a DNA test," Wicker says, throwing off the jacket. "I suspect you have his sample."

Lex is watching Wicker much the same way Verity is, like he's trying to find the resemblance. "I can... *get* his sample," he says, casting a strange glance at her.

"*Wait*," Rosi says again, this time holding up a hand. "Remy is really your brother?"

Scowling down at his feet, Wicker corrects, "*Half*-brother. Same mother. Different son-of-a-bitch fathers."

"*If* the test confirms it." Lex is trying to sound like there's an alternative, but I think we all know Maddox was telling the truth. Regardless, he shoots to his feet, headed straight for the door. "I need to get to the lab and confirm this."

I watch him rush out, because Lex can't confront something like this without hard data and concrete facts. But what would it matter, really? We've been floating in a sea, untethered by biological chains for as long as any of us can remember.

But not Wicker.

Not anymore.

I aim for the bottom drawer of my desk, shoulders tight as Verity approaches him.

"Look at me." She grabs his face by the cheeks, twisting it this way and that. She's so pretty tonight, already in her nightgown, the swell of her stomach more pronounced than ever.

Thirty weeks.

Coconut.

She looks infuriatingly awed as she inspects him. "This is just... wow. Okay. *Wow!* I can kind of see it. You have his chin." I clutch desperately for the bottle of rum hidden in the back, finding it so close to being empty that I barely get more than a swig.

Wicker balks. "Maybe he has *my* chin."

She steps back, still gaping. "How didn't I see it?"

"No fucking clue, Red." He turns his mouth into her hand, pressing a kiss against her palm.

"Remy doesn't even know, does he?" But before Wicker can answer, she gasps in delight, framing her stomach with two sprawling palms. "Oh my god, that means Remy's his uncle!"

Crash.

The rum bottle slams against the floor, the explosion of glass so loud that Effie's panicked flaps and squawks ring out from behind the sheet covering her cage.

"Can we please," I say through gritted teeth, "shut the fuck up about Remy?"

It only takes one glance at Verity's ashen face to make me regret it. "What's wrong?" she asks.

"Nothing," I lie, kicking at a shard of glass.

But Wicker's always had my number, and right now, he's glaring at me in astonishment. "Are you fucking kidding me?"

I fling an arm out, gesturing to Rosi. "It's bad enough the Dukes claim our Princess as family, but sure. Why not? They can have my brother and your kid, too." Sneering, I add, "Hell, let's call Lex back and arrange a marriage. Then all of you can live happily ever fucking after in that death trap of a clock tower."

Verity's face falls. "Oh, Pace, it's not—"

But Wicker is marching up to me, growling, "You jealous freak! You're more of a brother to me than any fucking West Ender will ever be. Blood or not." His nostrils flare with outrage, but I'm too frayed to care.

"He doesn't even know you, and now what? In the span of an hour, he's your brother?" I swing my glare on a stunned Verity, hating the way my voice cracks. "Our baby is more related to Remy than me?" I hiss, "It's not fucking fair."

"I know." Wicker's face softens in a way that *hurts*, but he doesn't back away. "Pace, it doesn't matter."

I burst, "Bullshit, it doesn't matter! We all like to say that—to feel it—but I saw the way you looked when Maddox told you. When we don't have blood ties, it doesn't matter." I take a ragged inhale. "But when we do... it *matters*, Wick."

Suddenly, Verity is there beside us, her eyes—a shade of green I could pick out of a lineup—pin me with a defiant stare. "We're still more yours than anyone else's. Me, Lex, Wicker," snagging my hand, she rests it on the swell of her belly, "*and* the baby."

She can't mean that.

There's no paper to tell Lex the data.

There's no shiny secret about it, traded to Wick in a dark, dusty room.

There's no long, entwined, shared history with her.

All the anger has rushed out of me, leaving a heavy, hollow feeling. "I'm not a creator," I tell her, unable to shake this abrupt awareness that her son has nothing of me. "All I have to offer any of you is... this." I nod at the monitors, thinking of long nights spent watching over them all, knowing this is my place.

Lex is the body.

Wick is the blood.

I'm just the empty, watching eyes.

She follows my gaze, mouth going slack. "Is that why you've been so on edge these past few months? Pace, you're more to us than just *the security guy*." She turns to me, the look on her face so achingly sincere that it makes my gut clench. "You're my

Prince." Resting her hand over mine, she insists, "You're his father."

Wicker's looking at me like I just slapped him in the face. "You're my brother."

I hear the words, but I can't reach them. Can't *feel* them. The panic is rolling like a rogue wave through my veins. "We only work as a family because we don't have anyone else," I tell him. It's how it's always been. We're the discarded remnants of Royal flukes. Stones that have been eroded into misshapen fragments that somehow lock together.

"Wick," Verity whispers, brimming eyes sliding to him. "Show him."

Before I can wonder how he could even begin, he has a handful of my shirt collar, hauling me into him. It's closer to a punch than a kiss, his mouth slamming into mine. There's an edge of pain, and then a familiar warmth, his tongue demanding against mine.

Without having to think about it, I grab his face in response, meeting his kiss with the sort of aggression I'd never inflict on Verity. It's bruising and consuming, and when Wicker tears himself away, his eyes burn like fire.

"You're right," he says, bending to pull that knife from his boot. "Blood matters."

The sight of him cutting into his wrist is somehow more confusing than the kiss, although it shouldn't be. How many times have the three of us done this? Promises and pacts—*on my blood*—it's the first part of Wicker's Baron heritage he ever embraced.

I stand still as he grabs my hand, exposing the ladder of scars made in dark, quiet places. These were etched to track the passage of time, and grasping my wrist, Wicker bisects them with a clean cut. "Family, always."

I barely feel the sting.

Verity gasps, watching as he clutches my forearm, the wounds meeting.

"On *our* blood," Wicker says, which isn't how the promise goes. It's supposed to be made on *his* blood. On Lex's blood.

On *our* blood?

Swallowing, I grasp his forearm, knowing it's a stupid ritual. A Baron ritual. A ritual Lex has always hated but tolerated.

But it's still ours.

"On our blood," I promise, squeezing.

The only thing that breaks me away from his gaze is the flash of crimson I see in my periphery. Immediately, I drop Wick's hand, sucking in a sharp hiss. "What the fuck are you doing?" I knock Wicker's knife out of Verity's hand, wondering when she even took it.

The blood trickles down her pale skin—shallow cut, thank fuck —but when I snatch her wrist, she just turns it in my grip, those obstinate green eyes trapping mine. "This is how it goes, right? Now our blood is yours?"

When she strains up to brush our lips together, my fingers flutter over the curve of her belly. "Don't," I whisper when we break away, resting my forehead against hers. "Don't take him away from me." She doesn't ask who I'm talking about—our son or Wicker, maybe even Lex too—which is good, because I couldn't give an answer.

I just know that I'm nothing without all four of them.

She responds by touching my cheek, the scent of blood and old rain heady in the air between us. "Never." She breathes, "On our blood."

I can feel Wicker's hungry energy beside us, this strange crackle I'm used to grazing the edge of my nerves. I'm not even surprised when he swoops in, taking Verity's mouth in a long, indulgent kiss.

He'd never admit it, but nothing makes him hornier than high emotions.

I wonder if she tastes me in his mouth, the way we mingle and settle, and the thought shudders through me like a quake. Maybe that's my own touch of madness, this inability to feel part of someone unless I've left a piece of me inside them.

Pulling back, Verity rakes her teeth over her plush lower lip. "Now him," she says, hooded eyes shifting to me.

I don't get a chance to enjoy the spark of excitement in her eyes because Wicker instantly turns, dragging me into a hard, slick kiss.

It's a dichotomy that becomes more of a buzz than the rum had given me, the contrast of her soft curves and Wicker's sharp angles.

My dick could cut glass.

"Which one of us, you think?" I rumble, both our gazes falling on Verity. She likes it. Likes watching us. It's clear as day in the glaze of her eyes, the flush that's running down her neck. If she only knew some of the shit we've gotten up to together...

"'One fuck per day' rule," I remind him.

Wicker makes a low, rough sound, reaching out to sweep her long locks of red hair over a shoulder, exposing her pulse point. He sees it, too. "For her, maybe. But me?" He glances at me, eyebrow ticking up. "I can have as many as I want."

There's a question in his eyes, cocky but somehow still careful, like he doesn't want to spook me with the suggestion.

In front of us, Verity stammers, "Oh, y-y-you mean..." She gestures between the two of us, eyelids growing heavier. "*Oh*," she says, and then, "Oh, *god*, yes."

Wicker's on her instantly, pushing her onto the couch. "You like the thought of that, don't you?" he asks, nudging in between her legs. "Pace inside of me while I'm inside of you?" Wicker's never been shy about carnal things, and he's not shy about this—the thought of me fucking him.

Her chest heaves with want, fingers scrabbling to bring him closer. "Please," she begs.

For the first time, I really regret not having a bed, although it doesn't worsen the view much. Wicker and Verity are a fucking sight. His long limbs and her blushing skin. His muscles and her curves. The way Wicker's slender fingers look as they push down the shoulder of her nightgown, stretching it over a soft, swollen tit. His rough groan as he palms her, and her musical moan as she arches into it.

They're the picture of creation.

I'm so drunk on the thought that I don't even see who takes off Wicker's shirt. I just know that he's suddenly miles of warm, bare flesh, and impatiently tearing off her gown. "Pace," he's panting, mouthing at one of her peaked, rosy nipples. "You've got about ten seconds to make a choice before I'm balls-deep here."

That's all I need to kick my body into gear, shucking off my shirt as I approach them.

I don't know who to go for first or where I even fit in. This thing where Wicker and I reach out to each other for pleasure or connection... it's something we've done as horny teens and rowdy frat boys. We're men now, whether we like it or not. Princes. Fathers.

Things changed today when Maddox revealed the truth.

If I'm the empty, watching eyes, then my fingers are lost, wondering where they belong. In the end, it's her hand that finds mine, dragging me onto the couch beside them. The moment Wick releases the peak of a full tit, I swoop in to taste her, licking down the elegant column of her neck to follow the vivid flush downward.

She squirms when I latch onto her nipple, her finger threading through my twists, and I can feel where Wick is touching her, getting her pussy ready for him with these low, soft moans.

I have to brace a knee against the cushions to get to Wicker's neck, burying a teeth-heavy kiss into the curve of his shoulder.

He emits a deep, impatient sound, thrusting against Verity, but just as soon as they make contact, he's fumbling between their bodies and undoing his fly. In a show of determined skill, Wicker manages to be the first one actually naked, flashing me a wicked smirk as he kicks his jeans across the floor.

"Don't pretend you don't have lube in your bottom drawer."

Shrugging, I say, "Who's pretending?" and tear myself away from her clutching hands to find it.

As I'm rummaging around in there, I hear Wicker enter her, Verity's breaths escalating into rapid gasps. When I turn, he's got her spread wide in the middle of the couch, his hands braced on the back.

"Fuck," I breathe, reaching down to squeeze myself through my jeans. There's something about her spread like this, her belly big and round. I don't know what I want to do first, kiss her stomach, or her pussy, touch his hair, or every inch of his skin. She's gorgeous, laid out just for the two of us. *He's* gorgeous, like he's always been.

The light hits the contours of Wick's back, highlighting the sinewy muscles that ripple as he seats himself inside her. His sculpted frame is a testament to disciplined power, each subtle shift revealing the harmony between muscle and bone. The parentheses of her slender, creamy thighs invite him inside, and it's gotta be true what they say about pregnancy because she's glowing. *Radiant.* Her glittering fingernails dig into the flesh of his back. The sight is a blend of raw masculinity and refined beauty as she throws her head back into the cushion, mouth gaping on a sweet, pleading cry.

"Come closer."

Maybe it's meant for me, maybe it's not. Either way, it's like some part of myself is completely incapable of not going to her, my fingers working my pants open and shoving them down my legs. She beckons me to her, and takes my length in her hands, stroking up and down.

Fuck.

It's then that I realize Wicker isn't moving; his muscles coiled tight as he hovers there, and his head drops between his shoulders.

"Hey," I tell him, pushing up against his back to speak the words into his ear. "Give her something, brother."

Still, I'm the one to reach around him, pushing my thumb into her folds.

When I find her clit, Verity's green eyes squinch tight. "Oh, god, Pace!" She bucks up into it, causing Wicker to shudder. "That feels incredible."

"She's so fucking tight," he hisses, hips giving a tense nudge. "How do you stand it?"

It's then I realize what he's doing—what he's asking. "When we fall asleep, you mean?" Grinning, I open the lube one-handed, getting my fingers slick for him as I work her clit with my thumb. "That tightness, the way she gets so wet for it, how her pussy sort of... flutters and clenches..." I reach between Wick and I, spreading his cheeks. "Fuck, sometimes that feels better than coming."

I punctuate this by sliding my forefinger into his ass, enjoying the way he tenses up—just for a split second—before completely melting into it.

"That's how I do it," I rumble, meeting Verity's gaze. "Isn't it, Rosi?"

She never actually lost her nightgown. It's just pushed under her breasts and above her belly, this long ribbon of gossamer holding her down. Her long eyelashes brush her rosy cheeks when she asks, "What are you doing?"

The question is so soft, so innocently curious, that my lips twitch.

"I'm fingering his ass," I answer, the bluntness of it making Wicker snort. "Stretching him open so he can take my cock, the same way I stretch your pussy."

Verity's eyes widen, landing on him. "You like it?" she asks, reaching up to touch his jaw.

Wicker leans into the touch, the move pushing his ass closer to me. "Don't you?"

She doesn't take much time to think about it. "Yes. Thick and warm. Safe."

Navigating the presence of her growing belly is getting more and more complicated, but Wicker somehow manages it, curling over her to lick at the seam of her lips. "Pace has impeccable fingerwork," he husks. I accept the compliment with the addition of a third finger, indulging myself in the rough groan he makes.

Dragging a lip through her teeth, she catches my gaze. "I know he does." For a moment, it's like she and I are in sync, her hips writhing with every thrust of my fingers into Wicker. I can tell she's getting hotter and hotter for it, beads of sweat springing up on Wick's forehead as I get him nice and open for me.

She knows the moment I pull my fingers away, something in her eyes sparking with anticipation. "Look at me," she rushes out, grabbing Wicker's face. Her mouth lingers against his, green eyes capturing him. "I wanna see your face when he fills you up."

There's a pause where her request sinks in.

At the same time, in the same ragged voice, Wicker and I both exclaim, "Jesus fucking Christ."

I have my cock slicked up before the groans even clip off.

In the past, fucking around with Wicker has always been good. Sometimes fine. Other times great. But when I sink into his tight ring of muscle, our bodies linked, watching Verity's expression transform from intrigue to utter fucking lustful abandon...

It's all I can do not to bust right then and there.

Our relationship is no longer just about one another, it's this—the bond—that ties us together. Our bodies; slick and wet. The baby; ours.

"Fuck," he spits, hands curling into fists against the leather. "It may be too much, brother."

"Don't fight it," she says, her voice soft as she soothes him through the invasion. "Let him in." Wick takes a deep breath, giving me room to take another inch. "He's big, isn't he?"

"Not as big as me," he says, even though I can feel how tightly strung he is. "But he'll do."

Scoffing, I slide in deeper, satisfied when he drops his head into the curve of her neck. "Oh," he mutters, a tremor going through him, "goddamn."

Verity's glazed eyes lock on mine, her fingers fluttering through his blonde hair. "Be nice," she chides, even though her mouth is tipped up in a little smirk.

It isn't like with Verity, where all I want to do is stay inside and hold and *possess*. With Wicker, I just want to *fuck*.

The first punch of my hips doesn't make it any better.

He grunts, the muscles in his back flexing, while Verity *whines*.

I run a palm down the span of his spine with one hand while the other seeks out her ankle, guiding it to my hip. She immediately catches on, her long, elegant legs winding around me and Wick as if we were one, writhing entity.

And that's exactly what we become.

I roll my hips into his, which rolls his hips into her. It might be the first time I've ever felt truly spoiled, having the two of them, so achingly beautiful, under my mercy. I grab Wicker's hips and fuck him just the way I know he likes—deep and forceful—and in response, he fucks Verity in the same way, my movements dictating his.

The spot of skin below his nape is salty when I taste it, the sweat building between us. It's not the best angle, but I wouldn't know it from the sounds Wicker is making, deep and body-wracking. It's all-consuming.

"How...." Verity is gasping, "how does it feel?"

The backs of Wicker's ears go a vivid pink. He doesn't blush for just anything. "Like he's filling every part of me," he grits, a particular wildness to his words. He touches her neck, fingers splayed against her flushed skin. "It feels like he's giving it to me so I can give it to you."

Some spark of excitement in Verity's expression collapses into desperation. "Because you're ours," she says, plucking a wet kiss from his parted lips. "Aren't you?"

"I'm..." Wicker stutters, reaching back to clutch my thigh. "*Fuck. Fuck, Pace, I'm going to—*"

"Wait," I grunt, reaching around to hold him. My mouth slides against the curve of his cheek. "Come with us."

I already know it won't take much for Verity, but I still reach between them to find her clit, beckoning her closer to the precipice. From my vantage, I can just barely catch the pinch of his brow as she seizes, the first wave of my orgasm slamming into me. I use the force to punch into him, holding him there as my cock surges.

Wicker's eyes fly open, locking with Verity's. "Oh, fuck," he gasps, grabbing her chin to find her gaze. "I can feel it. Both of you. It's —*fuck!*"

I know he's coming just by the feel of it, his ass clenching around me as he empties into her. She rises up, the best she can with her belly pushed between them, and captures my mouth with hers. The kiss is long and lazy, tongue sweeping around mine, and I feel the press of Wick's lips against my throat.

"Hey," he says, once we've cleaned Verity up and taken her to bed.

She dozes off instantly, her body curled between us. "We're always brothers, you know that, right?"

I turn, seeking out his gaze in the dim light. "Yeah, I do."

"What the three of us went through together, no one takes that away. Not a King," he quirks an eyebrow, "and definitely not a fucking Duke."

Nodding, I say, "I know. It just got under my skin for a second."

He leans back into the pillow, body shifting to look at me. "Hey, I just realized something." At my questioning hum, he adds, "You haven't checked security once since we got back."

"Huh." I wait for the panic to hit, the stress and worry, the compulsive need to just go *check*, but it doesn't come. I'm met with an unfamiliar sensation buried deep in my chest. It's warm and lax and void of fear.

I think it might be contentment.

Even though I'm exhausted, both mentally and physically, I don't fall asleep when they do. We're in the main bedroom now and Verity's curled into my side, her hand on my stomach, using me as a body pillow. Wick's on her other side, face buried into the back of her neck.

I watch them, feeling somewhat foolish at my insecurities, but a part of me understands that's the result of Father's parenting. Being his discarded sons—it's the thing that brought us together. It's all we know. We wear the name Ashby like a badge, but we feel it like a wound.

After he's gone, there'll be nothing else.

Nothing but this.

I flatten my palm over the baby, making a mental promise never to do to him what Father did to us—making us feel unfit in our skin. I stay that way until the sound of Lex's footsteps draw my eyes to the door. He lingers there for a long moment, his eyes sweeping over the bed, quiet and assessing. Somehow he *always* knows. I wouldn't put it past him to have stayed downstairs longer, just to give us some time.

"Is it true?" I ask before he crosses the threshold.

"Yes." He answers, eyes darkening. "But it doesn't change anything."

"I guess not." I stroke Verity's hair. Blood and last names mean everything in Forsyth, but neither can touch this. The way she chases my touch, even in sleep. How Wicker chases her, a divot digging into his brow. The twitch of Lex's fingers as he watches him, like he's anxious to get into bed alongside us. "They're still ours," I finally accept.

"They are," he agrees, so easily, as if it'd never occurred to him otherwise.

I can't imagine feeling that certain about anything. "How did you get it?" At his questioning stare, I elaborate, "Remington's DNA sample."

I'm expecting to hear something really elaborate, like the roach of the blunt we smoked that night Nick Bruin almost got killed, or rummaging through a trash bin for a soda can.

"I didn't." Lex shrugs. "I got *all* their samples."

I blink, taking this in, and realize he means all the Dukes. "How the fuck did—" And then, it hits me. "Oh, shit."

Not just the Dukes.

"The annual blood drive," he says, reaching up to tug off his shirt. "Hundreds of West End samples, ripe for the taking." He looks pretty proud of it too, smirking. "I have a near complete database of the West End bloodlines."

Everything about last month finally makes sense. Lex agreeing to do that blood drive, all the work in setting up, the cooperation and pretense...

I glance down at Rosi, still sound asleep. "She's not going to like that."

"Why not?" Lex wonders, tossing his shirt over the settee. "Forsyth is a fucking mess. Knowing the bloodlines and where they lead will solve a lot of problems."

My brother is like this sometimes, unable to understand why emotion and logic aren't always the best mix. I keep my voice low, afraid of waking her. "She thinks you're all buddy-buddy with them now, but you actually just used her trip to West End to trick her family."

Holy fuck.

She *is* going to flip her shit.

He frowns, head snapping back. "It wasn't like that. I saw an opportunity and decided to make the most of it."

"She won't see it that way. She'll think you betrayed them."

He corrects, "I saved them." At the look I give him, grave and unimpressed, he stresses, "It's not like I'm going to use it against them!" Although there's a strain in his voice.

My eyes narrow. "What aren't you telling me?"

Deflating, he begins emptying his pockets. Glasses, keys, wallet. He looks tired too, bags beneath his eyes. "I figured we didn't need any more surprises, so I checked the results of your DNA against the bones in the solarium."

Remembering him taking that swab weeks ago, a spike of anxiety hits my chest. "And?"

"There's no match." He watches me closely, a worried tilt to his mouth. "I don't know whether to say I'm sorry or congratulations."

It's not *the* answer, but it's *an* answer. "Thanks for checking."

But he watches me, amber eyes searching mine. "You were upset before," he says, glancing at Verity and Wick. "Because of Maddox?" But then he shakes his head, guessing, "Because of Remy."

"He's Wick's brother. And the baby," I say, resting my palm over the curve of her belly. "He's his uncle."

There's a stretch of silence, and I'm sure Lex is going to give me some lecture about how all families are complicated, and how it doesn't have to mean we can't all get along.

Instead, he looks at me, his mouth set into a grim line, and quietly declares, "He's a douchebag."

An abrupt laugh bursts from my chest that almost wakes her. The weariness I've been fighting off all day settles over me, and I yawn. "It's late. Come to bed."

"Scoot over," he says, yanking the band out of his hair and letting it fall over his shoulders. The mattress sinks next to me and he shucks off his pants before turning off the light. Lex has never been a cuddler, but tonight he throws his arm around my waist, and I feel the heat of his breath on my shoulder. Out of the darkness, he says, "The closer we get to removing Father, the more darts will come our way. People will try to dismantle us. Keep us unsteady. Make us question ourselves. But the one thing Father did was teach us that no matter what danger is coming our way, we protect one another because we're *family*." His fingers press down on my hip. "Wick loves you, Pace. I love you. Verity trusts you. And god, that baby is going to be so goddamn lucky to have you as one of his fathers."

It may be the longest, most sentimental speech I've ever heard him say.

"I need you to promise me something," I say, voice low. Wicker can't hear this. "Something that's been bothering me since Maddox dropped his bomb."

His forehead creases. "What?"

"Under no circumstances, in no lifetime, will my son be a goddamn gutter-trash boxer, understand?"

He grins, silent laughter shaking the bed, but in the dark, I see the shadow of his fist extended toward mine. "Agreed. I'll go to the death to ensure it."

12

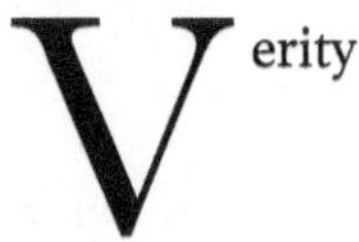erity

I DIDN'T REALIZE how it would feel to see the new nursery for the first time.

As I look upon it, cradling the swell of my belly, I find it psychologically freeing. It's as if we've shed the smallest piece of the Purple Palace for the most innocent of beings. It's not finished, but the hardwoods gleam with a fresh coat of polyurethane, and the walls are prepped with primer.

Fresh.

Ready for a new beginning.

The contractors tried to finish up before they were dismissed, sending me lookbooks and stacks of paint swatches for the walls, but I just can't make up my mind. Wall paint or not, we're nearing the final six weeks of this pregnancy and it's time to make other decisions, which is why Lex is following me around the room with a pencil and notepad while Pace and Wicker try to pretend like they're being helpful.

"We'll need a crib and a changing table," I comment, ignoring the focus of his amber eyes on me, "and a dresser can go over there."

"Got it," Lex says, a little too quickly. "Any other furniture?"

"Maybe a rocker for over in that corner. Or a glider?" I consider both, determined not to let the moment be spoiled by my own anger at him. "Those seem comfortable."

Lex tucks a lock of his hair behind an ear, the movement casual in its frustration. He's been fidgeting with it all day. It's all I can do not to snap at him to just put it up. If he thinks wearing his hair down all week can thaw the ice between us, he's wrong. "We can go try some out, see which one you like best."

"The crib needs to go on this wall," Pace says, pointing to the one wall without any other doors or windows. "I think it'll be the best coverage for security."

"No visible cameras," I remind him.

Pace grins in that soft, dark way that borders on condescending. "Nanny cams have come a long way. I'll make it totally innocuous."

"What about you?" I ask Wicker, who's been oddly quiet. I hold up the lookbook. "What do you think? Tigers, giraffes, or elephants?"

Wicker blinks. "Are we opening a slightly illegal petting zoo?"

Frowning, I flip to some other pages. "Well, there's also trains, bunnies, and baby ducks."

"For the tigers to eat?"

"For the theme," I whine, flashing him a page with a forest theme. "Gun to your head, which would you choose?"

"Can you just pull the trigger?" When my face falls, his lips turn up in a smirk. "Just fucking with you, Red. If you ask me, it already looks good. Bigger with everything taken out, you know?"

"It's an improvement," Pace says. He's wearing a tight, dark tee that strains at the upper arms. For the last three days, ever since he began sleeping in my bed without any surveillance equipment, he's been on a training kick. "I can't even smell the stench of sweat, weed, and masturbation anymore." He moves to the corner and waves his brother over. "Come give me a boost. I want to check this angle."

I lean against the closet door and prop my hand on my lower back, rubbing the sore muscles. I'm wearing a pair of oversized overalls with a cropped tank underneath. Thoroughly non-princessy.

"You okay?" Lex asks, taking any chance to touch my belly.

It doesn't matter that my body wants to lean into his touch. I still scowl, looking away. "Just achy."

The way I feel at thirty-two weeks makes me long for the first trimester and the days of morning sickness. At least then I was still skinny and didn't feel like I needed to pee every fifteen minutes. "Normal stuff. I promise."

"You need to rest? A bath?" His hand replaces mine, continuing to work his way up my side. "A massage?" His thumb grazes against the side of my breast, triggering a heaviness and tightened nipples.

"No," I say quickly. "I'm fine."

Lex's sigh reverberates more loudly than his whisper. "You're still pissed at me? *Really*? It's just some blood samples. We could unlock all of Forsyth's secrets if we just—"

I shoot him a sharp look, cutting him off. "You might want to sell that to someone who isn't the illegitimate daughter of Forsyth's worst King." Scoffing, I add, "You act like this city doesn't run on secrets for a reason. I know you're smarter than that."

His face falls. "I'm not going to tell anyone anything."

Before I can argue, Wicker's voice carries across the room. "He'll need a hockey kit. Skates." He shoots Lex an annoyed look. "A helmet obviously."

"Obviously," Lex mutters, looking frustrated at the interruption.

"Pads, a jersey," Pace continues, but frowns. "Guess he'll be too small for a stick at first?"

I turn away from their nonsense, just happy Lex and I aren't going to have this out yet again, and open the closet door. I take the moment to exhale and cup my breasts, getting a smidge of relief. Maybe I need a more supportive bra. Maybe something with more padding. Or less? Whatever style, I need something to help my nipples not be so sensitive.

Lex clears his throat. "Does the closet look good?"

This has essentially been the cycle of our arguing since Lex confessed his true intentions with the West End blood drive. I get angry, he pleads his case, nothing changes, and we focus on the baby because it's the only thing we actually agree on.

I drop my hands. "It's great. They did a really good job. We'll need some hangers," I say, still feeling grumpy, "those adorable little ones, and maybe a few baskets for smaller items."

The closet is smaller, having been divided with the majority of the space on the opposite side, in my room. Wicker's demand. This side has two bars for hanging clothes and several shelves. Plenty of room for our little pineapple and his tiny belongings.

"You know, I think we should add a few hooks." I turn to make sure Lex is including all of this on the list and find him standing so close that my belly brushes against his abdomen.

"You know, there are a few ways to help with that."

"Help with what?" I ask, exasperated. "Hooks?"

He gives my chest a pointed look, and fuck, he's like some kind of goddamn shampoo commercial. I'd swear a breeze floats by, billowing out his hair, all majestic and sexy-like. Instantly, my nipples get hard. Fine. Hard-*er*.

Why does he have to wear his hair down like that?

It doesn't help that he leans in, reaching out to graze the curve of my elbow with soft fingers. "With the aches and strain you're experiencing in your breasts. I know it's uncomfortable."

"You know, huh?" I snap. "You know what it's like to go from reasonably-sized tits for half of your life to carrying around two swollen melons that are constantly in a state of flux?"

"Well, er... no." He shifts uncomfortably, moving back a smidge. "I do not. Did you try the cold and warm compresses like I suggested?" At least this time, he's the one to get all throaty and glazed in the eyes. "Or light massaging when you're in the shower."

"I read the books," I tell him, not in the mood to be Dr. Daddysplained to right now. "Nothing is going to give me much relief until the baby comes." I cup my breasts with both hands, wincing. "They're just so big and ridiculously sensitive, and it seems to be getting worse." I glance over to where Pace and Wicker are discussing camera placement. Pace stretches his arms over his head, making that tight shirt rise up, giving me a peek at the sexy swath of skin right at the top of his ass. I cross my arms over my chest and wince. "Ouch. *Jesus.* See?"

His lips part on a slow, close exhale, "There are... *other* methods."

"Like what?" I ask, honestly desperate to try anything.

His eyes haven't risen from my tits once. "Methods we could help facilitate."

There's one word in that sentence that catches my attention. Tilting my head I ask, "What do you mean 'we'?"

"Some women find nipple play during pregnancy helpful—even to the point of engaging lactation." His throat jumps with a swallow. "Instead of suppressing it, you go all in, but..." Seeming to snap out of the daze, he reaches up to rub the back of his neck, grimacing. "Never mind."

"But what?" Because just hearing the words 'nipple play' has me on board.

"It has risks." He steps back, a divot of worry appearing in his brow. "Too big, in my opinion."

Of course he thinks that. "Like what?"

"Early labor for one thing." His hands drop to my belly. "As much as I want you to have some relief, I'm not comfortable with the risk."

I gawk at him, the anger rising. "Oh, *you're* not comfortable? Then heaven for-fucking-fend!" I glance over, realizing my outburst has caught his brothers' attention. "You hear that, guys? Lex is uncomfortable."

His jaw is set. "As the Prince in charge of our child's health—"

"But it's not," I argue, whipping my glare at him. "It's not just our child. It's not even just me. That's your problem, Lex! Me, the baby, the entirety of West End? You don't give people a choice over their own bodies, you just decide because you can take or save a life, it makes you God."

His eyes darken. "That's not even remotely true."

"But it is," I insist, noticing Pace and Wicker are awfully quiet. "Admit it. You think you know better, so you think you should control everything."

Lex is always composed. It's one of the first things I hated about him—that coldness. It's also one of the first things I found comfort in, this ability to remove myself from the emotion of a moment spread out before him. The way it made me feel even-keeled and distanced from the shame and embarrassment.

That composure leaves him suddenly—so abruptly that it's with all the force of a snapped wire.

He roars, "I *do* know better!" and I can't help it.

I flinch. I know he sees it, because he freezes, and even though traitorous hormonal tears spring to my eyes, I don't back down. "So did *he*." It doesn't matter that my voice is a cracked whisper. From the expression on his face, I might as well have screamed. "I'm Rufus' daughter, but..." I shake my head. "Are you willing to be his creation?"

Just as quickly as Lex snapped before, he snaps again—this time in stunned awe—watching as I spin on my heel and storm out.

I'M STILL upset about it that night while I get ready for bed. It was bad enough when they were making deposits, and now I'm starting to wonder if my body is ever going to feel like my own again. I can't choose how I nourish it, use it, or relieve it. It doesn't help that my breasts have been more sensitive than ever since Lex brought it up.

Or maybe I'm just horny.

God, it's probably some toxic mixture of all three.

It's not like any of this would be hard to do. Wick's eyes were glued to my rack before I got knocked up. And now that I have porn-star tits, he and Pace are aware of how easy it is to make me come just from stimulating them. It's not uncommon to wake up with Pace's cock buried in my body and Wick sucking on my nipple. It's probably another reason why they hurt so much lately. Inadvertently, those boys have lit a fire inside of me, and *fine.*

I want more.

So what?

The problem, as always, is Lex. It was his idea, but as soon as he said it, he immediately backtracked, listing his concerns and worries over doing something he considers a risk.

Dr. Daddy is a fucking tease.

"Ready for bed?" Wick asks when I walk out of the bathroom. I don't miss the way his eyes sweep over my fitted tank and the softest shorts I've found for sleeping.

"Not yet," I say, lowering myself next to him on the couch they moved in during the renovation. At first it was just to give them a place to hang out away from the chaos, but I like it here. The Princess bed is great for sleeping, but for anything else, it's a bit daunting in my current state. Sometimes it feels like they need to roll me out of it like a bowling ball.

Wick reaches out for my hips, guiding me down so I'm leaning into him.

Across the room Pace, dressed in nothing but sweats, gives Effie a treat and gathers the cover for her cage. "Say good night to everyone, pretty bird."

"Night, Princess."

"Night, Effie."

"Night, Wickkkker."

Wick smirks over at the bird, but obliges with a, "Night, Eff."

"Night, Pace."

"Good night." He lifts the cover. "See you in the morning."

"I have a question, Red." Wick's long fingers run down my arm, leaving a trail of goosebumps behind.

"What's that?"

"When the fuck did you start wearing a bra to bed? Is this some West End thing?" Wicker, I suppose, hadn't even heard the full breadth of our fight. If he had, he would have been on my side instantly.

As it is, he and Pace have just been uneasily tiptoeing around mine and Lex's spurious jabs.

"No, it's a pregnancy thing." I exhale, feeling my nipples tighten from his touch. It's not exactly a bra, but there is a built-in layer to the tank that keeps everything in place. Or, at least, tries to. These things have a mind of their own. "And it was around the time it started feeling like I was carrying two overripe cantaloupes twenty-four seven."

Pace's eyes drop to said melons, then he drags his gaze back to my face.

"I don't like it," Wick grumbles, tugging at the shoulder strap of the tank. "I like waking up with your bare tits in my hands, but see?" He tries again. "I can't get under this thing."

"I agree with him," Pace says, sitting down next to me. His hand grabs the neck of my tank and yanks it down, exposing the top swell. "These are too fucking pretty to hide."

His thumb sweeps over the top, dark brown over pale white. The jostling hurts, but it's that weird kind of pain where I want more, and I bite back a cry, arching my back into his brother. Never one to let an opportunity go to waste, Wicker releases my other breast from under the fabric and closes his wide palm over it.

"Damn," I exhale, sinking back into him

"Good? Bad?" Wick asks, hand stilling.

"A little of both, but don't stop." I look at Pace. "Either of you."

He doesn't hesitate, teasing his thumb over the tight peak of my nipple. That leads to a rush of euphoria, as if every nerve in my body is connected to that tiny nub. It must be why I barely hear the heavy footsteps padding down the hall or fully process Lex standing in front of us in nothing but a pair of shorts, face drawn.

"I told you this had too many risks," he sighs, looking strangely haggard. His hair is still down, but it looks like it's been tugged at all day long. "I'm trying to keep him safe."

I reply, "By telling me what to do with my own body." Unfortunately, my obstinate tone is belied by the crest of my moan.

"Okay, does someone want to explain what's happening here?" Wick asks, shifting his hips next to me. He's got a massive boner, and the movement does nothing to keep it from pressing into my hip. "I thought you two were fighting about that blood sample thing, which," Wicker holds up a finger, "was a boss fucking move, Lex."

Lex leans against the doorway, eyes rolling. "I told Verity earlier today that nipple play could possibly ease some of the strain she's having in her breasts right now." Pace opens his mouth to say something, but Lex cuts him a glare, adding, "But there's also a risk of inducing premature labor."

"I looked it up." I don't point out that while he's lecturing us all, he's staring at my tits. "And it's very unlikely."

"But there's still a chance!" He throws his hands in the air. "And you know I'm unwilling to—"

"Bruh," Pace says, "you need to chill."

Lex's eyes narrow at his brother. "What did you say?"

"He said to chill," Wick repeats. "We know you're stressed, and worried, and have gone over every single worst-case scenario, but the Princess isn't going to go into labor just because we suck on her tits."

"You don't know that," Lex argues.

"I've watched enough porn to confirm it," Pace states matter-of-factly, and a rush of heat travels between my legs. "If you want to supervise, then go for it," he continues. "Take a seat. Get comfortable. And if anything even remotely concerning happens, we'll stop."

Lex's amber eyes set on me, resignation clear on his face. "Is that what you want?"

"Yes." *Fuck. Yes.*

"Fine." He walks over to the armchair, drags it across from the couch, and sits. "If I see anything—one wince, one jerk, one sign that her body is going into labor—I'm stopping this." He looks between us. "Understand?"

Wick sighs. "Leave it to the Doc over there to make something erotically named 'nipple play' as unsexy as possible."

"It isn't about sex," Lex groans, running his palms down his face. "It's about stress relief."

He's wrong, of course, but after finally getting something resembling approval, I'm not going to push it. I lean back into Wicker, who isn't deterred by his brother's commanding presence whatsoever. If anything, he's probably more turned on, which is obvious when he goes straight for my breast.

That is, until Lex clears his throat. "You're going to want to get skin-to-skin."

"Huh?" Pace grunts.

Lex leans back in his seat, knees spread casually. "If Verity wants to stimulate real relief, you're going to have to trick her body into thinking it's ready for a change that's not just on a physical level, but a chemical one." His tongue darts out and licks his bottom lip. "We're in the third trimester. The reason her breasts are so tender is because they're already trying to acclimate to their new job: feeding."

"Skin-to-skin? No problem there," Wick mutters, pulling his T-shirt over his head. My belly drops, just like it does every time I see his body. I never get used to it—to any of them. With the extra layer of fabric gone, I can see how hard he is, and my nipples give a tingly pulse.

"You're next, Rosi," Pace says, and he and Wick work to peel off my shirt.

"Careful," I hiss. "That bra part is tight."

"Maybe you need one of those nursing tops," Pace mutters, his movements growing more gentle. "You know, with the flaps."

He's not wrong, and I've been looking at them in the catalog, but with the way they keep growing, I'm not sure what size I'll be. Together, they slip the tight tank over my breasts. The instant they're completely free, the heaviness sags against me, and I clutch them to my chest, which also makes them ache. It's impossible to find any comfort.

Pace's jaw slacks, and he lunges toward me, but a hand shoots out, grabbing his shoulder.

Lex.

"Slow," he directs. "It's not all about the nipple. She needs to get fully stimulated." His eyes wander over my tits, lids growing heavy. "Massage her first. Start at the back and push forward."

I feel more than ready. Hot, sweaty. But when Pace's hands start to gently rub the area just below my armpit, my body loosens, feeling like melted butter. I slump back into Wick's strong arms.

"That feel good, Red?" he whispers in my ear. His hands make their own passes, skimming from my neck to my shoulders, down over the slope of my breasts—*avoiding* the nipple entirely. "You like it when we touch you like this?"

There's a funny curiosity to his voice, like the thought of a woman enjoying a massage never occurred to him. Probably never has, until now.

"Uh huh," I mumble, hyperaware of the areas they're not touching. The brothers take their time—patient and diligent—until I'm about to crawl out of my skin. Fingers are everywhere, rubbing, sliding, and gliding. I'm so sensitive that I can feel each of their warm, excited exhalations tickling against my skin. A steady drumbeat pulses between my legs and I shift uncomfortably, wanting to be touched down there, too.

I dip my hand between my thighs.

"No." Lex's command comes with tight fingers wrapped around my wrist. Our eyes meet, and despite the fact this is supposed to be about Lex giving me control over my own body, I get the feeling he's enjoying his role a little too much. "This isn't about getting you off, Verity. That's easy when you're like this." His hand releases mine and drops to adjust the hard erection fighting against the front of his shorts. "Trust the process."

I want to kick him. I really do. And so does my pussy, but Wicker listens, his touch slowing, those long, skilled fingers turning gentle but firm. His thumb glides down the side of my breast, applying a deep pressure. "Too much?" he whispers against the shell of my ear.

"It's perfect," I swallow.

"How do they feel?" Lex asks.

"Hot and tingly." I close my eyes, feeling the sensation rushing to the tips of my nipples. "Painful."

I'd say heavier, but the boys are supporting their weight with those stupidly big hands. Vaguely, I recall watching the Baroness and her Williams that day by the elevators, months ago, and being completely unable to imagine my Princes ever worshiping me like that.

But that's exactly how this feels.

Lex asks, "Any pains in your abdomen?"

Feeling a slight pressure on the crown of my stomach, I look and see Pace kissing his way over the top. "No. None."

Lex's voice takes on a husky tone. "What do you want next, Verity?"

"For them to suck me." I gather my breasts in my hands, consumed by the ache. Pace and Wick eye them hungrily. "I want them to take this pressure away. *Please*," I beg, unabashed by my own whine.

Lex nods, giving a silent command, and when their mouths descend, latching onto my hardened nipples, I let out a long, delirious exhale. It feels so good. Better than anything I ever expected. Not just sexual—although my pussy is soaked—just this incredible sense of relief.

Resting my hands on the tops of their heads, I encourage them by stroking the back of their necks, guiding them closer. The contrast between them goes further than their complexion and hair color. I feel it in the way they latch on. Pace's mouth works greedily, using his tongue to work my nipple into a stiff peak, but he gets frustrated when he can't find a good rhythm and pops off.

"Hey," I ask, stroking his hairline, "what's wrong?"

Before he can answer, Wicker flattens his tongue across the top of my areola and then clamps down with a groan, giving me a sharp tug that zings across my nerves.

"*Oh*," I gasp, arching into Wicker's mouth. I take his face in both hands, holding him to my breast. "Yes, that."

"How?" Pace asks. "How are you doing that?"

It's disappointing when Wicker releases me, cutting off the growing buildup, until I see him sling his arm over his brother's shoulder. With spit-slick lips—and a little too cockily—he explains, "It's like Lex says, this isn't just some titty we're playing with. This is a titty ready to be milked. It's not about the outside, it's about the inside, drawing that delicious liquid to the surface." I watch as Wick places a wide hand on the back of his brother's head, encouraging him back on my breast. "Think about how you fuck her. Slow. Persistent," he says. "You need to coax it out of her."

"He's right," Lex says. The doctor steps in, instructing his brother how to hold my breast, taking me from the front with both hands. "Lift it up and get the angle right. Good, yeah. Now, use your fingers to pull down along the sides, stimulating the ducts."

I grow fuzzy when Wick continues talking about latching on, patiently showing him where to place his tongue and when to shift to a suckle. If I felt hot before, my temperature just elevated a million degrees, and it only intensifies when I look down and see my breast stuffed in Pace's hungry mouth.

"Feel good?" Wick asks, watching his brother feed.

I twist a lock of Pace's hair lazily around my finger.

"Yes, thank you."

Wick bends, kissing me with that sexy, dirty, *skilled* mouth, his hot tongue tangling with mine, before lifting my other breast to his hands and latching on. The sensation is different now. I feel the fullness all over. Stroking both of their heads, I look up at Lex, who has moved back to his seat across from us, stiff and observant. His jaw is locked tight, the hard line unyielding. He's staring at his brothers—studying them. Pushing my fingers through the fine hair on Wicker's nape, I offer, "You can, you know."

Amber eyes meet mine. "Can what?"

"Touch yourself."

"I wasn't—" he starts to lie, but there's no hiding his erection. Clearing his throat, he shifts. "It's a completely normal reaction in a situation like this."

"I never thought it wasn't. I don't know why you always—" My voice clips off, breath catching when Pace starts rubbing small circles just outside my areola.

"What?" Lex shoots upright. "What was that?"

"That was Pace, doing an excellent job." I glance down at Lex's crotch. "It may help this whole thing along, actually."

His brow wrinkles. "What do you mean?"

"I told you I did my own research," I explain, licking my lips, "and orgasms lead to the release of oxytocin, *and that* encourages milk production."

He almost looks annoyed that I know something. "That's... true. But I'll be distracted." Conflict wars on his handsome face, but he's still a man. A fucking horny one at that. "You'll tell me if something goes wrong?"

"Immediately."

I don't believe he'll truly relent until I see him lean back, pulling his length out from his shorts. He gives it a quick but fluid, jerking pump, and in the overhead light, the tip glistens, already dripping. A surge of prickling heat builds in my nipples. It's sharp and painful, but so, so good. That steady beating pulse throbs deeper in my pussy, creating a thrum throughout my body, one that grows with every suckle, every stroke of Lex's hand.

"Are you close?" I ask him, pressing my thighs together for any sense of friction.

He nods, his movements erratic. "Are you?"

I'm close to something, although I don't know what. My whole body feels like it's rushing over the edge.

"Don't waste it," I tell him, shifting my hips.

As if understanding exactly what I need, Wicker's fingers hook into my shorts, shoving them down my thighs. Wicker pops off my nipple. "You want his cum, don't you, Red?" I nod, and he tucks a hand between my bare thighs. "Come on, brother, give it to her."

In unison, Wicker and Pace each grab one of my knees, draping them over their laps to spread my thighs widely—obscenely—exposing where I'm slick and ready.

Exhaling, Lex drops to his knees, inching toward us as his hand jerks furiously, stripping up and down his cock. He stops between my thighs, and I reach for him, finally allowing myself to thread my fingers through his luscious hair.

I use my grip to yank him closer.

Lex hisses out a long, "Fuck," when the tip of his cock meets the slickness of my core. His eyebrows crash together as he looks down, spreading the wetness until he's slotted up against my entrance. My whole body is strung tight in anticipation. I've never felt so crowded before, one on each side while Lex hovers above me, his hand grasping the back of the couch over my shoulder.

But when he finally pushes in, trapped is the last thing I feel.

I *keen*.

If his brothers mind that Lex is grazing their heads with each of his grunted thrusts, they don't show it, the pressure of their mouths building a knot of tight need in my core.

"So wet, Verity," Lex says, face twisted in something that could be agony. "Your pussy's so fucking drenched for this. I can feel you getting wetter with each suck."

Pace groans, deep and gritty around my nipple, and warmth radiates across my breasts. Wick moans a garbled curse while Pace rises up, his mouth unlatching. He squeezes, pulling the nipple into a hard point, and Lex's wild gaze dips to my breast, all of us watching the drop of liquid beading at the tip.

"Please, Lex," I say, feeling hazy with the sensation of relief as Wick and Pace hungrily drop back to latch on, drawing out the fluid with little sucks. With my gaze never leaving him, I part the lips of my pussy with two fingers, "Put your baby in me."

His eyes meet mine and that's when I know he'll do it. That connection—that place we've been to so many times before. I don't need Lex to fuck me directly. Our intimacy lies in this. A look. A touch.

"Oh, fuck," Lex growls, lurching forward, and I feel the first pulse of his seed. It's hot and slick as his cock pulses inside me, his hips giving these small twitches, tense with restraint, as he empties into me. With a hard grunt, he pulls his cock free, making me whimper at the feel of his cum dribbling out.

"Don't worry," comes his quiet, ragged voice. "I'll give it back." I peer over his brothers' heads as he uses two thick fingers to scoop it up, eyes darkening as he watches himself pushing it back inside.

"Thank you," I moan, so lost in the lust-haze of it all that I can only feel grateful to have it back.

My hips rise to meet him, but he pulls out, swiping up the cum and giving it to me again. That, along with the sensation of release in my breasts, sends a shudder through me stemming from my nipples down to my clit and that's when it hits me.

My body isn't just made for this baby.

It's made for them.

I DON'T KNOW why I wake up at two every morning.

It's a new and very annoying feature of the pregnancy, as Lex had explained it. Something about hormones, as always. There's never a sound or a movement that does it, I just always find myself rousing, one of them—usually Wicker—wrapped around me as I struggle to fall back into slumber.

I blink into the darkness, unable to see much at first. Not that it matters. There's a feeling for each of my Princes, although they're hard to put into words. With Lex, there's a weight in the atmosphere, a strange density that changes the sound waves. With Pace, it's electric, like a hum sparking against my skin. With Wicker, it's always touch, the sensation of warmth and pressure.

When I wake up, the air is thin and far too calm.

Lex and Pace are missing.

I exhale as I lever myself up, cradling each tender breast. It's only been a few hours since Pace and Wicker—for lack of a better word—*milked* me, and I'm so relieved to find the pressure hasn't returned that I decide to get up and go searching, suddenly consumed by a spike of energy.

Wicker stirs when I extricate myself, flopping over to his other side. Even in slumber, he searches for someone, arms and legs grasping out to find contact. When he finds none, he emits a gruff, unhappy sound, but never fully wakes.

Satisfied, I reach for my dressing gown.

When I first came to the palace, I resented all the fine, silky Princess nightwear, but now that my tits are inflatables and my stomach is ridiculous, I find myself happy to pull on the robe that's been tailored for a pregnant body. The bust is low-cut, but allows my breasts to breathe. I cinch the gown right beneath them before padding out into the hallway.

There was a time when walking these halls at night would have frightened me. Now, I know the nooks and crannies, understanding the shadows are hiding corners that will be illuminated in the dawn.

Most of all, I know Pace has made this house secure.

It's why I don't startle when I reach the landing, seeing him coming up the stairs.

His dark eyes lock on mine, holding me captive for the whole climb. He's still shirtless, although he's put on sweatpants at some point, the waist riding low. He releases a dark chuckle. "Jesus, he was right on time," he mutters.

I rub my eyes, wondering, "Who? What?"

When he reaches me, his strong arms catch me around the waist, pulling me into him. "Nothing."

I instantly wind my arms around his neck. "You were gone," I say, trying not to sound accusing. He's been good about not checking the security at all hours, and even though his weird, new training routine is probably still meant to prepare him for a fight, at least he's not as obsessive about it.

"Sorry about that." He buries a kiss into my neck, the electric hum finally greeting me. "Had to help Lex with something."

I tilt my neck, giving him access. "With what?"

Humming, he pulls away. "Go down and see. You'll find it."

"But... Wicker," I say, frowning.

Pace cocks his head toward the hall. "I'll go give him something to latch onto. Just... listen to him, okay?" He gets two steps before pausing, turning back to me with an indecipherable expression. "There are fire extinguishers in each corner."

"Each corner of what?" I ask, startled. "There's fire?"

But instead of answering, he strides away toward the room, leaving me to descend the staircase with sleep-thick eyes and piqued curiosity.

Pace wasn't wrong though.

I do find it.

It's hard to miss the strange, eerie glow coming from the main downstairs corridor, not to mention the strains of classical music echoing down the hall. I follow it with a thread of worry, the train of my silk robe dragging behind me. It isn't until I get closer that I realize it's coming from the ballroom.

Stepping inside, I freeze.

The chandeliers are dark, but the tall candelabras glowing with fire around the cavernous room still catch the crystals, flinging glitter along the dance floor. Candles upon candles. There must be hundreds of them, both tall and stout, wide and slender. They cast everything in a warm, flickering light that reaches all the way to the dark corners.

And in the middle of the room, Lex is rising from his seat at a small, round table.

I blink furiously, because *oh*. Of course this is a dream.

I've had weirder.

I mean, he's in a tux and everything.

Lex adjusts the lapels of his suit, clearing his throat. "You always get a carb craving at two." His hair is down again, auburn tones reflecting the sparkling candlelight like embers.

I don't feel like I can really be blamed for not noticing the food on the table, although when I do, a laugh escapes my throat. I capture it with my palm, covering my mouth. "Okay, now I *know* this is a dream."

He's too far away to hear his exhale, but I see it, his shoulders inching down a notch. "Yeah?" He rocks back on his heels, right before barreling around to the other side of the table. "Here, let me..." Grabbing the back of the chair, he pulls it out.

For me.

I approach the table in a haze, thinking my imagination is pretty good.

It's only when I get closer that I see the dark circles under Lex's eyes, the tinge of strain in his features, and the way he holds himself so stiffly.

My smile falls. "Oh," I realize, glancing down at the covered platter. "Not a dream."

After a beat, Lex's stilted voice confesses, "Afraid not."

I still lower myself into the seat, eyes narrowed at the display in front of me. "What is this?"

"This?" he asks, reaching for the silver lid. He pulls it off with a flourish. "This is mint chocolate chip. And this..." He points to a box beside it, pushing it closer to me. "This is a gift. From all of us."

Lex has let me have real ice cream only once—the day after he saved Nick Bruin. And I had to hear about it for a week afterward. The box, small and made of black velvet, is wrapped in a red satin bow.

Maybe it's unfair, but I just hear Tommy's voice in my head.

"She's East End. They all want to be bought."

"Are you sure it isn't bribery?" I look up at him, arching a brow. "Because it's going to take a lot more than ice cream and jewelry to buy me off."

Lex's face falls. "I'm not trying to *buy*—" But his words cut off and he mutters a curse, raking his hair back with a harried expression. "You know what, you're right. This was fucking stupid. You can go back to bed."

Maybe it's the exhaustion on his face, or the dejected set of his shoulders, or the way everything about the setting looks so *intentional*, as if he and Pace had lit every single candle themselves.

And I know they did.

It's why I reach out before he can storm off, clasping my fingers around his wrist. "Sit down," I sigh. "Tell me what this is all about."

He gives me an exasperated look but obeys, sitting across from me all slumped and sad-looking. "Verity, I'm not good at this."

I unwrap the utensils. "You put the spoon in and grab a scoop."

His blank stare is unimpressed with my attempt at humor. "I've never had a girlfriend before, much less..." Nodding toward my belly, he shifts uncomfortably. "Whatever this is."

"You're trying to apologize," I acknowledge, dragging my spoon through a melting scoop of ice cream.

But his amber eyes capture mine. "This isn't an apology." My stomach sinks, and he must see it because he straightens. "I mean, I'm trying to explain something to you. The apology—that'll come after."

I watch him carefully. "And what is all this explaining?"

Lex folds his hands on the shimmery gold tablecloth, head bowed. "My brothers are the only thing I've ever cared about, and somehow, in some way, I showed it." He glances up, eyes filled with such anger that it takes me aback. "I showed it too much. I showed it to *him,* and he used them against me, time and time again." His jaw tightens, the candlelight throwing his angular features in sharp relief. "I want you to know that you're right." His face pinches, as if he's facing something unfathomably foul. "I am his creation, Verity. He tied it all together inside of me like tendons and muscles, where the smallest stretch of affection is always attached to the snap of a whip."

My spoon clatters against the bowl when I drop it, stomach flipping sickly. "Oh."

"I wasn't created to love," he goes on, head shaking. "But I *was* created to understand the body. To know how it works and *why* it works. So when I bully Pace into getting a vitamin shot or force Wicker into a dark room for three days after a bad hit on the ice, they let me, because they understand something that you don't." Reaching across the table, he takes the small velvet box, tugging the bow away. "Taking care of you and the baby, making you as healthy as I possibly can..."

He grasps the top, clicking it open to reveal a ring.

"It's the only way I know how to show that I want you," he says.

It's not just a ring, but a *Princess* ring, almost exactly like the one I'm wearing. "That I respect you," he adds, plucking something smaller from the bed of velvet beside it. I don't realize it's a key to the ring I'm wearing until he gathers up my hand, pushing the pointed end of the tool into the top stone. "That I care about you."

The ring on my finger expands, and for the first time since my coronation, it slips off the knuckle without sting or pain.

His amber eyes glow in the candlelight as they meet mine. "That I love you."

All the air leaves my lungs in a painful punch, that sagging tear finally brimming over, leading a track down my warm cheek. It's when I'm chasing it away, watching Lex tug the new ring from the box, that I notice the gold cursive imprinted in the velvet of the box.

To my beautiful Queen. May she reign.

"But I want you to know I'm trying to learn more." He stands, offering me an outstretched hand. "If you'll let me."

I stand on shaky legs, not having to wonder what this means. The ring he's holding won't hurt me—not like the one that was forged with tradition. This one slips on easily, snugly, but without the cinch of threat, and when I look into his eyes, I don't see the vacant depths of an empty man, nor the simmering resentment of a Prince forced to give it to me.

I see my future.

"I love you, too," I tell him, knowing that our journey to that future will be as thorny as the rose bushes surrounding this palace.

But knowing it'll be worth it.

The tension falls out of him in a long, measured exhale, and when he takes my hand in his, he brings it to his lips, brushing a kiss against my knuckles. "Wicker said I should dance with you now," he says, eyes sparkling.

Grimacing, I look down at myself. "Ever rolled a beach ball?"

Lex must take this as a challenge, because suddenly he's gathering me by the waist and leading me into an expert waltz. When I laugh, his lips tick up, and I'm hit with the memory of our first dance.

"When I saw you that night, you looked like Prince Charming," I say, tightening my hold on his hand. "You're finally living up to the hype."

He snorts. "You looked scared out of your wits."

Groaning, I recall, "Everyone was so cold to me..."

"I know I was," he replies, the mirth falling from his eyes. "You might not believe me, but that's why I took the samples, Verity."

I scoff when he spins, the bottom of my gown sweeping along the floor. "Because East End is full of snobs?"

"Because we're not 'Sides' and 'Ends'," he corrects. "We're all linked somewhere down the line, and maybe if people understood that, they'd stop trying to divide everything by streets and territories."

I'm more surprised than I should be at his answer, and in this moment, I look at him and see so much more than a father, brother, or lover.

I see a potential King.

"That's how you show you care about Forsyth," I realize.

If he's discomfited by his own transparency, he hides it well, his movements fluid and precise. "I guess it is. But if you asked me to," his face softens, "I'd destroy every sample."

I adjust my hold on his shoulder, following his next turn. "It's a nice thought, the idea of us all understanding how we're linked," I say tiredly. "But we're still divided, Lex. Imagine if Wicker or Remy found out about sharing a mother because of a test you did behind their backs. Imagine if Maddox never had the chance to give him context or closure." I give him a significant look. "There would have been bloodshed."

His mouth forms a grim line. "Does the truth always have to be so dangerous?"

I think about this for a long moment, letting the music and Lex sweep me across the candlelit dance floor. "Not always," I decide, turning my head to press a kiss against the cut of his jaw. "Which is why I do want you to destroy the samples." I grin, the warmth flaring in my chest like a firework. "After one last comparison."

13

L^{ex}

WHEN I GET Pace's text on Friday morning—*"drawing room, watch him"*—I'm not really sure what to expect. My brother's gotten really cryptic ever since he started kicking up training for the fall, as if it's taken so much energy, he can't even make a complete sentence.

What I'm *not* expecting to find, however, is Remington Maddox lounging on our settee.

I pause in the doorway, looking from him to Wicker, who's sitting on the sofa across from him. The room is deathly silent. Remy is staring at a spot on the floor with such searing intensity that I follow his gaze, finding nothing but the old hardwoods.

Wicker has his arms crossed, a scowl set on his face.

We'd been expecting him, of course.

The whole palace has been eager for Ballsack's—Eugene's—return ever since Agent Knight took him off the grounds in cuffs, and Remy was supposed to deliver him.

I don't see the DKS soldier, but I do see his Duke, a crevice carved in his forehead.

The silence lingers on and on, and I'm not compelled to break it, needing more data before I act.

But then Remy lets out this soft, scoffing laugh. "Nah."

"Yeah." Wicker's voice is firm. "Ask him yourself."

When Remy whips out his phone, it all clicks.

"You told him," I realize, unsure how to feel about that. On one hand, the fewer secrets, the better. On the other, Verity had a point. Letting information like this loose into the world could have unforeseen consequences.

Straightening, Remy puts the phone to his ear, eyes distant. Truthfully, I'm not sure how a normal Royal interacts with his father. If it were one of us, six months ago, it would have been stiff but respectful and polite.

Remy doesn't bother with any of that. "Is Wicker fucking Ashby my *brother*?" he seethes into the phone.

Obviously, I can't hear what's being said on the other end, but I do see Remy's reaction to it.

His face blanks out, bled of all expression.

Slowly, he says, "Right." And then, "Naturally." And then, "Hold on." He gives the phone a perplexing glance before holding it out toward Wicker. "He wants to talk to you."

Wicker pulls a face that's all hard edges and aggression, but strains over the distance to snatch it out of Remy's hand. "What?" he snaps into the phone, another silence stretching before us. "Hello?" Wicker pulls the phone away, gawking at it before raising his outraged gaze to Remy. "Did this fucker really ask you to give me the phone so he could hang up on me?"

Remy looks pale, springing to his feet. "I... I have to go," he mutters, lifting a hand to grip at his platinum hair. "I have to find a color that isn't gold." But when he goes to rush out, he freezes, spotting me in the doorway. "Oh. Hey." His eyes are a wild sort of green, zipping around like he's being hunted.

"Are you okay?" I'm not sure what makes me ask. Maybe seeing

Remy that night Nick Bruin got shot made me see him in a different light.

He's weirdly fragile for a Duke.

Remy plucks something from behind his ear—a marker—and taps a rapid rhythm with it against his thigh. "Yeah," he says, looking troubled. "I just need to see the sky and check my head, you know?"

I really don't. "Wait," I call as he rushes by. "This isn't why we asked you to come." When I shoot Wicker a disbelieving glare, all I get back is his middle finger. "I wanted to ask a favor."

Remy stops, turning to me, but his eyes never quite reach mine, stopping at my throat. "A favor?" he asks, shoving a fist in each pocket.

Hearing the skeptical tone in his voice, I elaborate. "A painting for the nursery. I was thinking..." Reaching up, I rub the back of my neck, pissed at Wicker for marring this. "Well, Verity thinks of you as family, and we thought it'd be a nice surprise if you painted something on the walls in there. They're completely bare."

Remy's gaze finally inches up, meeting mine. "They're *bare*?" he asks, disgust clear in his voice. "I'll—I'll be back."

And with that, he stalks down the hallway to the foyer, leaving.

I turn a blank look on my brother. "Seriously?"

Wick shrugs, spreading out on the couch. "He's the only person in this town who hates Maddox more than I do. Seemed like some fun shit to stir."

"We don't need to stir shit," I say, rubbing my temple. "Verity is going to give birth to our son in a month, and we still have our own fucking King held hostage."

Wick points out, "I wanted to kill him and get it over with. You're the one being all strategic and drag-ass about it."

"There are things," I say, teeth grinding, "we need to use him for."

He makes a flippant sound. "Like what?"

"Like the Royal Ascension!"

Wicker's eyes jump to mine and he straightens, mouth forming a slack moue. "We're doing the ascension? There hasn't been a Royal Ascension since—"

"Michael. I know." Shrugging, I remind him, "Our son is the heir to the kingdom. He deserves his birthright, and that's how people need to see him."

"Oh," he breathes. "Oh, fuck yeah."

"Yeah," I sigh, already cringing at the words I'm about to say. "So stop sowing discord and start taking Maddox's advice. We have a kingdom to lead."

I know I've driven the point home when Wicker rises to his feet. "I'll start the preparations then. We won't have much time."

The flash of malicious delight in his eyes doesn't bother me because I feel it, too. Upstairs, Pace probably has the same violently eager gleam in his own eyes.

But Verity doesn't even know what the ascension is.

And she hates getting blood on her dresses.

"IT'S DOWN HERE." I exchange a look with Rory Livingston as I walk down the hall. He nods in return, arms crossed over his chest. He's turned into a reliable asset for PNZ. Loyal. Adaptable. I know he'll have my back as I lead a rival into my house.

"The idea was to do it as a surprise, but unfortunately it became apparent very quickly that we're way outside of our wheelhouse," I explain. "That's when Ballsack suggested we ask you."

Ballsy's still getting settled back into his rooms downstairs. In truth, I was surprised he wanted to come back at all. If he wanted to stay in West End under his own King's protection, we wouldn't have held it against him. When I asked, he just laughed, saying Verity and our little cantaloupe need a chauffeur. It was said as a joke, but we both know it's true.

Everyone is growing more nervous with each day the birth approaches. A part of me feels relieved they do. I've had these nerves since she tested positive for pregnancy, tending the anxiety and pressure for long months.

It's about fucking time everyone else did, too.

"We aren't just outside our wheelhouse. We're in another stratosphere," Pace adds, appearing in the doorway. He eyes the man behind me dubiously. "Remy." He shoots me a glare. "I'm still on the record for this situation being fucked."

The *situation* is unprecedented, but so are a lot of other things lately. The night I made the decision to save Nick Bruin's life, I proved we were a house who could be reached out to if the links were there. Now that we know Remy and Wicker are biologically brothers, those links are even more unavoidable.

If we're going to make an ally, the Dukes are the most obvious and useful.

Remy must agree because he suddenly—awkwardly—thrusts his hand out to Pace, who stares at it much too hard, as if he's trying to find the resemblance between ink-stained Maddox hands and Wicker's.

In the end, Pace huffs, reaching out to grip it with a hard shake.

Remy doesn't give it back, though. He tugs Pace closer, bending down to assess my brother's tattoos. He purses his lips, using the tip of his ever-present capped marker to point to a whorl on Pace's forearm. "This prison work?"

"Yeah," Pace says, expression shuttered and hard.

Remy nods. "Violet."

I chuff a laugh, glancing at Rory. "They're gray, actually."

But Pace just says, "Yeah," looking weirdly impressed. "He did some of them."

Remy nods. "I noticed it when you capped Oakfield. Good work, by the way."

"Thanks." Pace looks down at his arm. "How'd you know Bo Violet inked these?"

"All the red mostly." He pops the marker back behind his ear. "And the thin lines. I've never met him, but some of the cubs have his ink. DK hooked you up, right?"

"What do you mean 'red'?" Pace asks. The tattoos on his dark arm are also in dark, non-colored ink.

Remy blinks. "You got them in the Pen, right?"

"Yeah."

Remy puts his inked fingers to a temple, and then mimics a trigger pull, saying, "Kapow! *Red*. Stay out of that place. It'll kill you."

"Sure." Pace's eyes slide to mine and I'm pretty sure he's reconsidering letting this man into our house. "I'll do that."

"Now," Remy rubs his hands together, "show me what we're dealing with."

Pace steps aside and allows Remy entry into the nursery. Wicker glances up from where he's made some progress taping the windows. The two make eye contact but don't speak. Wicker is probably the least on board with this idea, which is rich, considering his shit-stirring from earlier this morning.

I can't blame him. The interactions he's had lately with the Barons and Timothy Maddox surely are clouding his opinion. But when Ballsack heard we were struggling with a surprise decoration attempt for the nursery, he suggested we call in the only pro he trusted.

That's why Remington Maddox is inside the palace walls, up in our private wing, walking around the perimeter of the room, fingers out, barely grazing the primed surface. "How old is this painted lady? Forget all the new plaster and shit. When were her stones set?"

I frown. "You mean the palace? It was built in the late 1800s."

"Shit," he breathes, running his palm along the exterior wall. "She was born around the same time as the clock tower."

Confused, I wager, "I guess."

His green eyes are wide, following the path of his hand up the wall. "Imagine everything she's seen."

"A hundred years of East End jizz," Wicker mutters with a cold smirk. "I'll pass."

Remy stops, turning to Wick. "You don't like her."

Wicker glances at me, then back to Remy. "It's just a house."

"*Just* a house?" Remy gapes at him, an odd flash of anger building in his eyes. "She's sheltered you, hasn't she? Showed you her secret places? She's let you in, kept you safe, and made you a part of her soul." When all he gets is our silent, blank stare, Remy growls, pointing to a spot on the molding all the way in the top corner by the closet. "Here, you see? You put your initials—your *real* initials—into the heart of her. WCK."

Wicker squints his eyes. "What, that little carving? I put those there in fifth grade."

"Exactly," Remy says, nodding. "You showed her who you were. Called dibs. Don't be a fickle little bitch."

Wicker shoots to his feet. "Excuse me?!"

Before I can get between them, Remy explains, "I'm not putting my work in this house unless you intend to keep it." He turns to me, hands clasped behind his back in some kind of power move. It's like someone turning their back to a predator, signaling they're not intimidated. "Are you going to live here? I'm not doing art for the next Royal stock, am I?"

The best I can give him is this: "We don't intend to leave."

Seems good enough for Remy, thankfully. "Did she pick out a color?"

"No," Pace says, reaching into a bag from the paint shop. He hands him a palette of colors. "These seem to be the ones she's leaning toward."

Remy flips through them, his face transforming from one color to the next. His forehead tenses, jaw tightening with each one. "Just colors," he begins muttering. "Not feelings. Just colors. Not bad. Just colors." Eventually, he glances up, noticing our confused expressions, and freezes. He looks uncharacteristically embarrassed. "Oh, it's just.... Vinny and Sy say I need to find the good in every color. But, like—" He flashes a neon yellow swatch at us. "A guy can only handle so much."

"Not that one," Pace says, snatching it out of his hand and throwing it onto the floor. "I prefer our eyes not to bleed."

Remy exhales, shoulders loosening. "I'll need my kit for the mural."

"The mural?" I ask.

"Something right here," he lifts his hands, fingers making a picture square, "over the crib."

"How did you know the crib would be there?" Pace asks.

"Best angles for security, of course." He shrugs. "And the natural light, obviously." I'm starting to understand that Remy doesn't just see things that we don't. He sees everything all at once.

"That sounds good," I tell him. "Is there anything else you'll need?"

He rubs idly at his chest as he inspects the plaster. "I'll send you a list, and then we can figure out a schedule."

"Oh," I grimace. "Yeah, we can't do it on a schedule. It has to be on a certain day."

"And finished on the same day," Pace adds. "For the surprise."

"One day?" Remy asks, gaze going back to the wall, like he sees something already there. "That's going to be tight." He thinks on it for a moment longer. "But yeah. Okay." I'm not expecting his next question. "So what's he like?"

"Who?" I ask, only because Remy looks straight at me.

"The baby."

I give Wicker a confused look. "He's, uhhh…"

"Cantaloupe," Wicker drawls. "That's about the extent of our knowing him as *a fetus*."

But that's not entirely true, is it?

"He's really active at night," I say, thinking of Verity waking up at two every night.

Pace adds, "And she says he seems calmest when he hears music."

Remy's expression turns curious. "What kind of music?"

"Classical stuff," he answers, sliding his gaze to Wicker. "Cello."

Remy follows his gaze to Wicker. "Oh," he says, brow knitting together. "He's yours."

"Why does everyone keep saying that?" Wick bursts with a flare of annoyance. "He might come out brown like Pace—you fuckers don't know."

Remy just snorts. "It's like the molding. I know dibs when I see them." But he freezes abruptly, all the blood draining from his face. "Wait, would that make me…?"

I watch Pace carefully, knowing this is a point of tension for him.

We're different from other people. To us, blood ties are a big deal. Sometimes they're dangerous and worth keeping secret, but other times, they're enormous. Maybe, for once, they can even be something *good*. Something that doesn't need to be hidden and whispered about in dark, quiet places.

To my relief, Pace just shoves two fists in his pockets, head bowed. "Biologically, you'll be his uncle."

Remy blinks furiously, scanning the walls like he's seeing it for the first time. "Oh, fuck," he says. "That's... that's *heavy*. That's a lot of responsibility."

Wicker looks like he's about to lose it. "For you?! It's not like you'll be paying child support here."

But Remy just shakes his head, and since I can see it coming from a mile away, I step out of the doorway, anticipating his next words.

"I have to go—"

"Check your head?" I guess, moving aside. "See the sky?"

Remy stops, his green eyes locked on mine. "Yeah," he breathes, tucking the marker behind his ear. "Exactly. Fucking *exactly*."

Getting a better sense of this guy's mania, I ask, "But you'll come back and do it, right?"

"You saved Nicky," he says, as though that covers it. "And I'll do anything for Ver. She deserves the best."

If I've learned one thing that ties the Dukes and Princes together, it's that one simple fact.

Verity deserves the best.

～

"WILL AUGUST EVER END? Who thought it was a good idea to be pregnant in the summer?" Verity stands in front of the refrigerator, tugging at the collar of her shirt while letting the cool air rush out. To be clear, it's not hot in here. The thermostat is set on sixty-eight and runs continuously. "Also, do we have any more peaches?"

"I'll add it to the list," I say, giving Ballsack a look.

"Ver," he says, "we should probably head out, so you're not late."

She slams the refrigerator door shut and looks down at her dress. "I should change."

"I like that dress," I tell her, truthfully.

Her nose wrinkles. This has been a point of contention ever since we danced that night in the ballroom. "It's too tight."

"I think it hugs your curves perfectly."

"It's tight," she argues.

"It's flattering."

"I'm *fat*."

"You're literally the most gorgeous I've ever seen you." This isn't the first time I've said it, and it won't be the last. "The more your body progresses, the more beautiful you get. This," I say, taking a step toward her, "is a body of creation, ripe and full of life."

Her jaw sets. "Like a *melon*."

Fucking cantaloupe week.

Pinning her against the countertop, I trap her in with an arm on either side of her curvy body. "I know what you're doing."

She pointedly avoids my gaze. "What's that?"

"Procrastinating," I wager, leaning in to brush a kiss over the curve of her cheek. "You're worried about the shower."

She sighs, turning to graze my lips with hers. "I don't like being the center of attention."

"Too bad, because you're a Princess. You gave up the option of anonymity the moment you accepted the invitation to the masquerade." I push her hair off her neck, exposing the long line of her neck. "But I don't think that's it. I think you're worried about your court."

Her eyes flare with life. "Why wouldn't I be? The last time I went to the Gilded Rose with those bitches, they tried to ruin my hair. And then I ruined their relationships." Guilt flickers across her face. "We have a really complicated history."

"And you've done the work to repair it." The crown of her belly rubs against my lower belly, and *fuck*, I like it. "Tommy said he and Heather are back together."

A small grin tugs at her mouth, giving away her pride at her leadership, but all she says is, "Aw. I hope they're making each other miserable."

I laugh. "Yeah, neither is my idea of an ideal partner, but if it makes them happy…"

She touches my cheek, fingers tucking my hair behind my ear. "I like it when you laugh. You don't do it enough." A shiver of want runs down my spine, and then she frowns. "But what if the whole thing goes sideways?"

"It won't," I promise her.

"You can't know that."

"I know your mother will be there, and I'd pay good money to see what happens if someone decides to fuck with her daughter and grandson," I rest my hand on her stomach, "at their own baby shower."

She purses her lips. "You have a point."

"I usually do." I lift her chin, taking the opportunity to swipe a kiss. I do this more often now. Taking little pieces of her when she'll allow it. Getting closer because it feels like the only way I can breathe. "Go," I insist, "get spoiled."

I move, letting her out of my makeshift jail. Grabbing a banana off the counter she says, "I'm surprised one of you isn't driving me." She glances at Ballsack, who's doing his best impression of an inanimate object. "Not that I won't enjoy watching Ballsy get fussed over by thirty women."

Ballsack looks more hunted than he had when the agent dragged him out of here. "I don't have to go in." He looks at me, pleading. "I don't, right?"

The question was clear in her tone, so I choose my response carefully. "The rest of us have some frat business to take care of while all the women are busy. You'll be safe with your very own Ballsack escorting you." I pause, face scrunching. "Dude, your name makes for some really weird sentences," I tell him.

A ghost of a grin tugs at his lips. "One of the other guys I pledged with got 'Sphincter', so I count myself lucky."

She eyes us suspiciously, and I'm pretty sure our well-thought-out plan—decorating the nursery while she's at the shower—has been blown. Until she says, "You're going to kill him, aren't you?"

Huh. Plan not blown. I clear my throat. "No. Not today."

"You sure?" Her eyes narrow. "You're acting weird."

I pull her into another spontaneous kiss, assuring, "Princess, as much as we'd like to get rid of him, today is not the day."

"When then?" she asks, and I realize she's getting anxious to get the weight of Rufus Ashby off her shoulders. That, or she's still procrastinating.

Probably both.

"Soon. I promise." I nudge her toward Ballsack. "Drive safe."

"Will do," he says, ushering her down the front hall toward the car waiting out front.

Ballsack has barely driven through the front gates when I hear a knock on the back door. "Took you long enough to say goodbye," Remy mutters the instant I open it. "I thought maybe you were going to start going at it, and then I'd have to stab my ears out, but thankfully it didn't go that far."

"You were listening?" I ask, faintly disturbed.

He looks faintly insulted. "Only to see if it was safe to come in!"

There's movement in the SUV behind him and my eyes slide over his shoulder, catching sight of Sy climbing out of the front seat. He rolls his eyes at Remy, saying, "Ignore him."

I take in Sy's ratty T-shirt and old jeans. "What are you doing here?"

Sy sidles up to him, arms crossed. "Every time my Duke comes into this fucking place, he comes out with another family member. I'm here to make sure you're not about to ambush him with a long-lost sister or some shit."

Ah.

So he told him.

"That," I stress, "is between him and Wicker and whatever psycho is standing in as their father this week. I just wanted a nursery decorated for my Princess."

"Well, here we are. Even Picasso had an assistant." Sy walks back to the SUV, hauling a paint-splattered toolbox out of the back. "At least that's what Remy told me."

Remy gives me a look that doesn't brook an argument. "Your one day timeline means I need another set of hands I can trust." He grabs Sy by the wrist. "This is the hand of a man I can trust."

I lift my chin to Sy, holding the door open for them. "By the way, how's Bruin? I haven't gotten any calls lately."

"Pissy about having to take it easy for another few weeks, but he's healing up well." His expression turns awkward—maybe even *softens.* "Thanks, again."

Before I can reply, I hear, "Incoming," and Wicker's voice enters the room before his body. Sy and Remy jolt, turning around and seeming startled at his sudden appearance.

"Where the fuck did you come from?" Remy asks, eyes narrowed at Wick like he's seeing a ghost. I shoot my brother a look for using the hidden door next to the refrigerator, but the sound of wheels on the pavement takes precedence.

"Who is that?" Sy asks.

"Payne and Mercer," Pace says, coming down the stairs. "I told Tommy he could let them through the gate. They said they needed to drop something off and willingly checked their weapons at the bridge."

We have no business with the Lords, and from the tense set of Sy's shoulders, I don't think he does either.

Groaning, I demand, "No bloodshed!"

Sy holds up his hands. "No problem here. We promised Lav we'd be on our best behavior."

The vehicle, a big truck, pulls to a stop. Whatever is in the back has been covered with a gray tarp.

Killian exits the cab, and Mercer follows from the passenger side.

"Perilini," Killian says, nodding at Sy. "Maddox." He shifts his gaze to me and my brothers. "Ashbys. We've got a delivery."

"From our Lady," Tristian adds, gesturing to the truck. "For your Princess."

"A gift?" Wicker asks, eyes skeptical. "Why didn't she take it to the shower?"

"It's too big," Killian says, glancing at Sy. "And it's probably going to take three of us to get it upstairs unless you've got an elevator in this place."

Pace narrows his eyes. "How do you know the nursery is upstairs?"

Killian and Tristian exchange a look, but the King replies, "Don't get paranoid. I just assumed." None of us have forgotten the condition of the nursery that we abandoned or the rumors that followed. "Anyway, she said you'd be here working on the room today and it would be a good day to drop it off."

Remy assesses the two, apparently coming to a decision. "Sy, you can help Payne with that."

Sy frowns. "I thought I was your trusted hands?"

Remy nods at Tristian. "You need a delicate touch to handle explosives. An *artist's* touch. Mercer's with me."

Tristian manages to look both pleased and insulted. "The only thing I know how to draw is my Beretta, and Pace made me check it at the gate."

Killian sighs, relenting, "Whatever. Let Picasso and Matisse get started. I just need someone to help me get this upstairs."

As an undergrad, due to Father's influence, I've had the opportunity to observe physicians at the hospital. To witness the undeniable skill it takes to stitch a suture, keep a steady hand, set a bone. I've even experienced it myself when I'd saved Nick Bruin's life.

It feels like a higher power is in charge and working through you.

I never thought much about art or being an artist, but I've gotta give it to him. Remington Maddox has a gift. Somehow, by just using his hands, chalk, and a paintbrush, he's able to bring the walls of the nursery to life.

"This is pretty damn impressive," Tristian says, eyeing the mural. "You didn't do a draft or anything?"

"Psh," Remy scoffs, dabbing his brush into the makeshift palette he made out of a piece of cardboard. "Nah, I just visualize it and then bring it to life. Although Vinny did specifically demand I add the butterflies." He looks at Sy, fidgeting with a tube of paint. "This color is okay? You're sure?"

"All colors are okay," Sy answers, clasping his Duke on the shoulder. His voice is low and patient in a way I'm not expecting. "Plus, the blue and green make teal, right? Which makes it overpower the yellow."

Remy breathes out slowly, assessing the finished product. "Right. To the victor."

"Those stars are cool," Tristian adds. "I like how they look like they're hanging by a thread."

Remy follows his gaze, pushing his wild, platinum hair out of his eyes. "That's so the baby always knows how to get home, even when it's dark." He whips around, facing me. "Nightmares get in your head sometimes, Lex. You have to be watchful." His stare is almost too intense—seeking and pleading. "You'll watch him, right? Make sure he doesn't turn green? Because my mom," Remy's eyes flick to Wicker, "she gave that to me through her blood."

I straighten, startled. "Wait. You mean something hereditary?"

"I turned out fine," Wicker offers, looking unconcerned.

Still, I'm relieved when Sy dips close to say, "How about we go out for a drink tomorrow, and I'll fill you in on the medical history."

I exhale shakily. "Yeah. The colors are getting confusing." I catch Killian's eye and he shrugs. He and Pace have been building and arranging the furniture; a changing table and a bookshelf.

"She's going to like that," Wick says, gesturing to the chair in the corner. It's the gift from the Lords and Lady—a rocker. "She's going to love all of it."

I don't know how Maddox did it, but he managed to paint an entire garden on the wall. Roses rise from the floorboards, white and pure, while vines curl along the corners, hanging over the bed. There are the stars, a moon, and the silhouette of a bird taking flight.

When I point it out, Remy grins. "Oh yeah, that's Effie. She's a big soul. I bet the house loves her."

Pace opens his mouth to say something, but then closes it, thinking better of it.

Smart.

That is, until he turns to Payne, saying, "Your FBI agent showed up here the other day."

Killian instantly balks. "He's not *my* agent. And I heard he had a warrant." The muscle in the back of Killian's jaw tics. "Why are you pushing back on this anyway? I thought you wanted to find the girl."

"I'm not sure why finding a missing South Side girl means harassing one of my guys," Sy chimes in. "Ballsack is a good kid."

"He may be," Killian says, standing to his full height, "but he was in a relationship with her and one of the other girls who went missing. No one can name a better suspect."

"You're not going to find anything on him," Remy says, adding a flourish to a rose beneath the window. "Ballsy's been one of the sturdiest guys in the frat. Now he's..." he picks up a tube of yellow paint and twists it in his stained fingers. "Sad."

"For the record," Wick says, "we do want to know, but we're not too keen on Feds showing up at the palace gates, making accusations."

Killian rolls his eyes. "Let's face it. There's no way for there to be an impartial investigation by the locals. The corruption runs deep, and it leads back to every single one of our houses." Cops, judges, clerks, attorneys, politicians. He's right. No one is clean in Forsyth. "And I'm aware that it seems like we're meddling by using our federal contact, but it was the best we could do. We want answers."

"This is your fault, you know." Pace looks at Sy. "You and your fucking contracts, insisting on keeping an eye on Verity, and you swapped that kid across territory lines like a rubber band." He shifts his attention to the Lords. "And honestly, I'm not so sure you didn't have something to do with a girl from South Side conveniently applying to be an East End handmaiden."

"That wasn't us," Tristian says, hand pushing through his hair. "But it was orchestrated. By Story."

I frown. "Why?"

Mercer snorts. "You haven't noticed how close those girls are?"

Every guy in the room stares blankly, confirming that none of us had noticed, and I think about how I had to push her out the door to go to the shower today.

"None of you have sisters," Mercer continues, "but I do. There's a vibe. Our women have a connection."

Wick nods, face pensive. "I can see it. You know how women like to travel in packs. Ours don't have that option. Not even with their court or," he waves his hand at Sy and Remy, "or those cub-sluts of yours, or," he shoots the Lords a look, "the whores at your brothel. Sure, they have other women to talk to, but no one who gets what it's like to be Royal. It's an exclusive club."

"Tell me about it," Killian says, rubbing his forehead. "Is this a problem?"

The question seems to be directed at Sy—the other King in the room.

"Fuck if I know." He leans against the changing table, arms crossed over his chest. "The Duke in me wants to say hell no. But the psychology student in me..." He grimaces. "It says that if we want these women in our lives for the long haul, then they're going to need some kind of support outside of us. Someone who knows what it's like to carry the burden of being a Queen."

I shift uneasily. We've all just barely started speaking to one another, but the idea of Verity being a Queen of Forsyth...

It feels destined.

"Then we let it be," I say, knowing it's the right thing. And if it's not...

Then the three of our houses will deal with it in our own way.

Just like we always do.

erity

BALLSY PASSES through the palace gates, giving a quick nod to Matt Kramus. He's been quiet ever since he returned to East End, probably a little shell-shocked after spending forty-eight hours being interrogated by Agent Knight. Thankfully, Sy was able to get one of Saul's former attorneys to get him released. According to Sy, it turns out the arrest warrant had nothing to do with Stella or any of the other girls. That was bullshit. It was a simple bench warrant for failing to appear in traffic court six months ago. Since the FBI had no actual evidence that Ballsack had anything to do with the girls' disappearance, and the bench warrant was easily taken care of once he got in front of a judge, they had to release him.

Even after being out for days now, he still looks tired. He could be in West End laying low, except he wants to stay busy, so when he showed up to take me to the shower, I wasn't surprised. Concerned, but not surprised. "Ballsy," I start, "you don't have to do this. Any one of the guys can take me, and I don't expect there will be any trouble. Not with Mama there, and—"

"I need to ask a favor," he blurts, "but you have to promise not to put any attention on yourself."

I take in the stiff way he holds onto the steering wheel. The tight muscles in his neck. "Not sure I can promise that. I'm roughly the size of *a planet*."

He sighs, but goes on, "Remy's cousin called late last night, and that girl they found by the river? The dean's niece?" He glances over. "She's going to be initiated as the new Baroness in the next few days."

I freeze, taking this in. Classes start back up in a week so I was expecting a new Royal stock. "Well, that can't be a coincidence, can it? What have you found out so far?"

Pace has been shut-lipped about the whole thing, which is probably because every time I think of her, the sick feeling that's hovered over me since we found those bones in the solarium threatens to rise up the back of my throat.

I think of Odette. Or Amber Maddox. Posey Payne. Not all women who go missing are dead. Some are still missing. Others are hospitalized or in prison. I rest my hand on my stomach, relieved, not for the first time, that I'm carrying a boy and not a girl.

Although, I know firsthand that boys get hurt in Forsyth, too.

"We talked to the two kids who found her," he begins. "They were fishing that morning on the river, way out in the northern section."

"It's all forest out there, right?"

He nods. "They said she washed up completely unconscious. They thought she was a corpse at first, but one of them—some kind of fucking Eagle Scout or whatever—gave her CPR while the other called for help."

The hard line carved into his forehead makes me ask, "What aren't you telling me? You know I can handle it."

He shakes his head, huffing. "I know you can, it's just the way the boys described her. Like she'd been running for days. Makes it hard to pin down direction or territory."

That nauseous feeling from before intensifies. "Did anyone say anything else?"

"Not anything we don't already know about Arianette Hexley." Shrugging, he elaborates. "Nineteen-year-old black female, sophomore, pretty, related to the Dean of Admissions. All fairly surface-level details."

The Gilded Rose comes into view. "So what makes everyone sure she's connected to the other disappearances? She could have just fallen into the river, right? Or gotten lost. Or been a victim of something domestic."

"There were indicators," he says carefully.

"What kind?" I ask, needing to know.

"Implications she'd been held against her will. She was emaciated and covered in bruises. There were ligature marks around her wrists. Her knees had sores on them, and her feet... they looked like she hadn't been wearing shoes."

"She ran through the forest barefoot?" I wince. There's something barbaric about it, stripping a person of their basic needs. "Honestly, if Ashby wasn't locked in the basement and the Princes weren't sleeping in my bed every night, I'd accuse them. Sounds like torture."

He grunts, but we both know this isn't the Princes' work. Too sloppy and they're too preoccupied.

"There was something else. A wound just behind her ear." He touches the spot. "She'd been embedded with a tracker but it was removed. No idea how long she had it or who put it there."

It's common knowledge the Royals track their House Girls. Lionel Lucia and his penchant for sex trafficking set that into motion, but this girl was young, and not affiliated with any house or territory as far as I know.

His mouth forms a tense line. "But if she's told that FBI agent anything of actual value, they haven't been acting on it. The radios and the wires are suspiciously quiet. No one except me has been brought in for questioning."

My emotions rise and fall like I'm riding over the crests and dips of a roller coaster. Everyone's been interested in her story, but not like me, Pace, and Ballsy. A survivor's witness account has to be a huge break in Agent Knight's case.

So why hasn't anything come of it?

That's when it hits me. "The Barons. They have her under lock and key."

"Even more than usual." Face drawn, Ballsy pulls into the drive that leads to the Gilded Rose. "Pace and I can't get to her to ask her any questions."

I frown. "So where does the favor come in?"

Throwing the car into park, he turns to me. "Regina Thorn."

"Last year's Baroness?"

He gestures to the building in front of us. "She's going to be at this thing."

Slowly, I say, "Oh."

"We need to know what the Baroness' initiation is. Maybe there's some way we can get to her. Just," he stresses, "to ask her about what happened to her."

"So you want me to pump Regina for intel," I wager, shrugging. "No problem."

His eyes grow intense. "You have to be careful, though. I won't risk a sister to save a girlfriend. You understand? Plus," he shifts uncomfortably, "if your Princes find out I even asked you to do this, my nickname would become strictly symbolic."

My face softens. "I understand."

"It does make me wonder..." He turns his gaze to the building, grimacing. "I mean, I know it's not any of my business, but what are you going to do once classes start back up?"

This is easy to answer. "I'm taking the semester off."

He pins me with a look. "I mean as Princess. The masquerade should be gearing up in the next week. New Princess, new Princes—"

I cut him off. "We're not doing that."

"No?"

"A new Princess isn't chosen until the birth of the baby. The next masquerade is scheduled for the winter—just like mine."

"And you're okay with that? Another Princess? Another coronation?"

The expression on his face tells me he knows well enough what I went through, and what the next woman will go through as well.

"Let me get through this party and the birth of my son." I open the door. "Then we'll figure out what to do next."

IT'S BEEN forty-five minutes since I walked in the doors of the Gilded Rose, and I've had my stomach touched, my tits commented on, a pimple pointed out, and my glow discussed, along with how much weight I've gained, and one particularly invasive question about my bowel movements.

"What size bra are you up to?" That question is from Kira, who had her baby last month. She's already proudly told me how she's back to her pre-baby weight and shared a terrifying story about how at the hospital, after giving birth, they made her wear mesh, paper underpants for three days. "If you go up another size, which it looks like you probably will, you may as well just start getting nursing bras," she continues. "No reason to waste money on both."

I muster up a tight smile. "Thanks for the tip."

"Any time," she says. "No one told me anything about what the hospital stay would be like. I've vowed to share everything I learned."

Everyone needs a purpose, I suppose.

She continues, "And the sitz bath is your friend once you get home. It's the best way to get healed up down there."

I'm the Princess, I want to tell her. I became Princess by sitting on a ceremonial dildo. I know all about healing up an abused pussy. But I don't. I just nod and exhale in relief when she spots an empty seat across the room.

I wasn't faking my hesitation about coming to the shower today, but it's not about the women in my court or a wariness about watching West End Maggie in her tight body-con dress listen intently to Lakshmi as she talks about some new shampoo that makes her hair shine. Or Lavinia, with an empty plate, as she sits next to Kira, patiently looking at photo after photo of her baby. It's not Story and her herculean effort to make small talk with Regina over by the teacakes with tiny ice-blue booties on top.

It's not even my mother, Liberty Sinclaire, dressed absolutely nothing like a grandma-to-be in her leopard print dress, or the fact she's sitting in a tight circle, holding a delicate china tea cup, deep in discussion with Adeline and Mrs. Crane.

It's who *isn't* here.

Laura Walker. Kelsey Livingston. Stella St. James.

Stella would have loved everything about this, from the china pattern to the handmade banner over the door made out of felt and ribbon welcoming 'Baby Ashby' to the delicious food and tantalizing gossip.

The task Ballsack gave me on the way over is a useful distraction, but there's a nervousness there, too. I've only caught a couple glimpses of Regina, and the last time I saw her, she was twitching over by the front door, never really stepping into the fray.

This is important—something I can do to help Stella—and I don't want to mess it up. I want to be out there, searching. I could have gone to talk to those Boy Scouts who found her. I could be bursting into Maddox's crypt right now, demanding to speak to the new Baroness. No one would hurt a woman who's eight months pregnant.

Probably.

Right?

I hide my distress by taking a bite of a chicken salad sandwich, making a futile attempt to read Adeline's lips as she whispers something that makes my mother smirk.

"Fucking weird, right?" I spin and see the Duchess—Lavinia Lucia—making a neat pile of cheese on her plate. Her chin lifts to Mama and the others. "What do you think they're talking about?"

"I have no clue." I eye the room warily. "It's like a vault of Forsyth's secrets over there. They could probably bring this whole town to its knees if they conspired together." Yet, they don't. Looking around the room, I think I understand why. "I keep waiting for someone to whip out a curling iron and start a brawl."

"Please," she snorts. "As if those Princess wannabes would dare break a nail."

"They're tougher than you think." My attention falls on Heather, who showed up with two fake things: a smile and a tan. "And probably have more in common than you realize. I saw Adeline's weapons basket when I came in. It was full."

Lavinia's forehead lifts, considering, but doesn't look convinced. And that's why the women of Forsyth have never banded together. Someone felt the need to bring a switchblade to a baby shower, for Pete's sake.

Mistrust runs as deep as the Baron's crypt.

"So you finally talked to him?" Lakshmi's voice carries across the room. She, Heather, and Gina are huddled together, just like the first time I met them.

"I'd avoided him for weeks, but last night, he showed up when I was getting out of my date's car." A smile tugs at Heather's painted lips. "At first, I thought he was coming for me, but you know what he did? He went to the driver's side, dragged my date out, and punched the daylights out of him."

"Are you serious?" Gina gasps. The cutsluts perk up at the conversation, not-so-subtly leaning in. "He got in a *fight*? Tommy?!"

Heather nods. "He took a few punches, and I had to threaten to call campus security to break it up, but Tommy got one last punch in, told him to 'stay the fuck away from my girl', and ended it."

"Holy shit. Was this the LDZ?" Lakshmi asks, glancing over at Story.

Story sighs. "Oh god. Which one is it now?"

"Tucker," Heather replies. "You know him?"

"Oh, do I ever." She rolls her eyes. "Self-proclaimed South Side fuckboy. He has a thing for girls he perceives to be off-limits, including yours truly when I first arrived. He's probably run through everyone in the territory, so he decided to hit up East End."

"Ungrateful prick," Mrs. Crane mutters. "Hope your princey poodle boy tore him a new one."

"He did," Heather says, eyes going dreamy. "We're back together."

Mrs. Crane gives Heather a sour look. "For beating up a frilly frat boy? He better have gotten on his knees afterward and licked your pussy like a waffle cone."

Adeline gasps, but my mother just snorts, lifting her teacup in agreement. "Hear, hear."

"Tucker was just a rebound anyway." Again, Heather's lips curve. "I guess Tommy didn't know that."

The girls hover around and listen as she describes the altercation and the following grovel—minus the pussy-licking, much to Mrs. Crane's disappointment. I don't deny that I feel a smug sense of satisfaction that my advice to Tommy worked.

Maybe there are better ways to run East End than dungeons and bamboo shards under the fingernails.

Heather gushes, "I never realized how hot it would be for a guy to fight for me—literally!" She glances at the cutsluts. "You girls might be on to something."

"Of course we are," Maggie says. "A man all pumped up post-fight, high on victory and adrenaline? Best sex ever."

My mind goes to Wick taking me in the mausoleum.

She's not wrong.

"A fight is good," Mama says, voice rising above the girls'. Every eye swings in her direction. "But Delores is right, there's something about a man on his knees, groveling like his life depends on it, that just can't be matched."

"You mean like flowers and jewelry?" Lakshmi asks.

"No," Story interjects, twirling a lock of her dark hair around a finger. "Like when he comes to your door and carves your initial into his chest."

Lavinia blurts, "Or when he brings you the head of your enemy." At everyone's shocked stares, she shrinks into herself, quickly adding, "Or, you know, when he takes care of your kitten or helps you fix a clock."

Mrs. Crane's scraggly voice pipes in. "Severed heads are a messy business. Best stick with him taking care of your pussy."

Lavinia blinks. "Oh, I was being literal about the kitten. Although," she gives a sly smirk, "the other kitten is well taken care of, too."

I try to think if my Princes have ever groveled like that, with some big romantic gesture to prove their worth to me. Sure, there was Lex surprising me with the dance the other night. And I too know the charm of receiving a severed limb.

But what comes flooding back is the little stuff.

Lex bringing me coffee in the mornings, or Wicker sneaking treats to me in the dungeon. There was the time Pace washed the glue out of my hair with a gentle touch I didn't know he possessed, and then made me a second appointment to get pampered.

"This is the most Forsyth of all Forsyth discussions ever," Lavinia mutters, leaning in close. "But they can talk about pussy, beatdowns, and men doing sweet shit all day because I overheard Adeline say she had games to play." Lavinia shudders. "I'm not playing any stupid party games."

"Games?" Story asks, her expression reflecting my dread. "Like what?"

She flaps a hand. "You know, there's the one where they melt candy in the diapers and you have to guess which kind?"

"No," Story says, absolute horror overcoming her expression. "I don't know about that."

Two girls from West End wander over, joining in. Daphne points across the room, "That glass vase on the gift table filled with pacifiers and stuff? That's not just a decoration. It's a guessing game. And Adeline has some raffle planned, too."

"Oh," I reply, pulling a face. "Maybe I should fake a contraction or pretend like my water broke, and then maybe we can all just go home early."

"You can't go home!" Story shouts. Lavinia elbows her in the side and she winces. Rubbing her ribs she adds, "I mean, not yet. We have to open gifts!"

"In front of everyone?" Suddenly, it just all feels too much. I tug at the collar of my dress. It's like all the doilies and pastels are closing in on me. "I think I need some air."

"Is something wrong?" Story asks, forehead creased in concern. "Do you want us to come with you?"

"I'm okay," I rest my hands on my belly. "I'm just hot and hormonal. Give me five minutes, and I'll be ready for games and presents." I give them a tight smile. "Promise."

I can't get outside fast enough. As soon as I do, I gulp in the air, greeted by the scent of roses. There was a time when the smell would turn my stomach, but now it just makes me long for the sanctuary of the palace solarium.

However, the universe must be on my side, because perched on the bottom of the porch steps is none other than my coveted target, Regina Thorn.

She's resting her cheek on her knee as she fingers the bud of a new rose, eyes distant and wistful. Aside from Mama and Mrs. Crane, all the women inside are wearing bright, summery colors.

Not Regina.

She's in a long, black, lacy cardigan, which is covering a short, dark dress.

Maybe Wicker had a point before about Barons and their theatrics.

Clearing my throat, I watch as she jolts in surprise. "Sorry, I didn't know anyone was out here."

I start to go back inside but she straightens, insisting, "Stay, Princess. It's fine."

Turning, I offer her a small grin. I know we're outside, but there's a huge fucking elephant in the room; the fact I witnessed Wicker slitting the throat of her Baron. In a heartbeat, I can feel the warmth of his blood on my hands. I run them down my sides in an absurd attempt to wipe them clean.

"I don't know if we've ever actually met," I try. "I'm Verity."

"Regina," she says, giving me a nod. "I didn't mean to be rude by dipping out. Honestly, I was surprised to get the invitation at all. I figured after recent..." she grimaces, "*events*... I wouldn't have made the cut."

"Right." I take a deep breath, daring to take a seat on the top step. "About that..."

But she shakes her head. "Don't. My King told me what Will did. I wasn't even too surprised."

I tense, eyes scanning the parking lot for Ballsy's car. "You knew what he was going to do to me?"

Her head whips around, eyes wide. "Of course not. If I'd known, I would have told Father—I mean, the King." Frowning, she averts her gaze. "Do you know why the King chose them like he did? Why he wanted Williams last year?"

I cradle my belly, thinking of him—Will—staring down at me that night of the attack. "Not really."

Shrugging, she answers. "He always has a theme, doesn't he? My Freshman year, the Barons were all CS majors. The year before that, anatomy experts. The year before that, it was chemists. He always has a plan. But lately, he's been... hungry," she explains with a troubled tilt of her mouth. "To build a family. And William is his middle name. His father's middle name. His son's. They all knew what they were meant to be, but Liam and Bill understood it was symbolic. Will, though..." She inhales, jaw tightening. "He took it too literally. He wanted to protect his father's legacy. The wicked path can be like that, you know." Meeting my gaze, she stresses, "It's not just a title or a game. It's more than life or death. It's a skin we wear. They might take off the masks at the end of the ceremony, but the sense of self never returns."

I know this is a perfect lead-up to my question, but I can't help but ask another. "Has yours?"

Her brow knits up, surprise crossing her face. "I don't know," she answers, although, from the way she shifts her gaze to the distance, I get the impression this is the first time she's considered it.

"Your reign is over now," I say, fishing. "Maybe it's good that some other girl takes the path because now you can be anything."

She flexes her hands on her knees, watching them with a grim expression. "He's already chosen her and two of her Barons. But that's not the worst part. I visited the House of Night the other day, and it looks like they're preparing it for a—" But here, she pauses, body tensing. "I suppose I shouldn't say. Like you said, my reign is over." She glances at me. "Yours will be soon, won't it?"

Whatever the thing is she came close to telling me, it's like sand falling through my fingers. Sighing, I rub my stomach. "I'm not sure it'll be that simple for me."

She balks at the phrase. Simple. "For those of us on the wicked path, true self is about loyalty. Do you trust your lover enough to die? To give yourself over a hundred percent, body, mind, and soul? We're not just bound in this life, but also in the next. Will may be gone, but he's still tethered to me, waiting until I cross the veil."

I fail to repress a shiver. "That sure is some commitment."

Her smile is soft and unbearably sad. "It's our way."

"They're under a lot of pressure—the Royal men."

She nods. "They are."

"Although," I add, giving her a significant look. "I don't think they appreciate how much pressure they apply to us."

"No, I don't think so." Her eyes meet mine. "You're strong, though. If you hadn't been, my Will would have taken you. No doubt."

"I've had no choice but to be strong." I look down at my belly, working up the courage to be honest with this woman. This *rival* woman. "Have you ever heard how a Princess gets initiated?"

"No," she says, turning to me more fully. "Is it quite awful?"

I pause, thinking that this may be the first Royal woman to even assume that it *is* awful. "Well, first they take you to this room..."

And I tell her.

I tell Regina Thorn the whole sordid, disgusting, depraved thing. With each detail I lay bare before her, from the throning to the first deposit, to the fact my own biological father was there to witness and encourage the whole thing, her mouth purses up tighter and tighter.

When I'm done, I let the silence drag on. I wait for the crushing wave of shame, but it never arrives. The throning feels so far away now, as if I'd experienced it in a different life. Maybe we're not so different from the Barons, because being Princess—it's become a skin.

"But," I go on, playing coy, "I'm sure the Baroness has an easier initiation."

Living around DKS for so long, no one knows better than me that people are competitive. Not only in their wins, but also in their losses.

Her eyes flare. "Easy? There's nothing easy about the hunt."

I pause. "The hunt?"

"That's what they do," she explains. "The King sets the four of you loose in the forest behind the crypt, and the Barons hunt you. It's not just the Baroness' initiation. It's the Barons', too."

"They hunt you?" I ask, horrified. "Like an animal?"

For some reason, this makes her laugh. "It's a test, Princess. A Baron and his sinister sister have to be invisible. Silent. Ruthless. If a Baron catches the Baroness, that means he's good at hiding, following, adapting to the shadows."

"And if he doesn't?"

Her head cocks. "Doesn't what?"

"Catch her."

"Oh, Princess, he *always* catches her." The words are said without mirth. "The King chooses his darklings very well."

Reluctantly, I wonder, "What happens after they catch you?"

She hugs her knees, lifting a shoulder. "They bind you to their wicked path and worship death upon you."

Shaking my head, I admit, "I don't know what that means."

Barons and their stupid, cryptic bullshit.

"You couldn't. You're a creator." Smiling softly, Regina's arm stretches over the distance between us, hand brushing the swell of my belly. "You foster life and light. But we're servants of death, and this boy in your belly? He'll be a part of it, one way or another."

I watch her hand touch me, heart in my throat. "I'll never let that happen."

"Aren't you willing to die for your Princes?" Her eyes dart down to my stomach. "Your son?"

"I'm willing to do something a lot more dangerous than dying for them." Reaching out, I brush her hair over a delicate shoulder, heart clenching at the misery in her eyes. "I'm willing to live for them."

WE RETURN HOME with a carload of gifts and a deep desire for a nap.

"Where do you want all this?" Ballsy asks, parking in the front circle.

"I'm not sure." I eye the pile of boxes and bags. The women of Forsyth went all out, giving me everything I'll need for when the baby arrives. Everything I didn't even realize I would need. From binkies to boxes of diapers, to clothes and blankets. There are cute things like stuffed animals, and Lavinia gave us a starter set of children's books, but then Kira gave me some kind of paste for my nipples and a cream for stretch marks.

Ugh.

I forgot about stretch marks.

I decide, "Let's just leave it for now, and I'll talk to the guys about where we want to store it until the nursery is finished."

The nursery is another one of those things on my never-ending 'to do' list that's been weighing on me. It falls somewhere between fitting in my pregnancy yoga class and figuring out what to do with Danner down in his room. Yes, my 'to do' list involves everything from prenatal care to scheduled torture. I really may be an Ashby.

Danner doesn't seem to mind being locked up day and night. If I had to guess, this is probably closer to a vacation than anything he's had in years. Not having to pick up after and take care of three grown men and their father? Sounds like bliss. Although, I think we all know this has to come to an end soon. I get the feeling Wicker is the one dragging it out. I get it. Sometimes evil comes in difficult shades of gray.

Leaving the gifts behind, Ballsack and I walk in the front door. Without Danner manning the entry, there's a rotating crew of PNZ who stand guard, which is why Tommy is standing in the foyer.

"Hey," he says, looking bored, "how was the party?"

"Long, but fun." I rub the crown of my belly, feeling more and more of a strain when I'm on my feet for extended periods of time. "I saw your girlfriend."

He grins. "Yeah?"

"Sounds like you gave that Tucker kid the ass-kicking he needed."

"Turns out DKS isn't wrong *all* the time." He lifts his chin at Ballsack. "At least about this."

Tommy may be less hostile to me, but I doubt that extends to the rest of my West End family, so I distract him by saying, "There are leftovers in the backseat if you're interested."

His eyes light up, and once again, I'm reminded these hardened PNZ soldiers are really just boys. "I'm definitely interested, but I told the guys I'd take you upstairs when you got home. And..." He holds out his hand, revealing a strip of fabric, "that I'd make you wear this."

"Is..." I frown and peer at the scrap of fabric, "is that a thong?"

"Bro," Ballsack says, voice a low growl.

"What?" he shouts, eyes wide. "No! It's a blindfold." His words come out in a rush. "They want to surprise you with something upstairs."

"Oh." A laugh bubbles up. "Okay, that makes more sense."

"Does it?" Ballsack asks, skeptically. "I'll be right behind you."

Tommy rolls his eyes, but I turn and give him my back so he can tie the blindfold over my eyes. I consider this part of the process— showing him that I trust his best intentions lay with our house and kingdom.

And that trust, so far, hasn't been misplaced. Once the blindfold is secure, he takes my hand and leads me slowly, carefully up the stairs, pausing for me on each step. As we get closer to the landing, I catch the scent of fresh paint and sawdust. Did the workers come back?

"Okay," Tommy says, nudging me forward. "You can take it off."

Pushing the blindfold off my eyes, I gasp at the sight that greets me.

It's a garden, filled with blooming flowers and butterflies.

Monarch butterflies.

"Oh my god," I whisper, taking in the gorgeous mural on the wall.

The wall where we've decided the crib should go is decorated with a sprawling live oak, its Spanish moss seeming almost alive, as if I might catch it swaying in a breeze. Scanning the room, I gape at the new furniture—particularly the rocker in the corner—until my eyes fall on the three men huddled in the corner in paint-splattered clothes, watching me.

"You guys did this?" I ask, overcome with shock and emotion.

"With some help," Lex says, wiping his hands on a rag. He jerks his chin at the wall. "Remy's been working on a design for the mural, so he and Sy came over today. The Lords showed up unannounced with the rocker. We were on a time limit, so we all pitched in and helped to get it finished."

Now I'm even more shocked. "You worked with the Dukes *and* the Lords on this?" I ask, eyes darting to Pace. I can't believe he even let them all in the house.

"They passed security." He shrugs, looking strangely unconcerned. "And to be fair, Payne and Mercer just showed up bearing gifts."

"It wasn't as terrible as you'd think," Wick says. There are paint smears all over his expensive jeans.

Gently, I wonder, "With Remy?" I'm being vague on purpose. Ballsack and Tommy have no clue he and Remy are related. Luckily, when I glance at them, they throw us all a salute and retreat back into the hallway. "Was it... er, difficult?"

Wicker scoffs, toeing at a dried paint drip on the floorboard. "I might not know how to paint, but I'm sort of an expert at having brothers."

Lex cuts in, eyebrows hiked up. "So now that this is all done, you can relax and finish gestating our son."

Pace lurches forward, slamming his fist into Lex's shoulder. "Don't say 'gestate'! It's fucking gross."

Lex doesn't even flinch. "Except for the name," he adds, mouth strained. "You still need to decide on that, because every week from now until delivery is a melon, and if we start calling this kid 'pumpkin', I'll throw myself off a cliff."

I look around the room, overwhelmed by how easy it is to picture myself in here with the baby. Rocking him to sleep in the chair. Standing over his crib as I caress his fine hair. Leaning over the rail to brush a kiss against his perfect head.

"Don't worry." A small, soft smile touches my lips. "I've got a name all picked out."

15

"WE PAY PEOPLE TO CLEAN. You know that, right?" I say as Verity steps out of the pantry with an armful of canned goods to add to the pile on the counter. When one starts to fall, I jolt. "Shit." Reaching out, I snag it out of the air before taking a few more that look on the verge of toppling.

"Thanks." Her smile is grateful.

"And we *used* to pay people. Then Pace fired them all—or locked them up—because he doesn't trust them."

"True." I add the cans to the rest of the items she's cleared off the shelves. "Doesn't explain what you're doing."

She has her hair up today, but it's messy and wild, which is fitting. She's been a fucking tornado all week. I don't know where the sudden surge of energy has come from, but I've grown fascinated by watching her zip-waddle around the palace with that spark of aggressive determination in her eyes.

"For one thing," she says, dragging out a sack of flour, "Danner's pantry looks like it hasn't been cleaned out since before your father became King. I know you guys love your old shit, but I don't think expired salad dressing qualifies as an antique." I pick up a bottle of dressing, check the date, and make a face. Yikes. Arching a brow, she continues, "And for another, I realized we needed room for all the baby stuff."

"Red, the baby has a whole room." I hop up on the counter, my hip knocking over a few small boxes of *antique* cornbread mix. "Why does he need a pantry, too?"

She cuts me a look, like she's unsure if I'm being intentionally dumb or naturally dumb. I give her an expression of pure innocence, but honestly, I have no fucking clue.

"Well," she starts, using a slow voice she must use with the Dukes when explaining algebra, "there are things like bottles and formula, little bowls and spoons, bottle cleaners, whatever supplements Lex is surely going to—"

"Formula?" I lean back on my palms, eyes darting down to her tits. "Isn't that what those things are for?" My eyes are fixed on her chest and I don't even try to hide the fact that I want them. They're so full now, enough to cup one in both hands, and ever since I tasted the milk dripping from her tit I've wanted to do it again. That night had been such a rush for all of us, and given the chance, I'd do it again in a heartbeat. With the way her nipples tighten from me looking at her, I'm pretty sure she would, too.

Her cheeks grow the prettiest shade of pink. "Yes, but the moms at the shower were saying that some babies don't take to it, or maybe I won't produce enough, or possibly my nipples will get too sore—we just don't know." I frown and she sets two more boxes of crackers on the counter next to me. "It's just best to be prepared for any circumstance."

"I wouldn't worry about him not taking to it." I reach out and reel her in between my parted legs. "We all know the Ashbys are boob men."

She rolls her eyes, even though that flush on her face deepens. "You're ridiculous."

"Am I?" I shrug nonchalantly, but my stomach feels like I've just taken a leap off the sheer cliff over the river, and when the hell did *that* start happening? "Or am I just a man who knows what he likes?"

My fingers curl around her ribcage, thumb rubbing under the heavy weight of her breast. Verity's mouth parts, breath hitching. The need to taste her is intense.

"You know," I start tentatively, feeling it out, "I did come down here for a snack."

It'd be so easy to just pull down the front of her shirt and suck those pretty things until she feels relief.

Her eyes glaze over, but just as I hook my fingers into the neck of her tank top, she deflates. "No. We promised Lex this is something we'd only do with his supervision," she says.

Fucking. Lex.

But she's right. We did. And we have to be... what's the word?

Responsible?

Ew.

She wriggles away, taking a wide step back from temptation. "If you're going to keep distracting me with all your muscles and hair and *mouth*, then you can at least help me get the rest of this out of here. I'm pretty sure that bag of flour is older than I am."

I grunt in disappointment but slide off the counter, adjusting myself in the process. She seems surprised when I don't leave, instead opting to help her sort and remove everything from the pantry.

"What's that up there?" she asks, leaning against the door frame and cradling the baby with both hands. "That brown thing?"

The ceilings are high and the top shelf is almost out of my reach, but pushing up on my toes, I catch the corner and grab it. It's a wooden box, small yet big enough to require both hands. I carry it out and place it next to the other items from the pantry.

"I've seen this before," I say, blowing a layer of dust off the top. "It's Danner's tea box." Opening the lid, I'm greeted with the heady scent of trapped spices. The inside is divided into small slots, tea packages filling each one. Chamomile, peppermint, lemon-ginger.

Verity stretches her back. "Those are the teas he made me."

A strange sense of wistfulness overcomes me as I run a finger down the packages. "Danner made the best night-time drinks."

Verity pulls the box toward her and frowns. "It's heavier than expected, right?" She tilts her head and touches a corner. She then pinches her fingers on one of the dividers and lifts. The tray moves. "Look," she says, "there's a second layer."

"Or a secret compartment." I help her lift off the entire tray. "Sure enough, secret tea."

I'm joking, but the items at the bottom aren't the pre-packaged teas from the store. There's a small mortar and pestle, and bottles line the box, each with peeling labels on the side. A stack of thick cards rests against the back wall. Verity picks up one, squinting at the words, which are faded and in a squiggly cursive. I pluck up one of the bottles labeled in that same curled script. More old, weird shit. No matter how much Verity spruces, this house will never be rid of it. I drop the bottle back inside with disinterest.

"Can you read this?" Red asks, showing me the card. "Is that Danner's handwriting?"

"Maybe." Now, I squint, reading aloud, "Purple Mercy. Crush seeds—ten to twenty-five. Bring ten ounces of water to a boil in a saucepan. Add one tablespoon of fresh or one teaspoon of dried foxglove, reduce the heat, and simmer for five to ten minutes. Strain the tea into a cup with a sieve, add crushed seeds, and add honey to taste. Speak now a prayer for the fruitless..."

"Foxglove?" Verity rummages through the jars until she pulls one out with the name written on the label. "I think there's some of that in the solarium. They're pretty."

"Pretty," I agree, "but toxic."

Her eyebrow raises. "How toxic?"

I take out another jar. "I'd have to ask Lex, but I think it can cause serious cardiac issues. And look, all of these are weird. Like this one?"

I show her the bottle, giving it a rattle. "What's he doing with wisteria seeds in his tea box?"

All of the pretty color in Verity's cheeks drains away. "Crushed seeds," she says, eyeing the bottle with wide eyes. "Wisteria seeds are poisonous. Why would Danner have such toxic things in his tea box?" The question hangs there until she stiffens. "How many nights did he bring me chamomile tea before bed, or lemon-ginger to help with morning sickness?"

"I think we need to talk to Danner," I say quietly, dread building in my gut.

A prayer for the fruitless...

"When?"

I close the tea box lid, tucking it under my arm. "Now."

WE'RE JUST outside Danner's room when Lex grabs me by the arm, pulling me aside. "Are you sure you're ready for this? I know you've always had a closer relationship, but if this tea situation means what I think it does—"

"I came to you," I snap. "Immediately, I may add."

Lex brushes his hair away from his face. He'd never admit it, but he wears it down specifically because it gives Red the warm tinglies. I can barely remember the last time he had it up. "I just know it's been an emotional few months. Dealing with Father, learning about your biological family history, becoming a dad, and now Danner—"

"Lex." I try to keep the annoyance out of my voice as I grasp him by the shoulder.

He gives my hand a baffled look. "Yeah?"

"I know you're trying out this new thing where you try to feel your emotions and stuff, but now isn't the time." I nod down the hall where Verity and Pace are waiting. "This has been going on too long." Obviously, longer than we realized. "Let's go do this."

Eyes rolling, he nods, both of us watching as Pace unlocks the door.

A moment later we're all pushing into the room, Danner's eyes lighting up when he sees us. "Boys." His smile is weak. *He's* weak. Or maybe that's what he wants us to think. Maybe it's always been some demented act. "And Princess. How marvelous it is to see proof of your creation. My dear, you're positively glowing with life."

From the way her attention shifts, it's obvious that if he hadn't spoken, Verity wouldn't have seen him tucked away in the dim corner of the room. And not just because Pace has positioned himself between them. We haven't allowed her to see Danner since the attack, but now, trying to view him through her eyes, I imagine it's a shock. Danner's always been old, like *old*-old, but he always managed his job with a certain grace and agility. Now, he's a shadow of himself, pale skin wrinkled and withered. He seems smaller, but maybe that's just the circumstances, an old man who's finally about to have his reckoning.

Lex steps forward, lifting the box, and Danner's expression instantly registers understanding.

"Ah, my tea box," he says, reaching out with a shaky hand. "Belonged to my father."

Lex sets the heavy box on Danner's lap. "I've been running tests for weeks trying to figure out how the princesses died. There were no wounds, no bullet holes, signs of strangulation, or other trauma. It's like they just faded away. But I realize I missed something." He holds the old man's eye. "Poison."

"Purple Mercy," Pace sneers.

"You were always a smart boy, Lagan." He opens the lid and inhales deeply, expression softening. "I knew the day would come when you'd discover the truth. I just hoped I would be long gone before you did."

"So you admit it," Pace says, fists flexing. "You poisoned them."

Danner nods, seeming more frail by the moment. I can't tell if it's a ruse or some kind of trick, because if what we suspect is true, then Danner isn't just an accomplice to Father's crimes.

He's a perpetrator.

"How?" I ask sharply.

Danner removes the top tray to reveal the bottles underneath. "The nettle tea was my father's recipe. It has many holistic purposes and anti-inflammatory properties and soothes a variety of irritations. It can also be used to encourage contractions, and over the years we attempted to assist princesses who were beyond their due date. Stinging Nettle, although a vicious little plant, was not used to harm those women." He lifts another bottle out. "Purple Mercy had another purpose altogether. Think of me as monstrous if you like, but that's exactly what it was." He looks up. "A mercy."

This seems to hit Verity the hardest, her eyes brimming with horrified tears. "But why?"

Danner looks tired, but he doesn't shrink away from the question. "I already told you that he was relentless in his quest to create an heir, even if that meant using the failed princesses."

"I think you mean to say we know he *raped* them."

He makes a soft, dismissive sound. "I would argue that he was well within his rights as King and by the covenants signed when the girls accepted their role as Princess," he waves a tired hand, "but that's neither here nor there. What I didn't tell you before was the conditions of their tenure. While I was up here helping raise you, he was down there, spilling his seed into those former princesses who wouldn't produce him an heir."

It's Pace who speaks. "The dungeon. He imprisoned them in the dungeon."

All my life, I've been told how despicable and deranged my own bloodline is, but this? This proves he's worse than even Timothy Maddox. "Is that true?"

Danner nods, as if he's pleased we're finally unraveling the thread. "Naturally, he had to ensure any conception truly belonged to him. It was a very philanderous era in Forsyth history."

"So you killed them to... what?" Pace asks, face twisted in fury. "Erase the evidence?"

Danner's words are spoken with a patience that galls me. "I mean it when I called it mercy. None of them conceived because none of them could. In the chaos of his grief, Rufus kept trying, over and over, like a man possessed. He kept one of them trapped down there for a whole year. What else should I have done?" he wonders, head tilting curiously. "Releasing them wasn't an option. They would have destroyed your father's reign. But even if it were an option, there would have been nothing left of them. He blamed those women, treated them cruelly because he couldn't accept the truth." He nods, confirming all of our suspicions. "He's the one who's infertile. Well..." He beams at Verity, his wrinkled lips stretched grotesquely. "Mostly infertile. You were a miracle of miracles, my dear. Once he confirmed that you were his biological daughter, all of the rage lifted. The sun shone on his kingdom again. All of that angry determination turned to ash. He finally was at peace with having the chance at a new legacy." He looks up, engaging Pace. "My only regret was not giving that tea to your mother soon enough."

I sense Pace's lunge before Lex does, which is probably for the best. If it were up to our brother, he'd let the red-hot fury in Pace's eyes land on Danner like a hammer. I grab him before he can, hauling him back.

"You son of a bitch!" Pace roars, struggling against my hold. "I knew you were a conniving little fucking worm!"

And while I'm expecting all of this, I'm not expecting Verity to sweep forward, expression hard. "You love my father. I know you do. So tell us what happened to Odette, or I'll go down to the dungeon right now and tell him you betrayed him." It's fucking genius, which is apparent in the way Danner suddenly *expands*.

His spine stiffens, straightening. "You wouldn't deny an old man his life's work."

"I would," she insists, voice full of steel. "I'll say you spilled all his secrets. He'll go to his grave believing you were disloyal." Danner must see the credibility of the threat because his eyebrows crouch low in a glare. Red adds, "We already know she was a Princess," and Danner grins.

"She was a handmaiden before she was ever a Princess."

My hold on Pace goes slack, but he doesn't move a muscle.

At all of our stunned expressions, Danner nods. "Oh yes, Miranda's handmaiden, to be exact. They were the best of friends. She was a fixture to the family, after a time, not unlike your Miss St. James was to you. The bond between a Princess and her handmaiden is very special." His expression turns pensive. "She aided Miranda in her conception of Michael, and then once Miranda gave birth, she saw to the boy day and night. Changed him. Fed him. Rocked him to sleep. Gave him medicine when he turned sickly. She mourned him almost as badly as Miranda did when he died." Suddenly, he looks at Pace, frowning. "It's a shame you never met her because I believe motherhood rather suited her."

"But..." The wheels turn in my head, struggling to understand. "She became Princess."

Danner purses his lips. "Miranda drafted her invitation to the masquerade herself. They wanted to be mothers together. And not long into Odette's reign, she was confirmed to be pregnant." He gives a slow, grim blink. "Unfortunately, that was the year the roses died."

Lex's eyes narrow. "You mean Michael and Miranda."

Heavily, Danner nods. "Your father was overcome with grief, hardly able to perform his duties. I'm sure you can imagine how difficult it was for him to see such a creator thriving in his own home—and the creation not his own." His eyes grow misty. "But even early on in the pregnancy, there was... speculation as to the potential father of the child. Odette was overly familiar with a member of the West End frat, which is something I'm sure all of you can appreciate, and she fell pregnant so soon that it hardly seemed likely to be by one of her Princes."

"What did you do to her?" Pace snaps.

Danner balks. "Me? Not a blessed thing." Here, he sighs, tugging a weathered kerchief from his pocket. "But Rufus wasn't in his right mind back then."

"You're a broken record," Lex spits. "Always making excuses for him."

"You must understand," Danner pleads. "He was a wild, enraged animal in those early years. I think he saw it as a grave disrespect to Miranda and Michael's memories for Odette to have conceived under such illicit circumstances. It's an affront to the institution of East End." He twists the kerchief with his gnarled fingers, seeming to have difficulty with his next words. "So he locked her up. In fact, she was the first."

Pace staggers back, eyes filled with horror. "No."

"Yes," Danner says, meeting his gaze. "She was locked down in the dungeon for her entire third trimester, and then…"

Verity lifts a trembling hand to her mouth. "Pace was *born* down there?"

Danner scoots forward in the chair, eyes beseeching. "He couldn't let her keep you. It would have been unbearable to watch such a bastardization of motherhood in his state. He gave her a choice. Either they could both spend the rest of their lives in that cell, or they could both leave it—separately."

"He wouldn't let them out until she signed him away," Lex guesses, snarling. "That sick son of a bitch."

"After you were gone," Danner says to Pace, "Odette and your father made a… mutually beneficial deal." He gives the kerchief another twist, smiling at Pace. "I always thought you had her eyes."

Pace's hands ball into tight fists, jaw tight. "Is she dead? Did he use her and throw her away, just like all the others?"

Danner sinks back into his chair, shifting his gaze to the window. Outside of it, the wisteria has climbed the stone exterior, so thick that it obscures half the view. He watches as a passing breeze makes the petals shiver and sway.

"Perhaps," is his dull answer. "Perhaps not."

Lex and I share a glance, understanding that this discussion is roughly the equivalent of an old man's deathbed confession. If there's something else he knows—something he's taking to his grave—then there's no torture in the world that would get it out of him.

An hour later, Pace is still arguing against the truth of this. "We can still make him talk," he reasons, stalking back and forth across the parlor we've retreated to. His eyes are full of rage, fists flexing. "We should put him down in the dungeon with Father."

I sigh. "Dude, he's like a million years old. We'd pull his tooth and kill him."

"Then we start with fingernails," he snaps.

Lex and I have never been able to relate to Pace's dogged determination to find out who his parents were. We've always just known. They might be fuzzy and borderline mythical to us as adults, but we have a grasp on where we come from.

Pace deserves that.

Lex says, "I can't tell you what happened to your mother, but..." He looks at Verity, and I see understanding dawn on her face. "But I can tell you what happened to your father. Your *real* father."

Pace freezes, turning to meet my gaze. "What?"

Exhaling, Lex leans forward, propping his elbows on his knees. He gives his linked fists a long, considering look. "Remember when I took those blood samples from the West Enders?" The only thing that greets him is silence, and I watch as Pace hovers over him, brows knitted in confusion.

"You found a hit?" he asks. "Already?"

I raise my hand. "When the fuck did this happen?" Nobody keeps me in the loop anymore. *Assholes.*

"I didn't want to get anyone's hopes up," Lex explains, tossing me an apologetic look. "And you suck at keeping secrets from each other. *Don't,*" he warns, "deny it."

I roll my eyes.

Clearing her throat, Verity explains, "There was someone I sort of suspected. Someone I know. So, I asked Lex to compare his DNA with yours—just to speed things up and leave others their privacy."

Lex nods. "And she was right."

Pace sinks into the couch suddenly, my eyes tracking him the whole way. "Who is it?"

Verity straightens, voice reluctant. "You've met him, actually. It's, uh," she tosses me a nervous look, "Pauly. You know, from the gym?"

Pace's face goes slack as he takes this in. "That guy's my father?" he asks, but there's not a trace of skepticism in his tone. He knows

Lex would never bring him news like this without being completely certain. His brows crash together in a frown. "Does *he* know?"

Verity shrugs, a helpless tilt to her mouth. "I don't know. I mean... I haven't said or asked him anything."

"We should go there," I say, standing. Lex was right. This thing about keeping family revelations under lock and key? It's bullshit.

Secrets aren't the kind of power I want.

That's Rufus' MO.

"Pauly," Pace says the name like he's testing it out, rolling it around his tongue. He crosses his arms over his chest, and then uncrosses them. "Well." He crosses them *again*. "Fuck him."

Verity shoots Lex a stunned look. "What do you mean?"

Pace's jaw goes tight. "I mean he fucking left us to rot here, so he can rot in West End."

I watch, deflating as he storms off. When I turn my gaze to Lex, I raise an eyebrow. "Bet my secret family reveal with Remy is looking real smooth right about now, huh?"

Usually, after something unpleasant, I sleep like a baby. Torture sessions, nights out at Mayfield, championship losses. I chalk it up to years of desensitization. It's hard to be upset when everything is upsetting.

But tonight, I'm wide awake, staring straight up at the ceiling and holding Verity a little closer than before.

I think of all the nights Danner tucked us into our beds. The way he'd keep the light on in the hall for Pace, or move Lex's shoes out of the doorway in case he sleepwalked and stumbled. I think of the end of each day and the words I'd speak to his old, hunched, retreating silhouette.

Goodnight, Danner.

I lay there for so long that the overwhelming urgency I felt during her month in West End rises back up. It writhes inside of me, just like the monthly melon I can feel shifting in her belly. Like some incomprehensibly small appendage is reaching for me through her flesh.

It requires a lot of patience and care to slip out of bed without waking any of them. Once I do, I stand at the foot, assessing them all. As if sensing my absence, Lex rolls toward her, burying his nose in her hair. Pace is buried inside of her as she curls around the lingering warmth on my pillow.

It's them I think about as I grab Pace's T-shirt off the desk chair. While I'm pulling it on, in the muted darkness of this room I've come to see as safe and warm, it hits me that this isn't all just temporary. The nursery is finished, and it's been decorated with care—the kind you don't just throw away.

As I walk down the hall to the security room, I try to think of the palace in this light. *Home.* With all its nooks and crannies and secrets, it doesn't feel anything like the abomination I used to think of it as. It feels familiar and full of potential, and as I creep down the stairs to the kitchen, I do what Remy Maddox once accused me of.

I put dibs on it.

Mine, I think as I fill the kettle, and *mine* as I wait for the water to boil, and *mine-all-fucking-mine* as I pull the tray out of a cabinet, getting everything in order. I don't have very far to carry it, and when I reach Danner's door, I don't even consider knocking.

When I walk into the room, he's sitting up in bed, a book fanned open in front of him.

He doesn't look shocked to see me. "You're back, my boy," he says, offering me that same soft smile I've known all my life. "I thought you may be the one to return."

I set the tray down on his bedside table, making sure everything is prepared just-so. He's done this for me—for my brothers, for Red—so many times that it twists something in my gut to realize how close any of us may have come to the end.

"We had a discussion after we left earlier," I say, lingering at the foot of his bed. "They're going to kill you."

He doesn't look surprised at this, either. "I suspected as much."

I avert my gaze, wishing I could be stone like Lex, or angry like

Pace. "My brothers are good at killing, as I'm sure you know by now. But the kind of killing they're good at..." I shrug, accepting it at face value. "It's not quick. That's not what we were created to do. So I guess I'm going to give you something you probably never gave those women you buried out back." I square my shoulders. "A choice."

Danner glances at the tray. "I suppose you're not here to set me free, are you?" When all I do is stare at the cup of tea, he nods. "So you're going to kill me."

"Don't think of it as murder," I say, voice clipped and crisp. "Think of it as mercy."

It's difficult not to see this as a show of weakness. The death I'm offering him—a death of his own making—is the easy way out. A Duke like Remy would shoot him in the head. A Baron like my father would cut him until there was no more blood left to give.

But blood means nothing in this family, and I'm not them.

"I used to think I loved you," I say, looking around the squat room. He's lived here longer than even Rufus has been alive. "You were the closest thing we ever had to a real father. A grandfather, maybe."

Danner reaches for the cup. "Then I couldn't die prouder."

But I watch him take it, lifting the mug to his lips, and decide, "It was a lie. You were too loyal to him to defend us. To protect us. To save us." I watch his throat swell with the first gulp, stomach twisting. "I wanted to love you because I wanted to be loved, and I didn't know what it looked like—felt like." With a speed I didn't know he was still capable of, he tips back the cup and swallows the whole thing in three strong swallows. I exhale shakily, looking away, and he coughs.

"Whitaker, look at me." His voice is thin and wan, and when I meet his gaze, he offers me a gentle grin. "Don't despair over this. I'm not afraid. I've lived a long, loyal life, pledged to the glory of creation. I know you won't believe me, but my actions with you and your brothers were true. I did my best to protect you from him, to heal your wounds, and to keep you fed and safe." The cup rattles against the dish as he sets it back onto the tray. "I'm aware that what I did for you wasn't enough, but I feel peace knowing that any one of Rufus' children will be an excellent leader for East End."

If I was expecting to feel triumph, then I'm wrong. Mostly, I just feel sad. Danner's killed people, but so have we. There's no mercy in what my brothers and I do. No special teas. No quick ends. There's no satisfaction in watching this old, frail man grimace as the poison meets his stomach.

But I can't trust him with my life anymore.

Not with my brothers'.

Not with my Princess'.

Not with my son's.

When I place my hand on his, holding his foggy-eyed stare, I can only think of two words to part with. They're the same words I spoke to him every night as a child as he tucked me into bed.

"Goodnight, Danner."

He gives me a feeble smile, eyelids fluttering closed. "Goodnight, Whitaker."

I leave the tray and the old man behind. When I close the door behind me, locking it, I'm thinking that when Pace and Lex come for him in eight hours, all they'll find is a corpse. I'm so caught up in the notion that a shifting shadow across the hall startles me.

But as soon as my gaze jerks up, I catch the color of fire, Verity's wild hair framing a pale face. "You didn't have to do that alone," she says, stepping into the light. Her eyes are brimming with unshed tears. "How long will it take?"

Realizing that she heard the whole thing, I sigh, raking my fingers through my hair. "Three, four hours, maybe."

For some reason that I don't quite understand, she approaches me like I'm a spooked animal. She takes these tiny, slow steps, her eyes never leaving mine, until she's so close that the apex of her belly grazes mine.

Gently, she lifts a hand, placing a palm against my cheek. "You are loved, you know."

Her eyes are so unbearably penetrating that my stomach clenches. "Sometimes..." I start, needing to catch my breath. "Sometimes it really fucks me up to know that everything I've come to love was given to me by Father." I glance down at her belly, thinking even that hasn't been untainted by his influence. But when I push my hand out, grazing against the heat of her stomach, I don't feel the bitterness. "I used to wonder if it was even real, like maybe I'm just making the best of it, or maybe I'm so broken that I cling to the smallest crumb of warmth, claiming it like a parasite."

Immediately, she insists, "That's not true."

"It was with Danner," I argue, reaching up to take her face in my hands. I hold her there as I look into her eyes. "But it's not with you."

"I love you too," she says, repeating what I didn't exactly say, but she understood anyway. "And so will he."

I've tortured the truth out of men before. Their deepest, darkest secrets. But Verity's confession isn't something forced. It's what I'd hoped for, it's something *real*, tangible. I kiss her mouth and take her hand, leading her away from what I accept as my past, instead guiding her back upstairs to our future.

erity

"THIS CEREMONY WILL BE DIFFERENT," Pace says, not for the first time. He's huddled close, a finger hooked beneath my chin so I'll look him in the eye when he assures, "No one in there will hurt you. Don't forget," he adds, gently fingering one of the curls framing my face, "to create is to reign."

I stand in front of the same doors I entered the night of the masquerade when I was whisked from the ballroom into the ceremonial chamber. That night, I had no idea what I was getting into, only that there was an adventure ahead. I had no clue what was to come, but tonight is simple. It's planned.

Even so...

I feel Lex's hand on my lower back before I hear his words. "You're nervous."

"A little." I run my hands down the flowy gauze, thinking this might be the first ceremonial dress I've worn and liked. It's new, gifted to me by Rory Livingston's family, and comfortable. *So* comfortable, like wearing one of my nightdresses. It looks like something from an old Greek statue, the back of it slung around each shoulder and gathered below my breasts to make an empire waist. However, I do wonder, "Why do I always have to wear white to these?"

"Tradition," Lex says simply, his hand moving slowly up my spine, underneath my hair to the column of my neck. "And I like it, you look stunning."

"You look like a fucking goddess," Pace agrees, fingering the fabric covering my breasts. One tug would easily free them. "Jesus Christ, Rosi."

"Thank you." A warm blush heats every inch of my skin. "You two look pretty good, too."

Clad in dark suits, they're the embodiment of sex, distinction, and masculine power. Somewhere, underneath this massive belly, my panties feel damp.

"We can do this privately if you want," Lex says.

But I shake my head. This is the only ceremony I've ever felt good about—like it'll bring something positive to East End. "No, something formal seems right. I just..." I rest my hand on my stomach, the new Princess ring gleaming in the sconce light. I'm fully aware that as a shield, skin and bone will do nothing. "It's just that this room and I have a lot of history, and none of it's good."

There's an energy to this room I've been avoiding, and mine is only part of it. It needs a cleansing, and not the Royal kind. Something... spiritual. It's as if decades of thronings, cleansings, and de-crownings have left a lingering scum of negative vibes that permeate the plaster walls and marble floors. It's like it's embedded in the chandeliers and gold accents. Sometimes, I think we should do like Lavinia did and just blow the whole fucking place to smithereens.

But no.

I'm not letting *him* run my Princes out of their home—the home he forced on them. It's a pillar of Forsyth and it belongs to them, and since we're set on making this place into a home, we'll do what East Enders do.

We'll have a rebirth.

Announcing my son's name, his claim as heir, and gaining the approval of the frat is how we'll do it.

"Hopefully, this will be the end of it," Lex says, the way he tugs at the collar of his dress shirt telling me he feels it, too. "I think we've done the groundwork with the guys to gain their full support."

It's not all weekly luncheons, either. I had Story pull some strings with Dimitri Rathbone to get Baxter into the music program. Lex has been checking in with Loeffler's grandfather at the hospital every Wednesday night. Pace has been tutoring a couple of the CS guys, and Wicker donated Rufus' car to be auctioned off to benefit a charity run by Mitch's mother.

It's these tiny, incremental things over the last few months that have shaped a new, fragile brotherhood.

"And if they don't?" Wick asks. He tucks a flask into his jacket pocket as he walks up. I frown at the dark smudges under his eyes, which are still a touch troubled. He hasn't slept well since they found Danner, two mornings ago. At night, he curls next to me, holding on tighter than ever, but there's no sense of peace. Maybe this will help.

"They will," Pace says, with utter confidence. "Our son is the heir, and Verity is Father's blood..." He nods again. "They'll be on the side of creation."

I have to hope he's right, but I also know we're in Forsyth, a place where 'right' doesn't always mean much.

"You promised I'd get through the night without getting blood on my dress," I remind Lex.

For some reason, he glances at Pace, mouth tightening. "I'll do my best." He squeezes my hand. Pace's dark eyes hold mine as he places a hand on my belly and pulls me in for a kiss just hard enough to leave me breathless before he follows his brother to the door of the ceremonial room.

Wicker, as the father of the child, waits with me. It's another one of the reveals—officially, anyway. Word has spread, like gossip always does in Forsyth, that Wicker is most likely the biological father.

"Guess we're doing this." Running his hand through his hair, he tousles the blonde locks in that way I know is meant to make himself look like he doesn't care. They all have their armor on today. Lex's hair is pulled back. Pace has the palace crawling with security. Every inch of Wicker's body, from his hair to the casual way he stands, is adjusted into an air of giving zero fucks, which means he's on high alert. They've promised me everything will go smoothly, but I guess years of trauma-filled ceremonies will give even the strongest man some reservations. "But if you want to turn back now, hop in the car and go for burritos, I've got the keys."

It's all I can do not to drool, groaning instead. "As enticing as that sounds, they'll just drag us back and make us do it again later, so we may as well face it now." I adjust my dress, making sure my overripe tits aren't going to spill out. "I'm not sure I'm getting into this dress a second time anyway."

Lex gives Loeffler the go-ahead to open the doors, revealing the ceremonial room for us. We're met with the overpowering scent of roses. I asked Adeline for guidance, making sure to follow the traditions for an East End baby-naming ceremony. She'd been thrilled, digging through her archives with photographs and announcements for prior events. She helped me by contacting the caterer and Fran the florist, and even helped me unearth the traditional decor for the event.

'People, Verity,' she told me, while flipping through a photo book, 'especially like those in Forsyth, crave consistency. In a time of change, it's important to show them that you'll do whatever it takes to keep them safe.'

That's why, despite the chill of the massive room, there's warmth from the lit candelabras mounted in every arched window sill, and the purple carpet rolled out before us softens our footsteps on the marble floors. Wicker offers me the crook of his arm, and I slip mine into his.

For security reasons, Pace insisted we make this a PNZ-only event —no outsiders, not even Ballsy—and the men of the frat flank the carpet, creating a safe channel for us to walk through.

I look into each pair of eyes, skeptical but defiant.

It's impossible to forget the last time I made this walk. I'd been filled with both rage and fear. I was newly pregnant, the almost fully formed baby I'm carrying tonight barely a cluster of cells. I'd betrayed my Princes, publicly and harshly, and I'd been punished for it. Tonight, everything feels different, though. I'm not being forced down the aisle; I'm being escorted. The anger and hatred I felt directed at me by the PNZs that night are replaced by gentler expressions now, smiles, and even some genuine encouragement.

Part of me wants to yell and scream, to tell them to get on their knees and let me ruin them the way they ruined me, but I'm made for something bigger than a moment of revenge.

I'm made to be the mother of a king.

Ahead, at the end of the royal carpet, four men wait. Lex and Pace are in the center, while Matt and Rory stand on each side. As we get closer, they step aside, revealing a backward throne. It doesn't matter that it's not the throne I was forced to bleed and ache on. For a brief moment, I stiffen, remembering the sensation of being torn into and held down. Next to the backward throne is a table covered in a white cloth that's been embroidered in gold thread. There's an object in the center, wrapped in white linen, and the setting doesn't give me any comfort.

I didn't arrange or approve either of these.

"I never apologized for that night," Wick whispers, his eyes pinned to the table as well. "The way I claimed you after your throning..." His jaw tightens, which is the only reason I realize it's the same table he bent me over, stealing my virginity and innocence with untethered brutality. "I was just so fucking angry," he says, blue eyes swimming with the memory. It's impossible not to remember the words he said to me that night after giving Danner the tea.

Sometimes it really fucks me up to know that everything I've come to love was given to me by Father...

Wicker isn't the type to say words like that aloud. I understood what he was trying to tell me then, and I didn't need the words because I felt them.

So it brings me up short to hear him say these.

"I'm sorry." His voice is low but strained, and when he glances at me, I see the regret. "I thought he was chaining me to him, and I resented you—everything about you. But I'm starting to realize that's what he wanted. He never wanted us to think of you as a gift." He rests his hand on top of mine and gives it a squeeze. "But you were, Red. You were a gift. And that's what this is. Remember that."

An apology by Wicker Ashby is enough to steal my breath, but the gut punch comes a moment later when Rory and Matt move to turn the throne, and it's not empty.

My father is sitting in it.

A quiet murmur rushes through the crowd, revealing that I'm not the only one surprised. It's not just his presence that's shocking, but the state of him. Their King isn't just sitting on the throne, he's strapped in, limbs secured at the ankles and wrists. Someone cleaned him up and dressed him in a tux, but there's little hiding the abuse he suffered. A welt on his cheek. Burn marks peeking out from beneath his collar. Thin strips of tape suturing a deep, raw cut on his forehead. The hand resting on the arm of the throne is missing two fingers, the stumps purple and grotesque.

And that's just what they can *see*, the pentagram Wicker carved into his chest hidden from view.

The only reason Ashby isn't spewing his toxicity is the gag in his mouth. Unfortunately, he isn't blindfolded because his blue eyes are trained on me. They dip down to my stomach, widening, and he tugs futilely against his restraints. Wicker lifts his chin but keeps his gait easy as he encourages me to walk all the way to his brothers.

The first thing out of my mouth is, "Why the fuck is he here?"

The guys share a look.

"This isn't a naming ceremony," I guess, halting. "This is a... decrowning?"

Lex argues, "It is a naming ceremony," and lifts a hand to stroke my belly. "But if the frat blesses it, it'll also be the beginning of our son's ascension."

Pace adds, "We didn't want you worrying over the vote."

"Now?" I ask, feeling more than a bit blindsided, but the resolution in their expressions tells me this wasn't a sudden decision. I look back toward my father, and then sweep my gaze over the men in the room. Just like my Princes, they're dressed in their malicious best, black ties and coattails. The scent of their collective cologne and aftershave is a radiant, throbbing thing, but mostly I sense their restless energy.

These are terrible men, and in Forsyth, there's only two things to do with terrible men.

Kill them or recruit them.

I take a deep breath. "Okay."

Tommy, on the other hand, isn't okay. "What the hell is this? Why is the King bound and gagged?"

Lex steps forward, eyes hardening. "As you can see, your King hasn't been away on business for the last few months. He's been here, secure in the dungeon. He was placed there after we discovered that he was the one responsible for the attacks on the Princess and the palace."

"Bullshit," someone in the crowd mutters. "The King would never kill his daughter and grandson."

"You'd think that," I say, trying to keep my voice even, "but you've all seen—*and* participated in—the lengths my father will go to in order to keep me in line. There's not a man in the room who can deny that."

Gazes shift, feet shuffle, and no one does.

"He hired a Baron to do the dirty work," Wick announces, lifting his chin. "Their own King confirmed it before offering his Baron up to me as a sacrifice for the affront."

"You killed a Baron?" a voice says. "Fuck. That's savage."

"That's what a *real* father does for his son," Wicker replies, eyes sharp as blades. "Rufus made an attempt on my blood, and in return, he's paid the price, too."

"You're the father?" Matt asks, and I see it, the shift in respect as they all regard him. These men buy into this world hook, line, and sinker. The fact that Wicker's sperm fought its way upstream to fertilize my egg sheds him in a new light.

Dory barks a joyful laugh. "Fuck, man, congratulations!"

If I didn't know better, I'd think a spot of color rises to his cheeks. "This baby is mine and Verity's, and by the rules of Psi Nu Zeta, also my brothers'. But hear this," he adds, meeting the eyes of each man in the room. "Rufus Ashby has no claim to him, not after what we've learned."

Pace thrusts a hand out, pointing to the King. "This man is not a creator." Face hard, he looks at Rufus, lip curling in disgust. "He's nothing. He's firing blanks."

A wave of confused mutters rise over the room.

"What does that mean?" Tommy asks.

"He's medically infertile," Lex confirms as he approaches the throne. Seeming to derive satisfaction from the way Rufus pales, he leans forward, spitting the words like venom. "It seems that after Verity and Michael, he was unable to impregnate anyone else. And trust us," he slams his hands onto Rufus' arms, meeting his glare with a stony smirk, "he tried."

"Farrah Baxter." Pace clasps his hands behind his back as he strolls down the front row, pausing in front of Dorian Baxter. "Dethroned as Princess and held captive in the palace dungeon for ten months while Rufus raped her. She was abused—defiled—and then murdered."

Dory stares at him, face slack. "Farrah Baxter? My father's sister?" He shifts his gaze to Rufus. "That's not possible. She ran away to their grandparents' home in Korea forever ago. I never even met her."

"You can meet her now, if you like." Pace doesn't look happy to give the news, his own eyes swirling with turmoil. "Her bones are still in the basement. We kept them for you, so your family can put her to rest." Dory is still reeling from the news, but Pace suddenly spins, stalking down the aisle. "Margo Hampton. Held captive in the palace dungeon for five months. Murdered." He stops in front of Julian Carter, who for some reason seems to know the name.

"Hampton?" he asks, stunned. "Was she—"

"Chloe's second cousin," Pace confirms, and I realize why he stopped at Julian. Chloe is his girlfriend. "You wouldn't know the other three women whose bones we found buried in the solarium,"

Pace goes on, returning to the front of the room. "They were just women. No old money names or reputations. They never had the chance to build any."

The room falls silent as they all take in the horrific details of lives lost to this man. A man who forced his body and will on them until there was nothing left but bones and dirt.

"Yes," Pace says, turning his gaze to Ashby, "even Danner betrayed your pitiful ass."

It's a verbal hit, but the punch lands, Rufus unable to hide his shock at Danner ratting him out. If this were a coffin, his would have just been nailed shut.

"Rufus Ashby spent his life extolling the virtues of creation," Lex says, turning his back on his father. "We've learned that Rufus Ashby isn't a creator. He's an instrument of death, and nothing more. He's a selfish, narcissistic megalomaniac who's never made East End his priority. If he had, he would have stepped down two decades ago. He was focused on his own needs. His own failed desire to procreate. His lust for torture and control." Lex's amber eyes glow violently in the candlelight. "As his sons and Princes, it's true that we're trained to apply pressure when needed. But we don't do it for our own pleasure. We do it for the good of this kingdom. That's the difference."

It's almost like Wicker absorbs the energy because suddenly he's raising his voice. "He took our ideals and twisted them into something ugly and wasteful," he insists. "He *wasted* our women. Our creators. Our mothers and sisters. He used their flesh and discarded them when he was finished."

The room is quiet for a moment, until Dorian asks, "What are you asking us to do?"

"We handle situations like this internally. No police or external investigations." Lex pulls out the PNZ pledgebook and flips to a bookmarked page in the middle. "The King can abdicate, stepping down with grace and accepting his failed position. If he refuses, we can invoke an Oath of Fealty, where each member can decide if they want the King to continue to rule, despite the evidence presented today."

"And who'd be King instead?" Tommy asks, raising his voice over the din. "You?"

Lex is unfathomably steady as he puts down the book. "We've given a lot of thought to that, actually. I can't deny that I'd make an awful King. Since I'm about to begin med school, you're all aware I have ambitions that'd require too much of my dedication and attention." He gestures to his brothers. "Wick would make a fantastic King. He'd forge alliances that would enrich us, and he'd run the Royal businesses like a well-oiled machine. But he'd be miserable in a position that ties him to the obligations of ruling, and I won't ask it of him. And Pace," he adds, sighing. "My brother would make this kingdom prosperous and safe, but he'd never get to feel any peace, always looking over his shoulder."

Dorian looks confused. "If not any of you, then who?"

"All of us," Lex says, nodding at my belly. "Or rather, all of us until our son—the true heir—comes of age. And you can be assured," he calls out over the rising protests, "our child will be taught how to rule properly—"

"He'll be taught *kindness*," I snap, giving Lex a disbelieving staredown. Turning to the men in the audience, I say, "My child will be given a choice to rule or not, but if he does, it'll be to make East End a home that's safe for his mother, his sisters, and his future daughters as well as yours." I rest my hand on my belly, watching the way the dress tugs and pleats under the pressure. "If that's not a kingdom you're willing to serve, then de-crown me now. I'll take my Princes and child with me when I leave, because I'll—" I swallow, "—*we'll* want nothing to do with it."

A hush falls over the room, and I'm only mildly disarmed by Lex's apologetic grin. "What she said."

But Tommy shoots forward, demanding, "The King should get to say his piece, shouldn't he?"

My stomach builds with dread at the naked betrayal in Tommy's eyes. I'd come so far with him. For him to see this as deceit is disappointing.

"Fine." Pace gestures to the men next to Rufus and Matt yanks the gag out of his mouth. Ashby coughs, and then swallows repeatedly before clearing his throat one last time.

"Matthew." He gives him a look of disdain. "I always knew you didn't have what it took for true leadership, always chasing the next thing." He swings his gaze to Rory. "But you, Rory, I expected more of you. You come from fine Royal stock. If it hadn't been for my own children coming of age, you would have been Prince."

Rory's face flickers with annoyance. "And I'm sure in the next two years, my sister might have become Princess. I mean, if she weren't missing," he adds, tossing Rufus a searing glare. "A lot of Royal women seem to go missing around you."

Before Rufus can deny it, Wicker scoffs. "These are your final words, old man? Insults to the next generation?"

Ashby swings a glower around the room. "I have no fear of this generation, or the next, or the one after that. Your stories are nothing more than fabrications to justify your treasonous actions." He sniffs, able to put on an air of pretentiousness even while bound like a prisoner. "Even if it was true, I'm a King. I rule this territory. I choose who lives and dies. Who creates." His eyes land on his sons, and I feel the struggle between them. A father trying to get his children in line. Grown men, ready to forge their own lives. "Do they know what you've done? How you've locked away their King for months on end, and undoubtedly ruined everything I've spent the last two decades building in East End while you were playing house with my daughter?"

Dryly, Lex answers, "Well, we did just tell them."

"And did you tell them about all your new Royal friendships? Oh," he says at the looks on our faces. "You think I don't know that you've allowed the FBI into our gates, and forged relationships with our truest enemies, the Lords and Dukes." His eyes spark to life. "Yes, Lagan, I know you saved Nick Bruin's life." To Wicker, he adds, "I know you've tasted the curse of your bloodline." Rufus lifts his chin toward Pace. "I know you're still seeking a truth you'll never find. One I'll never give you." Rufus releases a chilling, ragged laugh. "And to you, daughter. You think I don't know you're thirty-five weeks pregnant, craving salted mango, still fretting over your missing hand-maiden, and trying your best to tame my sons?" He shifts his gaze to my Princes, snarling. "You think you're in control, that you've got a handle on this kingdom, but I always know what's happening in my house. In my kingdom. With my *creations.*"

I freeze, heart in my throat.

He shouldn't know these things, and from the look Wicker gives me, he's thinking the same thing. Wick's been so careful about keeping him contained like a quarantined virus. The things he knows are so precise, so personal, that he can't know them.

But somehow he does.

Grinning, Rufus declares, "No, I will not be abdicating my king-dom, nor my throne. Because I know what you don't. That the men of PNZ aren't behind you. They're behind me. As always."

His confidence is unwavering, and for a moment, I feel like I'm back kneeling on that carpet in front of the fireplace. We're all kneeling because we've taken a swing that we cannot miss. Yet the fist just whiffed past Rufus' head and, fuck.

We're screwed.

"Thomas," Rufus' voice rings out clear and controlled. "Start the proceeding."

Tommy emerges from the crowd and passes us, a smirk lifting his lips. There's no doubt I read the whole thing wrong with him. I'd never won him over. I'd never repaired the rift.

I didn't do my job.

A sense of hopelessness drapes over me like a weighted cloak as I watch, nearly disassociating from my body as Tommy steps up to the table and removes the cloth. Underneath sits a crystal bowl and a purple velvet pillow. Placed on top is a sharp-bladed dagger with a gold, jeweled handle, the hilt flared out in the design of a crown, similar to the bed up in my room. He lifts it, allowing the glint of light to pass over the metal, revealing the PNZ crest and letters forged into the blade.

"In the face of opposition," Tommy says, lifting the knife, "fealty must be declared."

His movements are slow and precise, and Wicker tenses next to me, ready to take action if Tommy makes a move. They called for this ceremony—I fucking planned it—but there's nothing we can do now but see it through.

Tommy stands before my father, shoulders tipped back. Pace's shoulders rise when Tommy lifts his left hand, and in a quick move, slices the tip of the blade across his palm. He turns to face his frat brothers, and as blood runs down his hand, he makes a fist. "I swear my fealty to the King of East End."

He turns, but not to face my father. Instead, he stares down at me with fire in his eyes. In the corner of my vision, a flash of purple falls to the floor—the pillow.

And then Tommy Wright drops to his knees.

Startled, I lurch back, but not before Tommy has thrust out his bloody hand, placing it on the crown of my distended stomach. Holding my stunned gaze, he dips his chin. "To create," he says, voice like steel, "*is* to reign."

Warmth from the blood seeps through the dress and into my flesh. Standing, he faces Rufus, whose expression is twisted in fury. "Don't trust him!" he hisses. "He's the one that came to me, spilling secrets of your ill-conceived mutiny."

"I've proven my loyalty," Tommy says, wiping the blade on his thigh. "Just not to you, but to the throne. You thought I was working for you," he smirks over his shoulder at Pace, "but in reality, I was working for them."

From there, the dominos fall. He hands the knife to Dorian, who makes his own long, deep cut before placing his blood-soaked hand against my belly. "To create is to reign."

Theodore Loeffler follows, and then Dexter, Mitchell, and Matt Kramus. I don't think I even break out of the shocked daze until Rory gets on his knees before me, raising a bloody palm to my stomach.

"To create is to reign," he says, and when I place my hand over his, holding it close, a tear slips down my cheek.

"I'm sorry we haven't found her, Ror."

Slowly, he shakes his head. "It wouldn't make a difference,

Princess. I know a kind heart when I see it. That's all we need from you."

Another twenty men kneel to stain my dress, but for the first time, I'm proud to have my white dress bloodied. With each man who looks me in the eye, pledging their oath to my son, the memory of the throning—the cleansing—grows more and more hazy and undefined. The men who watched and participated in those vile ceremonies didn't know me, and I hadn't yet realized how strangled their hearts were by Ashby's rule.

There could be no greater proof of Rufus Ashby's failed kingship than the knowledge he hadn't snuffed everything good out of his own men.

I just hope I can keep finding more of it.

It's harder when the line ends because now it's just the three of them.

My Princes.

Lex takes the knife first, kneeling on the pillow with a crooked grin. "I want you to know this is fucking disgusting, and I'm running a million tests on you tomorrow." Still, he slices his palm, placing it over the blood-soaked fabric with a grimace. "To create is to reign."

Pace follows, licking his lips as he kneels. "You're getting off on this, aren't you?"

My laugh is half delirious. "Absolutely."

He doesn't even flinch when he slices his palm, but then he drops the knife, taking my belly in both hands. "To create is to reign," he whispers, leaning in to brush his lips against my belly.

Wicker, however, is silent as he drops to his knees, cutting into his flesh. "To create is to reign," he breathes.

Reaching out, I stroke my fingers through his hair, watching his eyelashes flutter. "Are you okay with this?"

His blue eyes rise to meet mine, and there's no reservation there. Instead, the silence is heavy, filled with the weight of significance. "I never thought I'd be able to pass on a real legacy," he says, the candlelight glinting in his eyes. "This is..." Visibly struggling to find the words, he pauses, inhaling, "everything, Red. *Everything.*"

Lex steps in then, clearing his throat. "Rule of law says the new King has to kill the old one. But since our son's hands are a little too small to hold the knife, we decided it'd be—"

"The Princess," Rory calls out, gesturing to me. "Obviously."

No one's more surprised by the suggestion than me, but I can't deny the logic.

When I meet Lex's gaze, I don't waver. "Until he's born, I'm an extension of him," I explain, unwilling to bring a failure of tradition into this. "Any wrong move could put us at risk. I'll do it." But when I reach for the knife, Wicker pulls it away, frowning.

"Red..." he begins, shifting uncomfortably. "Murder isn't something you come back from."

"Neither is this," I insist, cradling my belly. *Creation and destruction, two sides of the same coin.* "I can handle it."

Pace looks like he wants to argue, but from one glance around the room, it's clear the men agree with Rory.

So he hands me the knife.

I've never killed a person before. Wicker is probably right. Murder isn't something I can wipe away from my inner slate. The knife is heavy in my hand, but it's also warm from the heat of forty hands. That's the notion that consumes me as I round the purple throne, unwilling to look my father in the eye one last time.

Rufus struggles against his binds again, thrashing and shrieking. "You will tell me!" he's crying out. "This is a naming ceremony. You will tell me the name of my heir. You will tell them it's Michael!"

It's sad is what it is. Rufus Ashby lost his family, and if there was ever a human morsel in his heart to begin with, he never got it back. I think of him strangling this kingdom and turning it to ash. I think of Lex's pained eyes after that whipping. I think of the way Pace can never quite relax until he's alone with me in a room. I think of Wicker, two nights before, and the agony in his eyes when he questioned if his love was real.

I think of my mother.

But mostly, when I grip a handful of Ashby's hair, yanking his head back to expose his throat, I think of my son.

Of making this kingdom a home for him.

Of hope and change.

Putting the blade to his neck, I take a deep breath, letting that anger—the West End fury that flows through my veins—infuse my voice with stone. "I'd never name my creation after you," I tell him, pushing the blade into his skin. "I'm naming him after *this*."

The knife slices as I yank it to the side, feeling the tendon cut. A wet gurgle sounds out, but I don't look down as I hold him by the hair. Not to watch his blood spill. Not to see the life fading from his eyes. Not even to see how long it takes for his final breath to spill out of his wound.

I watch my Princes, tall and strong, as I give them a gift almost as good as our creation.

"Justice." Dropping the knife, I square my shoulders. "Our son will be named Justice."

17

L^{ex}

I'M CHECKING the spray under my hand when I hear the sound of Verity's whisper.

Shaking my wrist, I walk back toward the bedroom, peeking through the doorway. She's walking—not pacing, not striding, just aimless, idle walking from one side of the room to the other. She looks tired but alert, a strange wildness in her eyes.

And she's talking. "You don't have to," she says, giving the side of her belly a mindless rub. "But if you want it, I'll make sure it's yours. Your dad, Wicker—he didn't get that. I think it's important. But not everyone wants to be King. It might be an awful lot of work."

I realize she's talking to him.

Justice.

We decided we'd let her name him long ago, but until tonight, she'd been keeping her choice to herself. Likewise, she doesn't know what my brothers and I chose for his middle name yet.

The blood on her dress doesn't bother me, either. Maybe it's because of my lessons in the art of torture, which Father started when we were young. Or learning to draw blood at the clinic. Or suturing older PNZs before I was even a pledge. It could be from seeing my own bloody back after Father's punishments. Maybe a lot of it's from a youth spent in hockey leagues where the more blood, the better.

But a small, secret part of me worries that it's older than medical training or hockey. Something so old that the sight of sticky, congealing crimson has become a stone in my foundation. Because maybe it's from that night, when my father killed my mother. I don't remember much, but I've seen the reports.

They found me caked in my mother's blood.

It's something Wicker and I always had in common—being brought into this strange house of decadence under a layer of death and decay.

Verity's origin in the palace is also marked in red, and as much as she hates it, there's something glorious about the way she looks in that white dress, bloody handprints covering her abdomen. To steal a phrase from her Dukes...

She's a fucking victor.

"It'll take a minute for the water to warm up."

She startles at the sound of my voice, but just looks up, giving me a small grin. "Oh. Sorry. I was just..." She gestures at her stomach. "Giving him the rundown." It's not the first time one of us has caught her doing that—giving baby Justice an outline of the day's events.

The shower pounds behind me. Since Wick and Pace stayed back to call the Barons and secure the palace, leaving me and Verity to get her cleaned up and into bed, I beckon her into the bathroom. Once she's there, I move behind her, unzipping the back of the dress to reveal creamy, soft skin. I push the fabric over her shoulders, down her arms, and over her belly, until it falls in a heap around her feet. "Anything hurt?" I ask. "Any pain?"

She shakes her head. "I feel fine. Just tired, yet also... wired?" She sighs, one I know is from exhaustion, and I place my hands under her belly and lift, taking some of the burden.

She shudders out a breath, leaning into me. "God, that's so much better."

I feel the weight of it—our son—and ask the question I've been dreading. "Are you... bothered? By what you did?" The first kill is always the worst. Victor or not, I don't like to think of Verity as a killer. To me, she's the embodiment of creation. To tarnish that with death and violence...

"Should I be?" She turns just enough to show me the curve of her cheek, brow furrowed. "I should feel remorse, right?"

I pull in the scent of her hair. "You should feel whatever you feel."

Her mouth works around a stilted reply. "I feel... relieved, mostly. He was a monster who helped bring me into this world, and I helped take him out of it."

I bend to kiss that place on her neck. "That's the Royal way."

She hums. "Do you think that makes me a terrible person?"

Pausing, I keep hold of the weight of her belly as I dredge up the memory. "I remember feeling fascinated with my first kill. The way his lungs shook—the sight of his flesh torn open—it was the first time I looked at a human body and saw a machine. And I was... well, annoyed, to be honest," I confess, hoping she doesn't think less of me. "I remember it taking a lot longer than I was expecting, and it made me super late for lunch."

She strains her neck to glance at me, like she's trying to decide if I'm lying or not.

Gravely, I explain, "It was my favorite casserole."

What I don't say is that my first murder victim was a rapist of princesses, too. An ex-Count, to be exact. Lionel Lucia and Father gave him to my brothers and me for experimenting. For training. For... experience.

Verity doesn't need to know that part. She only needs to know this: "You did such a good job tonight." I lave my tongue over her throat, tasting copper. "I'm sorry we didn't give you the heads-up. Everything had to play out just right." I let her lean into me, tipping her head back to rest on my shoulder. Her hand wanders above my head, finding the tie holding my hair back and tugging it loose.

She whispers, "I think I understand."

But I still explain, "There was no way of knowing if Rufus would come to his senses and actually abdicate, or if he did have a mole in the group and not just Tommy pretending to give him what he wanted. It needed to unfold as organically as possible so no one can say we manipulated it."

Her fingers comb idly through my hair. "Did you know they would choose him?"

"Honestly, we weren't sure. They could have picked any of us." I graze my thumbs up and down the underside of her belly. "But I think they made the right decision. We're more mature now, and we've proven we can manage East End in a crisis. The rest will sort itself out. Right now," I add, gazing down the curves of her body, "we have a baby to focus on."

She settles against me, her hands sliding over mine, and together, for a few quiet heartbeats, we carry this weight together. There's a small thump against my palm, and I jolt. She cranes her head to look at me, offering a tired smile. "He's *very* awake."

I flatten my hand over the area and revel in the feel of our son moving around. "Can I..." I begin, feeling inexplicably embarrassed. "Can I talk to him?"

Her smile widens. "Of course. He can't come out of there only recognizing me and Effie, can he?"

I snort. "Turn around," I tell her, wanting to check the rest of her before she gets under the water. Her front is a contrast from the pale, clean flesh on her back. My scrutiny goes to her abdomen first. Every inch of her bulging stomach is tinted red, the bloody handprints seeping past the linen and onto her flesh. Above, there's a slash of blood spatter from cutting Rufus' throat.

I scan her for injuries, although I know there are none—at least, not externally. She inflicted the wounds—the death blow.

She's the one who broke our chains.

As I kneel before her, just like I did when I swore my oath of fealty, that's the first thing I tell our creation. "Your mother is a real badass," I say, shivering at the sensation of her fingers carding through my hair. To her belly—to *Justice*—I whisper, "I know this is a weird family you're being born into. But we're really excited to meet you."

Thump.

Verity chuckles at the look on my face. "Actually, he already knows the sounds of all your voices."

I blink up at her, amazement clear in my voice. "How do you know?"

"It's all in the way he moves." She bites her lip, seeming to consider this deeply. "With Wicker, he sort of... stretches? I swear, it's like my belly gets bigger. And Pace's voice always makes him kick and twitch, these little punches that feel like flutters. And you..." She pushes my hair back, an unbearable softness in her eyes. "When he hears your voice, he squirms around, like he's turning, searching..."

A lump finds its way into my throat as I watch her belly shift, almost imperceptibly. "You're sure nothing hurts?" I ask, watching her carefully.

"Lex."

I know that tone, so I let it go, knowing she's ready to wash off and get into bed. I ease her panties down her legs before leading her into the shower, and it's difficult to step away once she has. It's getting hard not to let the excitement in—the knowledge that in a couple short weeks, we'll be holding our son in our arms.

Once she steps under the spray, she peers back out, owlishly asking, "Aren't you coming?"

Pausing, I ask, "You want me to?"

I don't know how women work in situations like these. My brothers and I always processed our kills in different ways. Wick's always preferred getting lost in pleasure, slamming his hand over that dopamine button again and again. Pace has always turned to weed and his attachment to Effie. I've always just wanted—*needed*—to sleep it off in peace.

"Please?" Verity, it seems, wants to be close. That, I can give her.

I strip quickly, yanking at the buttons of my shirt and not caring if it rips. I kick off my shoes and shuck my pants, then step into the steamy shower. She watches me, eyes dropping down to my thick erection. I've been hard since I first touched her, and I'm even harder now that we're standing close together, nothing between us but water and steam.

The water rushes down her body but does little to remove the stain of red. There are a million of Wicker's various bottles on the shelf, and I pick one at random, liking the idea of her being washed in our scents.

Once my hands are lathered up, I start at her neck, eventually running my hands over her shoulders and chest. I use my thumbs to scrub away the droplets of Rufus' blood that are spattered there. With a deep sigh, she leans against the wall, letting the water rush straight against her chest.

"Does that feel good?" I know the heat can relieve pressure.

"Yes," she manages, and I continue, massaging her collarbones and dipping my hands down the deep crevice between her breasts. Her chest rises and falls, and despite the warm water rushing down her body, her nipples tighten and peak, making my cock knock into the underside of her belly. I cup her tits and push them together, eliciting her airy groan. "They just feel so full all the time."

"I knew once you started, it would only get worse." Letting Wick and Pace nurse from her was probably the most erotic thing I've ever witnessed. There was something so primal about following the path, the knowledge that they put their seed into her, let her nurture it into life, and then nourished themselves with it.

If my first kill taught me that bodies are machines, then watching Verity's change, evolve, *create*, has taught me the opposite.

"Do you want a taste?"

Her question draws my eyes upward, and it's obvious I've been caught staring—fantasizing. My tongue flattens against my teeth, the urge so bad that I nearly push her against the wall, latch on, and give her a forceful suck. But I drop my hands and squeeze more gel between them, focusing on cleaning the last traces of blood off of her stomach.

I grab the nozzle of the shower head and lift it off the dock, bringing it down to spray off all of the soap. Her hand catches mine, wet lashes fluttering. "I made it weird. I'm sorry, it's just...is it always like this? I know it was for Wicker, but..." Her eyes dart down, "Well, Wick *always* is..."

I touch her chin and lift her face up. "What are you talking about?"

"Horny." Her green eyes are so wide, far too innocent considering what she's done tonight. "Is it normal to be horny after doing what I did to Rufus?"

I take her in again, this time looking for more than injuries and strain. The blown-out eyes, the shallow breathing, the pebbled nipples. I nudge her down on the seat in the corner of the shower and stand over her, considering.

"Wicker once explained it like... causing death makes him want to experience life." Tilting my head, I add, "Which, medically, makes a sort of sense. You're full of endorphins. Adrenaline is pumping through your veins. Your system is on alert, and," I touch her stomach, "you just went into some primal protective mother mode. It's normal."

"Good." She licks her bottom lip, cheeks rosy and glistening. "Then what I'm going to do now totally makes sense."

She reaches for me, gripping me tight around my shaft. Her touch is forceful, but somehow still soft, her hand stroking me upward, pushing the blood toward the tip. Her tongue darts out to taste me, and then her lips circle around the head.

Moaning, she sucks.

"Fuck, Verity," I say, dropping the spray nozzle and bracing my hand against the glass door. She grips the base of my shaft and takes me in deeper, jacking me off with every pull. Shuddering, I stroke my fingers through her hair, overcome by the heat of her mouth. "Jesus Christ, baby, slow down or I'm gonna pop off."

I don't think she's going to, but right when my balls seize up, she releases me. Exhaling, I struggle to catch my breath, but it's not to slow down or stop. I know my role in this fledgling family we're creating.

If there's something her body needs, I'm going to provide it.

She pulls me toward her, hand still on the base of my shaft, and guides my cock between her tits. "If you won't suck them," she whispers, gazing up at me with lust-drunk eyes, "then fuck them, Lagan."

It's impossible to say no.

Every fantasy. Every thought I've had since I saw Verity's tits for the first time. Every medical exam and night sleeping next to her comes down to this moment. I can't feel anything but the warmth of her tits engulfing me.

So fucking good.

"I used to dream of this," I confess, voice embarrassingly guttural as I watch my cock pump between her tits. "In the early days, all those times you were on my exam table, your pussy so pink and wet for me," she moans and I grunt, feeling the vibration against my shaft, "I'd look up at you and see them—these perfect tits—and daydream about how they'd look once our seed took hold."

"Oh, god," she breathes, eyes slamming shut.

"Lean back," I tell her, pumping up and down to keep the friction. I cup her tits in both hands and squeeze them together, increasing the sensation. Her boobs are huge, and before I think, I tweak her nipple, eliciting a cry. "You tell me if it's too rough."

With her head propped lazily against the tile, she says, "The pressure feels good, don't you dare stop."

I couldn't if I tried.

Pumping into her, I say, "It really pisses me off that I couldn't give my seed to you like they did. I would have been so good at it, baby." The words tumble out of gritted teeth, any sanity obscured by the sight of her, panting, eyes glazed with stunned arousal. "I would have bred you day and night, so fucking eager to be the one who put my baby into you. That's what I'm gonna do when you're fertile for me again. Won't let you be empty again, Verity..."

"Lex," she whines, expression collapsing. "Keep going."

The intensity of the night takes over—*Lagan* takes over—and I rock into her, increasing the pace. Her eyes hold mine and it's so good this way, looking down at her face, the lights on, no sleep between us.

Her hands cup my balls, kneading at the sensitive sack. "Fuck, baby," I grind out, trying to keep my wits, wanting this to last as long as it can. "I love your eyes. I love that freckle behind your ear, and the stretch mark on your right hip." I fuck in and out, delirious from it all. "I love your hands—soft enough to drive me wild, powerful enough to slay the monster in the palace." I hunch over her, lips pressed against her forehead, watching her nipples as they start to weep. I swipe a thumb over it and stick it in my mouth, tasting the nourishment that will feed our son. "I love this baby and *everything* it's doing to your body. I love you, Verity, so fucking much."

I thrust up one last time, the tip pushing through the top of her cleavage. Cum spurts out, thick and ropey, spilling all over her chest and the swell of her tits.

Her lips part, the crest of a moan tumbling from her throat, and her hand drops, sliding between her legs.

I stop her. "No."

She blinks, flushed and impatient. "Why?

Glancing over my shoulder toward the door, I explain, "Because odds are, you aren't the only one who's horny, and you need to be ready."

P ace

"Justice," I say, clearly enunciating the name.

Black, shrewd eyes look into mine as Effie cocks her head. "Pretty bird?"

"No." I hold the treat just out of her reach. "Justice. It's the baby."

"Baby." Effie inches closer to the treat, bobbing her head with a trilled, "Baby bird."

Chuckling, I concede, "Yes, you're my baby bird. Justice is our baby boy. Can you say Justice?"

She lifts a foot toward the treat, straining. "Baby bird. Fucking *baby* bird."

"Fair enough." Sighing, I relent, giving her the treat and scritching her ruff. "You're probably not the only one around here who'll need to get used to the concept of justice."

And that's not the only concept that's taking time to adjust to. It's been less than forty-eight hours since I found out I have a father, and not the corpse being collected by the Barons.

The real one.

Every spare moment I get, he pops in my head. That day at the gym, when he was sparring with me, I didn't take the time to really look at him. Talk to him. Know him. And even though a part of me is achingly curious, a bigger, much stronger part of me mostly just feels pissed the fuck off.

I'd never leave Verity here with that monster.

"They've been in there a while, right?" Wick glances over at the bathroom door. The shower slowed about fifteen minutes ago, then turned back on. Then shut off again.

Wicker obviously took a shower down the hall because he's got a towel around his waist, and I can smell the soap on his skin from across the room. Carefully, he places his knife and gun in the weapons compartment under the bed.

After alerting the Barons and leaving Rory and Tommy to deal with the exchange, we came upstairs to prepare for bed. We knew Lex would want to check Verity out, make sure the baby didn't suffer during the scene downstairs, but Wick is right, they've been in there a long fucking time.

"Night, Effie," I say, running my finger over her beak and dropping the cover over the cage. "Maybe I should go check—"

The door opens before I get the sentence out, and Verity and Lex emerge from a cloud of steam. Their skin is pink from the shower, and they're dressed for bed, Lex in a pair of gray boxers and Verity wrapped in a white robe. While the tight line that normally creases Lex's forehead is smoothed, Verity waddles out with short, tense steps.

Wicker props his hands on each hip, accusing, "You fucked."

"Not her pussy," Lex replies, snaking his arm around her waist.

"Her ass?" I ask, aware of Rosi's tongue darting out to wet her lips.

Lex ignores us, pressing a kiss to Verity's temple, and Wicker glares. "Her tits? You fucked her tits! Jesus Christ, why the hell didn't you let me watch?"

"Because it wasn't about you," Lex says, rolling his eyes. "But I did save her for you." He squeezes her side. "Didn't I?"

Verity swings a glassy gaze on me. "He didn't let me come."

The dilated eyes. The pink cheeks. Her clenched legs.

Approaching her, I don't think twice about grabbing the tie of her robe and tugging it free. It parts slowly, revealing her belly first, and then her tits, and I exhale shakily at the sight of her. I've watched this amazing body of hers grow throughout the whole pregnancy, but it still doesn't fail to fascinate me. Her areolas are darker than they used to be—almost as brown as my own skin. Her belly is rounded, the skin taut and smooth, and although I'm getting impatient to meet the baby inside of it, I won't deny a part of me will miss my slow, quiet morning ritual of rubbing a special cream for stretch marks onto it.

"But you want to," I wager, parting the robe to see her bush. The hair there is thin and delicate and soft. She still doesn't shave for me and when I push my fingers into it, venturing into her folds, I find her slicker than ever. She whimpers, face dropping to Lex's shoulder, and my cock leaps eagerly.

Lex gestures behind me. "Pull out the compartment at the foot of the bed."

Wick and I glance at one another, both aware of the function of that particular feature. Moving quickly, each of us grabs a handle and pulls the drawer out.

It's a purple velvet kneeler.

"Well, that's convenient," Verity says, taking it in. It's mostly a bench with the cushion hitting just below her knees.

"The bed was designed for all parts of creation. Sleep, safety, and comfort." Lex guides her over. "You're welcome to get in bed and find the position that works best for you, but the Princes who had this built knew what they were doing. Using the end of the bed will take some of the weight off, and by leaning forward..." He trails off, eyes dark.

"We can get to you," I say, cock thickening. "All of us."

The roundness of her body, although fucking glorious, is rapidly growing a bit problematic for more than one of us to navigate at a time. If we were more patient men, we'd wait until she's had the baby to try anything adventurous.

We're not patient men.

"You mean…" She bites her lip, shooting a smoldering glance between me and Wick. "Like, both of you? At the same time?" Then, she looks over her shoulder at Lex. "We can do that?"

He kisses her temple, watching as her eyes flutter shut. "If you want them to." He doesn't tell her that we talked about it last week, Lex deciding that her risk factors this close to the birth are so much slimmer than in her second trimester. He doesn't tell her that *he's* the one who brought the idea to me and Wick. And he definitely doesn't tell her about the one-hour argument between us over who gets her ass first.

Verity shudders. "We can try it." Her eagerness is on full display as she shrugs off the robe, letting it fall to the floor. For a brief moment, time stands still. I told her earlier tonight she looked like a goddess in that dress, but here? Naked? Fuck me. She's so ripe and swollen, full with life—creation—and the urge to sink into her isn't just a want.

It's a primal need.

Wick's towel drops to the ground and he already has his erect cock fisted in his hand. If anyone knows how to take command of a moment like this it's Whitaker Ashby.

"Fuck, you're gorgeous," he breathes, crossing the distance between them. He places his mouth on hers just as his hand finds her full tit, massaging the supple flesh with his palm. When he pulls away, lips red from the kiss, he tilts his head at Lex. "Did he drink from you?"

Verity chases his mouth, eyes dazed. "Not yet."

"He will tonight." To Lex, he commands, "Get on the bed."

Our brother obeys, climbing up and kneeling at the foot while Wicker hops up on the bench, his cock pointing upward like an arrow poised to fire. He pinches the base, then strokes up. "You're gonna straddle me like a good girl, and then I'm going to lick your pussy just how you like it." His eyes meet mine. "She need some lube?"

"For you, no. She's ready." I lick my bottom lip. "But for me?" I jerk my chin at Lex. "Toss me a bottle."

While Lex rummages inside the bedside table, I take her hand and guide her over to Wick, trying to sense any nerves. "I'll go slow," I assure her, taking the opportunity to stroke the side of her breast as she swings a leg over Wick's lap. "Just relax and let us do the work."

It's a little cumbersome, and nothing like the rough manhandling we're used to, but their safety comes first. She places her hands on each of Wick's shoulders, and with his help, we get a knee on each side of him. Her belly is in his face, and I can't help but notice how much he touches her there now. He spoke the words earlier tonight, declaring himself Justice's father, but saying and believing are two different things.

The way he looks at her—*worships her*—I have no doubt he meant every word.

"That's right," Wick says once she's over him, adjusting. "Good?"

"I think so. I won't fall?" She looks between him and Lex.

Lex is perched above Wicker, sitting on the edge of the bed, one hand on her ribcage and the other squeezing her bicep. "We've got you." He nods at me. "Pace'll be behind you."

"I'm right here." I kiss her shoulder and run a hand down her spine to the curve of her backside. Even her ass is bigger now; her cheeks and thighs are so supple and thick. Shoving my hand into my shorts, I pull out my cock and give it a long stroke.

Wick scooches down, and with two of his strong hands clutching her hips, pulls her pussy right to his mouth. I don't need to look to know when his tongue makes contact. It's audible in Verity's moan, visible in the way her shoulders deflate, hips rocking slightly. The movement topples her forward, but Lex catches her.

Wick groans, long and gruff. "Fuck, Red, you taste so fucking sweet..."

I might not be able to see, but Lex can. His amber eyes are trained downward on Wicker, and when Lex's hands skate down her arms, they make a detour, giving her tits a squeeze.

"Ah!" she cries out, throwing her head back, and I'm right there, sucking a kiss into the junction where her neck meets her shoulder.

"He any good at that?" I wonder, nipping at her earlobe. "Wick's sucked my dick a few times, but it was mostly just so I'd suck his. No skillmanship whatsoever."

The hand on her hip lifts, Wicker's middle finger extending.

I bat it away.

"So, so good." From a glance, I see her forehead knitted up in pleasure. "It's like he's kissing me. You know... you know how he kisses..."

Fuck, that *does* sound good.

"It's both gentle, but firm. Little licks, the swirl of his tongue, and then he—" she moans, "sucks."

She leans forward, rocking her hips into Wick's mouth. Seeing the opportunity for what it is, Lex dips down to lift her tit to his mouth. His tongue finds her nipple first, giving it a slow, slick lick, before he finally latches on.

She gasps, arm flailing out to find purchase, and I offer my own hand up, surprised at the strength in her grip. "Oh my fucking—" Her words cut off into a strangled cry.

I stand back for a moment to observe them, getting harder and harder as my brothers share her body like this. If tonight proved anything, it's that whatever we do—scheme, fight, kill, love, or create —we do it together.

"Suck harder," she whispers, holding her tit higher for Lex to suckle. "It feels so good."

I can almost taste the release, but that's not what draws the surge of pre-cum to the head of my cock. That happens when Wick's hands move around her ass, his long fingers pulling her cheeks apart for me. He's never been able to deny me what I want.

I push her hair aside and kiss her across the shoulder blades, then down her spine. Placing my hands over my brothers, I spread her wider, revealing the only hole of hers I haven't had the chance to burrow into.

Kissing the smooth skin of her inner cheek, I lick inward, broadcasting my intent and giving her a chance to stiffen or pull away. When she doesn't, I swipe my tongue over the tight ring of muscle, indulging in her sharp, stunned gasp.

"Pace! Oh, fuck, Pace..." She lurches forward, and both Lex and Wicker groan. It puts my tongue close enough to Wick's that we mingle, drawn into a slick, heady kiss, right against her taint.

Unable to take it, I jolt my hand toward the bed, searching for the bottle of lube. "I'm too hard to be still tonight, Rosi. I need to move. You can handle it?"

"Y-yes," she stutters, her body close to becoming overwhelmed. "But hurry."

"As fast as I can without hurting you or Justice," I say, pouring a liberal dose of lube in my hand. I get my fingers good and slick before gliding them over the puckered hole. She flinches again, but this time less dramatically.

There's a moment when I slip the tip of my finger in that she tenses.

Wicker senses it instantly, his rusty voice insistent. "Bear down into it, Red. It feels weird at first, but once you stretch—yeah, just like that, baby. Breathe for us." I get all the way to the second knuckle as Wicker coaches her through it, his hand making soothing patterns on her hip. He's saying, "His dick's gonna feel so good once you're ready for him. You're gonna feel him so deep, Red..."

It takes a while to get a second finger in alongside it, but when I do, I twist and curve, stretching her out slowly. Wick's left hand suddenly drops her cheek and grabs for my cock, giving a long, measured stroke.

"*Goddamn,*" I hiss, thrusting into his fist.

It takes a minute to understand what he's doing—synching me into a rhythm—and my fingers, three at this point, move in time with it, gentle but deep. Lex's eyes meet mine over her shoulder, his lips spit-shiny as he warns, "Get her nice and loose if that look in your eyes means what I think it means."

He's right.

I won't be able to be slow and gentle.

When she's good and stretched, I nudge Wick's hand away and slot my head at her entrance, and the next time she thrusts back, I push in, intending to seamlessly keep the pace.

But she fucking *screams.*

I freeze, terrified I've hurt her, but the first strong tremor, ass clenching like a vise around me, makes it obvious she's not hurt.

She's coming her fucking brains out.

icker

HER FINGERS LATCH on to the first thing they find, one hand fisted in my hair while the other is digging desperate divots into Lex's neck. "Oh god," she's crying, rocking back into Pace. "Fuck me, fuck me— Wick, *please.*"

I don't know who triggered the orgasm, but I felt it building on my tongue and tasted it in the rush of her sweet slickness.

Pace can go forever. That's what years of edging will do for you. But withholding pleasure isn't my style. I want to fuck, I want it now, and I'm for goddamn sure not going to wait for my brother to finish.

When Verity slumps forward, body still wracking with release, I look up at Lex. "A little help?"

He moves next to me on the bench, using his upper body to hold her against Pace's deep, punching thrusts. Her expression is the picture of a woman straining toward ecstasy, jaw dropped on these sharp, little cries.

"Just a little longer," I tell her, reaching under her belly to find her pussy. "You can do that?"

"Keep going," she says, teeth bearing down on her bottom lip. She's sloppy wet, and I'm one second from a stroke if I don't get inside of her.

Luckily, Lex is on the case.

Reaching down, he grabs the base of my cock and casually guides it to her warm entrance. "Just be careful," he mutters, assessing the three of us with sharp eyes.

Once the tip is firmly in place, I drag her down, sheathing myself in her tight heat.

Jesus Christ.

She's slick from my mouth and the juices from her orgasm, but the tight feel of Pace's cock buried in her ass is something else.

Awed, I ask him, "You feel that?" We've never been inside the same chick before—certainly not one we call our own—and it's fucking intense, the pressure and heat all-encompassing.

"I feel it," he grunts, thrusting in at the same time I do. "I feel your cock. *Fuck*, Wick."

I almost bust my nut right there. "You hear that?" I ask, cupping her warm cheeks in my hands. "It's like we're fucking inside of you." The sentence is completely, laughably nonsensical, but Red gets it. Her breath hitches and she does this little... *wriggle*... making me slam my hands down on her thighs. "Easy, Red, easy."

"It's so much," she breathes, pulling in this big gulp of air. Her hand curls around my neck, thumb pushing into my pulse point. "I can't believe you're both inside me..."

Reveling in how overcome she looks from it all, I guide her upward, directing her to fall. I can feel just how deep or shallow Pace and I can go, and it doesn't matter that it's too close, not enough drag of resistance to really feel it along my whole shaft. Watching her full tits sway as Verity rides the both of us is easily the most mind-blowing fucking thing that's probably ever happened to me.

On one of these restrained little bucks, she groans at the bounce of her tits, moving to cup them with her hands. Lex gets there first though, his big hands supporting their weight.

"Pace was right before," Lex whispers, leaning in just above my head to push a slow, wet kiss to her swollen lips. "You look like a fucking goddess, taking them both. I bet you feel so crowded, don't you? Do you want it harder, baby?"

Frantically, she nods. "Can... can I—"

Lex reaches out to brush a damp lock of hair from her cheek. "Take what you need."

Which is real sweet and special and whatever-the-fuck, but he's holding her fat titty right in front of my face, and my whole world becomes narrowed down to the droplet of milk beading at the tip of her nipple. I lick my lips. This strange, almost primal urge to consume—to *preserve*—is a new bit of mindfuckery that I lean all the way into.

But Lex, somehow sensing this, is the one to guide it to my mouth. "You too, little brother. Take what you need."

Not needing to be told twice, I flick out my tongue and taste it, groaning at the flavor. The sweetness is less muted than last time, and I latch on to suckle it, drawing it out with my lips. Sucking her tits like this... it's like nothing I've ever felt before, a rush of warmth and comfort mingled with white-hot lust. It makes me drive my hips up into hers just as I take another greedy pull of her milk.

"God, Wick," she whines, threading her fingers into my hair. "What are you three doing to me?" The question is delivered on the cusp of a breathless chuckle, and it's Pace who answers.

"Worshiping you." I feel his hand sliding over her ribs, searching until his fingers find the seal of my lips. "Although Wick's always had a bit of an oral fixation. Isn't that right?" Not missing a beat, I take his finger into my mouth, giving it a long suck, and he spits a sharp curse.

Glancing up, I smirk around his digit.

How's that for skillmanship, fucker?

I don't leave her tit to cool, latching on for another hard suck that makes her thighs quake. Pace wraps his hand around the column of her throat, guiding her into his chest. I know from the hard set of his jaw that he's close, and when he says, "Come here," I sense what he wants.

Pulling off her tit, I hold the milk in my mouth as I strain over the distance, unsurprised when he reaches for me, hauling me into a hard, desperate kiss, right next to her red cheek.

Pace sucks her milk from my tongue, and I don't need to feel the way his fingers clench around my neck to know he's coming.

I feel it against my cock. "Holy fuck, Pace." I grunt the words into his gasping mouth just before he buries his face into her neck, shoulders jolting with a final thrust.

"So much," she's saying, brow knitted up in pleasure. "God, Wicker, it's so much…"

I brush my lips against hers, soothing her through it. "You can take it," I assure, hearing the thread of worry in her voice. Worry, because the strong, pulsing surges I can feel against my cock don't stop. Pace comes and comes, pushing these tiny, guttural, animalistic sounds into her neck.

I'm powerless to stop it when my own balls draw up tight. Verity's perfect cunt is clenching around me, and deep inside, Pace's cock is massaging mine with every surge of cum. I can still taste her milk in my mouth, and behind me, his legs bracketing my torso on the bench, Lex urges, "Come on, Wick. Let it go."

"Son of a—" My words clip off into a grunt as I slam my hips up, the orgasm feeling pulled from me just like I'd pulled Verity's milk from her. I feel her fingers clamp in my hair as she follows me over, her pussy fluttering around me.

This, I think as my thrusts trail off and I gather her into my arms. Pace clings to her back, still buried inside, while Lex kisses her slow and lazy through the final tremors of her orgasm. *This* is what it feels like to be unencumbered. There's no obligation here, no man in the dungeon pulling the strings.

It's the best fucking feeling in the world.

~

SHE SLIPS out of my arms at two am.

I don't actually look at the clock when I open my eyes, seeing her silhouette retreating out the door. It's always at two. Usually, I roll over, elbow Pace until he gives me an in, and wrap around him instead.

Tonight, I roll out of bed to follow her.

She's on the landing to the first floor, perched on the top step. She's wearing her silk dressing gown, and there's a hand thrust out behind her, propping her up. She doesn't hear me until I'm right up on her, but even then, she doesn't flinch so much as animate.

"Hey," she says, blinking.

I take a seat beside her, reaching out to sweep her hair over a shoulder, and she leans into me. "You okay, Red?" She nods, but I can tell something is troubling her, and I don't have to wonder what it might be. Sighing, I try to think of something supportive and comforting to say. "Killing people isn't so bad."

She slings me a confused look. "What?"

"I mean, killing Rufus especially. No moral gray there." It'd been difficult with Danner, not because I didn't think he deserved it, but because it took me a long time to realize it. "Don't let it get in here," I urge, pressing the point of my finger to the center of her chest. "Don't give him that power, you know? The power to change your heart."

Her eyes soften. "I don't feel good about killing him, but I don't feel bad about it, either. Honestly, I'm not the first Royal woman to kill her dad. Lavinia blew hers to smithereens."

It's the trace of humorous snark in her voice that brings me up short. "So if you're not upset about that, then what?"

The smile falls, transforming into a frown. "It's just..." Glancing down, she places her hand over her belly, rubbing it in a long, round circuit. Her head cocks to the side, eyes sad and wistful. "Well, he really wants lasagna."

It takes me five full seconds to really register her words.

"He wants," I blink, "lasagna?"

She nods, glancing up at me with a face that's so forlorn, my chest twinges. "Really salty and cheesy like my mama makes it. With the little bits of garlic and thyme."

Ah. "Homesick, huh?" This was supposed to be her month in West End, but since there's a new stock of Dukes—and a new Duchess, fuck—in the clock tower, the old set has taken the loft Verity used to stay in.

She pulls a face, snorting. "God, no. If I were in West End, I'd be staying with my mom, and I might love her lasagna, but I'm not getting pestered daily about... who knows? Cleaning out my old high school clothes, or decluttering the chest freezer, or going over the gym ledgers." Her eyes roll dramatically. "Plus, can you imagine me giving birth in West End? Lex and Pace—and you—would totally lose it." Looking weirdly resolute, she shrugs. "I'm absolutely where I need to be."

"So if you're not homesick, then..." I pause, taking in her little pout. "Oh my fucking god, you really are out here brooding just because you want lasagna. And you call me melodramatic."

She turns to me more fully, expression halfway to devastated. "You don't understand! The cravings... they're insane, Wicker! This baby is insatiable. The other day, Rory gave me a handful of M&Ms—which you won't tell Lex about—and on the way outside to eat them in the solarium like I'm some kind of criminal, I dropped them in the mud and—"

"Red," I admonish, already knowing where this is going.

She flushes. "I washed them in the fountain first?"

Clearly, I'm not properly fulfilling my role of being her sweets dealer. "Well, there's only one thing to do," I say, pulling her to her feet. "If my Princess wants a lasagna, then I'm going to get her one."

"This is ridiculous," Lex says, still half asleep. Neither of us are even properly dressed, and when we climb out of my car, I can only pray no one in this territory catches me in sweats and an undershirt.

I march him to the little stoop. "What's ridiculous is you depriving the mother of our child vital sustenance."

Lex whines, "Can't we just go to the grocery store?"

"She doesn't want some pre-packaged frozen lasagna," I argue. "She specifically requested—"

Abruptly, the porch light flares to life, the door opening to reveal a ruffled Mama B. Her hair is down in loose waves and there's a thick cream on her face. Her face scrunches angrily. "Get your asses in here before someone sees you. I'm not dealing with forty twitchy cubs tomorrow."

Pace called before we came—we're not *that* stupid—and explained nicely why we were crossing territory lines in the middle of the night. He said she didn't say no to her daughter's cravings but that she was sure as hell "not a delivery service".

I've been to the gym out front plenty of times, but this is my first time in the home Verity grew up in. I take it in warily as I stamp my shoes on the doormat before ducking inside, Lex following closely behind.

The ceilings are lower than I'm used to and I walk in hunched and huddled. There's not even a foyer. We enter right into a living room that could probably fit in Pace's security room. There are framed drawings and banners covering the walls, a bookshelf against the back, and a mismatching furniture set, but it's not very girly. There are no frills or flowers anywhere. One of the shelves is just a collection of crude shot glasses and wrestling memorabilia.

Despite that, it's... cozy. And not even cozy in that contemptuous way where someone really means 'small and crappy', but like legitimately... homely.

Lex is checking it all out too, adjusting his glasses to inspect one of the framed drawings. "Verity did this," he says, sounding surprised.

Mama B shuffles past us, flicking a hand. "She did them all. Now, get your asses in here and start cooking, because I'm not about to become a pregnant woman's personal chef."

Lex and I exchange a short, panicked look.

"C-c-cooking?" I stutter, rushing to keep up with her steps. "That's the thing where you put food in a microwave, right?" The kitchen has roughly the square footage of a postal stamp, and Lex and I both have to duck to avoid smacking our heads on the doorway.

I'm met with a tea towel, smacking me right in the face. "Wash your hands first," she orders, watching with sharp eyes as Lex and I both crowd in around the sink. Maybe he had a point before. This *is* fucking ridiculous.

It doesn't get any less ridiculous when, ten minutes later, Mama B is giving us a lesson in onion cutting. "Not like that! *Thin* slices, blondie. And what are you smirking at?" she asks Lex, who's gotten a little too superior since she praised his onion-peeling abilities. "Aren't you supposed to be some bigshot surgeon guy? I could gnaw that with my teeth, and it'd make a cleaner cut. Goodness gracious, are you trying to dice it or punish it?"

He glowers at her through onion-tears. "You're really cranky when people wake you up."

She doesn't dispute this, sitting down on a stool to flip through a magazine. "So the cravings are hitting her hard, eh?"

"Every night."

"Sounds right. I couldn't get enough chocolate when I was at this point with her." She snorts. "Wait until she gives birth. Lactation is going to make her hungry as a horse."

Pausing, I wince. "Maybe that's why she's gotten so—oof." Lex's very not-discreet elbow lands right in my ribs, and he shoots me a watery glare. *Right.* Probably don't want to tell her mother that we've been nursing her tits.

"We can handle it," Lex insists, brows crouched low. "We'll just... have to learn to cook. Somehow." The brows get even lower. "Eventually."

At her blank stare, I explain, "He has his first lecture in about five hours."

"Med school?" she asks, eyeing him thoughtfully. "That plus a newborn is going to be fucking brutal."

I shrug. "That's why I'm taking the semester off with Red. And Pace is taking an easy course load, so he'll be around."

Defensively, Lex adds, "The whole frat and the Court is willing to help, too."

She doesn't look particularly assuaged by this statement. "Well, the cubs pitched in for a crib and got it all set up in Ver's room, so when—"

My knife clatters to the cutting board. "He's got a nursery already," I snap, overcome by a sudden flare of red-hot panic. "They're *not* coming to stay here every other month. The contract only covered her pregnancy."

She looks momentarily stunned at the outburst, the magazine fluttering to the counter in front of her. And then she reaches for the knife, pointing it at me with a stern look. "Look here, blondie. This has nothing to do with a contract. I'm *going* to see my grandbaby. And if you'd let me finish before having your possessive freakout, I would have gotten to the part where I offered to babysit—on occasion—to give all four of you a break now and again."

I blink. "Oh." Glancing at the tip of the knife, I swallow. "I guess that wouldn't be so bad."

Mama B harrumphs, handing the knife back to me. "I don't know what you're worried about. She made it very clear at the beginning of the month that she preferred being in the Penis Palace. God only knows why." Aggressively flipping a page, she adds, "Considering *he's* still there."

I exhale, trying to get that weird flare under wraps. Don't know what the hell that was about. I just know the thought of Verity and Justice living here makes me see fucking red.

Huh.

"He's dead." Lex's voice is quiet and grim, and when I look up, he's holding Mama B's stare.

Her jaw tics as she searches his eyes. "When?"

Throwing a handful of diced onions into the pot, he answers, "About ten hours ago."

She takes this in silently, seeming to absorb it as we get started on dicing the garlic. After a beat, she gets up and grabs three of the crude shot glasses, setting them in a row. Lex and I share a glance as she snags a bottle of liquor from the cabinet over the fridge.

"Wait," Lex says, frowning. "Is that...?"

She pops the cork. "Yep. Your brother brought it to Family Dinner after the mutiny." Pouring some into each glass, she raises her own. "To the victor go the spoils."

Grabbing for mine, I give it a sniff before raising it, correcting, "To create is to reign."

She laughs a low, scratchy laugh. "Oh, blondie. Same fucking thing."

20

erity

"It's mostly a formality," Wicker says as we whiz through town. "They already have proof Rufus is dead—the Barons collected his body. They'll need documentation that the frat voted Justice in, although the... er... specifics are allowed to remain secret. Each frat does it their own way. All of that is protocol. What isn't is..." his hand rests on my belly, "well, frankly, you."

The four of us sit in the back of the car while a pledge drives. It's tense because no matter how many times they assure me everything about the meeting is 'protocol', there's no denying that what's about to happen is unprecedented.

PNZ may accept this vague leadership decision, but the other Kings?

I guess we'll find out.

"I can handle Sy," I say with more confidence than I feel. The Dukes have made huge progress under Sy's new leadership, but their

King still sees me as a little sister. "And Killian seems reasonable. At least, sometimes." Pace snorts, muttering something that sounds suspiciously like the word 'meathead' but I ignore him and look back at Wick. "And if you can play nice with the Baron King, just for today, we can get this over with and go for lunch."

There's a suspended silence where each of my Princes simply stares at me.

"What?"

"You just ate six pancakes," Lex says, gaping. "And eggs. And a double serving of bacon."

"Seven," Pace corrects. "Seven pancakes. She stole one of mine."

My jaw drops in outrage. "Your *child* stole one of yours," I retort, not even the slightest bit ashamed. I knew carrying a baby would make me hungry, but something flipped once Rufus was no longer in the house. My appetite is insatiable—and not just for food. I woke up to Pace buried deep inside me, and then showered with both Lex and Wicker.

And it's not exactly easy now. Lex is dressed in a dark gray waistcoat and crisply pressed trousers, hair slicked back into its bun. He looks like a gentleman, but only I know how much of a lie it is. Four hours ago, he was pushing his spunk into me while muttering absolute filth into my ear.

Wicker is carefully rumpled in that way of his, the top three buttons of his shirt undone to reveal a white undershirt. His hair looks like it *was* slicked back, but has since fallen victim to an ambitious round of fucking. Another lie. We fucked before he even fixed his hair.

Pace is the only one who came as himself, his dark green button-down untucked, sleeves rolled up to the elbows. His jean-clad legs are spread enticingly, the outfit finished off with an expensive pair of sneakers. The arm he has slung around me is loose and deceptively casual, but every now and then, he'll give a lock of my hair a little twirl around his forefinger.

Shivering, I try to break myself out of the lust fog. "And I can't help it if Justice eats like his fathers."

The car makes a right turn, and Wick gives me a smirk. "We get through this with no new surprise family announcements, and I'll take you to that all-you-can-eat Chinese place down on the Avenue you like so much."

Lex's eyes pop wide. "You took her there? That food is filled with sodium and MSG. No wonder your ankles are swollen!"

"It's not the food." I roll my eyes. "You try carrying forty extra pounds without any side effects."

"Well, you can't go anyway." Lex leans against the door, a blaze of sun catching the amber in his eyes. For a second, they glow like fire. "I spent all night getting the new 4D ultrasound equipment set up, so we're breaking it in this afternoon."

Wicker snorts, fussing with his hair. "I still don't know why you needed to spend so much of Rufus' money on some fancy scan machine. She's only going to be pregnant for like three more weeks. I hope they take returns."

"I guess I should have spent it on another car," Lex drawls, flicking his brother a wry look. "And plus, it can be used for her next pregnancy."

"Another car would be—" Wicker freezes, brows slamming together. "Hold up. What do you mean her *next* pregnancy?"

Lex and I share a long, simmering stare.

"Guys." Pace cuts off our bickering with a pointed tap on the window. "We're here."

We pull up in front of the large building where two black SUVs are parked along the curb. *Shit.* I knew Wick spent too much time washing my hair, but it felt so good. "Looks like we're fashionably late," he says, sliding his fingers through mine. The driver opens the door, and I heave myself from the car with the help of the guys.

The stirrings of fall are in the air as we march toward the building, Lex's hand guiding on the small of my back. I must look ridiculous in my mid-length purple dress, like some sad, mutated grape, but I'm running out of things that fit.

Entering through the doors of the old courthouse, I can't help but drink in the interior. From the floors to the molding, everything looks old and historical, painfully intricate, and wildly out of place next to the trio of men waiting to check my Prince's weapons.

"Hey, Kaz," I greet, opening my purse as I eye the LDZ next to him. "Making friends?"

He doesn't look surprised at the fixed-blade I pull from my bag. "Ah, Jordan and I are enjoying the lesser parts of our new titles. Guard duty."

I grin at him. "Congratulations on making Duke, by the way."

"Thanks." Frowning, he takes Lex's pistol. "Shame Ballsy turned it down though. We would have run West End ragged with Porterfield." I don't miss the accusing look he gives my Princes. "Feels like he's more East than West these days."

"He stays in East End for *me*," I stress, not allowing that glint of animosity in his eyes to grow. "Eugene's one of my best friends, and he's gone through a lot. I don't blame him for needing to take some time."

Kaz shrugs, nodding his head. "Sure, I get it. Still sucks."

I pat him on the arm. "Maybe next year. He's only a junior, right?"

"Right."

With that, Lex impatiently leads me down the high-ceilinged hallway, and I try not to panic over what's about to happen. "Maybe we should have given them a heads-up about being late," I say, keeping my voice low. Everything in here echoes.

"It'll be fine," Lex says, jerking his chin at something—*someone*—down the hall. Nick Bruin, dressed in a black T-shirt, jeans, and scuffed-up boots, straightens when he sees us. There's no doubt his eyes linger on Wicker a beat longer than necessary, possibly trying to determine how he missed the family resemblance.

"Hey, Nick." I grin when I see him, unable to stop myself from looking at the puckered two-inch scar on his neck. "Looking all healed up."

He stretches his neck back and forth, demonstrating the statement. "Not sure I'd win any Furies right now, but at least I'm finally off that godforsaken bed rest." Nick's blue eyes drop to my belly. "But

Christ, look at you. You're fucking huge, Ver. You sure there aren't two in there?"

I glower at him.

"Positive," Lex says, stepping next to me. After an awkward moment, he thrusts his hand out, and after an even awkwarder moment, Nick slaps it, their fists meeting in one of those unflinchingly macho handshakes. "Looks like you're still doing the range-of-motion exercises. You got a clean scan from the guy I sent you to?"

Nick fingers the scar. "Yeah. You did good work." He looks back at me. "How much longer until this thing falls out of there?"

I grimace at the visual. "Any time in the next three weeks." Every time I say that, it feels surreal. It seems so far away, but also excitingly close. "But no rush. I've still got a lot to do before baby Justice gets here."

Nick smirks. "Justice, eh?"

I shrug. "Seemed appropriate."

"Lex," Wick calls out. "We better get inside."

"You guys go ahead," Nick says, jerking his chin toward the ominous set of doors ahead. "I'll keep an eye on Verity."

"Oh," I say, glancing at my Princes. "No. I'm, uh.... going in, too."

His eyebrow lifts. "It's an official meeting, sorry. Kings and Royal invitees only."

It takes everything in me not to explain, but it's not right to let him know before the Kings.

"I know," I say, feeling the warmth of Lex's fingers as they thread with mine. "Let's just say there's been some changes in the hierarchy in East End."

Those blue eyes pierce through me. "What does that mean?"

Lex drags me off before I can say more.

"Considering you're the ones who called this meeting," I hear Killian's drawl when the guys enter the room ahead of me, "you're skating right over the bounds of punctuality. Good thing the Baron King isn't here, or he would have nullified the meeting two minutes ago." Killian sighs, muttering, "Apparently there's a situation with their new Baroness."

Wicker raises his chin. "It's probably best he isn't here anyway, because I have a feeling he's not going to like what's about to happen." Stepping aside to allow me to enter the room, he adds, "You know, with the old guard being so obsessive about tradition."

The first thing I see, other than Sy and Killian's confused faces, is the long table in the center of the room. There are five chairs, each one designed for a King. Killian and Sy occupy theirs. On one side of the table, the Count's seat sits empty, as does Maddox's. On the other is East End's chair, which is being held for Rufus, and three standard folding chairs, which I presume are for the Princes. It's clear the second they see me that I shouldn't be here. They better get ready, because the rules in Forsyth are about to get real fuzzy.

"Verity?" Sy bolts to his feet when he sees me. "What are you doing here? Are you okay?"

I face them both, smoothing out my dress. "I'm here to update you on the current status of East End."

Sy eyes Killian, and then Lex, before making an uncomfortable expression that's about seventy-percent eyebrows. Gently, he says, "This is a meeting for Royal frat members only. House girls aren't included."

"Well, that's the thing." I move toward the East End King's chair and stand behind it, my men flanking me. "As of two nights ago, I'm a little bit more than a house girl."

"Explain," Killian looks between us. "Now."

After exchanging a nervous look with Pace, I begin, "My father, Rufus Ashby, was found guilty by the members of PNZ for carrying out the acts of kidnapping, rape, and murder during his reign over East End, as well as the attempted abduction and assault on me four months ago." My gaze meets Sy's. "These are not related to the current missing girls. I wish I could say it was, so that would be over, but it's not."

"Where is Rufus now?" Killian asks.

"Being processed by the Barons." My tone is flippant. It's hard to care. "He's dead."

Killian's spine straightens and Sy manages to speak through his shock. "About fucking time. Who took the crown?"

Here, I wring my hands, understanding that it's unconventional. "The frat gave my unborn son the Oath of Fealty, and once that was complete, Rufus was executed."

Killian looks between the Princes, eyes narrowed assessingly. "You're not answering my question—the only one that matters. Which one of you did it?"

I square my shoulders, looking him in the eye. "I did." And with that, Pace pulls out the chair, while Lex and Wicker each assist me and my cumbersome belly into it. It feels so good to get off my feet that I groan, long and loud. Insulting or not, Lex isn't wrong about my swollen ankles. "I killed my father and secured the throne for my son. But my Princes have agreed to help run the kingdom until he comes of age."

"What?" Killian balks. "He isn't born yet. That doesn't mean anything. Your territory needs a King, not a fucking—" He makes a wild, belligerent gesture. "Whatever the hell this is! Don't make this some weird group rule bullshit," he says, eyes pleading. "Sy and I— we're really trying to bring about change in Forsyth Royalty, but you're running before we've crawled. You get one King, just like the rest of us." He holds up a finger. "*One* King. Not three, a fetus, and his mommy."

On either side of my shoulders, Lex's hands squeeze the back of my chair. "The frat voted for this," he says, voice low and challenging. "They did it democratically, without threat or manipulation. You don't get to decide the future of our house. They do."

"This," Killian says confidently, "is a clusterfuck. We asked for a King and you brought us—"

"A solution," Pace says, eyes rolling. "So get over it and get on with it."

Sy shakes his head, mouth pressed into a tense line. "The Baron King will never accept it."

"We're taking his advice," Wicker cuts in, glaring at Sy, "and leading our fucking kingdom. Hell, we just added another King to his crypt."

Killian rubs his forehead, looking worn. "Do you not think I'd want to rule South Side with my brothers as equals?" He gestures to Sy. "Don't you think Perilini would rather share his kingship with a legit Bruin and a Maddox? There's a reason we choose one leader, and it's big enough that people like us sacrifice the hope of ruling alongside the people we care about."

"Simon." I hold Sy's gaze beseechingly. "We all know Nick and Remy rule alongside you in all but name. I'm sure it's the same for South Side."

Sy nods. "That might be true, but the name means something, Ver. It's a target I'd never put on my brothers' backs, and I'd never ask DKS to put their necks out there three times more than they already do in order to protect them."

There's a long beat of quiet where the only sound is Killian's gold pen tapping on the tabletop. Finally, he holds up a hand, jaw tight. "Let's just shelve this until the Baron King can be here to have a say."

I deflate, disappointed but unsurprised. "In that case, we can skip to the next topic we called this meeting for. The Barons' vote won't be necessary. It's a matter of the contract between East and West."

Sy frowns. "Your contract?"

"My contract was with the Princes," I correct, "and that's already been dissolved."

Understanding dawns on Sy's face. "You want us to dissolve ours."

"Verity can come and go as she pleases," Pace offers, laying a stack of papers on the table. "There's no reason to bind her to East or West —*but*," he adds, "if and when she goes to West End, she may not come alone. We need your assurance we'll be welcome as her escort."

Sy scratches his head. "Are you sure?" he asks, looking at me. "We've fully moved out of the tower and into the apartment, but there's still room for you there. Or we can find another location to—"

"No, thanks." I give him a gentle smile. "If I'm going to build a life for me and my son, I need to choose somewhere to do it. West End will always be home. I have roots there. But East End..." I glance behind me, meeting Lex's gaze. "It's where our presence as a Royal unit can do the most good. Not just for our family, but for Forsyth."

"You're really serious about this," Killian realizes, glancing between the four of us.

It's Wick who answers, "Verity may have held the knife, but we all killed Rufus Ashby. We didn't do it impulsively. We spent months building a plan, and we're committed to seeing it through."

Sy exhales, sliding the stack of papers closer. "Well, if it's what you want." He pales, eyes jerking up. "Oh, your mother is going to lose her shit."

I laugh, feeling Pace's fingers combing idly through my hair. "Who do you think gave me the idea? Don't worry, all of us are firmly required to attend as many family dinners as possible. But," I nod at the papers, "without contracts."

Sighing, he holds up the paper, ripping it in half. "Your call, Princess."

"See," Killian says, gesturing to the torn paper. "If the Baron King had done that with his contract, he might actually be here today."

Frowning, I wonder, "What do you mean?"

Sy folds his arms, his eyebrows doing that serious crouching thing yet again. "Let's just say... if what Remy says is true, we should all be expecting an invitation in the mail soon."

Wicker's eyes narrow. "An invitation for what?"

Killian kicks back in his seat, head cocked. "A black wedding."

"The first black wedding in four decades," Sy adds.

"What's a black wedding?" I ask, feeling confused.

"An arranged marriage between a Baron and Baroness," Sy explains. "Mom told us about it when we were kids. Apparently, there are times when a contract is signed between two families, agreeing for a Baron to take a formal bride. I thought it was an urban legend because she said it's always held on Halloween and everyone wears all black and masks," he shrugs his massive shoulders, "but apparently not." He smirks at Verity. "I guess it'll be your first official event."

"I've had my fill of Barons lately," Wicker says, squeezing my shoulder. "I think we'll pass."

"You'll be there," Killian says, rising from his seat in an indication that the meeting is officially over, "just like the rest of us. You think killing a King gives you power, but the truth is, all it gives you are obligations." He tilts his head at me. "Congratulations, Princess. Welcome to the club."

It's interesting to see the palace grounds transform with a new season. I've seen the crisp, dry decay of winter in its wilted vines and rattling branches. I've observed its springtime yawn of budding flowers and thawing fountains, an explosion of color across the courtyard and alongside the palace's exterior walls. I know all too well the lush green of its wet summer, the screams of cicadas, and the enchanting, speckled glow of its fireflies.

But the first peek of autumn is somehow the most magical of them all.

I stand in the circular drive, hypnotized by the rain of leaves. A strong breeze is enough to capture us in its tornado of yellows and oranges, the old oaks shedding them like a skin.

"We should take you out in the boat sometime," Pace says, and I realize the three of them have come to stand beside me, following my gaze to the landscape. It looks like a painting. "Out there on the water, it looks even less real."

Catching one of the oak leaves as it flutters past, I stroke it wistfully over the curve of my belly, imagining Justice can hear the slight papery crinkle. "I'd like that."

"Count me out," Lex says, pulling a face. "Algae is gross."

Wicker drawls, "Is it the algae, or is it that you can't swim for shit?"

Lex balks. "I can swim."

"Doggy-paddling and panic-treading don't count," Pace argues.

"I'm not the best swimmer, either," I say, grabbing Lex's arm in a loose hug. "Although I do have built-in floatation devices at the moment."

Wicker barks a delighted laugh that makes a smile spring to my face.

More and more, I'm convinced I made the right choice. The thought of raising our son—maybe even our *children*—in this place doesn't feel as nightmarish as it once had. The earth beneath our feet is pure and fertile. The stones that sit on it are strong and solid. And the people who dwell within it...

"We're better than the man who made us."

Not questioning the randomness of this thought, Lex gently takes the leaf from my hand, tucking it behind my ear like a flower. "And he'll be better than the men who made him," he agrees, brushing his knuckles against my belly.

My fingers itch to loosen his hair, but I don't.

Not until we're downstairs in the medical wing.

I hold back until then, and Lex winces when I snag the hair tie, giving a little, "Oof," as I pull it free. "Leave some hair on my scalp, would you?" Despite this, his cheeks color as he takes his stool. "This won't be much different than the regular ultrasound for you."

I'm lying on the exam table, my dress pulled up to reveal my belly. It's beginning to look weird with the skin pulled so thin, but a part of me can't imagine not having it there anymore.

"Careful with the joystick!" Lex snaps at Pace. "It took two hours to seat right."

"Pretty sure I've heard that one before."

All three of us startle at the sound of Wicker's voice. I've had more exams than I can count over the course of my pregnancy, and the only one I remember Wicker attending is the clandestine ultrasound where we discovered the baby's sex. I haven't pushed him about it, and Lex stopped pestering him to participate some time in my second trimester.

Now, he's closing the door behind him, looking reluctant as he shuffles into the room. "So, uh... what goes on at one of these things?"

Lex, still gawking at his brother, visibly shakes himself out of the shock. "I already drew her blood. We're just going to test out the new ultrasound machine. That is," he shoots a glare toward Pace, "if someone doesn't break it."

"I'm not breaking it," Pace snaps, and with a series of lightning-fast keystrokes, brings up some fancy interface. "See? I've been studying this software for days. I know it like the back of my hand."

Lex looks slightly stunned again. "Oh, er—good. You can operate the viz panel while I guide the transducer?"

Pace turns to level his brother with a stare. "Obviously."

Reaching for something on the table, Wick asks, "What should I do?" Realizing he's holding a pair of forceps, he flinches, setting it back down.

"Wick," I slowly say, "what's up?"

"Nothing." But despite his answer, he's glancing around the room like a caged animal, the tips of his ears reddening the longer we stare back at him. "Look," he bursts, "all this medical shit really freaks me out because he's going to come out of there someday soon, and there's going to be blood and goop and gross stuff, and honestly, the less I think about it, the better, but the baby has a name now, and like... fingers or whatever, and I want to see him in 4D too, so fucking get on with it."

Lex takes this in with a slack jaw. "Dude, you've watched me meticulously disembowel at least half a dozen men."

Pace adds, "You've cut off more fingers and toes than you *have*."

Lex points the transducer at him. "You've seen the inside of a brain."

"And hell, that was just a rough hockey practice," Pace says.

"Yeah." Wicker blinks, forehead knitting up. "And?"

Incredulously, I surmise, "But the baby being born will be too gross for you?"

Reaching up to scratch his temple, Wick seems to give this a lot of thought before coming to a conclusion. "Well, I didn't want to hold the brain, you know?"

It's the most ridiculous thing I've ever heard, but weirdly, maybe also the sweetest. "Wick."

He looks slightly aggrieved. "Yeah?"

"Come hold my hand, okay?"

Jolting forward to round the table, he releases a tense exhale, grabbing my hand. "Sure, yeah. Got it."

Lex shakes his head before squirting the ultrasound goo onto my belly. "Let's get started, shall we?"

The 4D ultrasound machine is enormous and looks overly complicated. There's a whole panel of buttons, dials, and switches. Pace navigates them expertly somehow, guiding Lex when the transducer goes too low or too high.

"Stop!" Pace says. "Right there. Look, Rosi."

I crane my neck to see the screen, awed at the image of our son's face on the screen. "Wow," I breathe through the tightness in my throat. He looks lumpy, but I can still make out all the details, from his round cheeks to his closed eyes. He looks like he's sleeping, and maybe it's the lumpiness, but I could swear there's a little divot right between his eyebrows, almost like he's—

"He looks so annoyed." Wicker shoots me a beaming grin that takes my breath away. "Maybe he's Lex's, eh?"

"Bro," Pace gasps, pointing at the screen, "look at his hand. Is he...?"

I groan. "Oh my god. You can't be serious."

Justice's hand is balled into a loose fist beneath his chin, but his middle finger is very clearly unfolded.

"He's absolutely flipping us off," Pace says.

Wicker's smile widens. "Then again, maybe he's Pace's."

When I hear nothing out of the third father, I glance at him, noticing how hard he's staring at the screen. "Lex?"

Straightening, he explains, "Just checking for any abnormalities. Craniofacial, skeletal, or abdominal. It'd be difficult to catch dysmorphisms on standard—"

"Lex." I put my hand over his on the transducer, waiting until he meets my gaze to command. "Stop looking at the fetus. Look at our son."

He stares at me for a long moment as it sinks in. He doesn't mean to see the specimen instead of the person. There was a time I didn't understand, but now I do. Lex needs us to pull him out of the lab jacket and into the moment.

And suddenly, he does.

Blinking, he turns to the screen, his grip on the probe going slack. "He's—" Lex pauses, back expanding with a sharp inhale. "He's perfect, Ver."

Wicker and I created this baby with blood and passion. Pace and I forged him in the heat of wild possession. But Lex and I made him right here, with a longing so fierce that it transcended things like science or territory lines.

Smiling softly, I stroke my thumb over his. "Yeah, he is."

"He has your nose," Lex says, tilting his head to follow Justice's curled angle. "He looks comfortable in there, doesn't he?"

There's a tiny moment where I think how nice it would be for everything to stay like this. That maybe I can stay pregnant just a little longer, and we can bask in the peace and harmony we've created, but then I remember: we're in Forsyth.

And nothing in Forsyth stays peaceful for long.

P ace

I TAKE a drag off the joint before blindly passing it to Bruin.

Family Dinner in West End, while not a contractual obligation, is still something Verity demands to attend. My first time at one of these things wasn't so bad. Decent food, good booze, and an orgasm on the rooftop. What's not to like?

But that was before I knew.

Bruin and I are outside in the alley. Despite the frankly great weed, he's twitchy, constantly glancing toward the door. Something about his girl giving him shit if she catches him smoking so soon after his throat injury.

But my eyes are focused on the old car at the mouth of the alley.

Or, rather, the man tinkering around beneath the hood.

When Bruin hands me the joint back, I ask, "You know him?"

He follows my gaze, lifting his chin. "Pauly? Yeah, he's the trainer."

I pull a deep drag, watching as the man in question reaches inside his rusty toolbox, pulling out a wrench. "What's his deal?"

Bruin shrugs. "No deal. He's been here longer than I've been alive."

"Is he," I work my jaw back and forth, "good?"

"At training?" Nick's eyebrow arches. "Sure. He's probably responsible for most of the frat's boxing acumen."

Exhaling, I say, "No—I mean, is he *good*? As a person."

When I pass the joint back, Nick's giving me this baffled look. "Spare me with the moral 'good' bullshit, Ashby. No one's *good*. On the scale of humanity, there's super-shit, kinda-shit, and lesser-shit." He points the joint at Pauly. "He's less shit than most. That's about the highest bar I've got."

I hum. "Right."

He twists to look at Pauly, the thick, raised scar on his neck stretching. "Are you worried about him with Ver or something? Because he's always been good to her and Mama B. Like a dad."

My eyes narrow. "A dad, huh?"

If I thought it'd make me feel better to know Pauly has been some upstanding guy to my Princess' family, then I'm sorely mistaken. Mostly I just get this hot flare of indignation, like... *how fucking dare he* give other people what should have been given to me and my mother.

Just then, the door behind us opens, and Nick mutters a sharp, "Shit, shit, shit," tossing the joint to the side. Lavinia's head pops out, blue-hair first, and she spots him instantly.

Her eyes harden. "Motherfucker, I *know* you aren't out here smoking weed when you were specifically told to lay off!"

Nick holds up his hands, cool as a cucumber. "Just shooting the shit, baby."

Her glower lands on me. "You. *Spill.*"

"We were smoking a joint."

Nick's fist bangs into me. "Dude, what the fuck?"

Shrugging, I say, "Her and Verity are friends. I'm not sacrificing pussy to cover up for a Duke. You'd do the same."

Still pissed, he replies, "Of course I'd do the same. Welcome to the super-shit club, Assby."

I flip him the finger as he trudges inside, the sound of Lavinia Lucia's growling admonishments disappearing behind the door. When it's just me, I look back at Pauly and think, *fuck it.*

"Shit," he says, almost banging his head when he realizes I'm lurking beside him. "Goddamn, son, wear a bell."

The term of endearment—little too fucking pointed—makes my stomach drop. "What are you working on?"

I inspect him more closely this time, trying to find any resemblance, and a part of me thinks Lex's test has to be wrong. This guy is a complete dud, with his scratchy beard and backwards baseball cap, which is probably hiding male pattern baldness. Maybe time was hard on him, but he looks older than the math would suggest. Aged. Worn.

"Changing an alternator for one of the girls," he explains, tugging a part up onto the engine block. "Hand me that belt tensioner, would you?" When all I do is stare blankly into the toolbox, he rears back, eyeing me. "The one that looks kind of like a bike pump."

Spotting it, I bend down to grab it, passing it over. "Did you used to be a Duke?"

The question catches me off guard as much as him, and when he props his forearm against the block, he swings a confused glance at me. "Afraid not. Almost—not quite."

I watch as he pulls a belt through some pulleys. "Why not?"

"Ah, just life," he answers, shrugging. "Heartbreak, drugs, and gambling. Went a little far west, you might say."

Watching him carefully, I ask, "You ever go east?"

He flinches, dropping the tensioner. "Goddamn it," he mutters, snatching it back up with a hard sigh. "Yeah, I played around in East End for a while. Not the kind of story a guy tells over a serpentine belt, though."

My eye twitches. "You ever play around with someone named Odette?"

The flinch this time is full-body and he jolts back, fixing me with a scowl. "How do you know about her?"

"She was a Princess," I reason, but already feel exhausted by the pretense. "Also, I'm her son."

He turns fully now, regarding me with a long, thoughtful stare. "You're—what, twenty-one? Twenty-two? That'd mean you were..." His frown falls away, understanding crossing his features. "So you were the kid she had with the Princes."

For some reason, it makes my blood boil. "Let me rephrase that, Paul." Crisply, I clarify, "I'm *your* son. Your son with Odette Delisle."

The blood drains from his face and he takes two steps back. "Look, that's not possible. Odette strung me along and then tossed me away more than once, and I think I'd know if she'd had my fucking kid."

"Well that's funny," I reply, "considering I've got a pretty credible paternity test that says otherwise."

His face goes slack. "Holy shit, you're serious." At my unflinching stare, he sucks in a breath that seems to never stop, his chest expanding comically. "Fuck, man, I've gotta sit down." But instead of sitting down, he leans against the wall, rubbing a palm over his chin. "When did this happen?"

Astonished, I throw my arms out wide. "How about you fucking tell me? It's not like I was there."

He looks shaken to his core, snagging a crumpled pack of cigarettes from his pocket. "Odette and I—we had a fling the summer before that kid and his mom died. Michael and Miranda, wasn't it?"

Nostrils flaring, I say, "My mother was her handmaiden."

He nods, eyes squinting. "But she had a lot of free time over the summer, and we became a bit of an item." Lighting the cigarette, he takes one shaky inhale before instantly tossing it on the ground, stamping it out with a grimace. "Once she became Princess, it got too complicated. She dropped me like a bad habit. I found her again a few years later, but there wasn't any kid with her."

"I was in foster care." My voice feels brittle and dry, and when I look up, Pauly's staring at me like he's seeing a ghost.

"You have her eyes."

I rub my forehead, grousing, "This isn't going how I expected." I thought I'd look this guy in the eye, tell him he's to blame for everything that went wrong in my life, and hopefully get a good shot in.

Instead, the anger fizzles to ash.

Pauly's face twists. "What *did* you expect, dropping a twenty-one-year-old bomb on a fuck-up like me?"

Spinning on my heel, I decide that I'm not equipped for this. Having a father I hate? I've got that shit down to a science. I could write a whole textbook on it. But having a father who was never given the chance to be one?

Good or not, I'm not ready to give anyone that opportunity.

It's quiet down in the dungeon.

The smell is mostly gone, replaced by the sharp scent of bleach and disinfectant. The cot is an empty metal frame, the thin mattress having been disposed of at some point in the last week. And it's dark.

Comfortingly dark.

It rankles to know that no matter how hard we try to make upstairs feel like home, nothing soothes the frantic vigilance quite like being in this darkness. Down here, nothing actually matters. The senses are so deprived that it dulls out even the twitchiest nerve.

I can't say what compelled me to come down here. One second, I was gathering my stuff for my first lecture of the day, and the next, I was tugging the sconce to open the passageway down here. Now, I'm standing in the doorway of the empty cell, gazing into its shadows.

Father is dead.

Gone.

He died knowing this blankness. This void. This aching expanse of loneliness.

My only regret is that he couldn't die in here.

"Hey."

The voice doesn't startle me. From down here, I know every

sound in this palace. I could hear her coming from the second-floor landing.

I flick one of the bars. "I don't like you being down here."

"Funny." When I glance behind me, she's giving me a tense grin. "I was going to say the exact same thing about you."

Shrugging, I bury my fists into my pockets. "Just seeing if the Barons earned that clean-up fee."

She steps next to me, winding her arms around my waist. "Maybe we should fill it in with concrete," she says, but I know I couldn't bear to.

"Then where will we run our lucrative torturing business?"

Humming, she takes a beat to consider this. "Port-o-potties."

Snorting, I place my hands over hers. "And damage the palace's curb appeal?"

"You could just," she burrows her face into my side, "*not* torture people."

I turn, tipping her face up to search her eyes. "You don't approve of what we do," I wager.

Frowning, she looks away. "I'm not saying people like Bruce and Rufus don't deserve it. And I know justice doesn't come without imparting a little pain. It's just..." She bites at her lip, wondering, "Doesn't it cling to you?"

I thumb her lip from her teeth. "What?"

"Inflicting hurt." Her eyes are so wide and innocent that another man might fold.

"Did it cling to you?"

Humming, she winds her arms around my neck. "If it did, it was more like... static cling. Easy to shake off." She shrugs, as if proving it. "But I've also only done it once."

"You hit Heather with a frying pan," I remind her.

She groans. "Am I never going to live that down? Of all my actions, that one was the most justifiable! She broke the girl code, and she knows it."

I point out, "You helped me kill Charlie."

"*That* was self-defense."

Tugging her closer, I add, "I bet, given half the chance, you'd castrate at least a dozen of the men in Forsyth," and she frowns.

"That's not true."

"Yes, it is." I lean down to kiss her, licking my way through the seam of her mouth. "And it wouldn't be because you're an Ashby, it'd be because they deserve it. This town doesn't raise happy, well-adjusted men, Rosi."

Maybe Nick Bruin had a point before.

Maybe there is no such thing as *good*.

She gives me a long, pitying look, like she wants to take away the pain—erase the past—but these are the men we are, the men we were raised to be.

Creation doesn't just happen in the womb.

"Things are going to be different." Curling her fingers at the nape of my neck, she draws my forehead to hers. "Our son will have the one thing none of you did—a mother. And mothers aren't just here to love and care for you. They're also here to kick asses, teach manners, and show you how to treat women. Mothers," she concludes, "show you something a father can't always teach."

Skeptically, I wonder, "And what's that?"

Rosi smirks. "How to be a real man."

I THINK about the dungeon cell a lot once I get to campus.

Voices seem louder, stares seem more pointed, and even with the mildness of an impending autumn, the warmth of the sun feels searing. I have no one walking at my side. Wicker and Verity are taking the semester off, and Lex is on a completely different campus almost an hour away. I start to regret coming back at all.

Until lunch.

"Hey, you dropped this." Hearing Ballsack's voice, I turn just in time to see a blonde snatch the charging cord out of his hand. Her lip curls in disgust and I'm pretty sure I hear her mutter "asshole" before she rushes off without so much as a 'thanks'.

"Ouch," I say when he walks by my table in the student union. "Smash and dash?"

He looks up, surprised to see me. "Huh?"

"That girl." I take a bite of my sandwich. "Old hookup?"

"Oh," Ballsy glances over the shoulder of his leather DKS jacket at her retreating form. "Nah. I don't even know her."

I pause. "You bang her sister? Break into her car?" I keep probing, but he just shrugs. "Dude, you did *something* for her to react like that."

"Nope." He drops into the seat next to mine, and I notice everyone at the table next to ours not-so-discreetly peek over. "The Royal Gazette just released an article identifying me as a 'person of interest' in the missing girls' case."

My eyebrows hike up. "But Agent Knight released you."

"On a technicality." He slumps back in his chair. This summer's been hard on him, the strain visible in the corners of his eyes. "And there are no other suspects yet, so I'm pretty fucked. Once you've been tagged as a criminal, it's impossible to shake."

Behind him, two girls whisper to one another. Our eyes lock and I realize that sitting next to me, an actual felon, isn't helping. Wryly, I respond, "Oh, I wouldn't know anything about that." I take a sip of my drink. "I'm sure they'll forget about it when Knight drags someone else in."

"Maybe." We're both aware of the number of eyes watching us, but although I'm used to hiding how it affects me, Ballsy shifts uncomfortably, hardening under the scrutiny. To be fair, cybercrimes are a far cry from kidnapping girls. "Honestly, I can't tell if they're staring at us because of the criminal thing, or if it's because we're from opposing frats." Sighing, he grabs his backpack off the floor. "Either way, I need to move."

"Fuck that. Stay." I push over my bag of chips, and he takes a few while I chew my mouthful of sub. "Did you do it?"

"Do what?" he snags another chip.

"Kidnap those girls?"

His head snaps up, face pinching. "Jesus, Ashby!" Leaning

forward, he gives his response with absolute conviction. "Hell no. Why are you even asking me that?"

"Because I just wanted to hear it for myself." I shove the last bits of my lunch into my mouth and stand. "Come on."

He squirms stiffly, eyeing a passing group of sophomore girls who give him an obnoxiously wide berth. "I've got class."

"Fine," I sigh. "I guess I'll go alone."

Despite the refusal, he stands pretty much instantly, because I know something about Ballsack that none of these sheep surrounding us have even considered.

He's innocent.

And sitting around doing nothing is going to drive him insane.

Looping his backpack over his shoulder, he follows me sullenly out the door. "Go where?"

I stop once we're outside, facing him. "My father hung me out to dry when I was arrested. I was fucked by him and the system. No one had my back, and I know we're not from the same crew, but you're a good kid, Eugene, and I don't want to see anyone go down for something they didn't do." I start walking again, this time toward the parking lot. "If Knight is going to have tunnel vision, then the only thing that'll shift him away is to give him an alternative."

Ballsy's footsteps sound out behind me. "You mean another suspect."

"Exactly."

The drive is spent in subdued silence, and I don't even argue when Ballsack reaches over to flick on the radio.

The DJ's low, smooth voice rings out. "Let's call that song a little tribute to a fallen brother. He paid the price of capturing a wicked heart. But who among us, right? Who among us..." His laugh is quiet and uncomfortably sinister.

I roll my eyes. "Jesus, my bird loves this fucking asshat."

Ballsy chuckles. "So do some of the cutsluts. Something about his voice, I guess."

"Well, it's definitely not his message. It's all Lit Major gibberish."

Proving my point, the DJ goes on, "But if not for the savagery of brittle lips and ruby blood, what would rattle the tin can of a Royal's hollow soul?" There's a long, hissing inhale, and then, "It's two-o-clock. Do you know where your brothers are?"

Ballsy glances over at me. "This guy smokes way too much weed."

I snort, turning off the Avenue toward North Side. "Seriously," I say. Then, after a beat, my gaze drifts to the glove compartment. "I've got a pen in there."

Ballsy deflates, saying, "Thank fucking god," and immediately pops it open to find the vape. He and I trade it back and forth for the rest of the drive—past East End, around the Barons' territory, through North Side, and over the river.

I know I'm good and stoned when the DJ starts making sense.

"These are the dark days, my friends," he's drawling, "because they have to be. The smallest slant of light would show us that we shift around in our little crews, pretending we're not part of the same rotting corpse, but we are. Limbs and corrupted organs. Hair follicles and fractured bones. Irises and perforated muscles. Our women keep getting plucked away like trophy molars because you've all forgotten. Your crowns are made of clay and straw and dead things." Another one of those chilling chuckles. "Remember that you will die. Wake up, Forsyth. Wake up and smell that sweet decay—"

The sound cuts with a flick of Ballsack's finger. "What's the over-under on agent Knight questioning that fucker?"

I glare at the radio, thinking it might be time to find out who this Sorrin dude is. "He sounds deranged enough to pique my interest."

When we arrive, I lead Ballsy to the front of the SUV, giving him a pointed glance as I check my clip.

"Are we where I think we are?" he asks, voice grim as he checks his own pistol.

I start walking. "Yep."

The forest here is thick and full of bramble patches. There's no path to walk, no treads in the mushy undergrowth, just limbs and thorns. Ballsack and I force our way through it, and I don't know this Arianette chick, but if she was running through this shit, she must be tough as nails. By the time we reach the riverbank, Ballsy and I are panting and soaked with sweat.

"This is where they found her?" he asks, bracing his hands on his knees.

There's a scrap of muddy police tape on the bank. "Looks like it." I take a second to assess the scene, noting the steep cliff face on the opposite bank of the river. "There's not much online about the girl they found. She's Dean Hexley's niece, nineteen years old, but I can't find any enrollment history at either Forsyth High or Preston Prep."

Ballsack hacks a breathless cough. "Maybe she was home-schooled."

I hum. "Maybe."

Picking through the overgrowth, I try to find a clue about any direction she might have come from, but it's too dense to say for sure.

"Who has access to this area?" he asks, inspecting a low-hanging branch.

I crouch down to pick up a smooth pebble. "Historically, it's kind of a no-man's land. Access to the river has always been public prop-erty—an easement owned by the city. The river cuts straight through town. If she was dumped upstream, it could have been the Counts. Sex trafficking was always their brand."

Ballsack doesn't seem convinced. "My intel says the Counts are still too disorganized for anything like that. They're barely able to keep up with the Scratch trade, let alone extracurriculars."

I rub my thumb over the pebble's glossy surface. "The current that runs through here can be strong, especially after a hard rain. The assumption that she came from upstream mostly came down to her injuries. Scrapes and bruises, like she'd hit the rocks on her way down."

He hedges. "Maybe she was dumped?"

My mind goes to the other option for sex trafficking in Forsyth, although no one would call it that. It's far more upscale and secretive than whatever the Counts could pull off with their Scratch whores. I wouldn't even know it existed if it weren't for Wicker.

Mayfield.

"I'm more interested in what's near here," I say, pulling out my phone. With a couple of taps, I have the map pulled up, waving Eugene over. "See here? That's where we are."

He looks, eyebrows knitting together. "There's nothing out here but forest and random ponds."

"Look closer," I press, zooming out. "Right there, in the corner." It's easily ten miles away, and it doesn't matter that their land has no river access. A girl who was running hard enough? She could make it here.

"Baron territory," he realizes, eyes hardening.

I nod. "It's where they do the hunt."

He wipes the sweat from his forehead, looking bothered. "It doesn't make sense. Why would they hunt her only to *re*-hunt her?"

"I don't think they did."

He huffs, swatting at a bug. "Explain."

"The Baron King..." I begin, leveling him with a look. "He has this real hard-on for the old ways. He doesn't like guns. He doesn't have a digital footprint. That time I was in the House of Night, everything was on paper."

Finally following, he snaps his fingers. "But Arianette had a tracker."

"The Barons wouldn't tag their prey," I conclude, tucking my phone back into my pocket. "There's no glory in a rigged hunt." I'm not sure what I was expecting to find out here. A footpath? Tire tracks?

Frustratingly, there's nothing.

On the trek back to the car, I broach a difficult topic. "We wouldn't think less of you if you just ran. None of us. The Dukes, Lex and Wick. Especially me."

Ballsy tosses me a glare. "Innocent men don't run."

Which is a nice sentiment, but... "There's a lot of innocent men who spend a lifetime in prison for crimes they didn't commit."

He stops in his tracks, turning to me with tired eyes. "Back home, our trainer has this saying. Some men hit rock bottom and bounce back up. But others hit rock bottom and ask for a shovel." He claps me on the shoulder, not realizing that it's the mention of Pauly that makes me stiffen—not the words. "I'm not a digger, Pace. I told Verity I'd do everything I could to find Stella, and I can't do that if I'm hiding like a little bitch."

"No one wants you free from this more than Verity," I insist, searching his eyes. "Why are you so hell-bent on going down with the ship?"

His shoulders sink, face falling. "I think..." Reaching up, he grasps a fistful of his shirt, right over his heart. "I think I love her, Pace. I was too chickenshit to say it, but I felt it, and she's out there right now, thinking she belongs to nobody. But she does." He exhales, asking, "I mean, what if it were Verity?"

This is easy to answer. "If it were Verity, I'd burn this whole fucking city to the ground to find her."

"Yeah." Ballsy nods, glancing back at the forest. "You're a Prince, you can do that. But I'm just a nobody who makes it easy to pin this shit on."

He's not wrong about that. Names, blood, and legacy control this city, and as far as I know, Ballsy is a regular soldier. It's a fucking tough pill to swallow and it's on my mind as we walk the rest of the way to the car.

"Just promise," he eventually says, "that no matter what happens with me, you'll keep looking for her."

I came out here to help him get his mind off his troubles, but I don't think it worked. For me, all I can see now are the thick woods and thorny brambles. The rushing, punishing water. Whatever that Hexley girl was running from was bad enough, but surviving the forest too? Those are shit odds.

Any girl that makes it out of here alive has to be made of steel. But I know what it's like to need hope, to be stuck in a dark pit of despair waiting for the light to shine in. If Ballsack needs me to be that light, then fuck, I'll be it.

"No one," I assure, "East or West, will stop until Stella St. James is found."

I just hope this is a promise I can keep.

WE GET HOME right before sunset.

It's weird enough to think of it as my home, but lately, it's felt a little like Ballsy's, too. "Do you think the Baron King would allow a search party?" he asks, gathering up his bag. "I could get DKS out there, maybe even LDZ. They keep what's theirs." He conspicuously doesn't request PNZ, even though we'd give them.

Shrugging, I admit, "I doubt it. But I'll ask." *I'll have his* son *ask.*

If Remy's going to be related to half my family, then he can damn well make himself useful to it.

We part ways in the foyer, Ballsack going left, me going right. I watch the dejected line of his shoulders as he trudges toward the room he once basically shared with Stella, and I feel a twinge in my chest.

What if it were Verity?

I find her in the solarium with Effie, hanging back a second to watch as she waddles from urn to pot, considering the plants inside. "This one won't make it through the winter. I guess we cull all these and find some evergreens, huh?" At first, I think she's talking to Effie, but then I see her stroke her belly. "I won't have much time to tend to it once you come, but maybe when you're a little older, you can help me in here. Would you like that?"

The sight of her soft smile makes my stomach swoop, that twinge in my chest transforming into a clutching fist. Sometimes she hardly seems real. How did she bloom her way into our lives, filling it with such soft, sweet, warm things? And how on fucking earth did we ever think of smothering it?

"Hey," she greets, eyes lighting up as she turns at the sound of my footfalls. "I was wondering when you'd—hey!"

"Come on," I say, tugging her by the hand toward the doors. "I need to show you something."

She protests with a sputtered, "But—" even though she follows easily. "Pace, I have Effie."

Pausing, I glance around the space. There's something I've kept in here for a few weeks now, trying to work up to the idea of actually using it again, while we've let Effie practice her flying. Snagging it from the bench, I decide, "Good. We'll take her outside with us."

Verity's eyes widen. "Really?"

"Just for the walk," I assure, clipping one end of the tether to my belt loop. "Effie. Pretty bird?" I click my tongue against my teeth, holding out my hand, and Effie effortlessly swoops down from the rafters to perch on my wrist.

It's not hard to clip it onto Effie's leg. She barely looks curious about it, instead walking up my arm to perch on my shoulder. Verity lets out a surprised, airy laugh as I take them both out the door.

Both of them are quiet as I lead us to the shore, eyes on Verity's footfalls as I navigate her over stones and branches. The back of the palace grounds is notoriously neglected, mainly an access to the waterfront that's never really used. The moat around the palace is actually a branch off the main Forsyth River, a creek that splits off before rejoining it upstream. It's nothing like the riverfront, the water mostly still and placid, a thick layer of algae resting on top.

The whole walk, Effie just stretches her neck, taking everything in with uncharacteristic stillness. When another bird squawks in the distance, she shrinks low into her plumage, crouching into my neck. But it's not long before she's curious again, twisting this way and that.

As soon as the jon boat comes into view, Verity gets a little buoyancy in her step. "Oh, you were serious about the boat ride."

"Deadly," I say, helping her into the boat with a steady hand—one foot over, then the other. Once she's seated on the little bench, I unclip the tether from my belt, handing it to Verity.

Effie looks dubious when I prod her onto Verity's knee, but ultimately lets out a trilled, *"Gentle, gentle."*

"That's my good girl," I say, giving her head a little scratch. "Hold on tight."

Verity's eyes hold mine as I push the boat into the water, planting my feet with a series of strong heaves that make the hull scrape against the muddy rocks. "We could wait for Wicker," she offers.

"No," I wheeze, giving another push. "Got it."

Just then, it slides into the water and I jump in, easing myself in behind her. The boat has a motor that probably hasn't been primed in a decade, so I give it a wincingly hopeful yank.

Luckily, it flares to life.

Unluckily, it scares the shit out of Effie, who flaps her wings with a panicked, "*Suck my balls!*" Making sure she'll stay put, I steer the boat into open water.

As soon as we get up to speed, Effie trills, spreading her wings against the wind.

Verity laughs. "She thinks she's flying!" That's exactly what she looks like, her wings extended to full span as the air speeds through her plumage. "This is a really big deal, Pace. Look at her—she's loving it."

Effie's little head sways in the breeze, her beady eyes taking it all in, and it's not quite what I was expecting. The worry of her escaping is there, but it's buried so far beneath the warm, happy feeling of hearing her delighted squawks that it's impossible to get to.

I take the boat out to a quiet cove surrounded by trees ablaze in yellows, oranges, and reds. Just like I promised. Satisfied with the location, I cut the engine, and the boat rocks gently, and everything around us is abruptly serene.

Well, everything but the hard-fast hammering of my heart.

Leaning over, I gently detach the tether from Effie's leg.

Verity frowns as she watches her, wondering, "Aren't you afraid she'll fly away?"

Truthfully, Verity sounds more nervous about it than I do. I'm not sure when that happened.

"Yes," I confess. But I look at Effie—at her wide eyes and craned neck as she takes in this big, wide world—and say, "I'd rather lose something I love than condemn it to a lifetime in a cage." When Verity glances back, I give her a wink. "You taught me that."

Effie takes a few more tentative hops on the edge of the boat, then flaps her wings, tottering around the edge. I hold my breath, not knowing if she's afraid of the next step. I sure as fuck am.

Rubbing my hands nervously over my knees, I explain, "I came to the palace with nothing but a bag that had exactly two changes of underwear, one extra outfit, a pair of race car pajamas, a toothbrush, and my teddy bear, Mr. Pickles." Verity's eyes lift from watching Effie to mine. "The social worker handed the bag to Danner, and once we stepped inside, I never saw it again. It wasn't much, but even as a kid, I knew it was mine. It was all I had."

"Oh, Pace..." Her face falls, eyes already shiny and close to brimming, but I don't want to make her cry. I just need her to know the truth.

So I lean down to brush my lips against the apple of her cheek. "Even though the house was bigger than anything I'd ever seen, I still had to share a bed with two boys I didn't know. I had uniforms for school and hockey, but nothing was mine. Not until I convinced Father to let me keep Effie."

I reach out and stroke her black feathers, remembering the day I brought her home. She was sick and badly neglected. Hardly talked at all. I looked at her and saw a sad, frightened, lonely soul—just like mine.

I spent weeks online learning about her. What she needed. How to care for her—make her safe and happy. I tried to give her all the things I always wanted but could never find.

"Over time, even after those boys became my brothers, and Ashby became my father," I gesture over my shoulder, where the palace sits behind the trees, "and that mansion became my home, I never felt like it belonged to me. It was always something that could be taken from me. Why wouldn't it? Nothing in my life had ever been permanent. But when Effie came to me," I watch as Verity reaches out to pet her, "she was already caged, and as long as she had someone to love, she didn't even mind it. She never knew any different. She couldn't... leave me. Not if I kept her locked inside."

Across the narrow space in the boat, Verity's hand reaches out and takes mine. Light against dark, scarred against soft. Wrong, but completely right.

I rub my thumb over her hand, as soft as that river stone. "I knew from the first moment I saw you on that dating app that I wanted you, and it wasn't just because of your perfect body or your gorgeous eyes." I touch her cheek, following the pink, warm flush down to her neck. "I wanted to keep you, Rosi, and I was blindsided by it. Obsessed. Messy. *Stupid*." Shaking my head, I try to remember that crazed, manic month I spent *consuming* her on the screen, but it feels so far away now. "I know it's dumb. I didn't even know you yet—not really. But I was sure that was love. It had to be, right? Because when you rejected me, it actually hurt."

"Pace," she starts, those big eyes full of sorrow, "I'd never even had a boyfriend before, and you were—"

I press my finger to her lips, stalling her words. "I was too intense, and it freaked you out. I know that now. And it took me a long time to realize that it wasn't even real." I watch as my finger drags against her bottom lip, falling away. "Whatever I was feeling back then... it wasn't love. It was desperation to *have* something to love. It was sad and pathetic, and I don't blame you for running. For striking back."

Miserably, she tries, "When I reported you, I didn't know—"

"You didn't need to know." My words brook no argument, and I turn my gaze out to the water, wondering how many living things are thriving there, just beneath the surface. "The truth is, I keep Effie in a cage because I love her. But blaming Father for going to prison... that meant acknowledging that he kept me in a cage because he hated me. I couldn't face that." Meeting her watery eyes, I confess, "So I blamed you instead. Someone who hurt me. Someone I could eventually punish for it."

She releases a long, shaky exhale. "Nothing about being an Ashby is easy, Pace." Her thumb rubs over mine, soothing me when I should be comforting her. "I forgave you for all of that a long time ago."

"God knows why, because I don't deserve it," I mutter before taking a steadying breath, summoning the courage I need to continue. "But I've thought about it a lot lately, and I want—no, I *need* you to know it's real this time."

A sad sort of hope swims in her eyes. "What is?"

I bring her hand to my lips, pushing a soft kiss into her delicate knuckles. "I love you, Rosilocks Sinclaire." Watching the force of my words sink in, the tears spilling over, I whisper, "So fucking much that every breath I take when you're nearby feels like a thousand daggers to the heart. So much that if you told me right now you wanted to leave and take our son to a better, safer place, I'd..." Pausing, I admit, "Well, I'd fucking hate it, and there's not a power in this world that could stop me from still watching over you, but—but I'd let you go." A fat tear rolls down her cheek and I catch it on the tip of my thumb. "I understand now that you don't cage the people you love."

She's quiet for a moment, and I sit before her, stripped and raw. Water laps at the edge of the boat and Effie lets a soft trill loose into the breeze. Finally, Verity says, "What we have is different from the others. We have a history, Pace, and it's complicated, but I also think that's what makes us able to work through anything that challenges us. You're going to be a good dad. You're going to keep Justice safe in a world that's filled with threats. I know you will because you already do that for your brothers, and for Effie, and for me." Her hand cups my cheek, and she gets as close to me as she can with the swell of her belly between us. "I love you too, Pace, and we are never going anywhere without you."

The boat twitches, and I realize it's Effie finally pushing off the edge, her wings unfurling like a flower. My breath hitches, and Verity clutches me back as we watch her silhouette rise against the fading sky. Each beat of her wings is a punch to the wind until she finally catches it. The sight of her soaring gracefully against a stream overhead is all at once terrifying and beautiful.

Just like life is supposed to be.

It's dark by the time we go back to shore.

My heart still feels vaguely outside my body, but every time I glance up, Effie is circling right above us, never straying too far.

"You know, we used to go out on the boat when we were kids," I say, helping Verity back onto the bank. If she slips and falls, Lex won't have to kick my ass—I'll do it myself. "Usually to get high or spy on the Princess." I point to a window on the west-facing wall. "You can see right into our window from the middle of the creek."

She shivers. "Well, that's creepy."

Laughing, I reply, "Why do you think I'm always closing those curtains?"

When we reach the garden, I plant my feet, take a deep breath, and raise my arm. "Effie, come." I punctuate this with a whistle, and it feels like Verity holds her breath with me as we wait.

Although it takes a heartbeat longer than I like, my stomach drops in relief when she swoops down, her black wings slicing through the twilight.

Her talons curl around my wrist when she lands. "*Sunshine*," she coos. "*Pretty sunshine bird.*"

Verity laughs, giving her head a little pet. "It's dark, pretty bird."

Satisfied, I release her back into the solarium and resolve to take a nice, long, hot shower with my Princess. I haven't had this much outdoorsing in a day since the time we went to hockey camp up north.

When we get back up to the house, both Lex and Wicker are in the kitchen preparing dinner, the latter glaring at his phone as he reads out instructions. "It says not to crowd the pan. You're clearly crowding the pan."

"You're crowding my last nerve," Lex gripes back, noticing us enter. "Hey, was that Effie I saw out the window earlier?"

"Yeah," I answer, ignoring their stunned stares.

"We took her flying." Verity lumbers up onto a stool, all grins. "You should have seen her! I think she was even catching bugs."

It's not the scent of grilled chicken or mashed potatoes that catches my attention. It's the black envelope sitting in the middle of the counter.

"What's that?" I interrupt, eyeing it skeptically.

"Came this afternoon," Lex says, drying his hands. "The Barons' seal is on the back. We waited until you got back to open it."

Verity picks up the envelope, studies the seal, and then runs her finger underneath it. She pulls out a sheet of black cardstock with silver ink across the front.

"Don't tell me it's another gift," Wicker mutters. "I don't know how Danner used to do it, but I've been trying to get the bloodstains out of my Versace for weeks. I'm on a murder fast."

"Not a gift. An invitation." She looks up, pulling a face. "To the black wedding. On Halloween, just like Sy said."

"Jesus, any chance we can get out of that?" I ask, looking between my brothers hopefully. "Pregnancy card? She'll be about ready to burst by then, right?"

Verity groans. "God help us all if the baby isn't here by the thirty-first." She rubs her belly. "By then, you'd have to roll me down the aisle."

Wicker decides, "Well, I don't care what Payne and Perilini say. I'm not going to some arranged wedding between an emo-gothy chick and one of the new Barons. Maybe it's going against my creepy pedigree, but those masks freak me the fuck out."

Verity inspects the invitation again, her jaw suddenly dropping. "Oh. My. God." She slides down off the stool, barely noticing when I lurch forward to catch and steady her. "*Oh my god!*"

"What?" Lex rushes over, hand clamping over hers, face paled. "Is it happening?"

"It's not the baby. It's this." She thrusts the invitation in his face, and his expression goes slack.

"Holy shit."

"For god's sake," Wick bitches, snatching the invitation out of Lex's hand. He begins reading aloud, *"You are cordially invited to bear witness to the eternal union of Baroness Arianette Gowen Hexley to The King of Barons on the evening of October thirty-first, at the House of Night."*

I grab the card to read it myself, but sure enough, in silver and red, the invitation is clear.

It's not just any Baron getting married. It's their King, and his new wife is twenty-five years younger.

"I guess Killian was right," Verity says, glancing between us. "Attending this wedding is a Royal obligation we can't refuse."

22

erity

"You sure you want all of this down?" Dylan, the kid who asks, is at the top of the ladder. Below him, giving support, is Chris. When I told Pace I needed help in the solarium, he sent me two kids who just went through rush and pledged PNZ. I guess grunt work goes to the newbies. They're both babies—in Prince terms—barely out of high school and thrust into a world they think is all frat parties, hook-ups, and future connections.

Instead, they're doing my gardening work.

"All of it," I tell him, pointing to the canopy. The leaves have already died off for the winter and it's just a hulk of gray, twisted, unassuming vines. Now, I know better. "Once you're done, drag it out back and we'll burn it."

Dylan nods, and gestures for Chris to hand him a small hatchet from the tool kit. They get to work with a gusto that makes me envious, all energy and optimism. The new pledges weren't at any of the ceremonies I've been involved in, but they've heard rumors about what transpired the night of the oaths. I see how they look at me, with a little bit of fear and a heavy dose of awe. They're obviously terrified of the upperclassmen, especially my Princes, and I've learned they'll do anything I ask them to without any questions.

It's pretty awesome.

"Hey," Ballsack says, walking out of the house and squinting at the light. "I thought you may be out here." He looks up at the guys. "What's going on?"

I lean against a pillar. "With all the renewal and rebirth going on around here, I figured the garden could use a little sprucing up before winter." Sighing, I prop my hand to support my lower back. It's been killing me all week. "Also, I'm bored to tears. Lex and Pace are back in classes while Wick is trying to get a handle on Rufus' business interests. No one's around to entertain me."

"You could take a nap instead of supervising freshmen hacking up your garden." He looks me up and down. "You look exhausted."

I make a face. "I *am* exhausted. Justice thinks it's fun to sleep on my bladder, making me get up every few hours. My cravings are ridiculous, and," I pull at the sleeveless dress I'm wearing, even though we're way past summer weather, "I'm hot all the time. At least it's cooler in here."

Ballsy tries and fails to hide his discomfort at my diatribe, and glances back at the guys hacking up the vines. "Damn, being a freshman pledge sucks. You wouldn't believe all the shit-work the guys gave me when I was first recruited."

"And look at you now," I smile, though a bit sadly. "They offered you a Dukeship and everything. Do you regret not taking it?"

"I don't know." He shakes his head, modestly, but I see the light in his eyes. "It's a strong class, and I'm not sure how great of a leader I'd be."

"Eugene." I give him a look. "You spent the last ten months living with a bunch of Princes in a completely volatile time, not only keeping me safe but managing to avoid a territory war. If that's not leadership, I don't know what is."

Ballsy's cheeks turn pink, and blushing at my compliments, his gaze flicks back up to Dylan, who's currently struggling to get his hatchet through the thick vine. "That's the purple stuff, right? Looks like big bunches of grapes?"

"Wisteria," I say, aware he's avoiding my compliment. "It is beautiful, but I've also learned it can be dangerous."

He studies me for a long moment. He hasn't asked any of us what happened with Rufus or Danner, but he's aware both are gone. "It makes it a lot brighter in here. I like it."

"*I like it.*" Effie trills from the branch of a camellia tree. "*I like it, Euuugene. I like it.*"

"Shit!" Ballsack jumps a foot off the ground. His hand lands on his heart. "I didn't know she was in here."

"I thought she probably needed to stretch her wings," I explain. Ever since Pace and I took her out on the water, she's been bursting with life, eager to go out again.

"Well, warn a guy next time." He exhales slowly. "I should kick Wick's ass for teaching that bird my name," he says, glaring up at Effie. "I told him in strict confidence that birds freak me out."

"No," I shake my head, fighting off a laugh, "you shouldn't have. These men are trained experts in the torture of their enemies. You're the dumbass who showed him a weak spot."

"They're just so unpredictable," he argues. After a blink, he adds, "*Birds.* Not Wicker, although that dude can definitely sneak up on a guy." He shakes his head. "It's their beady eyes, always looking like they're watching you, and the talons and beaks are strong enough to crack the shells off seeds and nuts." His eyes are wide and he quickly covers his crotch with his hands. "I don't want her to do that, or anything else, to me."

He's so serious that it's a struggle to hold back my laughter. "She's more likely to take a shit on you than to go after your genitals."

"Maybe." He scowls, keeping his eye on the black bird. "That bird is a—"

"*Pretty bird.*"

Ballsy flinches, but I can't help but smile up at Effie. "Yes, you're a pretty bird."

"Don't encourage her," he mutters.

"If she makes you that uncomfortable, you can go. I'm fine down here alone."

"Actually, I came to find you for a reason." He jerks his thumb back at the house. "There's a package that's been delivered for you."

I look over at the two guys hacking up my garden, unsure if they can be left without supervision. "Can you just leave it for me? Or have one of the guys take it up to our room?"

Ballsy's eyebrows do something complicated. "I think you're going to want to open this one sooner than later."

Relenting, I turn to the boys. "Dylan!" His clippers snip off a piece of fern. "Don't touch anything past that window!"

"Yes, ma'am."

I turn back to Ballsack. "What's so important that I need to see it now?"

Haltingly, he explains, "It's... from the Baron King."

THERE's no mistaking who the huge box is from. Although *box* isn't the right word. It's a massive wooden crate taking up the majority of the foyer floor. My name, *Princess Verity Sinclaire*, has been painted with a fine hand into the top while the BRN star is emblazoned on the sides.

"Ready?" Ballsack asks, standing next to the crate with a crowbar in hand, ready to pop the lid.

"Wait!" Wicker's voice carries down to the foyer. He rushes down with a scowl and unintentionally tousled hair. I can tell it's unintentional because he has this cowlick right beside his crown that he's always an expert at taming. Today, it's sticking straight up, the slight red rimming around his eyes evidence of his lack of sleep.

He's been pouring over Rufus' ledgers and accounts for days now, trying to determine the most profitable ventures worth keeping or selling off.

"Put the crowbar down, Eugene." When he reaches us, he snatches the tool out of Ballsack's hand. "Where did this come from?"

Ballsy shrugs. "Standard delivery at the gate. Your guys scanned it and brought it in."

"Not to sound vain," Wick eyes the container, "but I'm starting to think the King has a crush on me."

"Let's just open the box," I roll my eyes, "and worry about crushes later."

He wedges the tip of the crowbar under the lip of the box, and with Ballsack's help, they rip off the lid. The inside is stuffed with packing material, but an envelope, similar to the one sent to Wicker the day we went to the mausoleum, sits on top.

I gently pluck it up, opening it.

Dear Princess,

Congratulations on your son receiving the Oath of Fealty from the brothers of PNZ. Enclosed is a Baron heirloom that was Whitaker's as a child. I thought he might want to keep it in the family.

The Baron King

I give Wicker a questioning look, but he just shrugs and gestures for Ballsy to help him with the rest of the crate.

"The last time the Baron King gave us a gift, it was a human sacrifice," he mutters. "Stand back, Red."

I move because he's not wrong about the King and his gift giving. With my hand resting on my stomach, I watch as they pull off the sides, revealing the contents with a dramatic clatter of wood.

I notice the smooth, dark wood first, then the slats.

"It's a bassinet!" I exclaim in surprise. Wick stares at it before reaching out, running his hand along the railing. Then it hits me. "Oh, wow. Was it *your* bassinet?"

I move closer, brushing a touch to Wick's forearm while examining the head and foot of the bed. While I'd expect the usual macabre BRN iconography in the craftsmanship, I find just a beautiful design of curls and whorls carved into the wood. "Wick, it's beautiful."

My Prince is quiet, his hand clenched over the railing. Behind us, Ballsack's phone rings and he steps out the front door, probably grateful for the excuse to leave the room.

"Hey," I squeeze his arm, "are you okay?"

"I don't know," he admits, a complex combination of emotions coming over his face. "I've never been like Pace—wanting to know all his family history, needing these touchstones— but I... I can't shake it. It's chasing me like death itself, and then I see something like this," he grips the rail, "and I worry it's just bringing that darkness into our son's life."

"Maybe." I lift his arm and lean in against him, admiring the slight sheen of the wood's finish. "I've had those pledges cutting down the wisteria in the solarium all morning, trying to banish the house of every trace of evil connected to Rufus. But in the end, it's just a plant. A *harmless* plant. Only a psychopath would use it as a weapon. This..." I rest my hand over the railing, "it's just a bassinet, Wicker. A beautiful one that once cradled a beautiful towheaded baby who grew into the man I love." He looks down at me, his blue eyes softening. "Maybe the garden is just a place for beautiful vines. And maybe this is just a bassinet," I laugh, "which *is* something we still need, by the way."

Wicker seems to contemplate this heavily, a crevice carved into his forehead. "It's the people, not the things."

I nod. "Exactly."

The muscle in the back of his jaw tightens. "I think I'd like to keep it. If that's okay with you."

"It's absolutely okay."

He takes my face in his hands and kisses me in what I can only assume is gratitude. But it's not necessary. Our family will be an elaborate tapestry made from dark and light, hard and soft, pain and comfort.

And it'll warm our son.

Wicker decides, "Pace can check it for bugs or whatever voodoo the Barons put on it when he gets back from class, and then we'll move it upstairs."

"Perfect." I sigh. "I should probably go tell Dylan and Chris to stop hacking up my garden—"

The door swings open and Ballsack rushes in, phone still in his hand. The pallor of his face makes my stomach drop before the words even leave his mouth. "That was Remy," he says, voice tight. "They found a body. A girl."

The air knocks out of me, my knees going weak, but before I can crumble, Wicker catches me, holding me upright. I barely hear myself when I ask, "Is it her?"

"It's not Stella." Eugene swallows, but before the relief washes over me, he adds, "It's Laura."

"Laura?" It's not until he says her name that I realize how much I'd held out hope that she'd just left Forsyth for something better.

"She's dead?" Wicker asks, tightening his hold on me.

He nods. "Remy's uncle called because she's West End. There aren't a lot of details, but..." He looks pleadingly at Wick. "Are you okay if I head over to West End? Everyone's there and—"

"Sure, man. Fuck. Yes. Go, be with your people." He shoves his hand in his hair. "I'll start making some calls. Use a little of this newfound sway to see what I can find out. Verity and I can fill in the guys when they get home."

"I'm going, too," I announce, still feeling unsteady. "Let me get my bag."

"Red, you know you can't do that. Lex wants you close to home." His gaze drops down to my belly. "Just in case."

"I've got two weeks before this baby hits full term." My heart is pounding, and suddenly being over at the gym, with my mother and friends, is less of a want and more of a need. "There's no reason I can't ride two miles across town to be with my family."

"*Your family*," he repeats with a slow blink.

"You know what I mean." His jaw sets, but I'm already working my way out of his arms. The urge to go is tugging me to my old home like a magnet. "Wicker, she was my friend. They're all my friends. I just want to be with them."

After a moment, he relents, "Fine. But you're not going alone."

"Verity will be safe with me," Ballsack assures. "I promise."

Wicker is already snagging a set of keys from the hook against the wall. "I know she will be, but she'll be twice as safe with both of us."

I grab Wicker's hand and squeeze. "Thank you."

He tugs me close, pushing a lingering kiss into my hair. "It's the people, Red. Not the things."

LIFE IN WEST END has never been easy. We don't live in palaces made of gold or historic brownstones. Our territory is industrial, and our hobbies and work lean toward rougher, more physical trades. Both fighting and the gun business are dangerous. The years after Davis, Manny, and Sarah were run off, when the territory was under Saul's rule, were hard on the community. I might have been young when I lived here, but I well remember that. We've lost a few guys to Scratch and the other junk Lionel Lucia slung throughout Forsyth, but this...

I haven't seen the gym like this since Tatum Cross' suicide—well, murder. Not that we knew it at the time.

As soon as we enter, I almost wish I hadn't come. The anguish and grief feel like a low murmur in the cavernous building. Andrea has her arm around Maggie's shoulders, both of them with mascara-stained cheeks. Kaz has his arms wrapped around Kathleen, and Louie strokes Daphne's hair as he whispers something private into her ear. In the back, near Mama's shut office door, Sy rubs the back of his neck while Remy paces back and forth, his marker twirling erratically in his fingers. Nick and Lavinia stand off to the side, his forehead pressed against hers as he whispers to her, wiping his thumbs under her wet eyes.

It's only when Wicker and I approach that he looks up, straightening at the sight. "Ver," he says, giving Wicker a dubious look. "You didn't have to come."

"Yeah, I did," I reply, hoping that bringing a Prince into this vulnerable, hurt moment isn't adding to the strain of it.

When Lav sees me, most of that worry goes out the window. She both perks up and falls apart at the same time. The hug we share is awkward with my massive stomach between us, but she doesn't let go, clutching me tight.

"It's so fucked, V," she says. "She was one of the first girls to ever look at me and see someone other than a Lucia. When she disappeared, I hoped she'd just..." Her words choke off with a sob.

"Me, too," I tell her. "I thought maybe she got the fuck out of here. Was living at the beach or some place where she could just vanish and start over."

But even though neither of us probably wants to admit it, the scenario seemed unlikely. Laura was happy here. She and Ballsy didn't exactly have a romance for the ages, but she had someone who treated her well. She had friends, school, and ambitions. But that hope of her hightailing it out of this wretched city was better than the alternative.

The alternative, it seems, is unthinkable.

Lavinia's gaze lifts over my shoulder, where I know Eugene came in behind me. He's standing with the Dukes, hands shoved in his pockets. "How is he?" she asks, gathering herself in that special marriage of Lucia and West End armor.

Glancing at Wick, I sigh. "Numb, I think. He didn't say much on the way over." A twinge jolts up my spine and I step back. "I think we're both terrified of what it means for Stella."

Wicker jams his fists into his pockets, looking unsure of his place here. "They could have been unconnected. I wouldn't make any conclusions yet."

"This is Forsyth," Nick says, drawing Lavinia protectively into his side. "Everything is connected."

Wick nods, unable to argue that much. "Well, whatever we can do or offer," he tells Nick, shrugging. "Pace is good at getting into files if you need to know what the police know."

Lavinia sniffs, glancing up at Nick. "That might come in handy."

Nick neither accepts nor declines. "I should be out on the Avenue, sniffing out some leads," he says. But she strains up to press a kiss to the tattoo of her lip print on his neck—the side unmarred by the shrapnel scar—and I know from the way he looks at her that he won't be leaving her side anytime soon.

"The girls?" I ask, looking around. "Are they... handling it?"

Lav shakes her head. "They're a mess. And they're scared."

This knowledge makes it worse, and the grief combined with the anxious energy in the room spurs me to accept the only thing I know to do. "Tell me what I can do to help." I scan the room, eyes landing on Sy's. "Where's Mama?"

Nick nods toward the back. "She's talking to Laura's dad on the phone."

"Okay." I take a deep breath, feeling Wick's hand slipping into mine. "Anything else need doing?"

"Remy's keeping up with his uncle," Lav explains, and I see him off to the side, texting on his phone. "The girls are planning a vigil for later tonight."

"Oh, that sounds nice. Here?"

"At the tower."

Good. Staying busy is good, which is what we need to be doing, because I cannot think about what all of this means for Stella.

"Food," I say, as if it's the easiest solution in the world. "We'll need food."

Wicker perks up, saying, "Yeah, I've gotten good at the lasagna," and my heart clenches at these small, easy offers. "Just point me to a pot."

"I'll help," I say, unable to resist lifting our joined hands to my lips.

"And we'll need booze. A shit-ton," Lav adds, gaze dropping abruptly to my stomach, "well, for most of us."

"A couple more weeks," I say, ignoring another twinge.

Wicker doesn't, though. He frowns, leaning down to whisper, "You sure you can handle this? I know Lex says it's good for you to move, but—"

Interrupting him with a kiss, I explain, "I'll feel better if I do something."

Despite looking unconvinced, he sighs. "Just no heavy lifting. Get one of the fifty guys in here to do it, okay?"

Lav nods, looking a little more steady now that we have a plan. "We'll send a few of the guys out to stock the bar at the tower, and—"

Wicker tugs me away. "We can go see what's in the kitchen, in case we need to send someone to the store."

She exhales, taking a breath so deep I'm jealous. The baby has dropped a bit, settling more on my pelvis which is hell on my hips, but falling into the rhythm of work does the trick. Wicker and I pull out ingredients and heat the ovens. As he works cutting onions, other girls slowly begin finding their way into the kitchen, where I give each a job.

"I know Mama keeps a bunch of frozen bread in the chest freezer," I tell Daphne. "Go see how much there is? It'll defrost pretty fast if we set them out." I turn and eye some DKS recruits who look overwhelmed and lost. They never met Laura. "Hey, guys. See that stack of tables against the wall?" One pimply kid nods. "Start putting them out in rows—Family Dinner style. And then the chairs—"

"Verity Sinclaire!" I spin and my mother stands in the doorway. She looks like hell, eyes red and puffy. "What the hell are you doing?"

"We were just—"

"Getting off your feet," she answers for me, shooting Wicker an incredulous look. "She's thirty-eight weeks pregnant."

His jaw drops, the ladle in his hand thrust in my direction. "She said she had to! She gave me the big, sad eyes and everything."

Mama snorts. "Falling for the pout. Bush league, blondie."

I insist, "I'm fine, Mama." Although it is a little hot in here. "We're almost done."

"You're already done." Retreating, she holds up a finger in her infamous 'you have one minute' command.

"Go," Lav says, looking guilty. "You've already been a huge help. We'll finish getting this ready, and then we can all eat before the vigil."

I exit the kitchen, where Mama is waiting with her hand on her hip. She's mad, but she's also worried and sad and all the things that are swirling around in my stomach like a storm.

Pushing aside my anger, I beeline to her, collapsing into her arms.

She instantly gathers me up, sucking in a huge breath. "Oh, Ver Bear."

I inhale the scent of her, allowing myself this comfort. "I've seen a lot of bad things since becoming Princess, Mama. Things that were so bad, Rufus Ashby had to be eliminated, but whoever did this... *is* doing this..." My voice cracks. "He may be worse than Ashby or the other Kings combined."

At least Danner gave them a quiet way out.

"We'll find him," she says, stroking my hair back. "He's getting sloppy. One escaped girl, and another one shows up dead? He's not going to be able to hide for long."

It's there, in the warm silence of Mama's arms, that I hear the first phone go off.

The *ding* comes from somewhere behind me—barely a distraction—but then a series of other notification sounds swell all around the gym until Sy's booming voice punches through the room.

"237!"

erity

"LOAD THE GIRLS UP!"

Mama and I jolt back, her eyes flying wide. "No," she says, swinging around to watch as DKS members begin yanking guns out of their pants and jackets, handing them off to the nearest cutslut. "Not here. Not now!"

I spin as Maggie rushes past me toward the lounge, loaded up with three pistols. Behind her, the other girls scurry in the same fashion, and I don't need to ask what's going on. I was one of them once. A call of 237 to load the girls up?

Wick slams out of the kitchen with Kaz, his blue eyes meeting mine. "What is it?"

I run to him, wincing as my stomach clenches. "It's a raid. They're coming to—"

A deafening crash echoes as the front doors splinter open, the heavy thud of boots reverberating through the building.

"Everyone, down on the ground!" a voice bellows, and suddenly there are a dozen guns pointed at the room.

What erupts next is the embodiment of 237.

Mayhem.

Nick Bruin takes out his gun first, stepping in front of Lavinia as he points it at the cops. Weasel and Kent follow, drawing their pistols, and I'm stiff with panic as Wicker pulls me behind him. I don't even realize Remy's up in the loft section until he suddenly drops down, landing beside me, Kaz, and Wicker, poised to strike.

Shouts fill the room from either side, DKS enraged as the officers bark orders with a precision that doesn't even begin to cut through the chaos.

Not until Mama's voice rings out over the loudspeaker. "Every cub in this room better lower his fucking gun right this instant!" There's a tense beat where my heart hammers wildly, Wicker backing up into me as if he could hide me. Slowly, DKS begins obeying, guns being lowered with tense jaws and flared nostrils. Glancing over to the box seats, I catch sight of Mama leaning over the betting table, growling at the police through the microphone. "This is a vigil for one of our own. How dare you choose today to come bursting in here, guns blazing? Show some fucking respect."

"Sorry for your loss, ma'am." Agent Knight, not even bothering to remove his sunglasses, steps over shards of the gym's broken door and struts past the line of heavily armored enforcers. "But that's exactly why we're here today. We would have preferred to have apprehended our suspect peacefully." He throws a pointed look at Sy. "Inconveniently, that was made impossible since our entry into West End was obstructed. Something about a heavy barricade of stalled vehicles in the roadway?"

Sy offers him a cold grin. "Don't know what you mean."

Agent Knight doesn't look impressed. "Well, I'm sure you can understand how a premeditated defense might make us a little twitchy. Like you're trying to buy time," he glances over at the guns, "or hide something."

Wicker twists his head to glance at Remy, mouthing, "Stalled vehicles?"

Remy inches closer to Nick and Lav, whispering, "Failsafe. Our guys block the roads to buy us time to secure the gun stash."

Kaz adds, "The cutsluts are dumping any loose pieces they managed to snag."

Agent Knight's gaze sweeps over the men in the room, skating over Wicker before skittering back. "An Ashby in the bear den. Interesting. Mr. Perilini," he says, gesturing to Sy. "If you'd politely instruct your... cubs... to comply with procedure, I'm confident we can leave here promptly and without any loss of life."

Sy's lip curls, and for a moment, I'm terrified he's going to resist. I wouldn't even blame him. But in the end, Simon Perilini was made King for a reason.

He knows what's best for his boys.

Making a big show of it, Sy goes down to his knees, and in a breathtaking unison, every man around him follows, each of them going down to their front, flat on the ground.

With an annoyed sigh, Wicker does the same. "Can't keep a shirt clean to save my goddamn life. I don't know why I bother anymore."

"Versace?" Remy asks, looking him up and down.

Wick nods.

"That's why I stick to black."

The exchange isn't enough to calm the agony growing in my stomach, unable to even show solidarity by getting on the ground with anyone else. Sensing this, Wicker props up onto his elbow like he's just hanging out—the very picture of ennui—and curls a hand around my ankle.

"Just stand back and don't say anything, Red." His blue eyes flick up to mine, and I realize the bored air about him is entirely artificial. "One day, we're going to ruin this motherfucker."

"Goddamn right, we are," Remy mutters, glaring daggers as the police begin dragging up DKS members, one by one, and summarily search them. I don't know how many guns the cutsluts were able to grab before Knight burst in, but it couldn't have been very many. Dave, Nick, and Hernandez are all packing, and Weasel's frisk results in two glocks, a revolver, and a beaming grin as the frat all witness it.

Porterfield whistles. "Weasel is legion. Three points!" and the rest of the frat laughs, watching as Weasel is escorted out with a proud strut.

"What does the winner get?" Wicker asks, coming to the same conclusion I am.

They're turning it into a competition.

Kaz is the one to answer, smirking. "The final fight in the next Fury. I've got three myself."

Wicker raises an eyebrow. "Want a fourth?"

Kaz's gaze whips to him. "For real?"

"In my waistband," he says, watching the officers grab another guy up in the distance. "Now."

Smoothly, Kaz reaches over and takes the gun from the small of Wicker's back, tucking it into his own. "Thanks."

Wicker looks up, giving me a baffled glance. "Sure. Anytime."

The laughter and celebration that waves through the room with each arrest is neither happy nor bitter. It's a lot like Wicker, actually—putting on a show of this not mattering in the least.

And in a way, it doesn't. I actually start to relax as I'm ignored, and they work down the line, each confiscated gun resulting in sharp cheers and easy grins. Even Mama, down on the floor beside the table, barks a laugh at Dave, who moans as an officer grabs his junk.

When they reach our little side group—Wicker, Remy, Kaz, and I—one of the officers with a thin mustache and snapping gum asks, "Why aren't you on the ground?"

Wicker drawls, "Look at her. She's thirty-eight weeks pregnant. The fuck do you expect her to do?"

A cramp rips through me and I gasp, clutching my belly.

The cop sighs. "Fine. *You*. Up."

The wave of pain rushes away, and I realize they're motioning at Remy, who rises fluidly to his feet. He grabs the corner of his shirt and lifts it, revealing his body art, arms spread. "Bad day for you, buddy. I'm clean as a whistle."

Remy might be, but most of them get taken off—even the ones who don't have guns—for something or another. Traffic violations. Probation violations. Simple possession of paraphernalia. Kaz gets the loudest cheer at four guns, with chants of, "To the victor go the spoils!" and he obnoxiously bows as he's led away, handcuffed and skipping. But it's all small stuff, and from the way Remy is chuckling as he stands back—one of the only guys who couldn't be arrested—chances are, all of them will be out by tomorrow.

But then they get to Eugene.

Agent Knight is the one to step over his prone form, bending to gather Eugene's wrist for the handcuffs. It's nothing like it was with the other guys. There's no fun frisk to see who's won the raid's gun count.

Instead, Agent Knight clicks the cuffs, saying, "Eugene Warren, you're under arrest for suspicion in the murder of Laura Walker. You have the right to remain silent. Anything you say—"

It hits me as the room erupts in a different sound this time, full of indignation and hurled profanities, that this was the whole point. To clear the guns, the frat boys, even some cutsluts out of the room before they arrested him. The realization knocks me sideways, and I no longer hear what anyone is saying. The only thing swimming in my ears is an odd sort of ringing as I watch Ballsy turn to meet my gaze, all the blood draining from his face.

Everything falls apart.

The artifice of fun snaps away, and suddenly, a wave of fury fills the air.

I'm not even surprised when Remy rushes at Knight, slamming his tattooed fist into his face with a snarl. "That's bullshit, and you fucking know it!"

Knight staggers from the hit, his sunglasses flying off, but quickly collects himself, offering Remy a bloody grin. "Thank you. When we came here, I didn't have anything on you, and trust me, I looked." He jerks his head at the officer running over. "Book Mr. Maddox for assaulting a federal officer."

Remy puts his own hands behind his back, leaning in to sneer, "You're a pussy. You wouldn't make it ten seconds in a ring with one of us."

But Knight's already moving on.

To Wicker.

He stares down at him, dabbing his split lip. "I wonder what we're going to find in your pants, Ashby."

Wicker climbs slowly to his feet, a cocky smirk plastered to his face. "Just my throbbing, nine-inch cock."

"Why are you doing this to us?" I ask, the words tearing out of my throat like a sob. "Eugene didn't do anything. Why won't you leave him alone? Can't you see we've been through enough?"

Agent Knight gives me a long, searching look. "It's always the boyfriend, Miss Sinclaire. Or the fiancée. Or the husband." He steps closer, peering down into my eyes. It galls me to see the sympathy on his face. "You think I'm gunning for the people you care about, Princess, but I'm trying to protect you from them." Agent Knight glances back, watching as Ballsy's led out of the gym. "Something you may think about before that baby gets here."

Laura is dead.

Stella might be too, for all I know.

Eugene, the Dukes, DKS—everyone is being taken away in handcuffs.

And somewhere in that maelstrom of grief and anger and bone-deep helplessness, I feel a sudden trickle of warmth against my thighs, transforming to a gush, just as a cramp seizes me.

"Oh no!" I gasp. "No, no, no..." I grab for Wicker, but he's already there, shoulder slamming into Agent Knight as he catches me. I know he understands what's happening when his shoe slips, squeaking against the clear fluid pooling on the floor, because he inspects it with a frozen stare.

And then his blue eyes rise to mine. "We need to get you out of here." He swings that panicked gaze onto Agent Knight. "Her water just broke. You can frisk me, but make it quick. We have to get to the car to—shit, my leather. No," his head shakes, "don't worry about that. Oh, fuck."

"You're not going anywhere," Knight says, pushing him back. "This is an active raid, Ashby. How do I know she's not faking?"

"Her water broke! How's she going to fake that?"

Another cramp hits, and I suck in a breath. Knight glances over, grimacing. "If your girlfriend needs an ambulance, we'll call her one, but no one else is coming in or out of here until we're finished."

Only one problem with that. "They can't get through," says an officer, overhearing. "The tow companies here are giving us the runaround. We're having to call the county wreckers to get those stalled cars removed."

"County?!" Wicker snaps. "That'll take an hour, at least!"

Agent Knight holds up a finger as he pulls the officer to the side, leaning in to ask him something.

I gasp, another slice of pain ripping through me. "The... the barricade. *Wicker.*"

He's there instantly, grabbing my face to draw my gaze to his. "Hey, it's okay. It's fine. You don't need to worry. I've got this handled."

"How?" I whimper.

He pauses, mouth pulled back in a grimace. "Okay, so I don't actually know. Lex told me my job during labor was to keep you calm, so that's all I know how to do." His face falls. "But I swear in another circumstance, I'd be absolutely killing it. I had all these massages and—"

I double over with a moan. "Wick, we can't leave and an ambulance can't get to us. What do we do?"

There's a beat where a steel resolve comes over his features. "Maybe an ambulance can't," he agrees, whipping out his phone. "But nothing can stop Lex from getting to you."

~

I TAKE a deep breath as I pace in circles.

It's only been ten minutes and it's already getting harder to hold myself up. But sitting down had been worse, so I'm just walking. Breathing. *Listening.*

Mostly to my mother, who's giving Agent Knight the dressing down of his life.

"My baby is about to give birth, and your stubborn, incompetent, Barney Fife ass better cook up a quick way to get her to a goddamn hospital, or we're going to sue your ass to kingdom come!"

The agent scratches his head, looking a bit harried. Clearly, in all his planning, he hadn't been expecting a pregnant woman's labor to interrupt his grudge raid.

"We have EMS medics coming," he explains, watching the door. "They'll have supplies, and if it gets to that point, they'll know how to deliver—"

"Fuck your medics!" I shriek through another gritted wave of pain. I can't explain why, but I'd rather linger in pain than know this asshole played any part in Justice's birth. "Nobody working under your supervision is touching me. Not one fucking finger, or I swear to god, they'll lose it." I take a breath, trying to calm down. "He'll get here. I know he will."

Even my own mother looks stunned at the outburst, although also reluctantly impressed. She ultimately rolls her eyes. "Oh, fuck this guy. Someone grab Pauly!"

Pauly. I take a slow breath. Pace's father isn't exactly who I want but at the very least he'll have drugs.

Wicker approaches, the phone pressed to his ear. There's a sheen of sweat on his forehead that wasn't there before, and he thinks I don't notice him forcibly smoothing the bothered divot in his brow away. "He's on his way," he tells me, "breaking speed records."

"Don't worry," Mama says, watching my pacing. "Sinclaire women have the easiest labors, Ver Bear. You slipped right out of me like a slug from a water can."

A chorus of disgust sounds out, and I'm reminded once again of the ten DKS sitting against the wall, all their wrists cuffed behind them. The first paddywagon is full, and the second got blocked by the barricade, so they're all stuck here until Knight unfucks his own mess.

Fucking *perfect*.

Remy grins from his spot on the floor. "That's beautiful, Mama B. Red as fuck."

Wick turns away to hiss into the phone. "Lex, where are you? They're talking about slugs and gross stuff, and this isn't my area of expertise! I'm just supposed to be the soothing, calm guy. Listen to my voice, Lex. Do I fucking sound calm?"

I shake my head, as if I can shake the pain and panic away. "They won't let him in. We're trapped here, and they don't care." The hysteria of it all grips me just as another sharp contraction hits.

Lex and I had a plan. I'm delivering at Forsyth General, where he's going to assist for credit hours—a string that had been pulled almost eight months ago, the same week my pregnancy test came back positive. Wicker made me a playlist and Pace was going to be my anchor because they were both going to be in the room with us. There was supposed to be a full medical facility and *drugs*. It was a good plan. A solid plan. A plan that didn't involve ten detained cubs, an FBI agent, and a gym medic.

"I know a way in." I spin at the sound of Pace's voice, seeing him rush toward me. Looking around, I realize Knight and his officers are momentarily distracted outside, and I all but collapse into Pace's arms. His hair is windswept, and he's panting—a lot like me. "It's completely fucked out there. Cars stalled five deep with half the fucking police force clogged up behind them. I had to scale up the back and come in through the roof." He pulls back, searching my face. "Are you okay?"

"Yes," I lie.

Wicker, looking relieved to see at least one of his brothers, answers, "No. I've been timing her contractions for Lex, and—"

As if he's summoned it, I grip Pace's shirt in a tight, white-knuckled fist as another contraction grips me. The fierce, unyielding pressure radiates through my core, and I howl out a primal, "Fuck!"

It goes on for a stretch where all I see is blinding, white-hot pain behind my eyelids. But I also feel Pace in front of me and Wicker behind me, his fingers digging into my lower back.

I guess that's the massage he was talking about.

Slowly, the blinding pain ebbs, and when I open my eyes, it hits me that everyone in the room—even Remy—even Kaz—seems to have frozen with me in the agony. I exhale a trembling breath, looking up into Pace's eyes. It's such a relief to know he's here, his presence giving off that electric hum that I've grown accustomed to when all of us are in bed together, late at night.

I part my lips to say something gracious and profound, but what emerges is, "I'm *not* giving birth in front of ten frat boys."

Pace releases the breath he's been holding with a quiet, nervous laugh. "Well, these frat boys are about to become men, because it really seems like he's coming, Rosi."

Belligerently, I note, "They're not even our frat!" and Wicker gapes at me.

"*That's* what you're worried about?"

From across the room, Remy jerks his chin. "Excuse me—nine frat boys and an uncle." He grins at Kaz. "I'm going to be an uncle."

Pace shoots him an unamused glare. "We need to get you somewhere. Isn't there a lounge?"

Mama makes a wild, frustrated gesture. "It's being searched by those dumbfucks at the moment, along with my office."

Growling, Pace scans the room, his eyes coming to a stop on the ring in the middle of the gym. "Oh, hell no. The kitchen?"

Before I can fall to pieces at the thought of having my baby next to a fucking stove, Pauly appears. "The training room." He points to the door. "They're already done searching it. I've got sterilized mats and plenty of towels."

Pace doesn't waste any time. He bends, hooks a forearm behind my knees, and fluidly lifts me. "Let's go."

It's not much better than the kitchen, but when Pauly and Mama rush in ahead of us, I'm resigned to my fate. Together, Pauly and Wicker slam a thick blue sparring mat on the floor, gesturing for Pace to bring me over.

As he's lowering me to the mat, I hear, "You're going to have to check her, Pace. See how dilated she is." Lex's strained voice makes me startle, and I search out the sound, realizing Wicker has him on speaker.

"Lex?" I cry, the fear finding a foothold as Pace reaches under my dress, dragging my underwear down my thighs. "Where are you?"

His voice emerges in a panicked rush, "I'm about to hit West End now. Tell me where we are."

Terrified, I struggle to get the words out. "I don't know how to explain it. It feels..." I gasp as Pace's fingers enter me, his dark eyes holding mine. "... like a ton of pressure. He's close." In my periphery, I see Mama shooting Pauly a knowing grimace.

Pace deflates, glancing at the phone. "Look, dude, I don't know this centimeter shit, but I'm pretty sure all systems are go here."

I tense, a sharp intake of breath heralding the onset of another contraction. Pain surges through me like a tidal wave, starting deep in my abdomen and radiating outward in relentless pulses. I grip for the closest thing I find, fingers digging into hard flesh, eyes squeezed shut as I ride out the crest of the worst contraction yet. A bead of sweat trickles down my temple, and when it finally fades off, I emerge to find Wicker clutching my hand, his blue eyes wide and unwavering.

"You're fucking amazing, you know that?" To the phone, Wicker explains, "Another contraction. This one seemed worse."

Lex mutters a sharp curse. "Verity? Do you feel like you have to push?"

Already exhausted, I consider the way it feels deep inside, confessing, "Kind of."

"Goddamn it," Lex mutters. "I just hit the blockade. Pace and Wick are going to take care of you until I get there. If you have to push, just—you remember the breathing, right?"

The panic rises again, and I look at Pace, feeling the tears welling up. "Not without Lex," I cry, the misery threatening to overtake me. "I can't do this without Lex." I sob, long and pitiful, and it's pathetic. Nothing is right. I'm going to bring this baby into the world all wrong.

"Hey, hey, look at me," Wicker whispers, his drawn face coming into view. "Here soon, you're going to be holding Justice. That's good, isn't it?"

I pull in a sniffle, trying to imagine that lumpy little face I saw in the ultrasound. "Yeah," I decide, wiping my eyes.

"You're excited?" Wicker asks.

I nod, trying to gather myself. "Yeah, I am."

"Me too, Red." His grip tightens around my hand as he flashes me one of his prized grins. "You want to know the middle name we picked out for him?"

My heart skips a beat. I'd given them the task of choosing a middle name weeks ago, but since none of them brought it up again, I figured they just forgot or were unable to decide.

On a hitched breath, I ask, "What'd you pick?"

Wicker reaches up to swipe a tear away. "James," he says, cupping my cheek. "Like Stella St. James. So she can still be here with you."

The grief is like a punch to my heart, but more than that is the thought of it. She'd be right beside me wearing her pigtails and bright smile, rattling off some random bit of information that would completely distract me from what's about to happen. I worry for a second that the sadness is going to overtake me, but it doesn't.

Stella would tell me to be strong, like a Princess. Like Pace's mom. Like Miranda. Like all those women we found in the solarium.

Strong, like a Monarch.

"I love you," I tell Wicker, and his shoulders sag suddenly, forehead dipping to rest against mine.

"I love you too, Red." His voice is quiet and ragged, like he's giving away something much scarier than words. I don't need to wonder how many times he's said that to someone who wasn't one of his brothers.

When he pulls back, I shift my gaze to Pace. "And I love you. All of you." It's easy to sink into the peace of that because maybe the situation is wrong, but that?

That suddenly makes it more right than anything's ever felt.

Building my strength, I lever up on my elbows, breathing deep. "I need to push now."

Wicker sputters, but keeps his grip on my hand. "Lex said to wait, can you do that?" I'm not sure I can but then he adds, "We're right here with you, Red. Deep breaths, just like we practiced."

"We've got this," Pace says, kneeling between my parted thighs. He looks scared and nervous, his dark eyes a touch wild, but there's also a spark of confidence there. "Justice doesn't come without a little pain, right?"

24

L^{ex}

I'LL GO to the grave with this fact, but I'm not as good a climber as Pace.

This becomes increasingly maddening as I struggle to scale the back of the building, wondering how the fuck he managed to catch a toehold over the window to reach the metal ladder next to it. It doesn't help that hot, rushing panic is coursing through my veins, and the only thought that registers is that Verity is in there—*right there*—giving birth to our baby.

Without me.

The back lot is overgrown with things that must have been weeds at one point but are now approaching stalk status, which is good. It gives me a little bit of cover. Thankfully, Knight's little goon crew is too busy with the PNZ procession that met me at the barricade to notice my piss-poor impression of Spiderman. Even halfway up to the roof, I can still hear Tommy out front, ranting, "This is a witch-hunt! Do you know who my father is? Do you know what he'll do when he finds out what you've done?"

Who knew his obnoxious assholery would actually be an asset?

Grunting, I strain for the ladder, realizing that Pace probably made a jump for it. *Fucking psycho.* Taking a deep breath—*needs must*—I plant my toes into the brick ledge, flex my knees, and leap.

I catch the bottom of the ladder with one hand, thrusting the other out to pull myself up.

Riiiiip.

Jerking, I look over to see the neck of my shirt caught on a broken piece of metal. "Son of a..." With a huff, I duck my head through the neckhole, thrashing until I can pull my arms from the sleeves.

I don't give myself time to rest, the air cool against my sweaty, bare back as I scurry up the ladder the rest of the way to the roof. It's just like Pace described it, lush with plants and flowers, but I barely register it, spotting the hatch.

As soon as I open it, my stomach sinks.

"Fuuuck!" comes a ragged, distant voice that I'd know anywhere.

The rickety ladder beneath me clatters noisily as I dart down the length of it, surprised to find Mama B waiting for me at the bottom.

"Finally," she hisses, glancing out the door. "Two more minutes and they were going to insist on taking her out front to meet the ambulance on the other side of the barricade, and she's made it clear to everyone that she's not going anywhere without you."

I peek around her, feeling sweaty and borderline crazed as I watch Agent Knight in a standoff with Lavinia Lucia. "What the hell is taking so long?!" she shouts. "If you're holding back the EMS team because you're being a petty bit—"

"Watch it, Ms. Lucia," he growls. "I've got another pair of handcuffs." She steps back, arms crossed over her chest. "We're not doing anything. It's an absolute clusterfuck out there."

"Whose fault is that?"

"It's protocol to clear an area before we let anyone else in—including medical. There were enough guns in here to fill a warehouse, and my guys are still sweeping. We offered to take her out and meet the ambulance, but she's refusing." He exhales. "If you want to come out there with me and find the best route for the EMS team to get in and help your friend, I'm all ears."

He's not wrong about the clusterfuck. It's absolutely pandemonium out there. Every cop in the city is clogging the streets outside the gym. I'd broken every speed limit to cross town, and once I had, I got out of my car and sprinted half the length of West End to the back entry. "How close is she?" I ask, lungs heaving. "What's the timing on the contractions?"

It's only been minutes since I put my phone in my pocket to climb the building, but that scream I just heard...

"I don't know," Mama B says, voice quiet but cutting. "Those fucking animals came in, and everything has been a madhouse—" Her words bite off into a gasp, and when I twist to find out why, I see her gaze fixed on my back. "Sweet suffering Jehovah, what the fuck happened there?"

Annoyed that she's seeing my scars, I snap, "Not important. Come on, they're leaving."

As soon as Knight and Lavinia are out of sight, Mama B zips around me, leading me across the floor of the gym toward a door on the east wall. I crash through it with her, pulse thundering as I spot Verity on the floor.

She's lying down, knees up, thighs spread wide, and a pale Wicker is beside her, squeezing her hand.

"Told you, Red," he says, eyes lighting up. "Look—he made it."

I don't need to nudge Pace over. When he sees me, it's like all the tension falls out of him, and he shoots to his feet, backing away so fast, he bumps into Pauly. "Thank fuck you're here."

But mostly, I just see her. Cheeks red, eyes wet, chest heaving with exertion. "Lex," she pants, grabbing for me the moment my knees hit the mat before her. The kiss I give her is quick but searing, too full of the dread and terror I've been carrying with me ever since I got Wick's text. "Lex, I was so scared to do this without you."

"I've got you now," I say, struggling to catch my breath. It's more of a relief than it should be to look down and not see the baby's head.

"Okay, you're not crowning yet. Uh, it's Paul, right?" I glance at the trainer—at Pace's *dad*—whose haggard face looks a bit green.

"Pauly," he corrects. "I don't know much about births, but she's looking good."

"Did I hear something about towels before? Antiseptic? Something to clean my hands with."

Looking grateful for a task, he begins tossing me things from the shelves; sterile saline wipes, nitrile gloves, and a thick stack of hand towels that I try not to think too much about.

"Is it okay?" she asks, her green eyes full of fear. "Is everything happening right?" She reaches a trembling hand down to her core, wincing. "I don't feel him."

"Not yet, but that's fine. Good, actually," I assure. As I speed through the process of using the wipes, my hands are steadier than they have any right to be. "Wick," I call as I pull on the first glove. "How long since the last—"

"Now! Fuck!" Verity's whole body tenses before me, lips pulling back on a gnashed cry. Her hand reaches out, nails clawing into my forearm, and I freeze, absorbing the pain. I've seen women giving birth before, but none of those were women I love. Even the sight of Verity in pain cleaves through my chest like a hot knife, she looks like a force of nature as her body clenches in a push, a spray of rabid spittle flying out through gritted teeth. Wild tendrils of her red hair are plastered with sweat to her forehead, the capillaries closest to her skin already blooming, breaking.

She looks like a warrior.

A creator.

"Never mind." I don't wait for the contraction to ease before grabbing her knee with one hand and sliding my fingers into her with the other. Wicker presses his forehead to her temple, whispering quiet, intense, soothing things.

"That's right, Red," he murmurs. "You've got this. You're stronger than any of us are, that's for fucking sure."

"Tell me something I don't know," she snaps, and her mother snorts, muttering, "*Men.*"

"He's coming," I tell her, pitching forward to capture her gaze. "You're doing so good, baby. We're almost there, but not quite. You're fully dilated and a hundred-percent effaced, just like we talked about, but you have to work with your body and the contractions—not against it. You're going to need to wait to push until I tell you to, okay?"

She answers with a long, miserable sob. "They took Eugene, Lex." A tear rolls down her cheek, voice thick and ragged. "Laura's dead, and they think he—"

"Don't think of that right now," I urge. "Your job is to get that baby here."

Mama B leans down to catch Verity's gaze. "Listen to me. Ballsy would beat his own ass if he knew you were worrying about him at a time like this."

Jerking my chin at Wick, I order, "While you've got her hand, try to count her pulse."

In the minutes between contractions, the room grows electric with anticipation, each second stretched thin with expectation. But he's coming faster than I expected, and it's not long before I notice her stomach tightening up and nod at Verity.

"It's time. Do you think you can push now, baby?"

She responds with another of those body-seizing clenches, and Pace moves in behind her, giving her leverage. I brace her thighs as she bears down, releasing a guttural sound that might as well be a fist reaching into my chest. Her mother crouches down, almost like she's remembering her own labor—sense memory—the two of them connected through the pain.

When Verity collapses, fatigue warring with determination in her eyes, I urge, "Breathe," and watch her chest expand and contract. Reaching down, I enter her with two fingers, feeling our son, stretching her out to help keep her from tearing. "He's close," I say, glancing at the guys.

The air around Pace seems to hum with eagerness as he smooths her hair back, grinning. "Hear that, Rosi? Not much longer now."

Wicker just looks fucking terrified. "Should she push?"

I nod. "Push again when you're ready."

I don't hear the approaching footsteps, but I do hear Agent Knight's abrupt, commanding voice ringing out from the doorway. "Where the *hell* did the other two Ashbys come from?" My jaw tightens as I see a tight fist grabbing Pace by the neck of his shirt. "How did the two of you get in here? You can't be—"

There's a flurry of motion that I'm too distracted to see the progression of, but by the time I look up, Pauly's got Agent Knight pushed up against the wall, his tattooed forearm pushing hard against his throat. "Do not," he growls, teeth bared, "fucking touch him."

Knight glares back. "This is an active crime scene."

"Look around you, little piggy." Pauly backs off with a hard shove, standing between Knight and Pace. "This has fuck-all to do with you."

The air around us trembles with the strength of Verity's sudden roar. "Get out!" The bellow rides the crest of another deep, clenching contraction, and she follows it with a push, face twisting with the effort.

The agent, rightly, turns on his heel, muttering, "Stubborn East End bullshit," before shutting the door.

"Breathe!" I say, watching her suck in a hard breath. I glance down, and then nod rapidly at Verity. "He's crowning. This is the hardest part, baby. I want you to build your strength up for a bit, okay?"

"I'm scared." She exhales. "It hurts."

"There's no going back now. Look at me, you've got to push through the pain because on the other side of that is relief and our baby." She nods. "Try not to tense up, okay?"

When she obeys, I don't see the fatigue anymore. I see eyes filled with fire and steel resolve, and when the next push comes, it's with a strength I wouldn't believe her capable of. Here she is, this little slip of a girl, tendons popping, eyes squinching, mouth pulled into a grimace, and she's *giving life*.

Even if all my plans had fallen into place—my training, the fancy instruments, and diagnostics—it wouldn't matter.

I have no power here.

Mama B spurs her on as the head emerges. "That's right, Ver Bear, you've got it."

"One more push," I tell her, reaching down to hold his head, keeping his airway clear, and checking to make sure the umbilical cord isn't wrapped around his neck. "One more good push, baby, and it's over. Can you give me one more?"

Against my arms, her thighs are quivering, and she releases a loud, wet sob. But when I look up, she's bracing against Pace, sucking in a deep, deliberate breath.

Her final push is pure resilience, body shaking with the force of it. The room seems to hold its breath with her, listening as she grinds out another cry of raw fury.

I jolt forward when he emerges, gathering him close to flip him. Using my fingers, I clean the mucus and blood from his mouth and nose. He's flushed a light purple, skin wrinkled and slick, and my heart skips when he doesn't immediately begin breathing.

Frantically, I begin rubbing his back. "Come on, little guy. Let's see it."

Suddenly, he begins squirming.

"When he hears your voice, he squirms around, like he's turning, searching..."

His first breath is this tiny, quivering thing, released in a cry just as raw with fury as his mother's had been seconds ago. My vision swims as I take him in, and for a long moment, it hurts to breathe. He's so small—so unbelievably fragile—and we made him with our bodies, with our minds, with our hearts.

In two-hundred and sixty-four days.

It's only when I look up at Verity's anxious face that I feel the heat of tears in my eyes. Gruffly, I assure, "He's good," before carefully laying him on her belly. "And you're a fucking goddess."

The cord is still attached, and the afterbirth will come, but the sound of sirens seems like they're getting closer. Which is good, because at this moment, I seriously doubt my ability to function.

I'm too busy watching my family.

Verity releases a ragged gasp as she touches him for the first time, her wet eyes filled with awe and joy. His tiny body, warm and damp, settles instinctively against her skin, and she instantly gathers him closer, fingers grasping against his delicate skin. "Hey, Justice James," she sobs, voice trembling with emotion.

Glancing over, I laugh breathlessly at the looks on my brothers' faces, so full of astonishment and adoration.

The world narrows to just the five of us as we each meet our son in our own way.

Justice's minuscule fingers grasp at nothing and everything all at once, and as Pace reaches down to stroke the fine, downy hair covering his head, Wicker extends his own trembling finger, face slackening when Justice's flailing hand latches onto it.

Mama B tearfully says, "He's beautiful."

Wicker doesn't even make any smirking, vain comments about him taking after his father. He just swallows, speaking through a tight throat, "He's strong."

"Of course he's strong," Pace says, clapping Wicker on the back and pulling him in for a hug. "Just like his mom and dad."

It's barely five minutes later that the EMS crew comes in to load Verity and Justice onto a gurney. It's difficult to watch someone else touch them, a possessive heat coming over me as the medic covers her—*my* Princess—in a blanket.

"You did good." Mama B's warm palm comes to rest on my shoulder. "Let them take it from here." Glancing over, I'm taken aback by the tenderness in her eyes.

"Yeah," I agree, although my brothers and I may as well be fused to the stretcher as they wheel her from the gym, onto the crowded West End street.

Still shell-shocked in a way, I don't expect the sight that awaits us.

On one side of the street is a long row of handcuffed DKS.

On the other is a line of PNZ.

As soon as the gurney emerges through the doors, all of them turn to look our way, a sea of hopeful, nervous faces. But then Justice releases another one of those squawking, raspy cries, and the crowd erupts as one.

DKS cheers while PNZ claps, and we make our march to the ambulance with congratulatory shouts of, "'Atta girl, Princess!" and, "To the Victor, Ver!"

Maybe I never fully bought into Rufus' bullshit—maybe East End was built on a foundation of suffering and degradation—but looking at my Princess, no five words have ever rang truer.

"To create," I whisper, pressing a kiss to her damp forehead, "is to reign."

FRESH FROM A SHOWER, I pull the green scrub top over my head, and hear the nurse say, "Let's help you out of this."

Glancing over, I see her slipping Verity's stained dress over her head, revealing her post-birth body to the entire postpartum room. Despite knowing this is a purely medical arena, it bothers me. I'm used to it just being us down in the palace's medical wing, and right now, nurses are scrambling around us, in and out.

We were a mess when we came in, both of us covered in blood and fluid. They sent me to shower and get sterile, while the OB team checked both Verity and Justice.

"You did good work," Dr. Hoffman says. "Both of your patients are in perfect health."

"I didn't do much," I say, taking in Verity as they sponge her down. "She did the heavy lifting."

He shakes his head. "Modesty will get you nowhere in this business, Ashby. Take the compliment—and congratulations." He claps me on the back. "You're a lucky man."

When I turn back to where the team is assessing Justice, I lurch forward. "Can I do that?"

The nurse practitioner on staff pauses, holding up the syringe. "You want to administer the vitamin K injection?"

I take it. "Yes."

I swab my son's squirming thigh with an antiseptic wipe before uncapping the syringe. But when I look down at his tiny, writhing body, I freeze, a chill running through me at the thought of pushing the needle into him.

At causing him pain.

It twists in my stomach like sickness, the memory of all the times Father's whip lashed my back with hot, stinging slashes.

Yakov, the NP—a burly guy I worked with occasionally during my internship—gently takes the needle from my stiff hand. "I wasn't able to do it with mine, either. You wanna look away?"

Sighing, I turn, allowing him to administer the injection. "You've got kids?" I ask, watching Wicker pulling another scrub top over his head on his way out the door. He'd taken off his shirt right before EMS came to swaddle Justice in. So much for the sanctity of Versace.

"Two," Yakov says, and then, "Boy and girl. All done. Took it like a champ."

I spin right back around, not asking before I snatch up the bottle of prophylactic eye drops. This, I reason, won't cause him any pain, even though he squirms an awful lot. His eyes are a fascinating shade of gray-blue, and when I gather him up in my arms to take him back to Verity, he mostly looks annoyed.

"Here he is, all cleaned up," I announce, soothed by the weight of him against me. "Everything looks good. He's healthy. And the doc said you're doing good, too."

"Am I?" she asks, eyes swollen and drooping. Her hair is a knotted mess, and she's two shades paler, the white gown the nurse put her in doing nothing for her pallor. "I feel like I got run over by a truck."

Grinning down at Justice, I reason, "That's what happens when you have a six-pound, four-ounce baby on the floor of a gym."

"Sounds like a bruin to me." She laughs at my scowl but then winces. "Ouch."

"You ready for him?" I ask, even though I'm not ready to let him go. I could hold him forever.

She nods and slowly stretches out her arms. "The nurse said I should feed him right away."

Pausing, I glance at her chest. "Tell me what you need me to do."

This is the stuff they don't teach you in medical school; the stuff that happens after the procedure. The awkwardness and frustration of doing these things for the first time. Verity tugs the neck of her gown down, revealing a plump, ready tit, and I guide Justice to it as she takes him into her arms. Together, we adjust and readjust, nudging his mouth to her nipple.

"This is... weird," she whispers, sliding a nervous glance at Yakov, who's preparing the clear hospital bassinet.

Unable to disagree, I call out, "Hey, Yak, don't take this wrong way, but could you fuck off?"

He barks a laugh, situating the blanket. "Sure thing, Ashby. Push the button if you need me."

Once he's left, Verity throws me a look that's both admonishing and grateful. "Rude."

"I'll buy him dinner in the caf," I promise, fluttering my fingers over Justice's grasping hand. "Is he—"

"Oh," she says, eyes snapping wide as he finally gets with the program, lips latching onto her nipple. "There you go," she coos down at him. "You're such a quick learner."

We share a quiet, soft smile, and by the time I hear the tap on the door, Pace entering reluctantly, Justice is latched on.

"He's eating?" Pace says, perching on the other side of the bed. He leans down and kisses Verity on the forehead while resting his hand on Justice's little head.

"He's trying," she says, nose wrinkling.

"He'll figure it out in no time." Pace watches him closely, his thumb running over the soft hair on his head.

"Where's Wicker?" she asks, and I hate the line of worry on her forehead. I remember him leaving, but was too distracted to wonder why. "He didn't freak out, did he?"

"About being a father?" Pace asks, chuckling. "Not... exactly."

Before he can explain further, the door pushes open and Wick struts in. He's in a clean shirt that he must have gotten from the gift shop, because emblazoned on the front in chunky collegiate letters is the word 'DAD'. Clutched in one hand is a box of cigars, and in the other, a nondescript paper bag. I guess someone is finally embracing his role.

He stops short when he sees us, his eyes flicking over this wild little family of ours.

"Nice shirt," I say, mouth twitching.

"I got you both one, too," he hands Pace the gift bag. "But holy shit, Red. Look at you."

"What?" she asks, face falling. "Do I look that bad?"

"What? No," comes his instant response. "You just look so motherly and shit." He walks over and squeezes in beside me, lifting her chin to plant a slow, tender kiss on her mouth. "It's hot as fuck."

"Stop," she says, a small smile lifting her tired expression.

"He's right." Pace's hand rises from Justice's head to stroke the swell of Verity's tit. "You're like one of those fertility statues. If we put one in the garden, the frat would worship it."

She gives me an exasperated look, as if she's expecting me to talk some sense into them. But I can't. "Don't look at me," I tell her. "I already told you that you're a goddess."

Some of the color returns to her cheeks as she looks down at Justice, his mouth abandoning her teat. She frowns. "Well, that wasn't very much."

"It's okay," I assure, stroking the shell of his tiny ear. "He's not going to eat much at first. It's more about muscle memory at this point."

She looks at Wicker, a reluctant tilt to her smile. "Do you want to hold him?"

Neither he nor Pace have yet.

Wicker releases a long, tense breath as he reaches for him. Blue eyes dart to mine. "Tell me if I'm doing it wrong."

Wicker's palm cradles his head, the other hand tucked under Justice's body, and then he pulls him into his chest, stiff as he carefully adjusts. "Is this...?"

"You're good, Wick," I assure, but stand behind him, directing his arm.

The three of us watch as Wicker settles, gazing nervously down at his son. "What if he starts crying?" he frets. "What if he—" But then Justice's eyes flutter open, blue meeting blue, and Wicker looks *gutted*. "So, you're what all the fuss is about, huh?" His whisper is light but strained with emotion, and when he ducks down to gently brush his lips over Justice's forehead, Verity, Pace, and I share a long look, understanding the gravity of the moment.

Wicker, the person most afraid of loving something, has been captured, hook, line, and sinker.

"Pace," he suddenly says, rising to round the bed to his brother. "Your turn."

But my other brother fidgets, hands buried deep in his pockets. "You sure?" he asks. "You can take some time, Wick."

Wick just scoffs. "I have a lifetime to be a dad, but we only get to meet our son once. Come on, make the arms."

Amused by the clumsy directive, Pace holds his arms against his chest, pitching close as Wicker passes Justice into the cradle of his hold. When Wicker steps back, Pace *furls*. It's like his whole body is holding the baby, shoulders both high and curled inward, as if he's shielding him from something.

Up until this moment, I've been pretty well-versed in the field of Pace's emotions. He's never been as explosive as Wicker or as composed as me. Pace *feels*, but he expresses it tactically.

Nothing about the look on his face right now is tactical.

"I was so worried I'd feel different once I saw him," he says, voice ragged as he glances up at me. "Like I'd meet him and know he wasn't mine."

Verity struggles up in bed, anguish on her face. "Oh, Pace."

But he grins down at the baby, head shaking. "It's just the opposite, though," he says, eyes softening as he takes in Justice's tired face. "He's made of you and Wick—two people I love the most. Nothing has ever felt more mine than this." He looks up at me, eyes both curious and wrecked. "Is it like that for you?"

My chest throbs. "Yeah," I admit, taking Verity's hand in mine. "That's exactly what it's like."

Maybe Wick can't understand it yet, how something they made together can feel so inexplicably linked to us.

Maybe someday he will.

THE NEXT MORNING, Pace and Wick stand outside her room, wrangling a sort of schedule for the string of visitors—from various territories—currently crowding the maternity ward's lobby.

PNZ gets first dibs.

"Whoa." Tucking his bouquet of white roses beneath an arm, Rory ducks down to get a good look at Justice, still nestled in Verity's arms. "He's got the cutest little chin."

"I don't know," Tommy says, eyes narrowed as he assesses him. "He's all wrinkly and red and bald. Looks kind of like my grandpa, actually."

Rory smacks him with the bouquet. "He just came out of a *person*."

Verity gives a tired chuckle, meeting my gaze. "I'm assured he won't look like a ninety-eight-year-old man forever."

Shrugging, Tommy places his own bouquet on the pile below the mounted TV. "From me and Heather."

Verity's eyebrow ticks up. "Heather sent me flowers?"

"No," Tommy says, rocking back on his heels. "They're specifically for the baby."

A smile twitches at her lips. "I'm sure Justice appreciates it."

After that comes Kramus, Baxter, Loeffler, and Mitch, each with their own bouquets of white roses. By the time PNZ leaves, the whole console table is bursting with them, a shock of white amongst the bare furnishings. They seem content to hang out all day, until I kick them out, telling them Verity needs a break.

"You need a break," she says watching them exit the room. "You were up all night hovering."

"I wasn't hovering." I was checking vitals, and fluids, and listening for Justice's tiny, perfect breaths.

Her eyes harden into a threatening resolve. "When Pace and Wick get back, I want you to go home and sleep." Somewhere in the procession of PNZ visits, she'd sent them home with a list of things to bring back for the rest of her stay. *Hopefully, they remember to bring my glasses so I can take these godforsaken contacts out.*

I rub my eyes, refusing to acknowledge how gritty they feel. "Ver, I'm fine. I got a solid two hours around three—"

"Are you fucking me with this plaque?" Verity's mother's voice comes from the hallway. "'The Rufus Ashby Maternity Suite'. Jesus Christ, that son of a bitch never saw a room he didn't want to piss on." She walks in with a dramatic roll of her eyes. "Well, I wonder if rooms in the fiery pits of hell have plaques?"

"Hey, Mama," Verity says, eyes lighting up when she sees her mother. "I'd ask to move rooms, but this one is really nice."

The four of us came to an agreement when Verity killed Rufus. We're going to enjoy every privilege and indulgence he left for us, and the maternity suite is exactly that. Indulgent. From the coffee maker and mini-bar to the jetted tub in the bathroom. The only reason I managed those two hours of sleep last night came down to an accidental lounging on the guest bed six feet away from hers.

"Sure enough. It's a palace." She looks around, taking in the couch and small kitchenette. She spots the wall of roses. "I see the frat has been here."

"They just left," I say gently, "and Verity needs to rest and feed—"

"Lex Ashby, don't even think of kicking me out," she snaps, heading straight to the little bassinet where Justice is sleeping. "Verity can feed the baby in front of me. The girls, too. This is nothing we haven't seen."

"What girls?" I ask, but a moment later, Lavinia and Story appear in the doorway. A grin splits Verity's face at the sight of them, and I remember what Tristian said that day working on the nursery. These women aren't just contemporaries. They're friends.

"You came," Verity says, looking more alert than she has all day.

"And we brought food," Story says, holding up a greasy bag.

Verity inhales deeply, immediately sitting up. "Is that from Señor Mexicana?"

"Yep. Special number five."

"Oh my god, I love you." She snatches the bag from her. "I'm starving."

At Verity's defiant look, I hold up my hands. "Go for it. Your body needs fuel."

"Got you one too, Dr. Daddy," Lavinia says, thrusting a foil-covered burrito at me from another bag.

Since when does West End's Queen buy food for a Prince?

Unable to hide how touched I am by the gesture, I say, "Wow." My stomach rumbles, and I remember I haven't eaten either. "Thanks."

While Mama B is hunched over the bassinet and—there's no other word for it—*gushing*, the two girls plop on the couch.

Lavinia begins, "Okay, tell us everything. Like, on a scale of one to Sy's dick, how bad did it hurt?"

"Jesus." I choke on the first bite of spicy chicken, not even caring that Verity's exposing a breast for the hungry baby Mama B is bringing her. I can't be here for this discussion. "I'll, um, just go eat this down in the visitor's lounge."

The sound of giggling follows me out the door.

I wander down the hall until I find the little room set aside for visitors, and pull out a chair. The second bite is as good as the first, and I relish the grease and carbs, idly wondering if Wick and Pace can take a detour on the way back to buy me three more.

I'm halfway done when a massive figure in black stalks by, and I call out over beans and rice, "Hey. In here."

Sy loops back, exhaling in relief when he sees me. "This place is a fucking maze."

"You get used to it." I take another bite, and he nods at the burrito.

"The girls found you, I see."

"Yep. They're in there talking about—" *Your massive dick*, I don't say, "—well, stuff no one wants to hear. Not even me. And Verity's feeding the baby, which is still touch-and-go, so we may want to give her a few minutes."

"Cool. Remy and Nick are parking the car." He sits in the hard chair across from me, stretching his legs out, and I change the subject. "What's the news on Ballsack?"

Sy looks almost as tired as I feel, and I find myself curious about what a night in the city lockup with a couple dozen of your own frat brothers even looks like. "It's not good," he begins, crossing his arms in a way that signals discomfort more than machismo. "They've got hard evidence on him this time, and I'm not sure it'll be easy to beat."

I frown. "What evidence?"

His eyebrows crouch low. "Our lawyer says there was blood at the scene of the crime. Specifically, Ballsy's blood on Laura's teeth."

"Her teeth?" My blood runs cold. "So he did it?"

Sy's face snaps with shock. "Fuck no, he didn't do it. The coroner puts the time of death at about thirty-six hours ago, but they searched him over twice and couldn't even find a break in his skin, let alone a bite wound." Sy's eyes skitter around the hall, a touch of paranoia in them. "Simply put, he's being framed for this. Someone in Forsyth wants this pointed in our direction."

"But," I argue, "if he doesn't have any wounds, then how would someone even get his blood—"

My pulse stutters as it hits me.

The blood drive.

The samples I took.

The realization my little scheme may have played a part in this slams into me like a sack of bricks. *May* is the operative word here. Who would have gotten access to it? And how? It feels like a stretch to me, which means Knight will just think it's bullshit. And if Ballsack is being framed, then that just puts me as a suspect—the person with access to his blood.

Mother*fuck*.

"Hell if I know," Sy says, rubbing his face, "but we'll deal with it. The lawyer is top-notch. One of Saul's scumbags, so that's good." He looks over my shoulder, and I glance back, seeing Remy and Nick approaching. "The girls are down there now, and Verity's feeding the baby."

"Got it." Remy jerks his chin at me. "How's my nephew?"

It's Maddox's eager grin that makes me set aside worries about the blood evidence for the moment. Among the grief of Laura Walker's death, Ballsy's arrest, and missing women, it's not often people like us get something to celebrate. Even so, my appetite is gone, so I toss the rest of the burrito in the trash and stand, saying, "Let's go find out."

Before letting them in, I crack the door, checking to make sure she's decent. Verity can flash her tits to her mom and her girlfriends all she wants, but it'll be over my dead body that the Dukes get even a glimpse of her nipples. Seeing that she's put the goods away for now, I open the door for them to enter just as a burst of laughter comes from the women.

Nick eyes them skeptically, "I can't ever tell if that's a bad sign or not."

"They're happy," Sy says, coming to the same conclusion I had. "They deserve that—especially right now, with the rest of West End planning a funeral."

Death and birth.

No one understands the cycle more than a PNZ.

"Looking good, Ver," Remy says, approaching the bed. "Wanna see what I did this morning?"

She sits straighter, eyes narrowing. "What did you do?"

He thrusts out his arm and pulls back his sleeve, revealing a clear bandage. Nestled against his other ink, a small crown is visible beneath the translucent bandage. In a looping script, the initials *J.J.* interlock. "For my nephew."

Verity stares at it, her mouth pressed into a tight line as her eyes begin welling. "Oh, Remy," she gasps, wiping a tear from her eye. "Fuck you. You know I'm hormonal right now."

From the couch, Lavinia beams at him. "I helped with one of the roses on the bottom."

Verity's chin wobbles, and she looks at me, a plea in her eyes that I don't have to consider for long. "Do you want to hold him?"

Remy freezes, glancing at me. "Can I?" Shrugging, I wave my hand, having had my possessive instincts whittled down over the course of so many visitors already. The Dukes don't even feel like enemies anymore, which is something I might think to feel worried about later.

Right now, I watch as Justice meets his uncle.

"Oh," Remy breathes adoringly as he lifts him. "He's so small. Sy's got books that weigh more than you, little guy." He grins down at Justice, and if I inch a little closer as he adjusts to cradle him in his arms, then no one could blame me. "He's got my chin," he says, holding him up for the others to see.

Verity laughs. "Well, I think he's actually got Wic—"

"Ver," Lavinia says with a sigh, "just let him have it."

It's still weird as fuck that Remy and Wick are half-brothers, but now that I know, it also kind of makes sense.

"Vinny, look," he says, flashing her an excited grin. "Have you ever seen a brighter white than this?"

Brows knitting together, we all look toward Sy, and he snorts. "He doesn't mean his skin color. White means—"

"Fresh and clear, like a clean canvas." Remy's eyes light up, and he looks at Verity. "Can I give him his first tattoo?"

I jolt forward to take him. "Okay, enough of that."

He frowns, but hands Justice over to me. "Not *now*. I mean when he turns sixteen." At Nick's elbow jabbing into his side, he hisses, "Fine, eighteen."

Nick wraps his arm around Lavinia and places his hand over her belly, "Maybe it's about time we thought about putting a baby in you."

Verity perks. "Oh my god. Yes! It'd be fun to have a baby together," she pleads, looking hopefully at both girls.

"As much as watching Remy holding that baby has obliterated my ovaries, no freaking way," Lavina says, attempting to push Nick away. He just holds on tighter. "I can barely manage the three of you and the Archduke."

"I'm not ready either," Story says, giving Verity an apologetic grin. "I've got to finish school, and we're still getting situated in the new house. That basement renovation is taking forever. Have you ever worked with contractors?" Even as she rolls her eyes a small smile tugs at her lips. "But my guys will be great dads. I know that."

Sy leans against the end of the bed, dipping his chin at me. "So what is he going to call each of you? Dad? Papa?"

Verity and I share a look, and she admits, "We haven't talked about it yet."

Nick snorts. "Trust me, figure that shit out now. We've got two dads, and it gets confusing."

"But you call them by different names," Verity says. "Pops and Dad. How is that confusing?"

"Nick's right," Sy agrees. "It's a pain in the ass."

Giving Justice a gentle bounce, I try to imagine him calling out for me. What would it sound like? Rufus went by Father. It was all formal, and knowing him, intentionally stiff.

I think of the shirt Wicker got for all of us with the word Dad on it.

"I know one thing," Verity's mother says with certainty. "There's only one Mama in this family."

It's not until later, after everyone leaves and Pace and Wick return, crashing together in the bed, that I realize I'm still thinking about it. Not what the baby will call us—Mom, Dad, Papa, or whatever else he comes up with will be perfect.

I'm thinking of Verity.

She's finally asleep. I've got Justice bundled up in my arms, and it strikes me hard how amazing his mother is. In a single day, she's had the Queen of South Side delivering her food. The Queen of West End —born and raised North—giggling on her couch. Even Maddox and his young fiancée sent a bouquet of flowers and a card. Kings and Dukes, East End soldiers, PNZ members... people from every corner of this city.

They weren't drawn here because of a Royal birth.

It was *her*.

Justice isn't just a baby. He's our baby. A *Prince* who is going to need a hell of a long time to be ready to lead. Verity's already more than a mom and a partner.

More than a Princess.
She's a goddamn Queen.

erity

THE ROOM IS dark when I jolt upright, patting the spot next to me. It's filled with a hard, male body. Wicker.

I gasp. "The baby. Where's Justice?" I shake him awake, shifting over to make sure I didn't roll over him.

"Red," Wick mumbles, coming more awake. He squints up at me through one blue eye. "What are you doing?"

"I was feeding him and fell asleep." The panic rising into anguish, I shove him over, hands searching. "Oh my god, where is he?"

I'm hot, drenched in sweat, the front of my nightgown stuck to my skin. Wicker rises up next to me, searching the bed with his own clumsy hands.

"I've got him," a whisper carries from the doorway, and when I whip my head around, I see Pace's silhouette in the doorway. Relief rushes over me. I'm not the worst mother in the world. Just the most exhausted.

"Christ." Wick shoves his hand in his hair. "Scared the shit out of me."

I spy the tiny swaddled bundle in Pace's arms as he slowly makes his way over. He's shirtless and has been the case since we came home from the hospital, completely engrossed in our child. His dark eyes are fixed on Justice, a soft expression set on his face. "You fell asleep while nursing him, and when I came to put him in the bassinet, I realized he needed a change." He grins down at the baby. "Once I got him bundled back up, he was dozing again so I just held on to him while I went over some homework to give you two a little time to sleep."

"Thank you," I say, noticing the time. Two and a half hours. That's a record since we got home two weeks ago. "I obviously needed that."

I'd love to say we've been a well-oiled machine, superstars who are killing it at this parenting thing, but the last two weeks have been a total blur. I've never been so tired in my life. My body aches, and the guys are grumpy as hell, frequently snapping at each other—and I'm snapping at them. And on top of that, there are the fluids...

So many disgusting bodily fluids.

Although they're all putting in daddy duty, Wicker and I agreed that Lex and Pace should try to keep the most normal sleep schedule since they're both still in school. Even though that's true, they pitch in constantly. I have no idea how moms with only one sleep-deprived dad manage it. Or no partner at all. They're the real heroes.

"I'd tell you to go back to sleep," he says, sitting on the edge of the bed, "but I'm pretty sure he's getting hungry."

On cue, Justice squawks, and a heaviness followed by pinprick tingles tightens my nipples. This isn't like before when the guys had to draw the milk out of me. Justice and I are in sync. When he's hungry, my tits know it, and it's not just a dribble. It's a full-on flood.

"I'll go get you a towel and a dry shirt," Wick says, easing out of the bed.

I strip off the one I'm wearing, which is still damp from the last feeding, not to mention the hormonal sweat bath I had in my sleep.

The fabric snags on my breast, and I wince from the pain. Pace's nose wrinkles. "Still sore?"

I groan. "So fucking sore. God, I had no idea." Chapped, peeling, aching. How did I ever think these things were for pleasure? "Okay," I sigh, rolling on my side. This is the best way to feed at night. "I'm ready for him."

Pace unrolls Justice from his blanket burrito, and his little fists start waving. The closer he gets to me, the more he starts fussing, little mouth already making sucking movements as he waits for food. Pace doesn't quite hand him to me, but rolls him into my side, guiding his mouth to my dripping nipple. The first pull of suction hurts like a mother, but once he starts going, I just feel relief.

Pace takes that moment of stillness to duck down, pressing a kiss to my forehead.

"Here," Wick says, climbing back into the bed. His hand arcs over me, and he gives me a small washcloth to keep my other boob from dripping milk on the little guy before he's ready to swap sides. "You can change into the clean shirt when you're done." His voice is still sleep-thick and slurred, and when Wicker lays his head down, his eyelids immediately fall.

"Thank you," I rest my head on the pillow, feeling the hormones surge through me. Feeding the baby is comforting to both of us, and at night, it's hard not to fall asleep.

Wicker's hand reaches out to blindly smooth my hair. "Rest, okay? Pace and I have this."

"You sure?" I ask. Wicker may say he has this, but he's a fast and heavy sleeper. He'll conk out the minute we get quiet.

"Yep," Pace assures, lingering at the end of the bed. "I have to get up in an hour anyway. Early practice. You two get as much sleep as you can."

My eyes have already fluttered closed, soothed by the sucking motion of baby Justice and the fact I've got the best dads in the world watching over us.

∾

I LIE ON THE TABLE, fifteen pounds lighter than I was the last time Lex examined me, and watch him move fluidly around the room. I swear all three of them have gotten more attractive since the baby came. He's wearing these pants that are far too snug against his ass, and his sleeves are rolled up in that way that drives me crazy, veins and tendons shifting as he grabs for the clipboard.

As for me, well...

There's no swell of life in my stomach, just saggy, scarred skin. My tits are huge—like, *massive*—but they're painful and sore from overuse. *Utilitarian.* My once smooth skin is now splotchy and red. A strange rash showed up on my arms last week. Hormones, Lex tells me. *Perfectly normal.*

"You're still bleeding?" he asks, pushing his glasses up his nose. His hair is pulled back, and although I long to yank that band out, I suppress the urge, looking away.

"Less than the first week I got home."

He nods and jots it down in his file. "Lactation is going well," he notes, because he's witnessed it himself. "I know you were worried he wasn't getting enough milk, but that's resolved?"

Sighing, I agree, "He's a pig." The hour directly following a feeding are the only moments of the day I don't feel fit to burst. "I should've known he'd pick up on it quickly." I crack a smile. "Takes after his father."

Lex's mouth quirks in a small smile before he sets down his clipboard and pulls on the latex gloves.

"Let's check your abdomen."

Ugh.

In all the times I've been naked around these men, not once has it felt like this. I know I'm not the most beautiful girl in Forsyth, but I've never felt insecure. I knew they wanted me. Even when Lex had his erectile issues, he still made it known. But now? Still carrying the extra weight, the ring of puffy skin around my midsection, and the swollen, bleeding pussy, I feel like a sack of leaking meat.

And the fact none of them have even made an advance on me confirms it.

I'm disgusting.

Eyes laser-focused, Lex presses his fingers into the doughy skin that was once my flat, smooth abdomen. Literally, it's like he's kneading dough, but despite my mortification, he's seemingly pleased with whatever he's found.

"Looks good." Meeting my gaze, he dips his chin in a nod. "Remember, it's common to have abdominal swelling for a while. I expect that will improve soon." He moves to the end of the table, where he taps my knees and says, "Let's get a look down here."

Down *here*.

This from the man who's whispered all the dirty things he wants to do to my pussy, even when he couldn't get it up to do it himself. But it's not a 'pussy' anymore. It's just a portal to my reproductive organs.

Embarrassed, I spread my thighs for him, feeling the wash of heat over my cheeks. But the moment he touches me, fingers searching my folds, my knees snap together.

His amber eyes rise to mine, questioning.

Exhaling, I force my knees apart. "Sorry."

"Don't be sorry," he says in that calm, soothing tone. "You just went through some trauma down here. It's understandable."

"Sure," I choke out, feeling his fingers poke and prod.

He ducks his head to look at what his fingers are doing—entering me—and hums. "It looks like you're healing up nicely." Lex's hands are gentle on the insides of my thighs as he finishes up his examination. I look down, checking his crotch, and there's not even the slightest hint of an erection. For someone who has zero interest in sex right now, I'm still inexplicably disappointed. "The bleeding may last for another few weeks."

"What about sex?" I blurt, hating myself for asking. "I'm just... wondering."

He pulls off the latex gloves one at a time, his eyes searching mine. "The recommended time is two to twelve weeks." We're rolling into the three-week mark. "But you know I'm going to always err on the side of caution and say we can discuss it again at your next exam."

"Okay," I say, unsure of how to feel. I don't feel up to sex right now.

In fact, it seems absolutely terrifying after giving birth. But there are these little flickers of heat that I get—usually when I see the guys with the baby. I haven't lost all of my desire, it just feels different, like my maternal endorphins get mixed up with my horny endorphins.

If I have to watch any of them shirtless while lovingly rocking our son *one more time*, I'm going to burst.

Lex sighs, resting a palm on my knee. "I've already told the guys, and they're fine with it. Good, actually. No one is in any rush," he assures me. "Right now, the focus is on Justice and your recovery."

It's not until he turns away, giving me the opportunity to change in private, that I realize this is the first time in months that he hasn't taken his hair down for me.

Maybe all that talk about wanting to fill me up again when he could was just that—talk. Maybe their attraction to me was just about the creation of it all, and now that the baby is here, they're not interested.

The rational part of me understands it's not reasonable. I haven't even had the opportunity to mourn Laura, worry about Stella, or fret over Ballsy not being able to get bail. There are a million things happening in my life, and god knows the last thing I want right now is sex.

But all I do is nourish our baby, and I can't—I just *can't*—only be that.

Except maybe that's really all a Princess is.

FUMBLING WITH THE LAUNDRY BASKET, I approach the nursery to the sound of low, haunting cello notes.

The melody is both mournful and soothing, resonating in my chest like a wisp of shadow. As the melody swells and recedes, my eyes flutter closed, allowing the music to paint vivid pictures in my mind. The corridor fades away, leaving only the rich, velvety sound that wraps around me, each stroke of the bow pulling me further into repose.

When I peek inside, it's to the sight of Wicker in the rocking chair that Story and her Lords had gifted to me. In front of him, Justice is resting in the bassinet, silent and still.

Wicker is shirtless, and even from the doorway, I can smell a hint of his body wash, my body unwinding longingly at the scent. He looks deep in concentration as he draws the bow over the strings, his blonde hair damp and unruly, muscles shifting with each note.

He's fucking *exquisite*.

With a lump in my throat, I enter, going straight to the closet, and abruptly, the music ends.

"Hey, Red." There's a clatter, and then the sounds of him setting the cello against the wall, but I don't see it, engrossed in folding the laundry. "This kid goes through more clothes than a hockey team during an entire season," he says, coming up behind me. I wait for *something*—a kiss, a lingering touch—but nothing comes, and I take a small step to the side to open the dresser drawer and tuck a stack of onesies inside.

"Preaching to the choir." Picking up the basket, I start for the closet door when his hand clamps down on my arm.

His blue eyes pierce right through me. "Let me do that."

"I've got it." I wriggle from his grip and continue my chores, willing the lump in my throat away.

Sighing, he props himself against the closet door, his body a long, muscular line. "You okay? You seem... agitated."

Hot tears prick at my eyes. *Dammit.* "I'm fine."

He's quiet for a beat, then asks, "Did something happen at the exam?"

"No," I answer, recalling that Lex sent me off with a promise to buy more pads. "Nothing happened. I'm just tired."

He cocks his head, glancing at the bassinet. "Then stop cleaning and go take a nap. I just put J.J. down. He's kind of like the old fogies I played for at that insurance fundraiser over the summer. Hearing me play puts him right to sleep."

I shake out a small shirt. "The minute I fall asleep, he'll want to eat. It's just easier this way." I blink away the tears and focus on organizing the baby items over the changing table. Wipes, powder, rash cream, diapers...

"Red," he reaches for me again, this time wrapping his arms around me. His fingers graze my belly, and I try to push him off.

"Don't." I inhale, flinching away. "Please, don't touch me there."

His blue eyes are wide, palms held up in the air. "Why? Does it hurt?"

My fists clench. "No, Whitaker, it doesn't hurt." Humiliatingly, a tear escapes, and I watch as he realizes, his stunned gaze following its track down my cheek. "It's... gross. *I'm* gross. I'm fat and smushy," I wave my hands around my body, "my tits feel like they've been through a meat grinder, and my vagina had the equivalent of a watermelon pushed through it. I'm an abomination and you know it. You *all* know it."

"That," he says, swallowing long enough to gain his thoughts, "that was a lot. And not even remotely true, you are *not* gross."

I catch a glimpse of myself in the mirror beside the changing table. My hair hasn't been brushed in god knows how many days, my shirt has spit-up stains on it, my right boob is bigger than the left because Justice, like his father, seems to prefer it. Rubbing my eyes, I admit, "I mean, it's not like I thought I'd look like a celebrity after leaving the hospital, but I thought maybe I'd get to take a shower."

When was the last time that happened? Two? Three days ago?

Wicker deflates, reaching out to stroke my dry, knotty hair. "Red, it's only been a few weeks. The book said it's perfectly normal to take—"

I snap, "A few weeks, and not one of you has made a move on me."

He blinks slowly, utterly frozen. "You want... to have sex with us?"

"No," I admit, not completely sure what I *do* want.

"Okay." He tilts his head, mulling over his words like he really doesn't want to say the wrong thing. It's like I've always said. Whitaker Ashby may be pretty, but he isn't dumb. "You want us to want to have sex with you?"

I sigh. "Maybe. I just..." I grab my boob with both hands. "I want to be something other than a dairy cow."

Wicker's eyes drop to my tits, brow arching enticingly. "First of all, you have to know my cock gets hard when you do that." Pushing off the jamb of the closet door, he stalks toward me. "And second, I'm hard all the time—probably more than before—I've just gotten better at hiding it."

I roll my eyes. "Sure." The pandering just makes it worse.

"Hey," he tugs me closer, "we've been through a lot, haven't we?" At my stilted nod, he ducks down, pressing a kiss to my pulse point. "I had no doubt you were strong, but watching you give birth to Justice was next level. Anyone can slit a throat, but pushing out a six-and-a-half-pound baby and then feeding him and taking care of him? You're a goddamn superhero."

I squirm, feeling unfairly patronized. "Stop."

Wicker doesn't let me turn away, taking my face in his hands. "We know that your body needs to rest and recover." His blue eyes hold mine. "We've had to take breaks before. We survived. We can do it again."

I blink back the sting of tears. "But... before, I didn't look like this."

He stares at me, eyebrows raised. "What the fuck are you going on about?"

"Wicker," I beg, "don't be a dick."

Shrugging, he replies, "I don't know what you want me to say. Boobs are always hot. Big or small. Sagging or so filled with milk they're about to pop." He spins me, dragging my back against his chest, not letting me escape as he points me to the mirror. "Your tummy," he begins, digging his fingers into the give, "is soft because you carried our son in there. Your ass is wider because you were feeding him, helping him grow strong. The stretchmarks and chapped nipples... it's all just the story of our family written on your body. Just like Pace's tattoos and Lex's scars." He presses a kiss against my neck. "And if that's not convincing enough, I watched you eat bacon this morning and turn it into milk to feed our son. That shit is pure wizardry."

Now I'm crying harder, the tears streaming down my cheeks. Still behind me, his hands move to my face, wiping off the tears with his thumbs. "Look at me, Red."

I meet his eyes in the mirror.

"If you think I'm going to go looking for someone else, you don't get me, but that's fair. I haven't always put myself out there. Vulnerability isn't my forte." He tugs at my hair, letting it fall over my shoulders. "I love you, Verity—every part of you—because you made me see that I could be so much more than an object to be sold and traded." His cheek presses against mine and it's wet from his own tears. "You made me into a man, and then you gave me the chance to be a father, something I never even thought I wanted, but somehow, you knew I was worth it."

All those insecurities seem foolish as he wraps his arms around me and squeezes me tight.

"I love you, too." I tell him. Then after a big sniff—*ugh, fluids*—I add, "And you're really not pissed about the no-sex thing again?"

"I'm getting better at being patient." Since I can feel his boner against my leg, I roll my watery eyes, and he smirks at my reflection. "Okay, I'm *trying* to get better at being patient."

Sniffling, I try, "I won't get mad if you want to look at porn, or if you and Pace want to—"

He cuts me off with a sharp sound. "*That* is something we do with you, not alone. Seeing you with him is what turns me on, and it's the same for him. Understood?" I nod, feeling a flush wash over my skin as he assesses me, a divot in his brow. "And porn doesn't cut it for me anymore. Not when I've got the sexiest woman in the world in my bed. But let's make a deal." He turns me so he can look at me, head on. "If I get the urge to rub one off before we can do it safely," he offers, watching as his finger trails down my chest, "then I'll save it for you. But if you get the urge, you save it for us, okay? If you're getting off, I want to watch." In a deep voice, almost a groan, he adds, "And god do I want to watch that."

The flush returns to my cheeks. "Really?"

I search for any trace of a lie, but he holds my gaze unflinchingly. "You have no idea, Red."

The idea isn't unappealing. In fact, I feel a bit of a tingle at the thought. "It's something we do together," I agree, leaning into him, "even if 'together' looks a little different right now."

I'VE JUST WOKEN up from a small, half-hour nap, and I'm laying in bed with Justice, admiring his little button nose as he dozes. I've never taken care of a baby before, and I didn't really have many expectations for him to live up to, but he seems to be a good baby. He cries, but only for the usual things. Hunger, changing, temperature.

Each of the guys has their own way with him. Pace likes to walk him around the palace, through hallways and rooms, and sometimes even outside. When I watch Pace with Justice, I see a father who wants to show him the world as much as protect him from it.

Wicker likes to play for him. I haven't seen him with his cello so much the whole time I've known him. It's nice, the house being filled with music at the oddest hours. If I wake up, disoriented and alarmed, a calm always rushes through me when I hear Wicker's cello reverberating down the halls. When I do, I know he has him. When I watch Wicker with Justice, I see a father who wants to show him his heart.

Lex likes to relax with him. He'll scoop Justice up and take him to the sitting room, laying him on his chest as he watches TV, late at night, after classes are done. More than once, I've walked in on him, discovering his glasses askew as he sleeps, Justice fast asleep against him. When I watch Lex with Justice, I see a father who wants to show that time is precious, and he's eager to spend it doting on his child.

But I like doing this.

Just watching him.

"Good morning, J.J.," I whisper when he awakens, tickling his tiny feet. He's a skilled kicker, always full of energy at this time of morning. His gray-blue eyes are just like his hands, frenetic, searching out everything and nothing. I lean down to press a kiss to his tummy, bare since the little spit-up mishap that occurred after his feeding an hour ago. "What's on the agenda for today?"

"Today," comes Pace's voice, startling me, "you're going to have a break."

Looking over, I see him stalking into the room, throwing the drapes open wide. Bright sun fills the room, making my eyes squinch. "Gah! Too bright."

Pace doesn't relent, throwing open a dresser drawer. "My first lecture got canceled, so I have the morning free. And since Wick is a hopeless layabout—"

"Hey!" Wicker squawks, strutting into the room. "I do a lot of work around here, thank you very much. I don't see you or Lex cooking dinner on the reg."

Pace tosses him an unimpressed look. "Be that as it may, you're on Justice duty while I see to Rosi."

Wicker replies, "Deal," and zips over to scoop the baby up while I blink in confusion.

"See to what?" But Wicker is already gone, taking Justice with him, and I stare balefully at the empty spot on the bed.

Until I realize that Pace is undressing.

I turn to watch more fully as he pulls off his shirt and unbuttons his pants, shoving them down his thighs. His cock, limp but long, swings as he hops around, tugging the pants from his feet.

"Come on," he says, yanking the blankets off me.

I reach for them too late, nose wrinkling at the state of myself. My nightgown is crusty against my chest, the scent of Justice's spit-up lingering around me like a toxic cloud. "Ugh," I groan, feeling disgusting. "I guess I should do more laundry."

It never stops.

An infant, three men, and myself? I could possibly be doing laundry every day until I die, and the thought alone is enough to exhaust me.

But then Pace says, "Already did it," and grabs my hand, tugging me from the bed.

"You washed my clothes?" I ask, dubious as he leads me across the room.

Into the *hall.*

"Lex did," he explains.

"You're naked," I hiss, but Pace doesn't look bothered at all.

He just smirks at me over his shoulder, guiding me toward the staircase. "No one here but us, Rosi. Look all you wanna."

It's not a bad sight, the muscles of his ass shifting artfully with each step. His training must be going well because Pace's body is hard and more chiseled than ever. I feel even more insecure about my own body as I watch his, so tight and fit.

I'm so distracted by it, I don't even realize where he's leading me until we arrive.

I pause in the doorway, watching the candlelight throw his features into sharp relief. "What's this?"

Reaching out, Pace takes both my hands in his, dragging me into the large bathroom that used to belong to Rufus. "We never got to enjoy the jetted tub in the maternity suite," he explains, pushing my gown off my shoulders. His dark eyes sparkle in the light and he steps close, the gown pooling on the floor around my feet.

"Oh," I breathe, seeing that the large tub is full of aromatic bubbles.

Palms framing my face, he tips my gaze up to his. "I miss being inside you at night," he whispers, bending down to pluck a slow, shallow kiss from my lips. "I know we can't fuck, but I can still take care of you."

Immediately suspicious, I wonder, "Did Wicker put you up to this?"

Pace frowns, pulling back to search my eyes. "I put *him* up to this, if that's what you mean. We have a solid two hours to make ourselves feel human again. I know I'm all," he grimaces, fingering one of his silky twists, "covered in spit-up and shit, but I swear I can smell good again."

And with that, he tugs me to the edge of the tub, eyes beseeching.

It hits me then that maybe I'm not the only one who feels tired and gross all the time. Unable to smother my grin, I lift a leg, and then the other, listening as Pace gets in behind me.

"You'll wash my hair?" I ask, the excitement leaking into my voice.

He chuckles. "Dying to."

"And my back?"

He presses a kiss to my shoulder, guiding me into the bubbles. "Every glorious inch of you."

The water is hot—the kind of hot that's *almost* too much—and I inhale deeply as I settle into Pace's chest, letting the warmth seep into my sore, tired muscles.

His deep voice whispers into my ear, "I put some salts in. Lex said it's good for you, down there."

Down there.

The scent of lavender and eucalyptus wafts up from the bubbles, instantly relaxing me, and as I glide my fingers through the water, Pace uses a cup to douse my hair with water, fingers scritching along my hairline.

I'm already putty in his hands when he begins lathering it with a sweet-smelling shampoo.

"When I saw your picture on that app," he says, running his fingers over my scalp, "this was the first thing I was obsessed with. Your hair. It looked so silky and soft. I used to daydream about it against my face." It's a quiet, bashful confession that makes me grin.

Humming, I tip my head back, luxuriating in the feel of his fingers, frothing the suds. "It's all dry and coarse now."

He makes a small, dismissive sound. "It just needs a little TLC. Let me take care of it."

It's impossible to disagree, so I sit there as he tends to it, his long fingers working through the strands first with shampoo, and then a thick, floral cream.

"I miss it, too," I admit, somewhere in the midst of feeling like gelatin. "You being inside of me, when we go to sleep."

Pace follows my train of thought with a low, stilted, "It... wasn't always about sex."

Nodding, I tip my head back for another rinse, thinking that it's a lot like this. Just being wanted. Cared for. Touched. *Kept.* "I'm scared, Pace." My own confession is just as quiet and nervous, and it makes his movements slow to a halt.

"Of what?"

Turning, I face him, the water sloshing messily around us, and find his dark eyes full of worry. "Do you remember back when the three of you were giving... deposits?"

Pace frowns, rubbing some of the bubbles into my arm. "If that's what you want to call it."

Exhaling, I say, "You were all so... hungry. For me. For my body." Holding his gaze, I speak the fear that's been nestled inside me ever since Justice emerged. "Is that going to go away now that the job is done? Am I just... a mother now?"

"Oh, Rosi." Pace lets out this core-tingling, raspy laugh, tugging me closer. "That hunger didn't go away. It just... changed."

"But how?" I ask. "How did it change?"

He pauses, seeming to mull this over as he strokes my wrist. "Sometimes, when I'd fuck you, it'd be so... desperate. To have you." Brows knitting up, he shakes his head. "It was violent and greedy, but I know you're mine now. I can wait until *your* hunger comes back. Until *you* feel greedy." He glances down at my body, arching a brow. "And not to pressure you or anything, but I'm sort of counting the days."

I deflate at the naked want in his eyes. "You don't think I'm," I swallow, "disgusting now?"

"Disgusting?" His head snaps back, dark eyes pinning me. "Rosi, that hasn't changed. You're still beautiful. Do you see the way these PNZ fucks look at you when they're over here?"

Rolling my eyes, I say, "That's not about me, Pace. Everyone in East End has huge, throbbing Oedipus complexes. They're turned on by a motherly figure—not me, specifically."

He hums, reaching out to graze his knuckles over the curve of my breast. "The motherly thing is hot as fuck, but you're selling yourself short. You're a hot, fiery West End chick with a great rack and gorgeous eyes. Pushing out a kid didn't change that."

He punctuates this by pitching forward, taking my mouth in a leisurely kiss. He had a point before about our deposits being so rushed and desperate. We never got normal experiences, like dates and slowly building electricity.

But the electricity is building now.

His tongue is hot and slick as it licks slowly against mine, our lips fused in an unhurried, indulgent kiss. He grips my jaw with one hand and my hips with the other, scooting me into the cradle of his thighs as we make out.

"I love you," he says, easing off the kisses and grabbing the body wash. "And you make me feel safe in a way no one has before." He squeezes out a small dollop into his hand, rubbing it over my shoulders, and then down my arms, massaging soothingly. "Soon, I'll be back inside of you, but until then, let me take care of you the way you take care of us and Justice, okay?"

Leaning forward, I kiss him once more, feeling a pounding in my heart that is so different from before. He wanted me back then, hard and relentless, and maybe this feels tame by comparison, but he's fueled by something better than anger.

Love.

I turn my back to him, letting the warmth ease my aching muscles, and settle into him as he keeps his promise, cleaning every inch of my skin. From my neck to breasts, ribs to hips, thighs to calves, ankles to toes, Pace methodically bathes me, leaving no patch of skin untouched. And after, he sighs in contentment when I wash him back, my palms rubbing down his hard chest, mapping out this new form he's building. He reclines against the tub, head thrown back as my hand wanders, grabbing the hard, eager length of him.

He groans, but it's warm and unhurried, and when the water has cooled, I let him guide me out of the tub. Patting me dry, he wraps a fuzzy, purple robe around my body, not seeming to mind that his cock is still standing at full attention.

"Want me to brush it out? Dry it?" he asks, standing before me in nothing but a towel as he assesses my hair.

God, yes.

But also…

I wrinkle my nose, asking, "I wonder what Justice is doing right now?"

Pace dabs a towel over his face, pausing. "You miss him?"

"Is that silly?" I ask, knowing it must be. "We just left him. He's literally downstairs."

"Nah." He grins guiltily, checking his stubble in the mirror. "I was just thinking the same thing. I miss him, too."

I start for the door, but he grabs my hand and pulls me back, hand wrapping around my neck. His skin is still damp against my nose when I nestle it into the center of his chest, and for a long moment, we just stand there in the fading steam, enjoying the closeness.

And then, voice rough, he whispers, "Fuck, I can't wait to put another baby in you."

The idea is terrifying. Horrifying. My pussy actually clamps up at the thought, but then I look at him, those deep brown eyes, his sweet face and gentle hands, and realize there is no sacrifice too big to build a family with these men.

erity

I'M SWEATING by the time I wrangle my tits back into the black dress, checking my makeup and hair in the mirror. A little over three weeks since I had the baby, and I'm feeling a little more like myself. It helps that I get to dress up in something other than Lex's old hockey shirts and nightgowns, my hair cascading down in loose, shiny curls. Pace's commitment to taking care of it while I lack the energy to has done it a world of good. Where he'd once made me a part of his morning routine by rubbing anti-stretch-mark cream on my belly, he now brushes my hair, sometimes washing it or applying masks.

Unfortunately, there's no one around to do my makeup.

I settle for a light dab of foundation, warm blush, and a nude lipstick, exiting the bathroom with a steeling inhale.

That's when I hear Mama's soft, "He did it, didn't he? The scars on your back?"

Realizing I've just emerged into a sensitive discussion, I pause.

Peeking around the corner, I see Lex shifting awkwardly, reaching up to rub the back of his neck. He's in a black tuxedo, diaper bag hanging from his arm. "Yeah," he answers gruffly. "It's how he punished us."

I can't see Mama from where I'm eavesdropping, but I can hear the jangle of her bracelets, rhythmic and muted. She must be rocking Justice—maybe patting his butt. "When did it start?"

Lex clears his throat, and now more than maybe ever before, I long to take his hair out of its slicked-back ponytail. To free him from the memory of a life where he was forced to be proper and unfeeling and so hardened. "I was seven," he answers.

Mama's breath hitches. "Jesus Christ." And then a soft, "I'm sorry."

Lex shakes his head. "Don't be. I chose every wound. Each scar is a hit I took for my brothers. If I had to do it all over again, I would."

There's a suspended moment where Lex looks at his shoes, the backs of his ears flushed, and then Mama sighs. "My old man was a real hard ass. Not mean—not like yours. But he was very stalwart. Old-fashioned, you know? In another life, he could have probably been a Duke."

"Sounds a little like his daughter," he replies, a grin in his voice. "Where is he now?"

"Passed away my freshman year at Forsyth." Her voice is quieter than I think I've ever heard it. "I always regretted being so difficult for him—not getting to know him better. Not telling him how proud I was to have his last name." There's a long pause, and then Mama's gentle, "Would you like it?"

My heart stutters, squeezing painfully inside my chest.

Lex cocks his head. "Would I like what?"

"Sinclaire," Mama clarifies. Since Lex has his back to me, I can't see his reaction, but Mama suddenly rushes out, "I'm sorry if that's presumptuous of me. It's just... Verity is Sinclaire, and so is little J.J. here. I don't know what carrying the Ashby name around does for you, Wicker, and Pace. Maybe it gets you places and it's worth keeping. But," she hedges, "if the three of you ever get tired of lugging around that asshole's legacy, you're welcome to a name that'll help you build your own."

I don't hear Lex's answer because I have to duck back into the bathroom to punch down the swell of emotion in my chest. Frantically, I dab at the tears welling in my eyes.

So much for my mascara.

I give it a few minutes before gathering myself and exiting the bathroom, clearing my throat to make my presence known. Luckily, any residual anguish evaporates at the sight of my mother gazing down at a bundled up Justice, snug in her arms. He's freshly bathed and fed—quiet for the moment.

"He's the handsomest little fella, isn't he?" she says.

My mother, in a word, is smitten.

"I know."

Lex is lingering by the kitchen, expression indecipherable as he lugs the second diaper bag onto the counter. "I still say you could have come to the palace," he grunts, pulling out diapers and blankets. "It would have been easier than hauling all this stuff up here."

"I'm happy to watch Justice for you," Mama says, tapping Justice's nose with a sharp, lacquered fingernail as she beams down at him. "Thrilled even, but there is no chance in hell I'm stepping into that haunted mansion, even if it is to see my grandson. He's fine here."

'Here' is the apartment above Royal Ink. A compromise. There's nothing wrong with the little house I grew up in, but with all of the Royals in Forsyth headed to the black wedding, it seemed like the best option for the future King. Security here is top-notch, and Sy agreed to let two of our men stand guard downstairs. That, and the fact Mama likes the massive flat screen where she can watch her reality TV shows.

"How do I look?" I ask, adjusting the top of my dress again. I'd changed after feeding him, fighting my way into the first non-maternity clothing I've worn in months. Although, to be fair, the top is fashioned for nursing. "Tell me the truth, Mama, because he'll just tell me I look gorgeous, and I'm pretty sure the sleep deprivation has made us all delirious."

"Stop fidgeting, and let me look," she says, and I force myself to stand still. "You look beautiful."

"Really?" I worry, tugging at the bodice. "I don't look like a sausage stuffed in a casing?"

"Honey, you look amazing." My mother can't lie. She's a born truth-teller, and if I looked like shit, she'd just come out and say it. She appraises me head to toe. "Your tits look spectacular."

Lex smirks. "That's what I keep telling her."

I shoot him a glare, but he just grins back, shrugging. It's hard to stay mad at him when he's doling out compliments *and* wearing the hell out of a suit.

"Listen to your man," she tells me. "And you better get moving before he gets hungry again."

I squirm as I adjust my dress strap. "I've got, like... six nursing pads stuffed in my top. Hopefully that'll soak up any overflow."

Even though I fed him the minute we got here, topping him off to keep his belly full, we've probably only got two to three hours max before we need to get back. The clock is ticking.

"Everything you need is in the bag," Lex says. While the guys stayed downstairs going over the security procedure, Lex followed me up to oversee the hand-off. Just like old times. "Clothes if he needs a change, plenty of extra diapers, spit-up cloths, wipes, and some blankets." He pulls out a yellow blanket with ducks on it. "He likes to be swaddled in this one, not the dinosaur one—that one's for tummy time. The lilac blanket is for—"

"I'm sure we'll be fine," Mama says, only half listening.

Lex's forehead pinches. "If he gets fussy, it may be gas, so you can put him on his tummy to work it out—the dinosaur blanket. Specifically. Also, there's cream for his diaper rash, but don't put it on too thick. He'll get hungry in about two or three hours, so he should be able to wait until Verity gets back, but if he doesn't, there's an emergency bottle of milk in the refrigerator."

"Liquid gold," I mutter, thinking about how much of a challenge it was to pump those precious ounces.

"I can handle a baby for two hours, Dr. Daddy," Mama says,

rolling her eyes, then looking back down at Justice. In a sweet baby voice, she adds, "Tell your daddy to get out of here before I take off my shoe and—"

"We're leaving!" I announce, bending over and giving Justice a kiss on the forehead. He smells so good. Lex does the same, but before we leave, I make sure to pull my mama into a long, one-armed hug.

With my heart in my throat, I whisper, "You're a really good mom."

She turns to kiss my cheek, eyes softening. "You're not too bad yourself, kiddo."

"Learning from the best."

Before either of us can procrastinate any longer, Lex ushers me into the hallway to the elevator.

"He'll be fine," he says, as much for himself as for me.

I don't tell him the gratitude in my hug was more about Mama offering Lex our last name than for babysitting. "I know." The doors open and we step inside. "We're not going far, and if we have to leave, we leave. Who's going to notice?"

Lex adjusts his tie. "No one. Not with the epic wedding everyone is about to witness. What are they? Twenty? Twenty-five years apart?" He glances at me then, eyelids growing heavy. "Also, your mother is right." His hand cinches around my waist, and suddenly his body is against mine, pushing me against the elevator wall. Amber eyes sear into mine as he leans close with a velvety whisper. "Your tits look fucking spectacular. I can't help thinking about what my cock would look like, slick with milk, buried between them."

My knees almost buckle, nipples pebbling at his words, but it's followed by the sharp pinprick that I know leads to my milk letting down. His hand slides up my side, but I swallow thickly and stop him. "You absolutely can *not* touch my breasts, or it'll trigger a reaction that'll look like Niagra Falls right here in this elevator."

His tongue darts out on a smirk. "I'm not seeing the problem."

Lord have mercy.

"It'll ruin my dress," I whine, wishing we could indulge, "and then we'll have to miss the wedding, and something tells me that's not a good look for our first official outing as the representatives of East End and PNZ."

He groans but steps back, reaching down to adjust the bulge in his pants as the doors of the elevator open. I step forward to exit, but he grabs my arm and stops me, whispering in my ear, "Seriously, Verity. The three of us are going to be walking into enemy territory distracted by how fucking gorgeous you are. It's going to be a *very* long night."

My cheeks heat as we step out into the lobby. Wicker and Pace are focused on a tablet, both dressed in dark suits. We'd been told to wear black in honor of the wedding's theme. None of us have any idea what we're getting into.

Wicker glances up first, his gaze piercing through me as he stands straighter. "Christ, Red," he exhales, taking me in. He jabs his elbow at Pace, who draws his eyes away from the tablet, and sucks in a breath.

"Fuck me, Rosi." Pace's dark eyes assess me from head to toe before throwing Lex a pained look. "We're going straight into enemy territory with boners."

Lex points at him. "That's what I said."

My jaw drops. "How do you think I feel? You have to deal with one chick, but I've got three fucking underwear models to look at all night. Why do you keep letting Wicker dress you?" I demand. The man's got impeccable taste for menswear. Their suits are hugging all the right places.

Goddamn it, I want to *fuck*.

Lex shrugs, adjusting his shirt cuff. "We work with our strengths."

Let's just hope I have some left by the time this wedding is over with.

"God, I thought we'd never get out of there," Pace says, tugging at his tie as we all but sprint to the waiting car. "That whole thing—"

"Stop," Wick says, rubbing his temples. His hair is a rumpled mess from the mask he wore all night. "Let's swear right now—all four of us—that we'll never speak of *that* again."

"Deal," Lex agrees, helping me into the backseat of the car. They climb in behind me and Pace taps the roof, letting the pledge know we're ready to go. "We should get to West End in about fifteen minutes."

I groan, squirming in my dress, which has become itchy and annoying. "That's another reason we should have Mama stay at the palace. It's so much closer."

I'm not going to say I'm engorged, but I can feel the pads I'd stuffed in my built-in bra getting damp. It's been two hours and forty-five minutes. We're pushing the limits.

Wicker, sitting across from me, bends down to pluck up my foot, propping it onto his knee. Pulling off my shoe, he rubs tiny circles into my arch that make me positively melt. Sighing, I lean into Pace's side and inhale his warm scent.

As weird as the wedding was, I have to admit that it was fun to get out for a while. Lex and Pace still have school, and Wick sometimes has to attend to businessy things, but I never get out of the palace. I've put a lot of work into making it feel more like home, but the cabin fever is intense.

Lex's phone chimes and he picks it up, reading the name on the screen. "It's a text from your mom." He thumbs it open, scanning the words. "She says to stay as long as we want. Justice got fussy, so she gave him some tummy time—fuck, hopefully on the dinosaur blanket—and a bottle. He's back asleep." He sends a text in response. "I told her we're already on the way."

Smiling, I wager, "You also told her about the dinosaur blanket, didn't you?"

He pointedly ignores this question, and when the phone chimes back, his eyebrows rise. "She said to enjoy a few extra hours."

"You mean we've got two hours..." Pace asks, glancing between us, "alone?"

"We could go to the diner," Lex says, looking at me. "You hungry?"

My stomach drops as I realize I'm about to spoil all the fun. "Unfortunately, I'm going to need to get home and pump," I remind them, aware that I'm pretty much past the point of no return. "I feel like I'm about to burst."

Wick's eyes flick down to my chest and his tongue darts out. "I mean, you *could* pump," he says. It could be taken for casual, except for that hard, tense muscle in the back of his jaw. "Or we could take care of it."

The idea brings a rush of warmth between my legs and I confess, "I don't know if I can make it until we get home."

"Who said we needed to wait?" Pace says, wasting no time tugging at my top. "Let's at least relieve a little of the pressure."

Lex bangs on the window between the front and back seat, calling out, "Change of plans. Take us home."

The vee of my dress, made for easy nursing access, splits easily, exposing my breast. A drop of milk beads on my nipple, then slides over the round curve. Pace's thumb catches it, and I watch, hypnotized as he brings it to his lips, tongue snatching it off the tip. His eyelids droop. "You had almonds?"

I watch his Adam's apple bob. "This afternoon. How did you know?"

He smacks his lips. "Tastes sweet."

"I want some," Wick declares, pushing my leg off his lap and dropping to the small space between my knees. Pace's wide hand wraps around my breast, lifting it toward his brother, but the slightest bit of pressure is enough to send a spray arching into the air. It hits Wicker just below the eye.

"Oh god, sorry," I say, horrified.

"Don't apologize," he says, allowing the droplet to slide down his cheek to his mouth, where he licks it off. They get so hard and swollen now, a million times more than before I gave birth. He nods at his brother, "Do it again."

This time when he squeezes, Wick is ready with his mouth open. The liquid squirts inside but his eagerness takes over and he quickly latches on, mouth clamping over the mound of flesh and taking a long suck. Pace lifts the other side, already dripping, to Lex. "Want a taste?"

It's only then that I catch sight of Lex's hand on his crotch. He shifts, eyes boring into mine, and says, "I'll wait until we get home."

I hear the heat behind his words. It's not a deflection. It's a promise.

Pace moves to where he can reach me better, squeezing the sides of my breast as his tongue flattens out under my nipple, catching the milk as it spills. I moan, feeling a rush of relief at expressing both sides at once. "You have no fucking clue how good this feels," I say, my hands on the crowns of their heads, encouraging them to take as much as they can.

Glancing down, I realize Lex isn't the only one touching himself. Wicker fumbles for his zipper, reaching into his pants to draw out his flushed, rigid cock. From my vantage, I can only see the swollen head, glistening at the tip as he strokes it, but it makes my blood rush like fire.

Curling my fingers in Wick's hair, I pull him back, gazing down into lust-drunk eyes. "Go back to your seat."

He blinks, looking hilariously cowed as he jolts back, clumsily getting back in his seat. "What did I—" But his mouth clicks shut when I slide to my knees in front of him, eyes fixed to his leaking cock.

I curl my fingers around it, delighting in his long hiss. "You're not the only ones who can suck, you know."

And then I take him in my mouth.

It rushes through me like lava, a wave of want so strong that it drives my mouth down to his root. Suddenly, I feel so stupid for moping around these past two weeks, waiting for my men to remind me that I'm a sexual, desired creature.

They created Justice, but they didn't create that.

It was always in me, waiting.

Wicker releases a long, pitiful sound. "Fucking hell, Red," he gasps, fingers threading into my hair. Beneath my palms, I feel his thighs twitching upward, chasing the heat of my tongue.

I moan at the sparks that light inside me.

"You like that, Rosi?" Pace says, the electric hum of him getting closer, until I can feel his fingers on my neck. "You look so pretty sucking cock."

"Oh god, shut the fuck up," Wicker grinds out, his fingers tightening in my hair. "I'm so fucking close to busting, you have no fucking idea."

Pace husks, "I've got *some* idea," and I feel intoxicated by the sound that claws from Wicker's throat, so desperate and strained.

"Don't keep it from her," Lex says, pulling my hair back to watch as I slide my mouth up the shaft, sucking. "You want his cum, baby?"

Eagerly, I nod, my tongue laving the head of his cock, and Wicker *whimpers*.

Like, legitimately fucking whimpers.

The first burst of his cum tastes salty and hot, and I relish the vibration of his thighs as he trembles, thrusting into my lips with a long, unsteady groan.

Pulling off, I thumb the corner of my lips, but then Pace is there, chasing the taste of him off my tongue. "You're so fucking good to us," he whispers, and it takes me a moment to realize the airy rasp of his voice is owed to the way his arm is bobbing, fist stripping his cock.

I waste little time pushing him back, gathering my hair away from my face as I duck down, licking the glistening tip. Pace doesn't stop stroking himself, though. He points his cock at my slick, parted lips, and cradles the back of my head, softly commanding, "Open for me."

Obeying, I open my jaw, extending my tongue as I gaze up into his dark, hooded eyes.

"Fuck," he breathes, thumb pushing into the soft space below my ear. "You're so fucking beautiful. Are you ready for my cum?"

I answer with a flick of my tongue against his frenulum, entranced as I watch him seize, a long ribbon of cum landing in the crease of my mouth. Much like Wicker did before on my tit, I latch onto his cock, milking every grunted surge of cum.

"Almost home," Lex announces, and I slowly pull back.

A warmth blooms inside of me as I see my two Princes so lax and winded, their hair mussed. Glancing at Lex, we share a private smile, and by the time we go through the security checkpoint, any body part that couldn't be shown in polite company has been put away.

The car parks in the front circle, and Wicker and Pace get out first, each slightly stumbling. Still trying to catch my breath, Lex pins me with a hard, hungry look as he yanks the tie out of his hair and says, "My turn."

AFTER TELLING his brothers to go pick up our son, Lex carries me up the stairs.

I laugh breathlessly when he swoops me up, my shoe falling, and I watch with amusement as it clatters down the stairs behind us. "Someone's going to trip on that and break their neck."

"I'll fix them," he says, and as soon as we reach the landing, his mouth descends on mine, hard and unrelenting.

I respond by burying my fingers into the soft, cool tresses. It's easy to forget that Lex is a sturdy guy when he's pouring over books or doing delicate, exacting medical things, but right now, it's all I can focus on.

His chest is hard beneath my hand as he walks me back, guiding me to the bedroom without ever breaking the kiss. He tastes as sharp as his teeth, his fingers tugging erratically at my dress. "I know I can't," he says, panting against my lips, "but god, I want to fuck you."

"Tell me what you can do," I say, tugging him through the doorway.

He freezes before me in that black shirt and tie, slowly lifting a hand to his shirt collar. One by one, he loosens the buttons, the butterflies in my stomach roaring to life at the naked *want* in his stare. It's a core-deep tug that I haven't felt since Justice was born.

It explodes into violent flutters when his deep, silky voice asks, "You want me to make you feel good, baby?"

Swallowing, I admit, "Yes."

"Turn around," he tells me, voice gruff.

I turn, and his fingers move quickly, dragging down the zipper on my dress, pushing it over my shoulders, and letting it fall to the ground. His crotch brushes against my backside and I feel the hard steel pressing against his pants.

Sweeping my hair to the side, he kisses my neck, moving down my shoulder until he's spun me around. Gently, he lifts my breasts, kissing the nipple of each one. "You're going to let these fill up for me again," he demands, and all I can do is nod, already feeling the ache. "Until then, you're going to let me take care of you."

It's not a request, and I feel it in the way he pushes me to sit on the edge of the bed. I watch as he shucks off his shirt and pants, his amber eyes drinking me in hungrily. His cock springs upward as he drops his boxers to the floor, bobbing between his legs, fully erect, and I watch with jealousy as he strokes down the length, wishing he could be inside me. But when I cover my soft belly with my arm, he stops.

"Don't," he tells me, "I want to see you."

I remove my arm and place both hands on the mattress by my sides, mustering a confidence I don't feel. "I know I'm not as... smooth as I used to be."

Lex frowns, and then slowly crouches before me, palming each of my knees. "You mean these?" he asks, reaching up to brush gentle fingers against one of the worst stretch marks. At my grimace, he leans in, forcing me to meet his gaze. "Verity—baby— touch me."

Confused, I extend a hand to stroke the cut of his jaw, but he sighs, grabbing my wrist and directing it to his shoulder, and then back...

I suck in a breath, feeling his raised scars.

"Are they ugly?" he asks, a thread of misery in his voice. Before I can answer, he says, "They should be. They aren't like yours. They aren't there because I created life. They're just sour memories."

At once, I'm reminded of the words he spoke to my mother, hours earlier.

"They're more than bad memories, Lex. They're a testament to your strength. Your love and loyalty to your brothers." Leaning down, I press a kiss to his mouth, whispering, "I think they're beautiful."

His eyes flutter open, holding mine. "Then believe me when I say that's how I feel about yours." Ducking down, he plants a kiss on each of my knees while nudging them apart with his hands. "I know it might be too early, but can I show you?" He glances up at me through his lashes. "Can I eat your pussy?"

The words alone are enough to reignite the fire in my core. "I think I'm up to it, but," I place my hand on the one that's pushing my thighs apart, embarrassed. "I think I'm still bleeding a little."

He plants a kiss over my hand and then shifts it aside. "I know."

His tender kisses become tiny licks, traveling up my thigh, and ultimately shift to these lingering, tantalizing sucks.

My head falls back and I ask, "You know?"

His voice reverberates against the soft skin of my inner thigh. "There's nothing going on with your body that I don't know about, Verity. Everything happening to you is part of nature. Any change in you that's the result of carrying our son—those are a gift. The milk that you feed him with. The blood that kept him alive all those months he was in your belly. It's part of you and him."

His tongue flattens against my skin and he drags it upward, getting closer to the warmth between my legs.

"I can't fuck your pussy," he says, "but I can taste it." My breath hitches, and the first wet touch against my clit sends a shiver through my body. We're somewhere between the exam room and those late nights with Lagan. Less clinical, definitely not as rough. His warm breath feels good, the way his tongue darts into the folds of my pussy. Everything down there feels different now, the sensations dulled in some places, enhanced in others.

One flick of his tongue against my clit has my nerves zinging.

"Gentle," I tell him, thrusting my hands in his hair. His ministrations slow, languid to the point of driving me wild.

"That first night I had you on my exam table," he begins, speaking the words directly into my core, "I remember thinking that you had the prettiest, most perfect pussy I'd ever seen." Extending his tongue, he takes a long, languorous lick, his fingers digging into my thighs, holding them open for his searing gaze. "It's still so fucking pretty, baby. If you could see what I see…" A tense, slow shudder travels through him, and I whine.

"I need it… a little more," he sucks and my hips buck. A whine comes from my throat. "God, yes, like that." The pacing is different for us, so much slower, and I take in Lex's sweet, filthy words greedily, the tightness building deep in my belly. It's not long before the heady rush cascades, rippling across my nerves in a blissful orgasm.

Lex rises, working his way up my body. He pointedly dotes on my belly, kissing every inch of soft skin, and then up my chest, until he shifts next to me, his erection pressing into my hip. His mouth finds mine, and I taste myself, the tang of my pussy—and more, the metallic edge of blood. I roll toward him and reach for him, stroking from the base to the tip, spreading precum over the head. I'm distracted by his cock, by his mouth, and suddenly the orgasm I had isn't enough. I want to feel full. *I miss it.* "I want you inside."

His eyebrows crash together. "Baby, it's too soon."

"Maybe," I hedge, giving my wrist a twist, "for *that* hole." The words hit him and he exhales like he's been punched, his cock surging in my hand. I reason, "Pace and Wick won't do it. They're afraid. But you know my body better than anyone else." I wet my lips, watching as his eyes dart to the motion. "You know what I can handle and what I need."

He stares at me with parted lips, that dark glint of hunger filling his eyes. When he finally moves, it's to roll over me, situating himself between my thighs. His breath comes hot and eager against my mouth. "If you want this, you need to understand that I won't be able to moderate myself. I didn't fight Pace when he wanted to have you first, because you do this thing to me, Verity." His tongue traces the crease of my mouth. "This thing where I completely lose control."

When he pulls up, showing me his handsome, earnest face, I tell him the truth. "I trust you, Lagan."

He leans forward and captures my mouth with his, giving me a punishing kiss, hard and aggressive, an indicator of what's coming, and I wrap my legs around him, drawing him closer. I want it more than anything. To be clutched and grabbed and consumed.

I might wear the tiara.

But I'm still the same fiery redhead from West End.

The chuckle he releases as he reaches for the nightstand drawer, snagging the bottle of lube, shoots right to my core. "They're going to fucking kill me for getting this first."

I bury my own laugh in his warm shoulder, thinking that it's just enhancing the moment—this sense of furtive fumbling in the dark. "We'll make it up to them." My gaze dips between us, watching as he slicks his cock with the slippery lube, a rough sound escaping his throat when he ducks down to take my nipple in his mouth. I jolt at the sensation, which is accompanied by the prod of his slick fingertip, right against my asshole. His finger massages the area, then without warning, slips in.

I'm so desperate for it that I rock up to meet him.

"You want it that bad?" he asks, stretching me out as he laps the milk leaking from my nipple. "You missed having us inside, filling you up?"

My head thrashes more than it shakes. "You don't even know." I gasp, overcome by the way it feels when he sinks it further into me. The pull of his suckle on my breast meets the pressure of his finger in short, rhythmic pulses, like I'm being threaded. Spreading my legs wider for him, I get lost in the stretch of his knuckles as he drinks from me, my fingers tangled in his hair, holding him close.

"You taste so fucking good," he groans, changing to the other tit.

"More," I beg, rocking my hips. "Give me... *yes*."

His second finger merely teases at the feeling of fullness I want so badly, but the third is so close to being what I need. I gaze down his back, seeing the ridges of his raised scars, and can't help but touch him. He trembles when my fingertips glide over the slashes, memorizing their texture in slow, soothing, curious circuits.

I meant what I said before.

This *is* beauty.

It's been weeks since I've had one of them in me, but Lagan's hands work with precision. He knows my body inside and out, and it's no surprise that in just a few moments he has me panting.

His long, lean frame covers me as he abandons my breasts, trailing hot, wet kisses up my collarbone, to my throat, pausing at my mouth.

He's breathing hard as he gazes down at me. "Tell me you want it," he demands, stroking the lube up his cock.

Swallowing, I touch the tense line of his jaw. "I want you to fuck me," I whisper, watching my words ripple through him like a wave.

He pulls his fingers out and nudges up against me, slotting the wet tip of his cock against the ring of muscle. Growling, he pushes in, thick and long and painfully slow, knocking my breath from my lungs with each measured inch.

I grasp at his shoulders, my mouth falling open on a gasp. "Oh, god," I whimper, feeling the intensity of his gaze on me. "Oh, that feels so...*fuck.*"

His amber eyes never leave mine. Even when he begins carefully rocking into me, his cock dragging deliciously against my hole, he just... watches me. "I love you," he raggedly whispers, letting his cock stretch me wide. "You are my life. You know that, don't you?"

I answer by grabbing his face, and bringing him down for a deep, desperate kiss. He's *fucking* me, his hands fisted in the sheets as he drives his hips into mine, and it doesn't matter that he's only halfway in, or that he's clearly tuned in to my reactions for any proof of pain or discomfort.

It feels so good to be handled like this, my body used for nothing more than the pleasure we're both frantically chasing. His breath hits my chin, coming in short bursts, and his eyebrows pull tightly together, an odd distress coming over his face.

"How can you be this tight?" he mutters, digging his fist beneath my hips and using it to drag me upward, as close to him as I can get. "I'm not going to be able to hold it, baby."

I realize then that he's like Wick was earlier. Too close to the edge. So close to bursting.

The thought makes me *burn*, and I hold his chin, forcing his gaze to mine. "Give it to me," I plead, already seeing his face tighten as his thrusts grow deeper, more erratic. "Put your baby in me, Lagan."

His mouth opens on a shocked gasp, my hole fluttering around the first strong pulse of his cock. He holds my gaze when he comes, poised above me in a tense shudder. "Fuck," he growls, heat spreading through me with each surge. "Jesus, you've got us on a fucking hair-trigger."

He's barely finished his last shiver of pleasure when he pulls away. His cock slips wetly from my ass, and I try not to squirm as he instantly ducks down to check me, chest heaving as his fingers spread me open for his assessing eyes.

Seemingly satisfied that no damage has been done, he collapses next to me, turning to nuzzle his face into my breast. I hum when he licks lazily at my nipple, sucking away a rogue droplet of milk. We're both too tired to move, exhausted and satiated, and I comb my fingers idly through his auburn hair.

Slowly, he stirs. "Fuck," he mutters, "I think I passed out."

"It's okay." I yawn. "It's been a tiring few weeks."

"Let's get you cleaned up." Kissing my shoulder, he gets out of bed, walking to the bathroom. Stretching out on the massive bed, my fears from before have faded. My men love me—want me, *need* me—despite the changes in my body and our lives. We're different now. We're not just Princes and a Princess. Not even just lovers. We're more.

We're partners.

We're *creators.*

And I can't wait to see what we create next.

27

P ace

"So," I say, drawing out the word as I park. "You think Maddox is banging a twenty-year-old right now in his crypt?"

Wicker snaps, "Dude, we promised not to mention it!"

"*You* promised." I laugh, killing the ignition. We're parked in front of Royal Ink, and it hits me how often we're in West End these days. I still remember having to sneak into the territory to get to Verity that one night, months ago. Scaling this building, getting in through the skylight, and standing in wait as she showered up there. "I'm fucking fascinated by the entire thing. Like, how does it work with him and the other Barons? Do they share? Does she call him Dadd—"

He whips a hot glare on me. "I swear to god I will punch you in the junk if you don't stop."

Maybe Wicker having this whole extended family isn't such an issue, after all. I haven't seen him this riled up in years. "Fine," I agree, laughing. "Fine."

We pass Rory and Baxter on the way up, telling them to take off before riding the elevator up to the top floor. Since the Dukes and Lavinia didn't have a baby to come home to, they hung back to enjoy the post-wedding festivities, meaning Mama B is still alone with Justice.

"You're early," she says, when we walk through the door. The admonishment is clear in her voice, although it's hard to tell whether or not that's down to the trashy reality TV show she just paused on the big screen. "I told you, we're fine."

Wicker looks around the space, having never been here before. *Yes*, I want to say, *that's the table where Nick Bruin nearly bled to death.*

I bet they eat steaks on it now.

"Lex has been busy with med school and hasn't had much time with Verity." He shrugs, picking up a trophy on the side table and inspecting it. "We decided to come pick up Justice and give them a few minutes."

Resigned, Mama B turns off the TV, rising to her feet. "He's in the bedroom, out like a light," she says, walking over to the wine refrigerator. She pulls out a bottle and holds it up to Wick. "Want a glass?"

"No thanks," he says, pushing his fists into his pockets. "We've agreed to stay sober in solidarity while Verity was pregnant, and now, nursing."

She looks vaguely impressed. Then, she pops the cork. I hear the gurgle of wine pouring into the glass as I enter the guest room, seeking out our son. Justice is on his back in the portable crib, his pacifier resting next to his head, and like always, I have to take a long moment just to watch him, seeing his chest rise and fall with even breaths.

He's nothing like I thought he'd be.

Although he looks like the perfect combination of Wicker and Verity, sometimes these little peeks of mine and Lex's personality will already show through in him. Like how he wakes up in a furious tizzy, or when his curious eyes scan around each room I take him to.

There's nothing more soothing than walking him around the

palace, watching him explore how big the world is. Some nights, when he's fussy, I'll walk for hours, showing him the place where Effie first got out of her cage, or the sitting room we used to play Iceberg in, or the huge oak out front where I used to take my laptop during our weekends home.

I try to show him the good memories.

Unfortunately, the smell hits me before I even pick him up, and I turn, finding Wicker lingering in the doorway. "He needs a change." I grimace, and even from where he's standing, Wicker looks like he may hurl. "I'll do it if you'll get his stuff together and take it to the car."

Wick holds up his hands. "No argument here."

Verity makes fun of me for how precise I am with setting up for changing Justice's diapers, but I've learned it's a lot like torturing a mark down in the dungeon. It's smelly and super gross, and if you're not careful, you may get fluids on you, but everything goes smoothly if you're well prepared. Before I pick up the baby, I've already got the changing pad arranged on the bed and the packet of wipes ready. A diaper and fresh pajamas wait nearby.

"Okay, little guy, let's do this," I whisper, picking him up. I kiss his perfect little button nose before setting him on the pad, and start the process of undressing him.

"Dude, what did mommy eat before she fed you?" Definitely not almonds. Justice gurgles, not quite smiling yet, but energetically waving his fists around. "I'll make this fast if you promise not to pee on me, deal?"

I get to work, glancing over my shoulder when I sense someone behind me. Verity's mother stands in the doorway, a glass of red wine in her hand. "Sy kept Saul's collection, and I couldn't resist breaking into it," she explains, watching me and Justice with a soft grin. I wipe all of his crevices—there are so many—getting him squeaky clean. "You're good with him."

I toss her a smile. "Is that a surprise?"

It still is to me, sometimes.

"A little," she confesses, stepping into the room. She sits on the bed next to the baby, leaning over to kiss his forehead. "When I found out about Verity becoming Princess, I hated you. All three of you. Although, maybe hate isn't a strong enough word. Murder," she dryly adds, "wasn't off the table."

My smile hardens into a scowl. "Gee, thanks."

She shakes her head, looking rueful. "The only thing I knew about any of you was that your father was a monster. Maybe that was unfair."

I don't tell her how fair that actually might have been.

We did things to her daughter that I'd absolutely kill someone over if they were done to Justice. Even though Verity's forgiven us for those things, the thought still sits bitterly in the back of my throat.

Mama B goes on, "Even though I understand a little better now, I can't say I haven't been worried about my daughter and grandson this whole time. And I'll admit, I wasn't sure how you and Lex would feel about a baby that isn't biologically yours once he got here."

This makes me snort. "Family isn't about blood. It's about the people you love," I tell her. "You should know that. You see DKS as your family, don't you?" I grab the tiny diaper and slip it under Justice's body, giving his belly a little tickle. "Lex and Wicker are my brothers, and Justice is my son."

Her head cocks as she assesses me. "And Rufus?"

Freezing, I swallow back a lump in my throat at his name, head shaking. "He was never a father to us. He was a controlling prick who collected us for his own scheme to create a legacy." I fasten the tabs on the diaper, and Justice's little legs wiggle around, kicking against me. "A real father could never hurt his son. I understand that now." I stroke the bottom of his tiny foot, smiling when he squawks. Slowly, the smile falls, hardening. "He took my biological family away from me before I even understood what it meant, and Danner chose to take the secret of my father's identity to the grave."

When I glance over, she's watching me intently, an odd sadness swimming in her eyes. "I didn't know he was hurting the three of you.

If I'd known..." She sighs, long and hard, slipping her finger into Justice's grasping hand. "Sometimes I feel responsible."

My face twists. "Why the fuck would you feel responsible? Because you kept Verity away from him?" Snorting, I tell her, "That was probably the best decision you ever made."

But she shakes her head, a heaviness to the gesture. "If you spoke to Danner, then I'm sure you know about what Rufus was doing to those Princesses." She shifts, grimacing. "You realize he was infertile."

I shrug. "Yeah, he was shooting blanks. Danner told us."

"But he wasn't always," she says, the words slow and full of significance. "Not before I conceived Verity."

I do a double take at the glint in her eyes, realization dawning on me. "You mean..."

"The night he raped me, I got my revenge." She sniffs, the sound full of contempt. "The tip of my steel-toed boot, slamming right into his rotten testicles. I can't know for certain if that's what caused it, of course. But after, I know he was..." Her eyes sparkle menacingly. "Let's just say he was out of the game for a while."

I look at this woman in a new light, imagining her burying her boot into Father's nutsack, right after he made his final useful deposit.

Speak now a prayer for the fruitless...

And I *laugh*.

"Good on you," I say, not even caring about the implications. If Liberty Sinclaire took away Rufus' ability to create, then she's a fucking badass, and I'd tell it to anyone who asked.

"You're right about your father being a controlling prick." She takes a gulp of wine while handing me a clean pair of pajamas. "He had everyone who crossed his path in a chokehold. One wrong move and he'd make our lives hell. It's why I hid Verity from him for as long as I could." Justice grabs one of the bangles on her wrist and holds on. She offers him a smile, even though her eyes look haunted. "You know what he was capable of, Pace, and that's why I held onto the secrets. It's why Danner took them to the grave."

I look up at her, and from her expression, it's clear she has more to say, but can't bring herself to do it. I pick up Justice and nestle him carefully in the crook of my arm. "What are you trying to say?"

There's a long moment where I think she's just going to blow it off. But then she says, "Your mother—Odette. I knew her." She takes a deep breath. "We grew up together."

Tensing, anxiety tightens my throat. I've learned not to get my hopes up, but still, I ask, "You did?"

She gazes into her glass, a wistfulness crossing her features. "Non-Royals had a little more freedom to socialize together. We went to the same parties, hung out down by the river, flirted with boys at the Fury." She smiles at the memory. "We had a lot of fun, but then she applied for the job of handmaiden to the Princess. She was devoted to Miranda, and later, her son." An airy laugh escapes her. "We were all shocked when she was invited to the masquerade the next year. Even more so when she received the title." She touches a smudge of lipstick on the edge of her glass. "That, among other things, was the reason I hated to lose Verity to East End. I knew that a Princess would be so consumed with her 'duties' that she completely lost touch with the outside world. It's hard," she stresses, meeting my gaze, "being torn between the territory you love and the one you have a duty to."

I think back to how we managed every moment of Verity's day—how Father kept us busy with sports, school, and events. There's a certain kind of power in that type of discipline.

"Someone told me once that my birth father was DKS." The bitter taste Bruce Oakfield's intel used to give me has tempered over time.

"You know who your father is?" she asks, face showing surprise.

"Lex confirmed it." I'm not sure Pauly wants the world to know his business. When he's ready to claim it, he can.

Luckily, she doesn't ask for a name. "Odette would've kept it a secret for all of your safety. By the time word trickled over to West End that she was expecting, I was dealing with the fallout of the hurricane and my own pregnancy." She looks down at Justice. "But it makes sense for your father to be from West End. She was always drawn to the men on my side of town."

There's a heaviness in the air so I just cut to it. "I'm aware of what

Rufus did to my mother—Danner told me that much. I know he..." The words feel brittle in my throat, voice cracking. "He locked her up in the dungeon after she got pregnant as punishment for being unfaithful. I know I was... born there." The irony hits hard. All my wanting to lock away the people I love, yet I was born in a cell. I hold back the rage—barely. "I also know he agreed to send me away if she agreed to his terms. Danner just..." Frustrated, I huff. "He didn't tell me what those terms were."

Verity's mother takes a careful sip of her wine before looking at me, her eyes glassy and tired. "Do you want to know what happened? It's not pretty, but with Rufus gone, I feel..." Visibly struggling to find the words, she pauses, nodding. "I feel like I can finally tell the truth without retribution on any of us." She gives me a miserable smile. "But Pace, sometimes it's better to let things rest. You do have a family now. You have two brothers. My daughter loves you, and I know you love her as much as you love that sweet boy you're holding."

I look down at Justice, remembering the day Verity set us free. She looked so fierce and beautiful as she sliced that knife over Rufus' throat, announcing the name she'd given to our son. Only, it wasn't just a name. It was a promise all of us made to East End that night. And to each other.

"Justice can't be served without knowing the truth," I conclude, meeting Liberty's sad gaze. "Tell me."

She watches me perch on the edge of the bed with a drawn expression. "After you were born," she begins, wrapping her hands around the glass, "your father put Odette to work at the Gentlemen's Chamber."

"He made her strip?" I ask, clutching Justice close. When she nods, my stomach sinks. "That son of a fucking bitch."

"She was a novelty," Mama B explains, her eyes looking far away at the memory. "A former Princess available to the masses. Men could stuff her garter with cash, and she'd have to serve them. But he didn't just keep her around to humiliate her." Here, she shifts, her discomfort a palpable thing. "He knew she was fertile and he was still pissed at the betrayal. Bitter. Because she and some random West Ender created life out of thin air, and he couldn't get anyone pregnant. But god, did he try."

I think I understand the guilt in her eyes now, watching as she recalls the consequences of making a man like Rufus Ashby—a man who was raised to believe his own house motto—infertile.

I force myself to hear her words, already anticipating what's coming.

"Over the next few years, he raped her," she bluntly says, eyes growing flinty. "It wasn't called that, of course. Rufus was a King and Odette was his to do with as he pleased—especially since he was the only one who knew where her son was." Suddenly, she barks a dark, vicious laugh. "And she did eventually get pregnant, but here's the kicker. The baby didn't belong to him." Dipping her chin, she pins me with a significant look. "*They* didn't belong to him."

My tongue sticks in my mouth. "They?" A pain, like the tip of a dagger, pierces my heart. "She had twins," I realize.

She had *dungeon twins*.

Mama B mentioned them in the negotiations between Rufus and DKS. We'd watched the footage later. It was such a flippant comment, infuriatingly brief, but I remember it scaring him.

Now, I understand why.

"You have siblings." She nods, her smile jagged but bright. "Two of them."

I jolt to my feet at the way she speaks of them. I *have* siblings. Present-tense. "They're still alive? They're... out there somewhere? I don't—" Stuttering, I admit, "I don't understand. We know she wasn't with the other princesses' bodies in the solarium. Lex tested them all. If he didn't bury her there, then where is she?"

Mama B holds up a palm, stilling me. "Odette got pregnant again, but she had something this time she didn't have before." I don't understand the flash of pride in her eyes as she drains the last of her wine. "Help."

I raise an eyebrow. "Danner?"

"That wrinkly, poisoned toad? Hell no." Scoffing, she shakes her head, a slow, fond smile lighting her face. "She had something much better than him. *Me.*" Raising her glass, she says, "And a reigning Princess."

~

I DON'T REALIZE that I'm shaking until Adeline hands me the cup of tea.

"I always knew this day would come," she says, sitting across from me. Mama B, who offered to drive after Wicker took Justice home, is perched on the other armchair. "I just didn't expect it so soon. I guess I just figured the King was invincible, and we'd all go to our graves carrying his disgusting secrets." She's in a fuzzy pink robe, her hair twisted into a dozen or more rollers, and a pair of oversized eyeglasses are perched on her nose. No makeup or curls or accessories, just a pocketful of tissues.

It's like seeing behind the curtain.

Awkwardly, I shrug. "He thought he was, too. But turns out, he was mortal like the rest of us." I take a sip and realize she added a heavy dose of bourbon. Thank fuck. "You lied to me that day I was here," I say, recalling our discussion at the Gilded Rose.

"This woman, clearly someone you're related to, is a mystery. We've got no information on her at all. I was hoping you might know."

Adeline gives me a regretful smile. "I wasn't sure yet how much you knew. In truth, I wasn't even positive you were the baby Rufus forced her to give up. It was just a hunch. But I could tell you were curious. Searching." Her head tilts. "Duplicity isn't something I boast about, but I've learned to be good at it." She glances at Mama B, a proud grin on her face. "Fifteen years and the bastard never knew I was involved in getting Odette out of that cell."

Mama B chuckles. "No one ever suspects a woman in fuzzy pink slippers."

Adeline raises her glass in a toast. "Hear, hear."

I watch them with a sense of total disbelief, wondering, "How the hell did you do that? The dungeon is impenetrable. Ask me how I know."

Pushing her glasses up her nose, Adeline looks skyward, pulling up the recollection. "I remember I'd just been coronated—barely a month along in the pregnancy. My Princes were—and I'm sure you can relate, Pace—handsome and ambitious, and very eager with their deposits."

Mama B chokes on her tea, hacking a cough. "Christ, Adeline, I don't want to hear that shit."

She just shrugs, unbothered. "But they were dreadful at the uglier bits. The morning sickness and the constant puking were repulsive to them." Rolling her eyes, she recounts, "One day, after returning to the palace from campus, I was rushing up the stairs to get to the bathroom. But I didn't make it. Doubled over right there and hurled my guts out on the second- floor landing. I'd grabbed onto the nearest thing I could find to brace myself, which turned out to be a—"

"Wall sconce." I set my tea down slowly, sensing where this was going. "You found the secret passage."

"Yes!" she chirps, growing animated. "So, being the curious girl I was, I followed it down to the basement."

"The dungeon," I correct.

She nods impatiently. "And right there, in that awful cell, was none other than Odette Delisle." A hand flutters to her chest. "I was shocked to see her there, obviously pregnant, but far too thin. At first, I was so confused. Everyone had heard the rumors about the failed Princess that the King took pity on by giving her a job at the Gentlemen's Chamber. To the rest of Forsyth, she was entertainment, but to future princesses, she was a warning."

Swallowing, I ask, "What did you do?"

"Oh, I just talked to her." A tenderness fills her eyes as she stirs her tea. "For the next couple weeks, I'd bring her all the food that I couldn't manage to keep down anyway, and I tried to think of a way to help her. But," She pauses, pain filling her eyes. "I was weak and always sick. My pregnancy wasn't going so well." Twisting a tissue in her hands, she looks away. "And then, during the Lords' Christmas party, I met Liberty."

"I had a four-year-old, a babysitter, and five precious hours to spare." Mama B levels me with a look. "I was three sheets to the wind, ranting about Rufus fucking Ashby."

"I took a chance and told her about what I had found," Adeline explains, sitting to her full height. "And together, with the help of a couple of other Royal women, we organized a little rescue mission."

My heart races as I glance between them. "You got her out?"

Mama B nods. "We did. Right out the solarium, through the back lawn, and into a little jon boat anchored on the shore. Rufus never saw it coming." Her stare shifts to Adeline, who's grown conspicuously silent, that tissue in her hands being twisted to tatters. "Unfortunately, that was the night Addy lost her baby."

It grips my chest, the way the creation of life in Forsyth always seems to cling to death. Adeline's baby, Lex's parents, Wicker's father, Rufus and Laura Walker...

Can creation ever just come without destruction?

"I'm sorry," I say, voice tight.

Adeline shrugs this off with a breezy, "That miscarriage may have saved my life. I wasn't just a failed Princess. I was broken, and Rufus released me, none the wiser." But the anguish is there, right beneath the surface. "It was easier knowing I'd helped save three lives."

Taking a deep breath, I raise my plaintive gaze to hers. "If there's anything you know—anything you can tell me about my mother or siblings..." Pausing, I try, "I can... pay you, or—"

Adeline goes rigid, throwing Mama B a shocked look. "Heavens! What do you take me for?"

Mama B extends a palm. "He was raised by Rufus, Addy. Nothing's free in his world."

Now Adeline just looks sad, frowning. "Pace, I haven't had contact with your mother in years. My family ties to the Gilded Rose gave me a purpose, but you know better than anyone that Rufus watched our every move." Her eyes plead with me to understand. "It wasn't safe for her or the children, and she knew that. That's why she gave them up for adoption as soon as they were born."

I balk. "She got out with them, and then gave them up?" *What a waste.* That's all I can think as I take in the thought of her handing her babies—*fuck,* two of them—over to some stranger.

Some days, it's hard to even leave Justice to go to class.

"She did it to protect them," Mama B says. "She didn't care if Rufus found her, but the thought of him finding her children..."

Through the lump in my throat, I finish, "And doing to them what he did to me."

Scooting closer, Adeline explains, "She didn't get a choice with you, Pace. But with those two babies, she was able to choose the family. A nice couple with three kids, if memory serves."

I ask the question that I've been holding on to all night. "Do you know how I can find her?"

Them?

She and Mama B share a look. "I know where to start, although for everyone's safety, the information changes quickly. We took her to a safe house in Northridge, and from there, she went underground. I do know she had the babies—my contact showed me a picture. After that... the trail runs thin. Intentionally."

"That's all I need," I tell her, setting the teacup on the table. My heart and mind are racing. "I can hack into just about anything once I have a lead to go on, and this thing about Northridge—"

"Pace," Mama B says, resting her hand on my knee. "You can't hack your way into this one."

"Sure I can." I'm itching to get to my setup now.

"Hacking into a system like this will put women at risk," she explains. "Rufus may be gone, but other abusers are out there. You can't punch a hole in their privacy and security. It's too dangerous."

"We'll help you," Adeline says. "But you're going to have to trust us."

Trust two women I barely know with one of the most important details of my life?

"Fine," I breathe, rising to my feet. Mama B follows and I extend a hand to Adeline, watching surprise cross her face at the gesture. Gently, she takes it, giving my hand a shake.

"Pace," Adeline says, "always remember that your mother thought of you first. Every move, every sacrifice, was with the consideration of her children." She touches my cheek. "She loved you, and she'd be so proud to see the amazing man and father you've become."

Even though the words are coming from Adeline and not my mother herself, I feel the truth in them. Odette is a survivor. Just like I am.

And that's a bond we'll always share, even if I never get the chance to meet her.

erity

WICKER SHOOTS TO HIS FEET, eyes ablaze. "Are you serious about that call, Ref?!" Thrusting out an arm, he gestures to the penalty box, which is empty. "How is that fucking guy not—"

I grab Wicker by the arm and yank him down, giving him a stern look. Pulling a face, he mouths 'sorry' and tweaks J.J.'s beanie before continuing as if he never stopped, "How is that not a freaking high sticking? I mean, fuck." He glances down, wincing. "I mean, *fudge*." Rant over, he drops into the seat next to mine, grousing, "Face it, Red. This new no-cussing rule is hopeless."

"We can try," I stress, mouth twitching as I watch Wicker.

He perches on the edge of his seat, eyes fixed on the ice. A palpable energy radiates from him. Every play Pace makes is a symphony of emotion and Wicker's reactions mirror it, swift and intense. As soon as the Wittmore center gets the puck, Wicker leans forward, hands clenched, breath held, as if his sheer will could make

Forsyth's defense check him harder. Around us, the crowd is a blur because I'm unable to watch anything but him and Pace, their connection still tethered, even when they're separated by a rink full of people.

I nudge him. "You miss it."

Wicker exhales like a punch. "So fuck—" he gulps, "so *freaking* much." He takes J.J. from me, adjusting the miniature version of Pace's jersey—number three, Sinclaire —and holds him tight. "But if they advance, I'll get to travel with the team to Northridge next week. Plus, this is pretty cool, too. Introducing my man to the most epic sport in the world."

"You know," I hedge, "it's possible he won't want to play hockey."

I turn to Lex for support, but he and his brother just share an incredulous look. Lex decides, "Well, that's just crazy talk."

My phone rings, and now that my hands are empty, I pull it out of my pocket. It's Mama.

"Hey," I say, pressing a finger in my ear to dull the noise of the arena. "What's up?"

Her voice comes sharp. "Is there a reason Pace is ignoring my calls?"

Down on the ice, he chases the puck, smacking it down the ice to Anthony Giles, who waits in the wings.

Lex erupts this time, springing to his feet with a booming, "Thatta boy, number three!"

"Yeah, he's in the middle of a hockey game." I smile over at the baby, tight in his daddy's arms. "J.J.'s first, actually. It's a big deal."

She doesn't seem to take this as the monumental moment it so clearly is. "Well, I need him to call me back." She pauses. "A-S-A-P."

Rolling my eyes, I promise, "I'll tell him."

"Thank you," she says, but before hanging up, "and give that baby a kiss for me." Abruptly, the call ends, and I send it a glare. "It's really weird having my mom call you guys all the time. Don't get me wrong, it's better than her hating you, but it's a little much."

"Don't look at me." Lex holds up both hands. "She only calls me when she wants free medical advice. And most of it isn't even for her. I'm never recovering from that picture of Kaczinski's athlete's foot."

I wince, resting my temple on Lex's shoulder to gaze ruefully up at him. "I'm so sorry."

"Well, I don't mind it," Wick says, blue eyes still trained on the ice. "How else am I going to get her to talk me through her recipes?"

Like I said.

Weird.

It's not just me who's had to learn how to share my mother in a new way. After talking to Adeline, Pace has a better understanding of what his mother went through and why his biological father was absent. He's been making efforts to get to know Pauly a little better, and so far, so good. We even had Mama B and Pauly over to celebrate our first Thanksgiving with J.J.

I'm pretty sure the palace shuddered, Rufus rolling over in his grave at two West Enders drinking discount beer from his exquisite crystal goblets and fine china.

Down on the ice, Pace catches the puck and drops it down on the ice, already in movement toward the goal. Watching him makes gooseflesh rise on my arms. The way his body moves is so powerful and sure that I have to admit to feeling a little high on it.

He's mine, I think, knowing everyone in these stands is seeing the passion I feel from him every night when he's buried inside me. He passes the puck, then zig-zags down the ice, ready and waiting when Anthony slings it back over. Pace snags the puck and slaps it hard, zinging it to the back of the net. The buzzer rings and Wicker and I both shoot to our feet.

"Let's go!" Wick shouts, beaming down at J.J. "That's your dad! Suck it, Wittmore!"

The final score is three-one, and we head down to the waiting area just outside the locker room, buzzing on how we plan to celebrate.

"Burritos?" I suggest hopefully. "Pace loves burritos."

Lex sighs, shifting Justice's carrier to his other hand. "Fine, burritos."

"You just want to beat him at pool again," Wicker says, pausing to greet Anthony as he walks out of the locker room. "If we knew the key to convincing you to eat junk was billiards, we would have donated a pool table to Señor Mexicana years ago."

Ten minutes later, the door opens and Pace struts through, dressed in a dark suit. Unable to contain myself, I spring forward to leap into his arms, legs wrapping around his waist when he lifts me. "You were amazing," I say, capturing his smirk in a long kiss. "To the victor."

He nibbles my lip before letting me slide to my feet. "You the spoils, Rosi?"

"Me," grabbing his tie, I tug him toward his brothers, "*and* burritos."

Pace throws Lex a wry look. "Just can't let me have a win, can you? That pool table at Señor's was the worst idea."

"You killed it, bro," Wicker says, extending a fist that Pace bumps his against.

"Thanks. That netminder was some kind of sorcerer, and offense has been dogwater without you on center." He bumps his knuckles against Lex's fist next. "But our defense is solid, and we'll probably kill it in the tourney next week. You're still coming, right?"

Wicker answers without reservations. "Fuck—" He flinches when I slap his arm. "Fudge yeah, I am."

I watch as Pace squats, giving J.J. a breathtaking smile. "You rocking my number, little man?"

Justice kicks his feet happily when Pace tickles them, his eyes lighting up.

Loath as I am to break it up, I relay, "My mother wants you to call her immediately."

His eyebrow lifts and he rises, checking his phone. "She called three times." He presses the button, lifting it to his ear. "Hey, it's Pace. Everything okay?" He's quiet for a beat, and then, "Yeah, we won." My mother talks, her voice unintelligible as she speaks quickly. His forehead creases, but is otherwise blank as he nods. "Okay. Right. I appreciate it. Yeah." He grimaces, glancing at me. "Well, guess it's like a Band-Aid, huh? Time to rip that fu—" I glare at him. "Fuuudger off."

He hangs up, tucking the phone into his pocket.

Wick and I stare at him, until Lex asks, "What was that about?"

"Adeline called." He takes the carrier from Lex's grip, a nervous energy buzzing around him. "She found Odette."

PACE FIDGETS, circling the room like a caged animal. I took J.J. out of his arms five minutes ago, tucking him into the car seat where he's napping, which probably made it worse. Holding his son usually calms him down, but in this case, I don't think anything will help.

He's nervous about meeting his mother, and he's not the only one.

I don't mean me.

"I've been off hard drugs for a decade," Pauly admits, looking out of place among the pink and lavender decor of the Gilded Rose, "but if someone offered me a hit of Scratch right now, I'd probably take it."

"No, you wouldn't." Mama reaches out, taking Pauly's hand in hers. "You're going to be fine. It's been a long time since I've seen Odette, but I know her, and she's not blaming you."

"Yeah?" he asks, eyebrow raising. My mother gives him a warm, supportive smile.

Wait.

I look between the two, their hands, their expressions...

What the fuck—*heck*—is going on?

Before I can ask, Adeline, who's been peering impatiently out the window, drops the curtain to announce, "She's here."

I cross the room and take Pace's hand, feeling his fingers curl tight around mine as we wait for her knock.

And wait.

And wait.

Pace is frozen, dark eyes fixed on the door. "Did she leave?" he asks, his voice barely a whisper.

"No," Adeline says, peeking again. She releases a deflating sigh. "She's at the bottom step. She looks really nervous."

Join the club.

I squeeze Pace's fingers, turning to look up into his anxious eyes. "Maybe you should go out there."

His eyebrows twist into a frown. "Maybe she's having second thoughts?" I can see—*feel*—the insecurities rushing back.

"Think about it," I say carefully, keeping my voice low, private. "Can you imagine having to face J.J. after something like this? Explaining Rufus to him? All the horrible things you went through? The abuse and neglect?" I swallow, hating how every word is another wound. "Think about how you reacted to Pauly at first. Maybe she's scared you're angry."

He releases a measured, calming breath, and nods. "That's a good point." Meeting my gaze, he dips down to push a lingering kiss to my forehead, inhaling me. "You're so smart, you know that?"

"Well, some of us weren't raised in East End, where the average emotional intelligence falls somewhere around narcissists and megalomaniacs."

He squeezes my hand and grabs his coat, shrugging it on as he walks out the door.

I exhale, but it does nothing to quell my own anxiety, and now I'm the one who's pacing. Adeline gives me a warm smile. "He's right. You are smart."

I'm also *nosy*, so I dart to the window and discreetly pull back the curtain.

The first thing I notice about her is how short she is. She barely comes to Pace's shoulders, and as he approaches her, hands buried deep in his pockets, she turns enough that I can see her features.

She's beautiful.

Her hair is longer than it was in the picture from her coronation, but the curls are still there, elegant and shiny. She's wearing a long coat, cinched at the waist, but even from here, I can see that she's shivering, her eyes full of emotion as Pace's lips move.

"What's happening?" Wicker asks from across the room.

"They're talking." Immediately, I see the resemblance between mother and son—not so much in looks, but in how they carry themselves, intense and on edge. Odette has her hands shoved into her pockets too, both of their shoulders drawn high. I get the ridiculous notion that Odette also has a lot of security cameras around her house.

"No one looks mad. Odette does look like she's been crying." Sure enough, she extricates a hand from her pocket to wipe away a tear, her brown eyes big and full of grief. Her lips move, and even though I don't hear it, I see the sob rip through her.

Suddenly, they're colliding. Her arms wrap around Pace's waist, and he tucks her into his chest, the embrace hard and so still. I watch for a few moments longer, wondering if this is wrong—if I should give them some privacy. But then Pace turns to rest his cheek on her head and our eyes meet.

Instantly.

He gives me a sad but sweet grin.

Working through the lump in my throat, I let the curtain fall closed. "They're hugging," I tell the room, tears welling in my eyes. I know it's not the same, but something in my chest twists at the return of one of Forsyth's missing women—even if it isn't one of my own.

I look at Mama. "I think it's going to be okay."

J.J. squawks from the car seat, and I bend over to pick him up. Just as I'm settling him against my shoulder, the door swings open, bringing in a cold gust of air with Pace and Odette's entrance.

I stand, holding onto the baby as Pace shuts the door behind them.

There's a brief stretch of electric silence as Odette looks around the room, taking in our expectant faces.

"You know Adeline and Liberty," Pace says, pointing to the two women. His voice is thick, like he's holding back tears, too. "And Paul."

If she's shocked to see any of them, she doesn't show it. Pace must have given her a heads-up.

"Pauly," she says, looking at him fondly. "You haven't changed a bit."

He lets out a deep, thick laugh, reaching up to rub his hair-covered chin. "Neither have you. Still fibbing."

Her face falls and she lingers in front of him, hands wringing. "I couldn't tell you. I couldn't tell *anyone*. If he'd found out who the father was…" Her breath hitches miserably. "Please forgive me."

Pauly reaches out to tug her into his chest, wrapping her in a hug. "There's nothing to forgive, Detty. We were both done dirty." So quiet that I can scarcely make out the words, he whispers, "We made a damn good one, though."

She pulls back, giving him a tearful smile. "To create is to reign." Hearing her say the house motto—feeling her conviction in it, even after all she's been through as a result of it—makes my chest clench. But then she's turning to my mom, throwing out her arms. "Libby Sinclaire, as I live and breathe. You're even more beautiful than I remember."

"Flattery will get you everywhere," Mama says, hugging her back. "The years have been good to you, Detty."

"It was more than the years that were good to me." She pulls away, approaching Adeline with adoring eyes. "Adeline—my dearest friend." Their hug seems to last a little longer. A bit tighter. "How did a heart as kind as yours end up in this wretched place?" Odette wonders.

"Sheer stubbornness." Adeline rubs her back, sending me a wink. "It's the Princess' way."

After greeting her old friends, Odette turns misty eyes onto my Princes.

Pace points. "These are my brothers. Lex and Wicker."

She approaches them with a calm, radiant smile. "You," she says to Lex, head tilting as she inspects him. "You're the protector, aren't you? I can see it in your eyes."

He blinks, checking everyone else for our reactions. "You can see what?"

Odette reaches up to cup his cheek, nodding. "An old, fierce soul."

The words themselves might as well be a hug for how stunned he looks at hearing them, a quiet, tender emotion on his face.

"Hey." Wicker waves, always a pro at breaking the tension. "I'm the pretty one." He shrugs, sniffing. "It's been said."

Pace snorts. "Modest, too."

Odette steps up to him, her eyes locking on Wicker's nervous gaze. Ultimately, she smiles. "You're much more than that. A ferocious heart, I bet. The mask you wear is all Kayes."

His face goes slack. "You can see that in my eyes?"

"Just as clearly as I can see the shadow of your father, Benji."

Wicker jolts in surprise. "You knew my father?"

"A little." Odette takes his hand, urging him, "And you can let that shadow go. Whoever killed him did you a favor, and this," she stresses, "is coming from someone who knew Rufus Ashby."

Wicker absorbs this with a stunned expression. She's barely known him for a full minute, and just like that, she's gotten right to the heart of him. How many years did he spend wondering if life as Benji's son would have saved him from all that hurt?

In one sentence, Odette Delisle completely obliterated a million what-ifs.

"Thank you," he breathes.

Pace gives his brother's arm a squeeze before turning to meet my gaze. "And this—"

"I know who this is." Odette approaches me with an eager grin. "This is your Princess. She saved you. And even though she doesn't know it, she saved me, too." My throat tightens as she pulls me into a loose hug, careful of Justice, still in my arms. Through a thick voice, she whispers in my ear, "Thank you for loving my son."

It takes me a couple swallows to make my own voice work. "Thank you for creating him." When she pulls back, her eyes dip down to the bundle in my arms. "This is Justice," I say, turning to show her. "Justice James Sinclaire. Your grandson."

"Oh, my word." Her hand flutters over her awestruck smile. "Pace, he's beautiful."

"Do you want to hold him?" I ask, lifting my arms.

Handing him over doesn't feel like I'm giving away a piece of my heart, just adding another layer of people who love and protect him. I step back, letting Pace and his mother fuss over Justice.

Eventually, she looks up, addressing Pauly. "Have you met him yet?"

Pauly reaches up to rub his neck. "It's a long story that's about fifty percent firearms and profanities, but I basically watched him be born."

I toss Pauly a dry smile. "Fifty percent is generous."

He lifts a hand, waving it back and forth. "Seventy-eighty."

Odette's eyes flare to life. "Long or not, that's a story I want to hear." She looks down at Justice, her gaze growing wistful. "I have a quiet life now. Bare, because it's had to be. But I'd like to visit Forsyth again, I think." She glances at Mama and Pauly. "See how much our children are changing it for the better."

Later, when all of us are sitting around the table, the elders trade stories as my Princes and I laugh along, struggling to think of our parents once having been as young as us. Driving fast cars down the Avenue, causing trouble at Friday Night Fury, traversing territories like bandits. We drink it in, never having heard these stories before.

The good stories.

"I didn't steal the birthday cake," Mama insists, pointing at Pauly. "I stole the booze, and those fuckers had it coming."

"Mama!" I chide, covering Justice's ears.

"He's asleep." She gestures to him, conked out, draped over Lex's shoulder. "Anyway, we stole these freshmen's booze—"

Pauly pointedly adds, "And their birthday cake."

She flaps a hand, bangles jangling. "And the Psi Nus declared all-out war."

Adeline gasps, setting down her tea. "Oh, gosh, I remember that weekend! You've never seen so many pouting boys in your life."

Odette releases a melodic laugh. "Even Miranda was on the warpath. No one," she stresses, "steals cake from a Princess' frat boys. Didn't she put sugar in your gas tank?"

Pauly groans, head dropping back in misery. "*My Pontiac.* It took me years before I could get that thing up and running down the Avenue again."

Odette smiles sadly. "I remember that, too."

The fondness that runs between them might not be full of heat, but there's still an unmistakable warmth. When Pace looks at me, I realize it might take a while for him to feel it—to find a place to put the bursting shock of having so much family—but in his eyes, I see a man made whole.

Gazing over at Justice, I wonder if he'll be where I am one day, listening to me and his dads relay the blinding brightness of our reigning days. If he does, I decide I want it to be just like this.

No dungeons or pain or death.

Just love.

I REMEMBER my coronation feeling like a wedding.

It was almost a year ago that I entered the ceremonial room with Rufus Ashby giving me away to his three vicious sons. I think about that and my throning—even the cleansing—less and less these days. It feels so far away, as if it happened in a different place with different people. And I suppose, in a way, it did.

But today feels a lot like a wedding, too.

Not between me and a man—or three men. It's the Royal Ascension; a ceremony to bind me as the mother of the next leader of East End.

"Okay, turn and let me look."

I turn and face my mother, who adjusts the neck of my dress. I made a decision weeks ago that East End wasn't going to hold women to some bullshit purity standard anymore. Nothing about being Royal is pure. Maybe that's why they covet the idea of it so much.

This new idea of mine begins with the dresses. No more fucking white.

The one I'm wearing is a deep, emerald green.

The color of thriving life.

That's what East End should be about.

"Never thought I'd say it," Mama tells me, eyes darting up, "but goddamn, you look good in a tiara."

I grin, reaching up to fidget with it. "You don't hate it?"

"Because Rufus gave it to you?" She scoffs, giving Justice, who's nestled in the crook of her arm, a gentle bounce. "Isn't like that fucker ever wore it. You know who did? Miranda. Odette. Adeline..."

Getting her point, I inhale deeply, turning to the mirror. It's been almost two months since I had Justice. I'm not quite back into my pre-pregnancy clothes, and my tits are still massive, but slowly, I'm starting to feel like myself again.

"Thank you, Mama." I stand still while she fusses with one of my curls with her free hand. Justice, still sleepy from a feeding, will hopefully stay mostly quiet for the event. "And thank you for coming. I know none of this makes sense to you. Why I've embraced this world."

"It's definitely not what I expected," she says.

Even though I don't hear disapproval in her tone, I still feel compelled to put it into words. But it's hard to explain something that's so fragile and new. "I'm trying to change things for the women of Forsyth, just like Story and Lavinia." I think of my mother and Adeline, rescuing Odette from the dungeon, and add, "Like you."

Her face softens, a sad smile springing to her lips. "I'm afraid I didn't accomplish much, Ver Bear."

I argue, "Because it's not easy. It's definitely not fast. And it's come with a lot of pain, which I only survived because of the strength you gave me." I stress, "You did more than you give yourself credit for."

"Son of a—" Blinking, she dabs under a watery eye. "You're going to make me mess up my goddamn eyeliner." I laugh, because my mother isn't good at emotion, but her hand still clasps mine, squeezing.

"I thought you were raising me to be a Duchess, but it turns out the draw to East End came naturally." I peer through the glass doors, down to where my Princes wait for me. Taking a steeling breath, I tell her, "The guys want to take our name."

She blinks harder. "They do?"

I nod. "I love them, and they love me. I have a family, and all of us consider you part of it, territory lines be damned."

She presses a kiss to the baby's head. "I see the way they look at you and J.J." Her chin lifts, mouth set in an angry frown. "I also saw the marks on Lex's back. I can only imagine the scars Wicker and Pace carry run just as deep. Those men went through hell to get where they are today, to get to you."

"They did," I agree, so relieved and grateful she's able to see not just the pain in them, but also their devotion.

She bobs her chin. "Then I'll be proud to call all four of you Sinclaires."

Overcome with it, I pull her into a hug, careful not to squish J.J. My whisper comes thick and quiet. "I love you, Mama."

Hers is just as lumpy-sounding. "I love you too, Ver Bear."

The door opens, and Adeline slips into the room, dressed to the nines in a sparkling golden gown. "Oh, attendance is just fantastic, Princess! That baby sure does know how to draw a crowd." I already know what she's going to ask when her eyes fall on him, fists balled beneath her chin. "Can I hold him?"

Mama hands him right over, and I watch with a pang in my chest as she cradles him close, beaming.

"What a blessing you are," she whispers, eyes full of adoration. "I've thought about it a lot, and you know what?" Glancing between Mama and me, she squares her shoulders. "I want to foster or adopt. Rufus is gone, the Princes are letting me keep the Gilded Rose, and there's three bedrooms upstairs. There's nothing stopping me anymore."

"Good for you!" Mama says.

I give Adeline an excited smile. "You're going to be a great mom, Adeline."

I hear a knock behind us, and I turn to see Pace peeking his head through. "You decent, pretty girl?"

"Yes," I answer, giving my dress a spin. "What do you think?"

He lets out a low whistle, pushing through the door. "I think that dress is going to look fantastic on our bedroom floor in about five hours." Before Mama can voice her passionate disapproval of the comment, her hand dramatically covering Justice's ears, he saunters in, holding the door open behind him. "But I wanted to introduce the three of you to someone." He quirks a brow. "Or *someones*."

"Oh, my god," I breathe when the two kids enter. They're fresh-faced teenagers, their complexion as dark as Pace's. The boy is almost as tall as him too, sporting a bright green suit. The girl has long, curly hair, and her bright green dress is a perfect match to her brother's. Both of them are wearing intricately creative makeup, sparkles of gold stars around their brown eyes.

And they look like Pace.

"This is Micha," Pace says, gesturing to the boy, who does an exaggerated curtsy. "And Michaela." The girl gives us a spin much like the one I'd just performed for Pace.

"Pleased to meet you," Micha says. And then, "Your house is fucking dope."

"Well." I prop a hand on my hip as my mother snorts. "I guess the cursing is genetic."

Michaela nods. "Damn right."

"But don't tell our mom," Micha adds, pulling a face. "I hope the green's okay. Pace said there was a theme." He places a palm over his heart and I see his nails also match. "I *live* for a theme."

Wearily, Michaela explains, "We went through five shades of green before landing on this one. Be careful," she urges, "with the themes."

"Got it," Pace says, nudging them forward. "So, this is my girl, Verity. Her mother—we all call her Mama B. And this little guy," he says, stepping forward to kiss J.J.'s cheek, "is my son, Justice."

I worry at first they're going to ask questions. I knew they were coming, but we haven't had the discussion yet about how to explain our weird little family. In the end, all the worry is for nothing, though.

Micha just leans in to look, saying, "What a cutie."

After a pause, Michaela glances at me. "We don't babysit."

I laugh. "No problem. We have plenty of volunteers."

"And this," Pace says, addressing the stunned woman still holding our son, "is Adeline. It's a long story that I'm definitely never telling you, but she saved your lives once."

Adeline gazes upon them, clearly overwhelmed with emotion. "I never thought I'd get a chance to meet either of you. It's such a pleasure."

Micha looks at her, the glint in his eyes screaming that he's dying to ask. "Who does your makeup?"

Pace and I share a look.

Not quite the question I was expecting.

Adeline stammers, "I-I do."

He raises a hand, making an 'o' with his forefinger and thumb. "Flawless."

Adeline blushes. "Thank you."

"Okay," Pace says, dipping down to give me a slow kiss. He pulls back a scant inch, grinning. "Just wanted to see you before the Ascension."

I grab his tie—green silk—and adjust the knot. "Your game is really on point today."

"Every day," he calls, tossing a wave as he ushers his siblings out the door.

Adeline visibly gathers herself. "Are we ready then?"

She oversaw the planning of the entire event, from the chairs to the place we put them. Even though she's a stickler for preserving East End tradition, she's well aware of the pain and trauma associated with the ceremonial room in the palace. The harm it's caused so many Princesses, including herself, can't be ignored. So we didn't.

She embraced the idea of something fresh and new—a place that truly represents the ideas of creation.

My solarium.

The result is something out of a fairytale. The enclosed space is filled with winter plants, primarily the bright red from the poinsettias, which, along with a metric-ton of fairy lights, give the room a lush warmth.

"Now," Adeline begins, passing J.J. to me, "you'll just head down the aisle carrying the baby. Obviously, this ceremony is a little unconventional since the King is only seven weeks old, but the protocol is the same. Your Princes will take the lead."

I give her a gentle grin. "Thank you, Adeline."

"No, Verity," she says, touching her heart. "Thank you for giving me the opportunity to be part of this historic moment." With a deep breath and a flourish, she leads us out of the parlor and toward the doors of the solarium.

Immediately, I hear the first strains of music.

Cello music.

Peering past the people crowding between the edges of the flower beds and the purple carpet, I see Wicker playing, body curled around the instrument as he draws the bow back. His blonde hair is in fine form, swaying with each drag of the bow.

Leaning down, I whisper to Justice, "That's your talented daddy," and take the first step.

The walk down this aisle feels different than it did those times in the ceremonial room. There's no pain waiting for me at the end of it. Justice has the blessing of the members of PNZ, who are flanking the aisle, along with the women from our court. I see the faces of my tormentors, now my supporters. Tommy and Heather. Lakshmi and Kira.

I also see the faces of friends. Rory Livingston. Lavinia Lucia. Story Austin. My West End brothers—all three—are attending, as well as some of the cutsluts, Maggie and Kathleen close to Lav.

Pace's new family sits near the front, his mother beautiful in a darker green, while Micha and Michaela turn to watch my progress up the aisle.

Even the Baron King is here, donned in his bronze devil's mask, a veiled woman at his side. His *wife*.

And then, there's *them*. I look toward the end of the path, seeing my Princes. Lex's amber eyes glow as he watches me grow nearer, and Pace stands with his hands clasped behind his back, chin held high.

But even through the brightness and eagerness, I can't help but think of the people who can't be here, but should.

Eugene.

Laura.

Stella.

As in all PNZ ceremonies, there's a throne, but as in all things newly Sinclarian, it's been renovated. We had the throne I became Princess on stripped down, the insertion device removed. Now, the seat is covered in a plush, green velvet.

When I reach the head of the aisle, Pace shifts to make room for me, ducking down to kiss me on the cheek, and then Justice. "On. The. Floor," he whispers, winking. "Five hours. Maybe four."

I shiver.

Lex's hand grazes my lower back before he steps in front of the throne, facing the audience. It's uncharacteristic for him to wear his hair down at these sorts of events, but it's draped over his shoulders in loose waves, the gold of his eyes accentuated by his own green tie.

The final strains of Wicker's song come to a close, and he places his cello on the stand, rising to take his place next to me.

"That was beautiful," I whisper, leaning in close.

"I wrote it for him," Wick whispers back, blue eyes darting down to my mouth. Without hesitation or shyness, he captures my mouth in a slick, searching kiss.

In front of the Royalty.

In front of *my mother*.

Fatherhood has changed Whitaker Ashby in a lot of ways, but it hasn't changed how passionately he loves.

Remy's groan rings out. "Come on, get a room."

Wicker pulls away with a scowl. "How about you come over here and make me?"

Remy shoots to his feet, smirking. "Maybe I will."

"Hey!" I snap, pointing at Remy. "In your seat, right now! And you." I give Wicker an exasperated look. "Behave."

He sniffs, looking away. "He started it."

Lex and I trade a glance that says the same thing.

These two are getting a little too good at being brothers, although there's enough heat behind their words that I wouldn't leave them alone without expecting bloodshed.

Clearing his throat, Lex steps forward, pulling the book from beneath his arm. "I'd like to say I know how to do this, that there was a book in the library that laid it all out but," he holds up the pledge book before tossing it aside, "there isn't one. There's no easy way to claim a legacy."

A row over, Killian coughs, and in the corner of my vision, I see Lavinia taking Sy's hand.

Those are three legacies that definitely had to be fought for.

Lex continues, "My brothers and I aren't Ashby blood, which is good, because Rufus never wanted to make us his sons. He collected us as instruments." Pace stiffens as Lex's gaze lands on him. "He wanted someone to be the eyes and ears on everyone and everything in Forsyth." He looks at Wicker, his jaw tightening. "He wanted someone to sell, to trade for secrets and leverage." Then he holds his hand to his chest. "He wanted a carver. Someone without remorse who'd hold his scalpel as he cut down his enemies." His eyes drop to me, and then to Justice, still dozing in my arms. "And more than anything else, he wanted an heir."

Absolutely no one can argue with that.

Lex gestures to Justice. "You all came here today to anoint the new Psi Nu Zeta leader of East End. A leader who will have the best interests of our community at heart." He pauses, eyes scanning the crowd with a wry tone, "Although our son *is* the most amazing baby in the world—and no, I will not be taking any questions—I think that's something we all agree an infant can't do."

There's a chorus of chuckles and I shoot him a concerned glance. We agreed that although there are some things about our Royal arrangement that are true, it wouldn't benefit us to call attention to them here.

But then Lex raises his voice, saying, "A Queen can, though."

I whip my gaze to him, frowning. "What are you doing?" I mouth. The audience murmurs in equal confusion. I feel Wicker's arm slide around my waist as Lex takes a step forward, speaking both to me and the crowd at my back.

"The members of PNZ have taken a vote, and we've all offered our Oath of Fealty to Verity Sinclaire." His eyes meet mine, smile spreading. "It was unanimous."

"Over my dead bodies," a voice calls out. I only realize it's the Baron King when he stands, adjusting his black gloves. "Women may not take the place of a King."

"*Actually*," Wicker says, leaving my side to stand next to my brother. "There's nothing in any of the bylaws that say anything about what's between the person's legs."

From the front row, Micha gives a quiet, "Awesome."

"It's almost as if you forgot about women entirely," Pace adds, shrugging. "But accidental as it may be, the language specifying heirs is largely gender neutral. Verity is Rufus Ashby's only surviving heir."

Lex sighs, pinning the Baron King with a fed-up stare. "You and the other Kings wanted us to choose one ruler. Take it or *take it*."

Flabbergasted, I step closer, pitching my voice humiliatingly low. "But I don't know anything about ruling."

Pace scoffs, waving over the crowd. "Verity Sinclaire, you've done more for East End in a year than Rufus Ashby did in two decades. I can't wait to see what you do with an entire lifetime."

"He's right, Red," Wicker says, grinning roguishly. "And I, for one, am completely ready to be your pretty, kept Prince, so get up there and claim that title."

Lex cups my cheek, drawing me closer, and in his eyes, I see a promise that I don't understand yet. "You'll *never* be doing this alone."

I blink, trying to follow everything, but slowly, it all comes together. My men want me as their leader. And so do the rest of PNZ. I glance over at Lavinia and Story, who both watch on with wide eyes, and it hits me that I can use this position to help more than just my family, my friends, and this fragile, new territory I now call home.

I can use it to help a cause.

The Monarchs.

Too stunned to speak, I bend to brush a kiss against Justice's forehead, throat tight as I pass him into Pace's waiting arms. Wicker takes my hand and leads me up the steps where Lex steps aside, giving me access to the throne. It's so strange to look upon this seat and think of something other than misery, pain, and humiliation.

I look at it now and see change.

Turning, I scan the faces of the crowd, seeing my past and my present, but when I look into the eyes of my Princes—brown, blue, and gold—I see my future.

"Are you sure about this?" I ask, knowing the only thing about this I'd regret would be letting all of these people down—them most of all.

"Positive," Lex says, taking my hands in his. "The vote was recorded and witnessed by a member of good standing from each house, *including* BRN. This is what we want, Verity." He holds my shocked stare, insisting, "East End doesn't need another troubled, self-involved man to weigh it down with his baggage. It needs..." He pauses, searching. And then the divot in his brow smoothes away. "It needs kindness. You're the only person who's ever promised that to them."

I take a deep breath, looking at Tommy, Rory, Baxter, Dory, Loeffler, and Mitch—men who could grow into monsters under the pressure of a system that demands it of them. Or men who can grow into something better, if only they have the guidance.

Since that decision doesn't seem very difficult at all, I take a deep breath, bend my knees, and sit.

"Let's begin."

29

EPILOGUE

J*anuary*

"Wᴀɪᴛ, ᴡᴀɪᴛ, ᴡᴀɪᴛ," I urge, stopping Baxter on his way to the champagne cart. "Your tie's crooked," I explain, adjusting the knot. He lifts his chin, giving me room to fiddle. When I'm happy, I give him a pat on the shoulder. "Easy on the booze, Bax."

He throws me a salute. "Yes, ma'am."

Looking around at everyone in the ballroom, I find it amusing how I can recognize every single PNZ member and their date, even with masks covering their eyes. Sending out the invitations for East End's seventy-ninth annual masquerade ball had been an affair I struggled through, remembering receiving mine. I spent a week hammering everything out with Adeline, Wicker, and Rory Livingston, calling up the memories and trying to remember the good parts.

The throning has, obviously, been re-imagined into a much

different sort of ceremony, and on my way to check in with Pace, I hear Gina, Heather, and Lakshmi gossiping about who has what it takes.

"She's got great tits," Heather says, glaring at one of the candidates, "but only because she's overweight. I don't think they'd choose someone without a waistline."

The insecurity bubbles up, partly from the memory of them criticizing me in the same way, exactly a year ago. Another part is that, although I'm almost back to my pre-pregnancy sizes, I still look different.

"They probably want something new," Gina is musing. "Do you think we'll still get to wear the tiara?"

Nudging in, I say, "Yep."

They jolt in surprise, turning to me. "Princess," Lakshmi greets, and then stutters. "I mean, Queen."

"Nervous about the announcement?" I ask, clasping my hands together. "We have a really impressive field of candidates this year." My grin is pointed. "Finally."

From the way Heather goes stiff, she takes it as the insult it's meant to be. "Well, we were just discussing the," her eyes dart down, "*size* of the pool."

Smiling primly, I explain, "We're looking at different qualities this year. Strength and resilience. Leadership." *Brains.*

Heather nods at something behind me. "What about her? She has good, child-birthing hips."

Twisting, I see a curvy girl dancing with one of the Prince candidates. What neither of them knows is that they both chose each other on the preference card attached to their invitations.

This year's Princess and Princes will have a say in who they make a covenant with.

"That's Sophia Lark," I say. "She's a graphic artist with a minor in visual. She's definitely a creator."

It hasn't been lost on any of us that we'll be sharing the palace with whoever is chosen. Quite plainly, none of us are willing to move out of the home we've made on the second floor. But the changes we've made for the new royalty are still fresh, and I want to keep an eye on them—to make sure they're adhering to the new covenants—not the old. As a result, the new crop of East End royalty will be living downstairs, which has been empty for months.

Ever since Stella went missing.

Ever since Eugene got taken away.

Ever since Danner died.

I'm not sure if it'll make it easier to have people in the house again or unbearably more difficult. Following that train of thought, I wave at the girls and continue my search for Pace. He's not by the buffet table, nor is he at the door, covering security. I look for him for so long that by the time realization dawns on me, I've greeted every guest.

The air is crisp when I step out onto the balcony overlooking the grounds. I feel him before I see him, that inexplicable hum sparking over my nerve endings.

"Hiding?" I ask, turning to find Pace slouched low on the bench, his masked face tipped up to the starry night sky.

"Absolutely." He rolls his head to the side, meeting my gaze. "I hate these things."

Sighing, I approach when he holds out his arms, folding myself down onto his lap. "It's only once a year," I reason, worry building in my gut. "How'd it go?"

Pace had driven up to the Forsyth Pen this afternoon to visit with Eugene.

"Okay," Pace says, looping his arms around me. "He's angry."

My jaw tenses. "He fucking should be."

Pace shoots me an amused look at the language, and I shrug. The baby's not here to hear it. "The lawyer is building a strong defense," he assures, thumb rubbing soothingly against my ribcage. "Everything they have is bullshit. He just has to fight this shit."

"He will." This much is certain. "We're West End. Fighting is what we do best."

"And East End?" he asks, tucking my head against his warm neck. "What do we do best?"

"You glitter like diamonds, and you survive. But mostly," I press a kiss to his pulse point, relishing in the thrum of his heart, "you love the hurt out of each other."

There's a long pause before he reaches up, fingering the jewel in my tiara. "Then you're definitely one of us now."

For a while, we just sit there in the cold January air, drinking in the night. "How do you think they'll take it?" I ponder, thinking of the men my Princes chose to succeed them.

"They'll probably cream their pants, wasting our precious Royal seed." Pace laughs when I shoot him an exasperated look. "What? I did. Right here, in fact."

Deciding that I've hidden for long enough, I push to my feet, extending a palm. "Will you come and watch over me while I glitter?"

"Always, Rosi." He slips his hand into mine as he rises, using it to tug me close. His promise is made in an exhalation, warm and damp against my temple. "Always."

When we re-enter the ballroom, Pace takes his spot against the wall, hands in his pockets as his dark eyes follow me from guest to guest.

I know it'll take the rest of Forsyth a while to understand the changes underway. We're still looking for creators, but breeding? Well, there's only one Royal in West End who counts it as her job.

"Hey," a voice comes in my ear, forcing me to spin.

When I do, I let out a low whistle. "Who might you be?"

Wicker shrugs, his blue eyes shining through the mask. "Just some regular schmuck. No one important."

A mask, indeed.

I hum, flipping my hair. "That's too bad. I have it on good authority that the masquerade ball is about finding the perfect connection between me and someone's trust fund."

He laughs, winding his arms around my waist and pulling me close. "No one's trust fund is bigger than mine." He punctuates this by pushing his crotch into my thigh. "Oh, wait. That's my *thrust* fund."

I groan, sagging in his arms. "Come on, really? Enough with the dad jokes."

"Can't help it, Red." He pulls me into an artful spin. "I've ascended."

"Where's the baby?" I ask, fighting a smile.

He grips my hand, and idiotically, it takes me a moment to realize we're dancing. "Lex is putting him down."

Chuckling, I guess, "He's hassling Adeline about the importance of the dinosaur blanket, isn't he?"

"Tummy time isn't for ducks," Wicker mocks in a staunch, definitely not-Lex-like voice. "You know, I remember the first time I saw you."

I search my memory. "Out on the dance floor?"

"At the Fury," he corrects, "when I beat Oakfield into a weeping pulp."

"Oh, right." That night seems like a million years ago. "You upset a lot of DKS that night."

He smirks charmingly. "I could tell you were the only prize worth winning, even before I knew your name." He bends and tugs on the lobe of my ear with his teeth before whispering, "Maybe later we can head upstairs for some tummy time of our own."

Leave it to Wicker to get my panties wet while I have actual work to do.

"If we can get through the night without any actual bloodshed, I think it's an excellent idea."

He kisses me, slow and lazy. When he pulls away he searches over my head and asks, "Have you seen the waiter? The little cakes are on-fucking-point. Highly recommended."

I make a face. "My stomach's been crazy with nerves all day. Could you pilfer one away for me later?"

He spins me. "Anything for the Queen."

When he snaps me back, Lex is there, scowling. "I'm supposed to do that."

Wicker smoothly spins me into his brother's waiting arms. "Just limbering her up for you, caveman."

Lex is stunning in this three-piece suit, the gold mask tied neatly around his loose hair, and not for the first time tonight, I feel my knees go a little weak at his touch. "Let's see if I can remember how this goes," he says, leading me into a waltz.

Rolling my eyes, I ask, "Who are you fooling? I know all your moves."

He raises an eyebrow. "Do you?" Abruptly, he dips me, the move flashy and quick. I bark an embarrassing laugh, the sound inelegant but full of delight. His movements are just as exacting and confident as they had been that night a year ago. Back then, he'd seemed so stiff and cold. *Scary.* Now, he's anything but. His amber eyes bore into me when he snaps me upright. "I know all of *your* moves," he claims.

This time, I raise the eyebrow, winding my arms around his neck. "I've got a move you haven't seen before."

He nods, spinning us expertly past another couple. "Let's see it then."

Wetting my lips, I look around before straining up on my toes, pressing my whisper right into the shell of his ear.

Our movements come to a jarring and sudden halt as Lex freezes, jolting back to meet my gaze. "What?"

My heart hammers inside my chest, but I gather the courage to speak the words again. "I'm pregnant."

His lips part on an aborted inhale, and then he glances down at my stomach, as if he could possibly see a baby there already. Skeptically, he asks, "Are you *sure*?"

Searching his eyes for a reaction, I assure, "I took five tests. But you can—" My words slip away when he yanks me into a hard, unyielding embrace.

He crushes me against him, breaths erratic. "Justice is going to have a brother or a sister?"

Laughing, I let the worry I've been carrying all night melt away. It'd be a lie to say I'm not scared. Carrying Justice was an experience that I haven't even completely recovered from. It's far too soon to create again.

But life is also far too short not to.

"Yes," I say, breathing in the spicy, masculine scent of him.

He pushes me back to look at me again, this time with more assessing eyes. "How far along? When did you find out?"

"This morning," I answer, excitement thrumming through my veins. I'd been feeling off for a few days, but when I couldn't hold down my breakfast, I knew. "I can't be more than four weeks along, which could mean..."

Understanding sparks in his wide eyes. "You think?"

The week Wicker and Pace spent at the tourney in Northridge was hectic for me and Lex. We'd fall into bed at night deliriously tired, doing a quick video chat with his brothers before settling in for sleep.

But sleep never came immediately.

Every night, he'd push inside me, amber eyes locked on mine as we fucked, sweet and slow, or hard and fast. We played it loose, never getting back on birth control. It took a couple of months last time, and I figured the next one would be the same, but apparently, Lex at full strength was more potent than we'd realized.

He cradles my face in his palms, staring at me with awe. "You're saying it could be mine," he realizes, voice thick and ragged.

"No, Lex. I'm saying it is."

He presses his forehead to mine. "You haven't told the guys?"

I smile so big that it hurts. "I wanted the dad to know first, but I figured we could tell them after the throning."

I'd think this would crush Wicker's plans about tummy time, but nothing makes my men hotter than a baby, even if it is faster than we thought.

"They're going to flip out," he says, and we both look over to where they're standing, laughing with guys from the hockey team.

"Good flipping out, or bad?" I ask, suddenly unsure.

"Both," he admits, pressing his hand to my stomach, "but this is what we do, Verity. This is who we are and building a family is our priority above anything else."

A year ago, I never would have dreamed that I'd want to someday transform a group of hurt, angry boys into men. I never would have thought I'd want it *so much*, and so achingly, and so impatiently. It wasn't just because I became a woman in this beautiful, haunting place. It wasn't even because I became a mother, and then a Queen.

It was the fierceness of Lex's soul, the blaze of Pace's devotion, and the ferocity of Wicker's heart that made me a creator.

And ours will be a legacy of hope.

To FIND *out what's next for the Royals of Forsyth, keep reading!*

AFTERWORD

The royals of Royals of Forsyth U will continue in 2025, with Barons of Decay.

For anyone wanting more about Micha and Michaela these are crossover characters from our Preston Prep series, primarily Devil May Care and Devil Incarnate. Preston Prep is a standalone prep-school romance that is less dark than ROFU with a more enemies to lovers, high-angst vibe. Devil Incarnate is the most similar in tone/vibe to ROFU. Find the series HERE.

An extra, special, release month only surprise!!! For an exclusive, early bird, Princes bonus scene, sign up here! Please note, this scene isn't available yet so you'll only receive an email once it's ready to go.

FORSYTH universe
LORDS
ΛΔZ
DUKES
ΔΚΣ
PRINCES
ΨΝΖ
BARONS
ΒΡΝ
COUNTS
ΚΝΓ
COMPLETED TRILOGY
COMPLETED TRILOGY
ONGOING TRILOGY
FUTURE TRILOGY
FUTURE TRILOGY
LORDS OF PAIN
ANGEL LAWSON SAMANTHA RUE
DUKES OF RUIN
ANGEL LAWSON SAMANTHA RUE
PRINCES OF CHAOS
ANGEL LAWSON SAMANTHA RUE
BARONS OF DECAY
ANGEL LAWSON SAMANTHA RUE
13
LORDS OF WRATH
ANGEL LAWSON SAMANTHA RUE
DUKES OF MADNESS
ANGEL LAWSON SAMANTHA RUE
PRINCES OF ANU
ANGEL LAWSON SAMANTHA RUE
11
14
LORDS OF MERCY
ANGEL LAWSON SAMANTHA RUE
DUKES OF PERIL
ANGEL LAWSON SAMANTHA RUE
PRINCES OF LEGACY
ANGEL LAWSON SAMANTHA RUE
12
15

ACKNOWLEDGMENTS

Monarchs,

Over the last few months, I've seen posts in our groups from newer readers questioning some of the actions and scenes in the Prince's books. These are valid, but what warms my heart every time is when our Monarchs rise to the occasion and say, '*Trust the Process*,' or there's '*Method in the Mayhem*.' Those two phrases feel like they embody more than just the books themself but Samgel at the core. That trust allows us to write these books the way we want to write them and try to give you all the best version of this world we can come up with.

We had no real idea when we wrote Lords of Pain how big the world of Forsyth would become, but I did know that venturing into a potential fifteen-book series was a massive concept. Sam and I don't do small, especially when we work together. I have a million plot ideas and she has the most incredible character concepts and graphic inspirations, and together it gets complicated. And messy. And hugely fun while also overwhelming.

Although the Royals of Forsyth U is filled with a lot of drama, trauma, sex, and violence, believe it or not, we're not here for the gratuity. We think long and hard about these characters and how to give them their HEA. We've taken you on a wild ride, and we knew the Princes would be *a lot*. They are a lot and we hope to have given them a complete story, wrapping up as many loose threads as possible. (*while leaving a few for the upcoming books! Eeee!)

If you're in our group Monarchs or on our Discord you'll know that the past three years have been a lot in the Lawson household. I appreciate the patience and support from everyone. This book was written from hospital rooms (3 visits this year! And Mr Lawson is at the ER as I write this. On his way home soon tho!) hotel rooms, a weird Airbnb in Texas that had an open-concept bathroom clearly made for an OnlyFans set (@steffgreen), a historic mansion in Maine, and my cozy office.

Thank you to all our Monarchs and Queens, and a special one to our Empresses. Christina, Nadia, Lisa, and Vicki, who truly understand how we need every single one of you to get these books written and coherent at this point. We are a ball of chaos ourselves, and you guys make it happen!

I know I'll miss people. Just know you are appreciated.

Angel

*

Holy fucko, this was a hard book. What's that about? Idk, but this might be the last birth I ever write until we collectively, as a community, bring back the stork meta. Y'all, a bird coming to drop you a baby? That's solid. Let's make it happen.

We have literally the best team of people, and for me, this book is all for them. They kept picking me up off the ground, dusting me off, and helping me to not feel so isolated and alone. So Christina and Nadia, all my love for giving me digital shoulders to cry on and reminding me to sleep and eat and walk and shower. Being a human is really annoying sometimes, I think Lex will agree.

Big thanks to Lisa, Nikki, the Royal Ink staff (which, yes, is just my brother and my cats), and the Royal Ink VIPs; Taryn A., Christine K., Mollee C., Chloe S., Kaylin W., Nicole M, Michelle R, Erin G., Autumn G, Jennifer F., Rayna H., Jessica S., Haley B., Anne A., Julie T., Elizabeth W., Felicia B., Kristie-Anna B., Stephanie W., Jennifer F., Tammy T., Dee Dee R., and Jacki G.

Vicki. You are my life. Thank you for accepting the bonkers skin-of-our-teeth vibes that our time management mistakes keep creating. You deserve the world.

But mostly, an enormous thanks to all of YOU who waited so long to receive the Princes' legacy. As with all the other Royals, this is not the end of the Princes, only the end of their trilogy.

Much love from my gnarled demon fingers!

Sam

www.ingramcontent.com/pod-product-compliance
Lightning Source LLC
Chambersburg PA
CBHW032103310726
48972CB00001B/76